NOT ALL ANGELS
SOME ARE CALLED TO BATTLE

# THE DOLL

## AND THE DOMINATION

BOOK FOUR

BRANDI ELISE SZEKER

**<u>The Pawn and The Puppet Series</u>**
*The Pawn and The Puppet*
*The Master and The Marionette*
*The Puppeteer and The Poisoned Pawn*
*The Doll and The Domination*
*Novella (2024)*
*Book 5 (2024)*

# Content Warning

*Hey, you're still here? If so, this is probably your shopping list! Enjoy!*

Disclaimer: This book contains explicit content and dark elements and may be considered offensive to some readers. Check trigger warnings before reading. It is not intended for anyone under 18 years of age. Please store your files wisely, where they cannot be accessed by underage readers.

This is a dark dystopian society that is intended to be problematic. Please note that this is a fictional world and in no way reflects on the author's personal beliefs. We will see the society grow and correct its moral compass over the series.

This book contains: gratuitous violence, mental health journey, grief, depression, death of a loved one, mention of suicide, gratuitous/detailed torture, physical injuries (such as burn wounds), hallucinations, misogyny, mention of pedophilia, romanticized mental illness, gore, child abuse, mention of animal cruelty and death, dismemberment, mention of incest (off page), female oppression, degradation, starvation, body shaming, sexually explicit scenes, explicit language, religious trauma, horror, demeaning language, power imbalance, emotional manipulation, abuse of power, sexual assault, consensual-non-consent, exploitative situations, drowning, barbaric and degrading imagery, eating disorders, negative body image, dubcon, sadism.

Do not continue if you're unsure of the contents of this book.

*For you, the reader that does a little*
*fist pump to a long list of trigger warnings.*
*Grab your vibrator and vodka.*
*This one is fucked.*

*"He who fights with monsters might take care lest he thereby become a monster. And if you gaze for long into an abyss, the abyss gazes also into you."*

**-Friedrich Nietzsche**

MIDNIGHT SEA

ONDOGRAVES JUNGLE

VEXAMEN

EAST-VEXELLO MOUNTAINS

MADMAZ VILLAGE

MEAT CARNIVAL

FOUL FALCON FOREST

VEXAMEN PRISON

# Author's Note

*"DID is about survival. As more people begin to appreciate this concept, individuals with DID will start to feel less as though they have to hide in shame."*

*-Deborah Bray Haddock*

The representation of DID in this novel is a morally gray, dangerous character. This is NOT an accurate representation of DID. It is a symbolic representation of how DID appears to modern society—feared, misunderstood, and a mystery of the mind to gawk at. Please know that the rest of the series will be a journey for this fictional society and the characters to understand and accurately represent. But allow me to set the record straight for this nonfictional world. This community of people is NOT the monster. They are NOT the villains. They are kind, intelligent, wonderful human beings that were the victims of horrendous injustice and abuse.

Let this message encourage you to ask the right questions and seek to better understand. For more information about DID, please visit these sources:

https://did-research.org/home/map

http://traumadissociation.com/index

P.S. If you disagree with representations to different forms of trauma in this series, please be considerate of those who cope differently and feel accurately represented as a survivor of their experience. Everyone has their own encounters and ways of healing. If certain descriptions, situations, or explanations aren't for you, they may help or empower someone else.

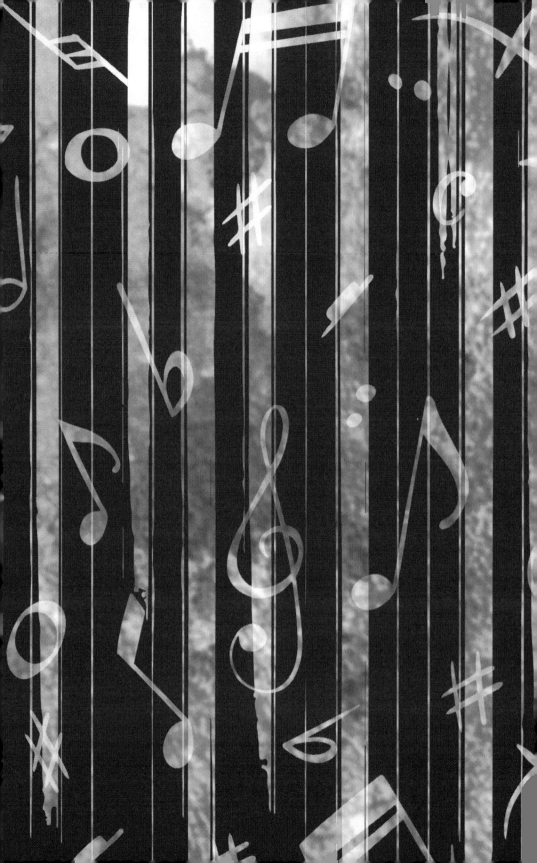

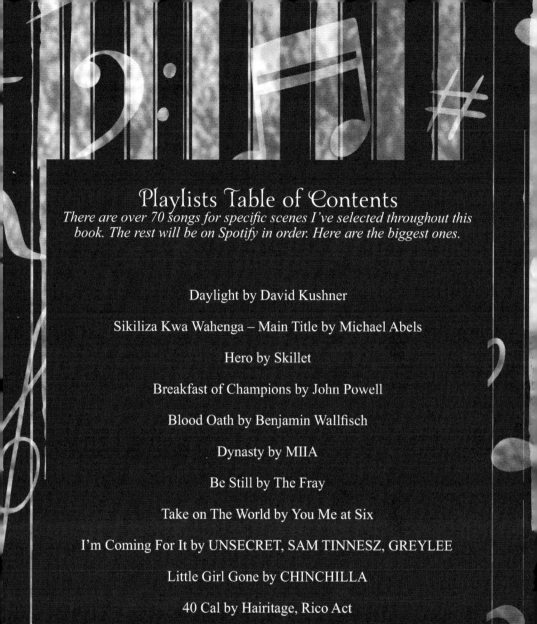

# Playlists Table of Contents

*There are over 70 songs for specific scenes I've selected throughout this book. The rest will be on Spotify in order. Here are the biggest ones.*

Daylight by David Kushner

Sikiliza Kwa Wahenga – Main Title by Michael Abels

Hero by Skillet

Breakfast of Champions by John Powell

Blood Oath by Benjamin Wallfisch

Dynasty by MIIA

Be Still by The Fray

Take on The World by You Me at Six

I'm Coming For It by UNSECRET, SAM TINNESZ, GREYLEE

Little Girl Gone by CHINCHILLA

40 Cal by Hairitage, Rico Act

# 1.

# The
# Commander

## Skylenna

"Cat got your tongue, brother?"

Collectively, we all look to Dessin with our jaws dragging across the brimstone floor. They look alike; that much is obvious. But it's so clear that their surroundings were different. Their upbringings turned them into separate creatures.

Kaspias Valdawell doesn't have that warmth in his dark brown eyes. There isn't that beating heart buried within his cold gaze. He's almost…hard to look at. In the dim light of the yellow and red bulbs, I make out the uneven layer of skin on his face and neck. Scars that cover more scars. A beard and black ink lining under his eyes. He's big, strong, rigid with bulging muscles like Dessin, but there's something sick about how he looks at his twin brother.

A twisted eagerness to cause him pain.

"We were told you were stillborn." Dessin doesn't blink.

Kaspias smiles for several creepy seconds. "So, I've heard. It's a little sad how easy it is for Vexamen spies to invade your delicate city, isn't it? I was taken the moment I was pulled from our mother and brought to my new home."

"Did they—experiment on you?" Dessin asks.

"I am not like you and your"—he taps two fingers to his temple—"horde of personalities. If they raise you without compassion, it makes the subject harder to break."

"There are two of you?!" Niles blurts out in disgust, eyes darting back and forth between each twin.

"*Niles,*" Ruth warns under her breath.

I can't even look away to shoot Niles a scolding glare. Kaspias was taken as a baby. A *baby*. An infant directly from birth. Sophia didn't even have a chance to hold him for the first time.

Dessin releases a quick breath. "You're one of them. A soldier in the Vexamen Breed."

I want to reach my hand between the bars and touch him. Let him know I'm here for him. He doesn't have to process this news alone.

"I am a commander in the Vexamen Breed." Kaspias runs a curious hand through his short beard. "And you're an experiment that went wrong. A product of insanity. A test subject that was released into the public."

Has he kept an eye on Dessin all these years? The thought triggers a tickle of a memory beneath the surface. I try not to get lost in it as I let it suck me in. Darkness swallows me quicker than expected, and I'm tossed into the forest. The scent of rain sinking into the dirt and pine trees swirling around me. Dessin is on the motorcycle, and *Past* Skylenna clutches his waist. We're outrunning—someone. Another motorcycle. A figure that wouldn't show their face.

Dessin fishtails the bike and throws his legs out to kick the stalker off their seat. They flee the scene before the person chasing them removes their helmet.

I see the beard first, and dread sinks into my gut. Kaspias has been following us. *Watching* us.

I'm back in my cage, knees painfully pressed against the jagged brimstone, blinking away the memory that threw off my equilibrium. How long has this been going on? Did Dessin really not have any idea that this was a possibility?

"You were the one that set the hunter's trap I fell into with the nadaskar. And the person on the motorcycle who chased us after we left the asylum to go find Ruth." A painful chill runs down my back as Kaspias blinks. And the moment he opens his eyes again, they're on me. Dark and hollow.

"Skylenna," he says as if testing the feel of my name on his tongue. "The other lab rat. How could you possibly know I was behind the hunter's trap?"

I stare at him. Too proud to break the long moment of eye contact even though I'm severely uncomfortable.

"You saw it in your head, didn't you?" he pushes.

I look back at Dessin, whose jaw is so tightly clenched; I wouldn't be surprised if he breaks a tooth.

"Has he not given his little pet permission to speak? Is that why you're looking to him? For approval?" His words scrape against my skin like sandpaper.

Dessin is on his feet, quick and dangerous, like a heart attack. "You may be my blood, but make no mistake. I'll rip out your tongue if you speak to her that way again."

I stand slowly, noting how little clothing I have on. A red one-piece…brassiere and panties. They're connected with a metal shackle around my throat. The neckline is deep and plunging, the sides are hanging loose in shreds along my hips, and the back is entirely open with a halter around my neck. I peek over at Ruth and Marilynn. We're all dressed this way. What a strange contrast from the white patient gowns in the asylum.

"She's your lover." Kaspias raises an eyebrow. "I couldn't tell. You were close but never…*touched*. Must be exhausting, threatening every man that looks at her with hunger in his eyes. She is enticing, isn't she?"

"I am not his pet, and he does not speak for me. I'll gladly cut that tongue out myself," I say with a level of calm that is both disturbing and confident.

And for the first time since we got here, Dessin smiles.

# 2. Good Morning

## Skylenna

"I'll make this brief." Kaspias ignores my threat, taking a bored look at the rest of our group. "Make any attempts to escape, and your equilibrium will leave you sick and disoriented. This is a prison, and yet, it's so much more. You'll have to endure the new culture until the Mazonist Twins are ready to meet you."

"Mazonist Twins?" Ruth asks.

I remember Aurick teaching me about the founders of Dementia and Vexamen. Orin Blackforth and Abraham Demechnef. Malcolm and Maxwell Mazonist. Looks like they're still alive and kicking.

"The leaders of Vexamen," Warrose mutters. "What are they like, a hundred now?"

"Pretty close," Dessin responds without tearing his eyes from his brother.

"There is only one rule. Since you can't escape, consent is essential, ladies." Kaspias points his eerie glare at me, then Ruth, then Marilynn. "This is a co-ed prison. But if you consent to pleasing soldiers or commanders, you'll be exempt from participating in the Fun House Nights."

*Consent?* I look to Dessin, who is seething at the word.

"What's Fun House Night?" I ask.

But the commander is unnaturally still as he pins a long, unsettling stare on his twin brother. The cords in his neck flex outward, shifting back and forth as he grinds his teeth. Those dark caramel eyes twitch like he's forgotten about the rest of us while he examines the physical appearance of Dessin. Is he comparing their similarities? Judging their differences? Inspecting any weaknesses Dessin might have?

The length of this piercing stretch of quiet rings in my ears. I would be lying if I said I'm not affected by the layers of intimidation bleeding from this commander's pores. So similar to Dessin. Yet cold dread has never crept into my very bones just by being in the same proximity as him.

Kaspias steps back into the shadows of the long hallway filled with creepy music from an old-fashioned pipe organ, a distorted trumpet, and incoherent gibberish from other prisoners banging against their cages. The exit is as smooth and seamless as smoke dissipating in the wind.

Our group is silent, but our thoughts are loud. We take several minutes to adjust to our new situation. To process the information Kaspias threw in our faces.

"How the fuck is it possible that he's scarier than you, Dess?" Niles breaks the silence.

"*Please.*" Dessin sighs. "Don't give me a nickname."

I sit against the bars of my cage, taking deep, calming breaths, and rack my brain to figure out what comes next. And I can feel Dessin doing the same.

In one loud clank, our cage doors open. And judging by the echoes of metal hitting stone, feet shuffling, prisoners groaning, and the floor rumbling, it's safe to say that they're releasing us for the day. A stampede of male and female prisoners stumble from the darkness into the hall, shoving one another, gripping the bars of other cages for support.

Dessin gives us the signal to stay put as they pass. It's like we're invisible. No one seems to care about the new arrivals. Some inmates limp with bloody, bare feet. Some crawl across the jagged, rough floor.

And based on the blur of moving faces, they all seem bruised, beaten, and raw.

I shift my gaze to Dessin. His eyes move over the mass of people quickly. Studying them. Assessing their injuries. His mind moves puzzle pieces around.

We wait until the hallways clear and step out cautiously. Before we follow the last stragglers, Dessin turns to me, dragging me into the safety of his arms, caging me against his bare chest. My arms close around his waist, feeling the raised burn scars across his back. I stroke them lovingly.

"Are you okay?" he asks, lips pressed against my hair, hot breath warming my ear.

I nod against his shoulder with tears burning my eyes. Emotion clogs my throat, not because I'm afraid, but because I *needed* this. His muscular body pressed against my soft curves. His steel arms gripping me so tightly I'm not sure he'll ever let go.

"You're not leaving my side while we're here." He fists the hair on the back of my head, drawing me in closer. "You understand?"

I melt a little at his words. "Okay." I don't want to be separated from him either. But I'm not sure if that's something we can control.

We part so I can hug Ruth and Niles. Warrose and Dessin nod at each other, still clearly not on good terms. And I peek over Niles's shoulder at Marilynn, watching us with tired sapphire blue eyes and pursed lips.

"I bet you're wishing you stayed back with Aurick, huh?" I tease.

Her round, dreamy eyes glide back to me. "It's not like fate gave me a choice in the matter." Her tone is layered with thorns and broken glass. I step away, deciding now really isn't the time to learn more about her prickly personality.

"Should we do another group hug?" Niles chirps.

We groan in unison.

Dessin turns to face us, his presence thick with cold calculation and a plan brewing in his mind. His burly arms cross over his shirtless chest. And God, I want to touch him again.

"Don't show any signs of weakness. Keep your chin up. Keep your eyes straight ahead. We don't know what kind of social system this is or the way of the hierarchy."

We all nod hesitantly. My stomach grumbles with hunger and twists with anticipation.

"But aren't you *the* alpha in captivity? You're the infamous Patient Thirteen. Shouldn't we be safe for that reason?" Niles asks.

"I don't show my cards until I know the game we're playing." His eyes flick from Niles to Ruth. "If there are any physical altercations, you step out of the way and let Warrose or me handle it. Understand?"

"Or me," Marilynn and I say at the same time.

Dessin gives me a relenting look, then narrows his eyes at Marilynn. "You can defend yourself?" We've already been over this, but no one has actually seen Marilynn in a fight.

"I can," she deadpans.

No one questions the confidence in her statement.

"So, Ruthie and I are the freaking infants you all have to protect?" Niles huffs.

"That's right. Stay in your crib, and let the adults handle this." Warrose slaps him on the back with a smirk.

Ruth lowers her eyes to the floor, gulping down an emotion I can't read. Something angry or helpless. Insecurity blossoms over her freckled cheeks.

Dessin snaps his fingers, scowling for us to lower our voices. "We won't speak of our weaknesses again." He taps his ear once, then points at the ceiling. "*We don't know who's listening,*" he mouths.

We walk through the long hallway without another word, following the flickering yellow and red bulbs and eerie music mixed with white noise. The sharp-edged floor pokes and agitates our bare feet, and the stale air smells of buttery popcorn and candy with a hidden aroma of rotten fruit.

I wonder how this place will compare to the Emerald Lake Asylum. If this prison will be better or worse. I push myself to keep positive thoughts until I remember that these are the same people who steal babies from their mothers' breasts. This is the same country that hosts the "Meat Carnival."

It must be worse. People like this don't have pleasant housing for prisoners.

I take in a stuttering breath. Clench and unclench my hands. What the hell have we gotten ourselves into? And why did we have to bring

Niles and Ruth along? I couldn't bear it if anything happened to them...

"You grind your teeth when you're stressed," Dessin says, eyes on the dark hall ahead.

"I've got a bad feeling."

He nods. "So do I."

*Well, fuck.*

I think of Chekiss, DaiSzek, and Knightingale. A wave of relief warms my skin. At least they're safe. They're far away from the brutality of this place. But I can't help but miss them.

"Are we not going to talk about the slinky outfits the girls are wearing?" Niles asks from the back.

I hear Dessin growl deep in his chest.

"I'm trying not to think about it, Niles," Warrose grumbles.

We're not the only ones, though. The men aren't wearing shirts. Just scrappy black pants with holes and a waistband that's loose around the hips.

"It's not a bad look," Niles adds, then pauses to think. "Way better than those cotton gowns and grippy socks, amiright?"

Silence.

"Who misses the grippy socks?" he asks again.

A longer stretch of silence.

Niles chuckles to himself. "I just had a mental image of Dessin wearing grippy socks."

Dessin whips back, lunging at Niles and getting in his face like a tornado grazing the earth. "I'm trying to focus on getting us the fuck out of here, Niles. And I was stressed *before* you started talking. But now I'm way past that. Why? Because at this moment, I'm thinking about my girl, wearing nothing but a shred of floss, walking in the vicinity of prisoners. Do you want to know what happens when I get the mental image of other men staring at Skylenna's perfect ass?"

Niles shakes his head, green eyes wider than I've ever seen them.

"I kill people."

Niles doesn't breathe. Doesn't blink.

"Just this once, can you make my life a little easier?" Dessin says in a slow exhale.

"Shutting up, sir."

Dessin nods once, turning back to me with damn near black eyes and a lasting scowl on his face.

I crack a smile. "He copes with humor."

"If I'm not allowed to cope, neither is he."

"How would you like to cope?"

"With my fist in your hair and my cock buried inside your wet cunt," he rasps in my ear, voice strained and laced with venom.

Heat shoots straight to my lower belly. I clench my inner walls. "Gotcha."

He smirks, the simmering rage starting to melt over his features.

"Niles actually makes a pretty good point," Warrose says, taking a quick glance down at Ruth. "There's got to be something else the girls can wear."

"You didn't like the dresses that were Demechnef-approved, and now you don't like my skimpy prisoner bathing suit?" Ruth retorts.

"I fucking hate it. One extreme to the other. You're"—he glances down at her body, then looks away with a grunt—"half naked."

Ruth shrugs. "It's kinda comfy."

Warrose shakes his head with a tightly clenched jaw. He stands out like a massive oak tree in a desert. Bare chest with raised tattoos, beautiful bronze skin, and hazel eyes that could light up this hallway all by themselves. He ties his dark hair back with a string.

I catch Ruth assessing his muscles, too. "You are also half naked, hypocrite." She scowls.

"It's not the same," Dessin calls over his shoulder.

"Exactly. No one's going to follow us men back to our cages. It's you three we'll have to guard around the clock." Warrose refuses to look back down at Ruth.

"Speak for yourself," Niles scoffs from the back, clearly forgetting about Dessin's outburst. "I'm a sex magnet. Any women in the vicinity will flock to me once they see my tan chest and shredded back."

"Your *hairless* chest," Ruth corrects.

Warrose and Dessin burst into deep, rumbling laughter.

I smile. God, I hope this place doesn't beat the humor out of us.

I TAKE A SLOW STEP back from the packed room before me.

"Jesus," Warrose breathes.

"Do we"—Ruth pauses long enough to gulp loudly—"have to do that?"

I want to run back to my oversized birdcage. At least we got more privacy than *this* in the asylum.

The ceiling is a pointed dome, like the tent of a circus. The walls are a black, rocky texture. The floors are wet and sudsy. And giant broken pipes protrude from the ceiling, spraying down like a raging waterfall.

And underneath that downpour? A room full of naked men and women taking their morning showers. A group shower.

Sentinels stand at either side of the entrance, wearing leather shoulder armor plates, straps with spiked edges, and dull brass studs. They watch the naked figures swiveling around each other with amusement twinkling in their eyes.

The entrance is still filled with prisoners stripping off their raggedy clothes and flinging them down a hole in the wall. But we don't move. Even Dessin seems caught off guard by the lack of privacy.

"Move!" a sentinel with a long beard and bloodshot eyes bellows at us. "You won't get fucked unless you ask for it. Now, strip!"

Dessin grunts and then glances over his shoulder at the rest of us.

"No eye contact. Get in and get out."

We all nod. But fuck, my heart is racing. My stomach is screaming into my esophagus. And every muscle is contracting, begging me to run for it. I watch Dessin unbutton his black pants, but I quickly look away. It doesn't feel right to appreciate his body when we're being treated like cattle.

With a quick shimmy, I step out of the strappy rags that keep the essential parts of my body covered. Hands and arms stretch out to throw their uniforms in the large hole in the brimstone wall, like a laundry chute. I mimic the action while holding my breath, throwing my hands over my breasts and between my thighs. Dessin doesn't bother covering himself. I'm sure it's easier for men to walk freely with what God gave them.

Dessin, Warrose, and Niles herd us to the center of the room, bumping into naked bodies as they force their way under the downpour. I hiss as the spray hits me like pebbles of ice. Goose bumps prickle over every inch of my skin.

Ruth and Marilynn huddle close to me, elbows smashed against mine as we cover our chests and press our foreheads together, blocking out the scenery we'd rather not see. I'm unsure if our men realize they're doing it, but they've formed a circle around us.

I look up through the uneven torrent of pipe water at Dessin's scarred back, Warrose's tattooed shoulders, and Niles's tan arms, blocking us in a tightly bound circle. They face the other prisoners, ensuring no one comes near us. Making sure there aren't any lingering eyes that land on us while we're indecent.

*You won't be able to keep this up, Dessin.* My heart tugs at the thought of what's going through his head right now. He must be out of his mind with territorial alpha energy pumping through his veins. I'm naked, and a bunch of wild Vexamen prisoners get to see.

I catch Ruth's round brown eyes, and she offers a supportive smile.

"It's better than the simulated drowning, right?" She chuckles, trying to see the bright side.

I scoff. "Sure is."

"Is this how we're going to shower the entire time we're here?" Marilynn asks, her dark red hair hanging in wet strings over her shoulders and chest.

"Sure is," Dessin says over his shoulder, running his fingers through his wet hair.

"They're just being protective," I whisper.

Marilynn nods, glancing at Niles's back like she's trying to figure something out.

"Don't let his goofy personality fool you." I lean in closer. "Niles is fiercely loyal and very protective, just like the rest of them."

"Even though he doesn't have the masculinity to back it up," Ruth whispers, snickering as Niles elbows her in the back.

At the other end of the room, prisoners begin to exit, grabbing rags off the hooks on the wall to dry themselves.

"We'll wait until the room clears," Dessin murmurs to Warrose and Niles, then hands us bars of soap. They look used already. Smeared in dried blood and dirt. I grimace but accept it anyway. Beggars can't be choosers.

We lather ourselves quickly, and by accident, my eyes trail up

Marilynn's body. She's bustier than Ruth and me. By a lot. Curvy, like she's never tried to abide by the lady-doll regimen.

"*Defemúrox egex domïnozoz yuevezezï?*"

We turn our heads at the soft male voice behind us. Short. Skinny. Bald. Long braided platinum blond beard.

And a fully erect dick pointing at Marilynn.

"He wants to know why you boys are keeping the new—juicy *cunts* to yourselves," Ruth chokes out the last of the translation like it physically pains her to repeat it.

"Yeah, I gathered that much from his tiny manhood standing at attention," Dessin says.

"Is it his manhood, though?" Warrose slowly turns to the blond-bearded man as if to show off his masculine physique. "Because it looks more like a clit."

Ruth gags on the water, still pouring over us from the ceiling. Warrose grins at the sound of her trying to breathe and laugh simultaneously.

The man glares at Warrose, then points at Ruth with a reddening face and quivering finger. "*Haxasfertiú mehzezï damö nadastraskazez!*"

His small, naked body storms out of the shower room.

"He says…I'll have this one bouncing in my lap by the end of the week."

Warrose exchanges a look with Dessin. "I'll kill him first."

We shuffle to the wall rack of rags. Dessin tosses them to us and turns away as we all dry off. Niles nudges Ruth, yet still keeps his eyes on the ground. "Look at you, Ruthie. Already making friends."

She sighs. "This morning is off to a great start."

"Should we invite Baldie Baby Dick to eat breakfast with us?" Niles pulls on a clean pair of black pants just as I slip into my new skimpy uniform. It smells like sweat and greasy food. I try not to gag.

"He'll be dead before then, Niles," Warrose grumbles.

"No killing. At least not yet. We need to keep a low profile until an escape plan is cooked up," I whisper to the group.

Dessin nods reluctantly.

"Now, let's try to eat breakfast without getting into a confrontation," I say after helping Ruth slip into the pathetic shreds of her uniform.

I'm thankful that I'm not in this alone. I'm not showering with strangers. They're my family. I'm not plotting by myself; I'm plotting with some of the greatest minds of our time. We have each other's backs.

We follow the length of the hallway until we reach an opening. The music is louder, and the yellow and red light bulbs cover the ceiling completely. It's bright, like one giant chandelier. Circular tables fill up as prisoners take their seats to eat their breakfast.

And that smell...

Raw fish and something sour. Like milk that's been left out for several days.

Dessin and I share a look, and I wrinkle my nose at him. The corner of his mouth tilts up, not enough to be counted as a smile, but his subtle way of telling me he likes when we silently communicate.

Heads turn to get a better look at us. Eyes trailing over each member of our group, speaking to each other without looking away.

"Are they serving bile with a side of poo?" Niles pinches his nose to block out the stench.

"Shhh," I hiss, baring my teeth at him. "You really want to draw attention to us right now?"

He sighs dramatically, running a hand through his mess of wet, golden hair.

"Let's get in line to eat," Dessin says, nodding toward the counter where prisoners grab plates and cups.

"I'd rather starve," Niles mumbles under his breath.

Stepping up to the metal counter, I avoid looking directly at anyone. Today is for laying low and observing. We need to understand how this place is run; then, we can make trouble if it suits our plans.

Prisoners in black aprons stand on the other side of the counter, passing out metal plates and cups, stirring pots of steaming gray goop, and making small talk in another language. They're older, maybe in their sixties or seventies, and perhaps that's why their job is to serve meals.

"What is it?" Niles asks the woman with long, stringy hair the color of storm clouds.

Her aged blue eyes flick up to him, and she raises a hairless eyebrow.

"*Haujezez nos gelecknezez demornatéz Demechnef?*" Her tone is accusatory. Sharper than a sword.

*Welp, I heard Demechnef in there, and that can't be good.*

"Come again?" Niles taps his ear like he simply didn't hear her.

*God, he's going to get us all killed.*

"She wants to know if we're soldiers from Demechnef," Ruth says hesitantly, glancing between Dessin and me.

I pause. Judging by the old woman's tone, being a Demechnef soldier in a Vexamen prison is not a good thing. I shake my head at Ruth. "Tell her no."

"*Nexéz,*" Ruth utters.

But the old woman is already shouting something, pointing at Dessin and me, babbling so quickly it sounds like one solid word. Other prisoners from the kitchen look up at us with a mix of curiosity and conviction in their eyes. Then, the rest of the room goes silent.

I try to get my lungs to fill with air, but they've decided it's best to retire for the day. In fact, it's so quiet that I can hear Warrose sigh and Dessin growl deeply in the base of his throat.

Without another word, the prisoners serving the food pour the gray goop onto the floor in front of our feet. I flinch, stepping back to avoid the chunky mess. But Dessin doesn't even look down. His bare feet are coated with the splatter, and he doesn't take his darkening glare off the woman before us.

"You sure you want to play this game with me?" he asks her, knowing she can't understand a word he's saying. But a wave of chills tumbles down my arms and legs at the challenge in his baritone voice, rough and edged with an intent to make her suffer.

The elderly cook spits at his feet, mumbling a phrase I'm sure is meant to offend.

I lightly touch Dessin's rigid, unrelenting arm. The muscles are flexed to the point of impassable stone. "Low profile," I remind him. But he doesn't seem to hear me. His lowered lids and clenched jaw are aimed at the lady with a crinkled scowl on her face. She's covered in scars and what looks like fresh wounds across her neck. I wonder how many years of her life she's been a prisoner.

"Let's sit down." Warrose nudges Dessin with his elbow.

Dessin casts her one final look, then turns to the crowd of prisoners.

Some are standing to watch the confrontation. Others are still sitting, but they've stopped eating. Stopped talking. Stopped moving.

And the room is so hushed that I can hear our feet pad across the floor until we reach an empty table.

I'm guessing it isn't every day they get Demechnef citizens in this prison. That should make our stay *enjoyable*.

We stare at each other, waiting for the room to fill with casual conversation and spoons scraping the bottoms of bowls. But it doesn't; all eyes are on us as if time has actually stopped. So, Warrose slams his fist down on the metal table, causing Ruth, Marilynn, and me to jump.

"Fuck," he grunts.

The room slowly returns to its previous volume. And I can breathe again. Air whooshes from my chest, and my clenched muscles loosen, turning to slime under my skin.

"We're fine," I reassure the table, although my hands are trembling in my lap, and my stomach is growling like an animal is trapped in there, trying to claw its way up my esophagus to escape.

"I hope this is only a *day-one-initiation* kind of thing." Warrose looks up at Dessin as if he can clarify how this will go.

But Dessin just shakes his head, calm rage seeping from his presence.

"It's going to be okay. We're used to not eating. Right, girls?" Ruth perks up.

Dessin's jaw tics. *Yeah, not the way to lighten his mood, Ruth.*

"Wow, somehow that pissed me off even more," Warrose says.

I look up at Marilynn, wondering what she's thinking right about now. She doesn't say much. Even her facial expression is unreadable. And honestly, I'm not too fond of that. We need to be able to trust each other implicitly here. No questioning who she's really working for. We are in enemy territory and only have each other to rely on.

"You've been quiet," I say, watching her reaction like a hawk.

Marilynn looks up, her sapphire eyes narrowing. "I'm always quiet."

The interaction grabs the attention of our table. They look back and forth between the two of us.

"I thought you might have more to say now that we're in prison and only have each other to speak to."

34

Dessin's dark gaze slides toward Marilynn suspiciously.

She shrugs, though the movement is laced with irritation, twisting her wet hair between her fingers. "I've lived a pretty isolated life. Talking isn't a strength of mine."

"Weird. I love to talk," Niles interrupts. "And can I just say how hungry I am?"

"We're in this situation because *you* opened your mouth, Niles." Ruth shifts in her seat, adjusting her shredded leotard in hopes of covering more skin.

Warrose leans across the table toward Dessin. "You don't think they'll try to starve us out, do you?"

"No." Dessin shakes his head. "We're too valuable to the Mazonist Brothers. They'd never let us die in here."

*But they can certainly make us think we're going to die.*

I reach under the table, caressing my hand over Dessin's thigh. He sighs in response. The tension clouding his vision and furrowing his brow begins to dissipate. I want to sit on his lap, run my hands through his hair, kiss his sharp jawline, and bring him out of this bad mood.

But with this many eyes on us, I'll have to settle for—

With the speed of a viper, his hand snatches mine, gripping my palm and my fingers, swallowing them whole in his massiveness. My entire body relaxes. Warmth radiates from his skin, tingling up my wrist and into my arm.

I didn't realize how much I needed his touch. How much I needed to be close to him. But that's our weakness, isn't it? We need each other. The way we need air to fill our lungs.

"How is everyone handling our recent events in the inner world?" I ask him quietly while everyone else discusses the smell that's coming from the kitchen.

Dessin peeks at me from the corner of his eye. "Not great."

"And Kane?"

He shakes his head.

"Because of—Kaspias?"

His throat bobs in response.

I squeeze his hand. God, I wish I could talk to Kane now. He needs to know I'm here for him. He's probably confused and devastated that his twin brother has been alive this entire time. And even worse—he's been here, in Vexamen.

"We're going to get out of here," I assure him. "This is just—another adventure. No, actually, it's another game."

"Oh?"

An idea illuminates my thoughts. "Let's make it interesting, shall we? Your part of the game is to map out an escape route. Mine is to free us from whatever they put in our ears."

"And what do I get if I find our escape route first?"

"What do you want?"

He leans in, lips brushing my ear. "I want to fuck you in your cage. I want you to hold on to the bars while I wrap your legs around my hips and pound my cock into you so hard that the entire prison hears you screaming my name."

A jolt of pleasure rushes to my inner thighs, and my clit throbs with heat. It's all I can do not to moan right here at his words.

"Deal," I say too quickly.

"And what shall I give you if you win, baby?" His mouth is still hot and breathy against my ear, sending chills racing down my spine.

I think about this a moment. "When this is all over. When the war has ended…" I trail off, unsure if I should even say it.

"Yes?"

I turn to him, dropping my voice low and soft. "I want you to put a baby inside me. I want you to marry me."

He blinks, and those beautiful hickory brown eyes widen. I instantly regret bringing this up now. Yes, I've always wanted the fairytale. And when I was a little girl, I used to imagine my wedding day with Kane. But who am I to bring this up while we're locked up? While we're currently being starved out?

Something flashes across his face. An emotion that isn't usually there. Something warm and hopeful. Something powerful and unmatched.

"Deal."

We look at each other for a long moment. And I know he's thinking what I'm thinking now. I want nothing more than to straddle him, pull his cock out of his pants, and push this stringy uniform to the side so he can fill me with everything he has. I want his baby. I want all of them to be the fathers of our children.

"That's some potent sexual tension."

Dessin and I turn our heads, and my eyes instantly land on Niles nodding at us proudly.

"Seriously, how are you two going to go this long without fucking?" he asks.

"Shut up, Niles," I hiss.

The creepy music surges through the speakers as the lights flash. Every prisoner rises, putting away their utensils to leave the room.

We rise to follow with empty stomachs. Yes, it's unfortunate. But Meridei did the same thing to me when I was her patient. And Ruth's right; if anything, the lady-doll regimen taught us to manage our hunger.

# 3. Regale Hour

## Skylenna

We're ushered into a stadium. A grand hall, like a theater, but with flashing lights, mirrors, rotating red and white wheels, swinging contraptions, and a stage at the center of it all.

The prisoners spread out, lounging in the chairs, using the swinging contraptions to exercise, and socializing with each other casually.

"It's like…recess?" Niles asks.

"Looks like it." Warrose scans the area suspiciously. "Probably keeps the prisoners from going stir-crazy."

"Maybe this is better than the asylum, after all," I say.

Only something is off. The stage is stained, and the air smells of burning wood, copper, and vomit. My gaze is instantly drawn to the corner of the stage. Prisoners hover around someone moaning.

I nudge Dessin and point to it.

We move closer to investigate. Careful not to walk too fast or get too close. Low profile. Don't draw any more attention than we already have.

Suddenly, the moans turn into throaty howls of pain. We stop a few feet from the crowd as someone moves out of the way, revealing an old man clutching his forearm for dear life as he groans through his teeth. An old woman next to him pours brown liquid over his—

"Shit," Warrose utters, pressing a hand back to keep Ruth from taking a step forward.

The old man's hand is *missing*. All that's left is a bloody stump. A sharp, protruding bone. Shreds of flesh hanging from where his hand once was.

"*Devmez ezeakaz ubne bileadéf!*" the old woman yells, holding his face in her hands as the others hold him down.

"We can't let it get infected," Ruth translates in horror.

"How did he lose his hand?" I ask, but the question comes out as a whisper, a single breath disappearing in the nervous energy around us.

The old man vomits across the old woman's thighs, but she doesn't seem to notice as the others wrap his wrist in gauze.

"Courtesy of Fun House Night," a strong female voice announces from behind us.

I turn away from the writhing old man to two giant women with crossed arms—short curly hair, splotchy red cheeks, and a towering height nearly matching Dessin's.

"God bless," Niles gasps, flinching away from her.

The first is a thick oak tree of a woman. Broad and beefy. I stare with my mouth parted, looking up and up and up.

"The name's Helga Bee," she says proudly. "This here is Gerta." She points to the shorter woman next to her. But not by much.

"You don't speak Old Alkadonian like the others?" Ruth asks.

"No, we do. But we knew the Demechnef Experiments don't." Her wide, buggy eyes dissect us individually, like a child holding a magnifying glass over a cluster of insects.

I hesitate for a moment. "How many prisoners speak our language?"

Helga Bee scratches her shoulder, causing the milky white skin to turn cherry red. "About seventy-five percent of them."

Dessin raises his eyebrows. "We haven't heard anything other than Old Alkadonian."

She shrugs innocently. "That's because anyone from our sister country is shunned and isolated here, Beetle Brain."

*Beetle Brain.* I nearly laugh.

Warrose beats me to it.

"I like her." He chuckles, looking back to Dessin to observe his reaction to the new nickname. Dessin clenches his jaw, grimacing at Helga Bee like he wants to do something—anything—to put her in her place.

Warrose laughs harder.

I look around at the prisoners spread out through the arena, watching us closely, scowling at our interaction with Helga Bee and Gerta.

"Why are you talking to us if the status quo is to ignore us?" Marilynn asks.

"We've never followed the lackluster trends here," she explains, sitting on the edge of the stage. "Gerta and I are from the East-Vexallo Mountains, the only territory exempt from the Vexamen Law. We're born rebels!"

That must be like the Bear Traps. A place outside of the social norms. A section of land that is exempt from the extreme way of life.

"How'd you end up here?" Ruth asks.

Helga Bee tsks. "Bad form. Never ask another prisoner what they did to get them thrown into the circus!"

It isn't until I glance at Gerta that I notice why Niles has been so quiet. She's been grinning at him silently, twirling her frizzy brown hair around her finger with blushing cheeks and swaying hips.

Niles tries not to look at her.

"You sure are a pretty man," Gerta says, voice a little deeper than I would have expected.

Niles doesn't look up. "Thank you, I know."

I roll my eyes.

"You said something about a Fun House Night?" Dessin asks with a clipped tone.

Helga Bee straightens. "Yep. Dates chosen at random, we have Fun House Night in this big ole' room." She circles her hands in a sweeping motion. "Vexamen Breed's finest come to watch whatever the Circus Orchestrators have planned to entertain them."

"Entertain...*how?*" Dessin asks cautiously.

Helga Bee smirks at him, waggling her strawberry-blonde eyebrows as if to ask, *do you really want to know?*

"Oh, you know, the usual. The Guzzle Ride, Ecstasy Dance, Swing Pit, Hunting Rally…"

"I'm going to need a definition for everything you just listed," Dessin deadpans.

"And then, of course, there are the Vex-Reaper nights for those who get three strikes. That's when soldiers get to watch misbehaving prisoners get punished."

"What kind of punishments?" I ask, dread sinking to the bottom of my stomach like a rock.

"Okay, so there's the Blood Falcon. You don't really want a description of that—but I'll give you a less disgusting explanation. They cut out your lungs and spread them like wings until you slowly die on the stage."

"How the hell is that the *less* disgusting version?" Niles cringes, inching away from Gerta, who has been subtly trying to stand close to Niles.

"And then there's the Vexamen Candles when a prisoner, who got caught trying to escape, gets dipped in oil and set ablaze."

I feel Niles stiffen; his entire body seems to turn to stone.

My stomach rolls. I shake my head at the graphic images flooding through my mind. *Okay, this place might be worse than the asylum.*

"How do we avoid getting strikes?" Warrose asks, voice sounding low and scratchy like he's bottling up a bout of rage swimming to the surface.

"Trying to escape, murder, suicide attempts, failure to attend a Fun House Night," Gerta answers as she reaches out to caress Niles's face.

I exchange a pained look with Dessin. *Great.* If we get caught at any point trying to break out of here, we get a strike, which could lead to a blood falcon situation or being burned alive.

"Dammit," I breathe. But I see the wheels turning in Dessin's head. This is his specialty. He can form an escape plan anywhere. Only now, he isn't just thinking of himself. He has to consider each detail carefully because it could result in one of our friends getting a strike.

"When's the next Fun House Night?" Dessin breaks the silence, rolling his neck to relieve built-up tension.

"Maybe a couple of days." Helga Bee grins, popping up from her seated position. "My advice? Get through it without making a fuss. Days like this are for us to nurse our wounds and recover." She nods to the man howling from his bleeding wrist.

Instinctively, I reach for Dessin's hand, curling my fingers around his warm palm. It's like my own comfort blanket. A slight touch to soothe the anxiety building within me, making it hard to take an even breath. That large hand shifts, wrapping itself around mine in a way that's both protective and sweet.

Helga Bee watches us curiously. "You two are mated?" She looks at Warrose and Ruth, then practically flinches toward Niles and Marilynn. "Are all of you paired up?"

"No!" The word half explodes from Ruth and Warrose's mouths. They grimace at each other and take a small step away.

Mated? "Dessin and I are together." And his hand tightens around mine in response.

She pulls her thin lips into her mouth skeptically. "The rest of you should at least fake being paired up." Her words are low and crass, a violent whisper as she looks around to ensure no one else hears.

"Why?" I ask her.

She shrugs her wide shoulders. "It'll help keep the male prisoners away from your ladies."

Dessin pulls me closer to his side, but the rest of our group makes no effort to do as Helga Bee says. I clear my throat, eyeing Warrose. He huffs, taking a step closer to Ruth, then shrugs at me like that's the best he can do. Ruth rolls her eyes.

"Better," Helga Bee says, still eyeing our body language with suspicion. "But you all should work on your acting skills. Get inspired by the mama and papa of the group. I could cut their sexual tension with a pair of bladed needle globbers."

"I don't know what you just said, but I agree." Niles nods, then balks with a curse as Gerta nuzzles her plump face against his bicep.

Marilynn's lips curl upward, not enough to be counted as a smirk, but it's a subtle change of her mouth, a silent adjustment that says she's amused by Niles. And honestly, I wouldn't trust her if she wasn't. Niles, although he can be very annoying, is relentlessly amusing.

"How does not being paired up affect Fun House Nights?" Dessin asks.

"They'll give you the option to participate in a private lust hour with a Vexamen Breed soldier. Most individuals put up a good fight but end up taking the deal when the alternative is grueling humiliation and punishments. And the longer you hold out, the more desirable you'll be to the commanders. It'll become a game for them to see you grovel for their attention." She takes a long breath, scratching her milky skin with overgrown yellow fingernails. "It's dirty and barbaric but makes for juicy drama when bored."

I groan. That's why that blond-bearded man got so testy this morning in the showers. He was looking for any women who aren't paired up or mated.

"Wait," I call for Helga Bee as she turns to leave. "They didn't give us food today. How long will that last?"

If we're going to survive through Fun House Nights, we need to have our strength. And right now, my tummy is gurgling loud enough for everyone to hear.

Helga Bee winces. "Yeah, that's shitty luck, isn't it? I dunno. If anyone gives you a portion of their meals, they'll get starved out, too."

"Then what do we do?" Dessin steps forward, dragging me with him.

"Figure it out, Beetle Brain. I'm a six-meals-a-day kind of woman. Can't afford to help you on this one."

# 4. Alters

## Dessin

I want to gut someone.

Watching Skylenna walk into her cage without a proper meal today punctured a hole in my chest. She tried not to rub her stomach. Hell, she even tried to cover the gurgling sound of her hunger with a pathetic little cough.

It's my job to provide for this family. I don't know when I elected myself to this position; the exact moment isn't clear. I suppose it happened the moment I met Skylenna in that asylum. I watched her from the inner world, paid attention as she and Kane grew up, had fights, played in the rain, cried about Jack, swam in the lagoon. I knew her in a way, or at least I felt like I did.

But that moment when she walked into the thirteenth room, my eyes scaled the length of her smooth legs, and my heart beat like a war drum in my chest as she locked those beautiful emerald eyes on me.

I expected her to tremble. To avoid eye contact. I was fully aware of the reputation I had. Proud of it, actually. I worked damn hard to make each person fear my presence. Careful not to let them get too close so Demechnef wouldn't target them for information. But my girl didn't recoil. She reached out and shook my hand and didn't shy away from my stare. I couldn't take my eyes off her. I mean, I remember her being a sweet, cute, little girl. I remember Kane's childish dreams of marrying her one day. But my God, she was devastating.

It's not in my nature as an avenging alter to bow to anyone's needs but my system. To protect the other alters. To harm those who have hurt us. Therefore, it took me by complete surprise when, at that exact moment, I would do anything to protect her, do anything to make her happy.

Sure, I would have protected her for Kane. She was all he could think about. But I was fucked, because I was the alter that was supposed to carry out her insane plan with ease. I was the one who was not expected to let feelings for her get in the way. That's one of the reasons Kane had to retreat to the inner world. He couldn't bear lying to her, keeping her in the dark, even if she was the one who orchestrated the damn thing.

It makes this situation so much worse.

I have this rot growing in my core, this aching desire to escape this prison and keep us all safe.

*This isn't your fault, man,* Kane whispers. But he isn't fooling me. The heart-wrenching guilt is pouring from him to me in a slow, poisonous trickle.

*I usually have time to work out an escape plan,* I tell him angrily. *But now, I feel like each moment that passes increases the odds of one of them dying. That blood is on my hands.*

Kane sighs but doesn't respond.

*Losing us to death or* fake *death left an irreversible mark on her soul. I can't let her lose anyone else she loves.*

Kane hums his agreement. But he can't stop the endless flow of remorse pouring off him. I'm suddenly shown a memory of him telling Skylenna he had a bad feeling about the warship. The mission. He wishes he would have tried harder to convince us to stay put.

*Go rest in the Ambrose Oasis,* I say to him with a layer of calm. *I need a clear head if I'm going to pull off the best escape to date. Your guilt is going to eat me alive, brother.*

Kane's quiet for a long time, but I know he's still lingering.

*Tell her I love her, okay? I love her so much.* The pain in his words is enough to paralyze me. I nod, and in a single moment, I'm drained of the heavy surplus of guilt and back to being pissed.

"Get out of your head." A charming, delicate voice flutters through my cage. I turn my head to look at her, forehead pressed against the crooked black bars between us. "Pay attention to me." Skylenna smiles sweetly, sending a rush of pleasure straight to my cock.

"My attention is always on you, baby."

"Who were you with just now?" she asks quietly, a level just above a whisper, like she wants to keep details about what goes on in my head private. Between us.

"Kane." I blow out a breath.

Her brow wrinkles. I resist the urge to rub my thumb across her worry lines.

"He wants me to tell you that he loves you."

Her green eyes shine with tears as she smiles, looking away with a blush touching her cheeks. "And what about you?" she asks without meeting my eyes. "Do *you* love me?"

She knows the answer to this. I can see it as clear as the morning sky across her softened expression. Yet she still asks, wanting that affirmation. I wait until she glances over at me, then nod once.

Skylenna smirks to herself, rubbing her hands up and down the backs of her arms, subconsciously trying to gather heat.

"Are you hungry?" I ask. Not sure why I'm even bringing it up. I have no food to offer her. An angry, stretching pain swells under my chest. The clamoring need to kill the prisoners that run that kitchen. The pricks that decided to starve us out.

She shakes her head. "No." *Lie.* "I am cold, though."

I shift closer to the bars that separate us, reaching my hands to pull her closer, wrapping my arms around her lean frame as much as I can manage.

Fuck, she feels good against me. My hands trail up and down her soft curves.

She inhales through her nose slowly, letting out an audible sigh against my bare chest. A little noise I've come to recognize as her enjoying my scent. I can relate. She always smells so sweet and pretty.

Raindrops, jasmine, and lilies. And it's always most robust on the top of her head. My cock twitches as she lets out a happy, sleepy, quiet moan.

"If you could be anywhere in the world right now, where would it be?" I ask, trying to distract myself from the primal need to run my fingers up her warm center and push them into my mouth just so I can taste her again.

"Easy. Under the stars. In the Red Oaks."

Classic. I remember lighting a fire for us that night she told me how Scarlett died. It felt so damn good to have my own special moment with her. After getting to know her, I grew jealous of the history Kane shared with her. I became hungry to make my own history with her. And that night, she let me comfort her, let me in on the darkest part of her...it was our moment. It was mine to keep.

And it meant the world to me.

"With a fire," I add, and she shivers.

"And DaiSzek to cuddle with."

"You don't want to cuddle with Knightingale?" I smirk.

She gives me a pointed look. "Uh, not really, no."

I laugh.

"She's so prickly," she muses. "Kind of like you."

"Aw, that's sweet."

She snickers, adjusting herself against the bars.

"She doesn't really seem like the cuddling type," she says.

"Neither does DaiSzek."

"Nah, he's a big baby."

My heart thumps in my chest. Fuck, he's the biggest baby. I miss him like crazy right now. He's my good boy. My fire-breathing dragon. I want to fight alongside him again. Tear this Vexamen Breed to shreds. We have such a bond when we go into battle; it's like this silent communication that no one else can hear or understand. This promise that he has my back, that he'd cover any weak spots I might overlook, that he'd cut through a forest, run through a hurricane, fly over a mountain, just to eliminate any threats I face.

"Do you think he's okay?" Skylenna asks with worry weakening her tone.

I shake my head. "No, I don't. He's bonded to us, baby. He's probably going out of his mind trying to cross that ocean."

She shudders in my arms. "We have to get back to him. To Knightingale. To Chekiss."

"I know."

Skylenna clears her throat, forcing away the tears that must be gathering in her eyes.

"If Skylenna is giving Dessin a blow job right now, I'm going to hurl," Niles states in a hushed tone. "Or get turned on. Not sure which yet."

Skylenna stiffens in my arms.

"We can hear you, you little monster!" I bark, shooting him a glare that could slice through that stupid, finely coiffed hair of his.

"*Whoops*. Am I really that loud?"

Ruth chuckles.

"No one is getting blown tonight," Warrose says with a hand draped over his eyes.

"Exactly," Ruth adds. "So, at least Warrose's nightly routine is perfectly intact."

Skylenna and I burst out laughing, her shoulders shaking against my arms.

Warrose pops up from his relaxed position on the cold floor.

"Is that going to help you sleep at night, little queen?" His husky voice is taunting, daring her to travel through this topic with him.

"Not if you're obnoxiously loud putting that right hand to work," she retorts.

We all laugh again, louder this time.

*Damn. Get him, Ruth.*

"I'd like to retract my little queen nickname. You're a little rebel talking to me like that." Warrose cracks a smile. "I guess I'll keep us both awake with this right hand. Every. Night."

Ruth loses her tickled expression, and her olive cheeks blossom with color.

"You're disgusting," she seethes, yet she shakes her head, biting back a smile.

"How about we have a no masturbation rule while we're here," I offer.

Niles groans dramatically. "Who invited the prude?"

At this, Skylenna giggles. And I want to bottle up that sound. Play it over and over again in my mind. She's so pretty when she laughs. In the asylum, she seemed so drained of life, so heartbroken. It took so long to hear that cute little noise.

She turns into me, her pink lips grazing my ear as much as she can with the bars keeping us apart. "I don't get to touch myself tonight?"

My cock takes notice, filling with heat at her question, her sultry tone, and her warm breath. "Did you *want* to touch yourself?" I whisper back.

She nods slowly. "My clit is throbbing, and I'm so wet."

"*Fuck*, baby," I growl.

The sexual energy races through my veins. It's enough to give me the strength to rip these bars apart like they're made of cardboard. I want her in my lap so fucking bad.

Greystone's dark, ravenous presence closes in on the front. My vision blurs slightly, the first sign I can feel myself start to dissociate.

*Get back,* I warn him. *We're in the Vexamen Prison.*

*I'm beginning to not care about dangerous surroundings when it comes to Skylenna,* he replies casually.

I ignore him and focus on how her long fingers travel through my hair, tracing the nape of my neck. "When this is all over, can we move far away from here?"

"Where would you like to go?" *I'd follow you through hell, baby.*

"Maybe there's a nice country out there? Somewhere that doesn't have a fucked-up government. Somewhere no one knows our names."

I nod, breathing in the scent of rain and lilies from her hair. *Where no one knows our names.* Wouldn't that be nice? But would our system of alters still have a need for me? Or would I simply disappear?

Is there life for me outside of this chaos?

I want that to be true.

"We could build our own house," she mutters, looking up at me with childlike hope blooming in her eyes.

"I'll build you your own castle."

Her smile widens. And that fucking settles it. To see that smile again, I'll do just that. One day, I'll build my girl a castle.

"And you'll build a special door for DaiSzek, where he can go in and out as he pleases?"

"Of course."

"And a big room in the castle for Chekiss. So, we can take care of him when he gets really old?"

I sigh. Her heart is so big. "Yes."

"And—"

"If you say a room for Niles, I'm taking it all back."

She laughs as I tickle her sides.

Now that I think about it, this could all be so much worse. I could be on the other side of the prison, somewhere far from her cage. Somewhere I can't touch, see, or comfort her in the night.

For this, I'm grateful.

"Would you like to live near the forest or the ocean?" I ask. Hearing the ocean waves at night might be nice and peaceful. It would be quite the change to—

Skylenna's eyes darken. A cold, stormy, seafoam green. And they flicker like she's watching a single, terrifying moment play out that no one else can see. A moment that seems to alter every small detail on her beautiful face. And then, with a few blinks, she's back, wincing in my arms. Visibly aching, trembling, retreating inwardly.

"Where did you go?"

I regret asking the moment she meets my eyes. I see the woman who created her own puppets out of orderlies. The same woman who chewed off Meridei's arm. She's quickly so cold, so detached, so withdrawn. It reminds me of myself. Back in Demechnef training, I'd look at myself in the mirror, feeling no connection to the reflection looking back at me.

It suddenly clicks—the *ocean*.

"I'm a fool," I say with a clenched jaw. "That was thoughtless."

I've known a trigger of hers is a basement. Confined, dark spaces. But I've now doomed her with another trigger. The beach. The sand. The ocean. The sound of the waves crashing on top of each other. That fact alone clenches my stomach in a tight fist. If only I could take away that memory, absorb it into myself.

I would.

She shakes her head. "I don't know what you're talking about."

Deflection. *I invented that, Skylenna.*

"I can't apologize enough."

51

She waves me off. A quick dismissal and nearly a command for me to stop talking about it. Now.

"Can you tell me more about your system? The other alters? How it all works?" she asks, changing the subject in a seamless transition.

"Your idea of a bedtime story?"

She nods with a happy little yawn.

I stroke the back of her soft arm, savoring the sensation of goose bumps rising under my fingertips.

I've told her about a few of the others. About the different reasons they split. But we're not exactly fond of explaining what goes on in our heads. No one really understands. At least, no one that we've met.

"Prompt me," I say quietly, low enough for only her ears. "What would you like to know?"

She's quiet for a moment, biting her bottom lip in thought. An intense urge to pull that lip with my teeth sends a burst of fire through my gut.

"Will I eventually meet all of the alters?"

"No."

"Why not?"

I shrug. "There are some that were split to stay in the inner world."

"For what reason?"

"To hold certain memories. Both good and bad. To act as a caretaker for those that can't cope or care for themselves."

"Like children?" She sits up straighter. A note of concern thickening her voice.

"We call them littles."

She turns to look at me, face pinched with sadness. "There are child alters in the inner world?"

I nod.

"What are their names?"

"Arthur and Little Kane." I don't see them often, but Kane does.

Her hand shakes as she covers her mouth in surprise. "There's an alter for Kane's brother and his younger self?"

"Mm-hmm. I call them introjects. An alter based on an outside person." I adjust my legs to stretch out, trying to relax. "Little Kane is kind of frozen in time at the age of six. Unable to accept that anything

52

has changed past the moment he lost Sophia and Arthur. He has it rough. Kind of stuck in this endless flashback of his trauma."

Skylenna gasps. "He's stuck in his own personal hell?"

I give her a soft smile. "He's taken care of, though, and so is Arthur. By a caretaker alter."

"What's their name?"

"Sophia."

"Wow, an alter for his mom." Her eyes turn round and glossy. I try to rein it in, not wanting to upset my girl tonight.

"Kane sees them every once in a while. It's good for him."

"And they never come to the front? Never join the outside world?"

I shake my head. "Once. But it was upsetting for Little Kane to see himself in an adult body. He was deeply disturbed and retreated further into the inner world. But every now and then, Sophia will come close to the front, offering advice and emotional support in moments of heartache." I pull Skylenna's hand to my lips and kiss softly. "The way a mother would."

"Do you have any other—*introjects*?" She melts as my lips peck her hand a few more times.

"Absinthe." The name unfurls an unsettling rage in the pit of my stomach. I was so angry with myself for not killing Absinthe before she could ever get her hands on Skylenna.

*Fuck*, even now, the urge to do unspeakable acts to torture that old woman rings in my ears and makes my fingers twitch.

"Why would you want that crazy bitch to be an alter?" Skylenna questions in horror.

"We don't get to choose how alters are split or who they become. They manifest into their own person. And at the time, she was abusing us. She's what we call a persecutor. An alter that was split to hurt our system."

"I'm sorry," Skylenna fusses, shaking her head. "I didn't mean to make stupid assumptions of how everything works."

"The fact that you're taking the time to learn about us is very kind, Skylenna. Most people would be too scared to ask or think it was a hoax."

"Why would an alter harm your system?" She jumps right back into it. I fight the urge to smile at her endless curiosity.

"A persecuting alter holds self-hatred and internalized abuse. They abuse the rest of the alters to teach everyone how to behave in order to prevent more abuse—especially from the real Absinthe."

"Oh my god. That's awful."

"She would reenact abuse to make sure future abuse wasn't harder on us. It's fucked up, I know. But she never comes to the front. We've found a way to keep her hidden and locked away so she can't hurt us anymore." I really need to talk about a lighter topic. I can tell by how her brow furrows and her fingers curl into her palms that this is upsetting her too much.

"There is a female alter that stays hidden from everyone," I say, searching for a lighter topic. "Her name is Bloom."

"Bloom." Skylenna smiles. "What kind of alter is she?"

"A memory holder. She keeps bad memories from the other alters. Occasionally works with other trauma holders, like me."

"What's she like?"

"Honestly? Soulless. Inhuman. She has to be, though, in order to cope with the memories she bears alone."

"Does she hold the worst of all the traumatic memories?"

I shake my head. *We're supposed to keep this light.* But now that the truth is out, I'll never keep her in the dark again.

"There are *deeper alters*. I've never met them. None of us have, actually. They reside so deep in the inner world, so far away from all of us, that I'm not sure if we could even find them. They hold the most severe, devastating memories that would likely kill us if we ever knew about them."

It's dark. I know.

"How horrible could something be that they can't come anywhere near you?" she asks, voice trembling.

I shrug. "Memories can sometimes bleed from one alter to another. Not intentionally. The ones the *deeper alters* cope with are too horrible ever to risk coming to light."

Skylenna holds me closer, pressing our bodies painfully against the bars.

"Is this why you never talk about it? Because of how heavy the topic is?"

I nod. "It isn't a happy story."

54

At that, her stomach gurgles loudly.

I close my eyes, letting my head fall back to the bars in silent hatred for this place. Our situation. The fact that they're all probably starving right now.

"When we fall asleep, maybe I'll join you in the inner world," Skylenna breathes, sleep draping over her eyes. "Maybe we can stay there a while."

I kiss the top of her head.

"It's a date."

# 5. Night Lurkers

## Ruth

The floor is cold and sharp. It's like trying to sleep on a bed of glass.

There is no blanket, no pillow, no silk sheets to caress my skin. I'm not lathered in body creams or hair oils. I'm not soft from my lady-doll regimen in a bathtub of milk and honey. The only familiar sensation is trying to sleep with an empty tummy.

I haven't voiced my terror to others, but it's there. Screaming in my bloodstream. Banging on the inside of my skull like a child throwing a tantrum. I've seen the inside walls of the asylum. But I was never a prisoner. Never helpless at the cruel hands of the staff. The constant urge to run and hide, stay in my cage, and avoid all signs of human life is unbearably intense.

But they can't know that. I don't want to be the weak link. I want to be fierce, strong, an asset to this family. But right now, as I shiver against the cold draft in the air, I feel like a massive liability. A burden they can't get rid of.

I roll over to my side, noticing Warrose staring at the cage ceiling. No doubt annoyed at the constant eerie music of a distorted trumpet and an old-fashioned pipe organ. They play it constantly—no peaceful silence.

I sigh, closing my eyes, trying to fall asleep. But his presence is like a lightning storm. Impossible to keep your eyes closed when the sky is demanding attention above your head.

I force my eyes into small slits, doing my best to hide the fact that I'm watching him. My gaze trails over the largeness of his chest, the taut muscles along his stomach contracting as he breathes.

I wonder how much his muscles would tense if I ran my hand up his abdomen and—

Okay. *No.* Stop that.

He's the chicken coward. He's rude and crass, and I don't like him.

But his black hair falls around his head in shiny waves. And in the strange lights, those big eyes look bluer than the midnight sea.

"My hand is securely at my side. You can stop waiting for a show," Warrose purrs, a smirk glinting in his eyes without looking over at me.

"*Pfff.*" I roll my eyes, a little embarrassed that I've been caught staring. "No one wants tickets to that show."

His tattooed chest rumbles with a laugh, but he doesn't respond, so I keep going.

"And another thing—"

I'm interrupted by a low, guttural growl. Labored breathing. Slow, thumping steps. Warrose and I perk up at the same time, instantly zeroing in on a massive figure passing our cages. *Slowly.* A gargantuan man that's over six foot seven with hair so long, it grazes the floor behind him. No shirt. Black pants. And a metal cage around his head. Rusted iron like a muzzle for a dog.

The collar around his throat is attached to a long chain that drags against the floor behind him. I flinch as he stops in front of my cage, hand gripping my bars.

I hold my breath, and every muscle of Warrose's body seems to turn to stone.

*There's a prisoner out of his cage!*

He doesn't look at me, though he lingers close as if he's waiting for me to make a movement he can track.

And I smell him. Months of built-up *rank* body odor mixed with a waft of wet dog. I wince, and that's all it takes. The giant, long-haired, muzzled man turns to me. His movements mechanical and awkward.

I gulp loudly as his beady eyes meet mine through the slits of his cage.

"Don't move," Warrose breathes, low and gruff.

I force myself to turn into a concrete statue. But my hands tremble at my sides, and my stomach drops as if I'm falling off a cliff. *Someone get him to stop staring at me!*

"He can't hear us. But stay very still," Dessin says quietly. I shift my gaze to him from the corner of my eye. He's holding Skylenna's sleeping body against the bars. And it's clear he doesn't want this little disturbance to wake her. In fact, Warrose, Dessin, and I are the only ones awake.

I almost ask Dessin how he knows the monstrous man can't hear us, but I quickly see the raised, jagged scars where his ears once were.

"Keep still, little rebel. His eyes are planted on you." And if I'm not mistaken, there's a hint of agitation in Warrose's voice. A territorial tone.

The prisoner grunts after a long moment, then continues to walk in a slow, dazed path.

I let myself relax back down to the floor with a long sigh. "What the hell?"

"It looks like there are some prisoners only allowed out at night," Dessin comments before closing his eyes and resting his head back against his cage.

I nod against the chill that rakes down my flesh. Flexing my fingers, I feel a weight covering my right hand. It's rough and warm. I nearly jerk it away before realizing it's a hand. A strong, calloused, bronze hand.

"Are you alright?" Warrose asks without paying me a glance.

"I guess," I say, still watching his large hand completely enveloping my own.

Warrose nods stiffly.

I remain still, afraid that if I move at all, his hand will return to his cage without another thought. I should want that. But for some reason, I hold my breath. I like the surge of heat pouring from his hand to mine.

It's so unbelievably comforting. A touch of solace I've been desperate for.

I don't want him to let go.

It could be anyone's hand, of course. I still don't like him or his bad attitude. But considering this situation, I accept the fate.

"Sleeping is going to be fun with these big scary men walking around at night," I say in a hushed tone. *I just want to snuggle against that warm hand.*

"Isn't it, though?" Warrose chuckles. "This place just keeps getting better and better."

I let my head settle back down on the rocky ground. I'm deeply uncomfortable. My stomach twists with the need for warm bread or a glass of milk. But at least my stomach will look flat while I'm in this revealing uniform. My thighs won't touch. My shoulders will remain sharp and pointed. All is right.

"Is this the worst place you've ever had to sleep?" I ask. I'm not sure I want to know the answer. But I need a distraction. Something to help me fall asleep in this cage. Something to make me forget about the giant, earless man that stalks the halls of this prison.

"Sadly, no."

"Top five?"

He nods.

"What was the worst?" My heart jumps as Warrose adjusts his hands on top of mine. But he doesn't take it away.

"Uh"—he scratches the facial hair growing thicker along his jaw— "I had to hide from a nadaskar once. By sleeping under a dead bear."

"*What?*" I hiss, trying not to wake the others.

Warrose nods. "I was eleven. Part of my training was to track down a rabid nadaskar. It ended up tracking me. Nearly tore my leg off. The only way to get it to forget about my scent was to sleep under a dead bear for a while."

I have no words. Not a single appropriate response. Do I apologize? Tell him I can relate? I understand? I cannot. Hopefully, I never will.

"What about you?"

"This is definitely the worst. But the time you made me sleep in a tree comes to a close second."

One night, while we were following Skylenna, Warrose was sure we were being followed. He made us climb a tree while we watched Demechnef soldiers trying to track where we went next. I complained all night, only stopping when Niles fell out and screamed in pain as he landed on his burned skin.

He scoffs. "You're such a brat. The only thing that made sleeping in a tree unbearable was hearing you whine about it."

"I've been told my whining is quite cute. Sexy, even."

"You have been lied to."

I snort. "Men don't lie when they're in the thrusts of passion."

Okay, so I've never actually experienced thrusts of *passion*. I did, however, lose my virginity to Benjamin Darthmunt, who lasted a good three pumps before grunting like a dying engine and landing on top of me in a sweaty heap. We did it three more times after that over the span of two months. I kept thinking it would get better. Maybe he'd last longer.

He did not.

It was awful.

Warrose's scratchy hand flexes over mine, gripping my knuckles like he wants to yank my arm and pull me into his cage. The sheer strength of his grip sends a rush of heat to my belly, sliding down my thighs.

"So, these men that are thrusting with passion are making you *whine* in bed, then?" His voice is dark and smoky, like a massive campfire at midnight.

"That's right." Not true. The only noise I made was to ask, *is it over?*

"It was bad sex," he states.

"Uh, no. It was really good. Like *really* good. So good."

Warrose turns his head, giving me an amused look of disbelief.

"Good," I add again like an idiot.

"If it was so *good*, then you wouldn't be whining. You'd be screaming your lover's name as each orgasm crashes into you. That's good sex, little rebel." That entire sentence is like diving off a cliff and falling into warm honey. I'm wet. Shamefully slick between my legs. Warrose's dreamy hazel-blue eyes flick down to my bobbing throat.

I huff. "You don't look like the screaming type, War-Man."

"You're right. I'm the growling, groaning, roaring into your neck as I slam into the hilt *type*. I'm the type that will have my face buried between your thighs for hours before I let myself come." His gaze turns dark, hazy even. I've never seen a man's eyes dilate to the point of black saucers.

I can't help it. My hand opens for him. And for just a moment, he's surprised. A brief glint of shock. But he acts quickly. Those large fingers curl through my own, and his thumb traces over my skin slowly. A gentle tease. A steady pulse of pleasure zings up my arm.

I pinch my thighs together as if my life depends on it.

What am I doing? I don't want to give him the wrong idea. But this feels so good. I imagine the sound of him growling in my ear. The feel of his weight rocking over my body.

I let out a quick breath as if to force out this attraction seeping through my veins, tightening my muscles, and making me involuntarily clench around air.

Warrose is not my type. I've always been attracted to gentlemen. Golden boys with blond hair, soft features, and charming personalities. That's what I was raised to find handsome. Romantic. Stable.

"Promise me something?" he asks, breaking the silence.

"Never." I smile.

"You can mouth off with me in private, be your usual bratty self. But you need to keep your attitude in check when we're out in the open."

"Excuse me?" My chest tightens.

"Behave."

I yank my hand from his grip. "That's cute. How did you see this conversation going in your head, chicken coward?" Steam practically bursts from my ears. *Behave.* I already feel like a helpless child in this group. And now I'm being told not to get in the way. I'm not *big-mouth Niles*. I know how to keep a low profile. "*Behave,*" I mock.

"I didn't mean it like that."

"Please. Stick your foot further into your mouth and explain."

Warrose looks down at his empty hand. "This place is full of men that…" he growls under his breath, running his other hand through his hair.

"That what?"

"And you're *you*, Ruth."

I stiffen at the sound his voice makes when he says my name. He never uses my name.

"I'm me?"

"I'm going to lose my mind if any of them try..." He trails off again, grunting at his inability to express whatever is frustrating him.

"Are you going to finish any of these sentences?" I ask.

His throat bobs, and his eyes fall closed.

"Warrose?"

"Forget it, little rebel."

Forget what? He hasn't said anything.

I watch as he pulls his hand back into his own cage, turning onto his side before his breathing turns rough and heavy.

# 6. Restless Fire

## Niles

"GO, DAISZEK! GO!" I scream at the top of my lungs, tears running wild down my face as I throw the giant lock to the sand.

*I did it! I fucking did it.*

But I'm unable to celebrate. Sweat drenches my tunic. My lungs seize up at the sudden shock of pain rippling through flesh, through organs, through my goddammed soul.

I look down as I start flailing about.

Bright orange flames eat at my skin like a fast-acting virus.

I howl in agony as it spreads up my arm and over my neck. It's a thousand blades slicing through my skin. It's acid melting through my veins.

All I can do is launch my body toward the sand and pray that I can extinguish this fire myself. I get lucky when I see DaiSzek bulldoze through the flaming pikes. The sheer force of his gallop is unstoppable.

*Yes, I've made the right choice. But all I can think about is my body* exploding in yellow light. The smell of burning flesh and smoke surrounded me at every turn.

"*Help meeeeee!*" I wail, crawling through the opening and rolling toward the ocean waves.

Water. I need water.

I'm going to die here.

But at least I'll have saved them all by freeing the black beast.

Sand rains in my vision like a storm of fine mist. I don't even know which direction I'm throwing my body as the motion of flames, waves, and the searing pain blur together.

I didn't get to say goodbye to Chekiss.

I didn't get to find a one true love. A soul mate. A person I'll love until my last breath. Maybe they knew I'd die young. Maybe they're waiting for me in heaven.

"*I'm here, Niles.*" A soft, soothing voice wraps around my sweltering body, shaking in terror. "*I'm here.*"

I jolt awake with a shaky gasp. Cold, cold, cold, yet burning on the inside. It was a nightmare. A reoccurring hellhole I fall into when I close my eyes. A prison far worse than this Vexamen trap. I blink away the warm tears pooling in my eyes, search my surroundings for an anchor. Bars. Black brimstone walls. Flickering red and yellow lights. And the disturbing tune that sounds like a broken record.

But the pain of the fire hasn't gone away. My arm vibrates with a sting so severe, I have to grit my teeth, clench every muscle, and hiss to release some of the tension.

*Where's my cream?*

We're in prison. We didn't bring the medicine that takes this agony away.

What the fuck am I supposed to do? I'll die if I must endure this pain without the salve I need. Do I wake the others? Do I start screaming? I'm two seconds from this becoming unbearable. A force that won't let me suffer in silence.

"I'm here." That voice from my nightmare scares the shit out of me. I jerk away from the sound, gawking in the dark at the cage to my left.

It's Marilynn. She's pressing herself against the bars, reaching for me with a cold panic tightening her cheeks.

"Hi." I try to wave, but the heat flares across my shoulder at the gesture. "Sorry. Did I wake you?" I grit through clenched teeth.

"I can help," Marilynn says, still reaching her arm out for me.

Like an idiot, I take her hand and shake it.

"No, give me your foot." Her voice is like steam from a hot bath, but her face still wears that grumpy, unapproachable mask.

*Oh.* Foot. "Why?" I hiss but stretch my leg out to her anyway. "It's kind of dirty. Normally I'm very hygienic. But as you can see, we're in prison and barefoot." Every word comes out strained like I'm moments from screaming.

She throws her long red hair over her shoulder and begins massaging my foot. I raise my eyebrows. "What're you doing?" I ask.

"It's for chronic pain. I'm trying to find the spot...*ah*, there it is."

Her fingers pinch a spot in the center of my foot. At first, it's painful, sharp, but after a moment I sigh loudly. It's as if she unplugged the drain that is holding my suffering. It's a slow release. But fuck, it feels amazing.

"Holy shit," I breathe. "How'd you do that?"

The fire under my skin isn't gone. Not even close. But it certainly reeled it in, taming the eternal flames.

"Just a technique I learned from one of the colonies."

I nod, lowering myself with a slow exhale. Relief. Sweet, sweet relief.

"Thank you. I would have woken up the entire prison if left to manage it alone."

Marilynn doesn't respond. Her ocean-blue eyes watch me with an unreadable expression. My eyes trail over her lazily. Her cherry-red lips. Her attire, intended as a uniform, struggles to rein in her generous form. Creamy white skin covered in freckles.

"You don't say much, huh?" I whisper.

"Not nearly as much as you."

I chuckle.

"We need to get you medicine for these burns," she muses, still adding pressure to my foot. "You think this prison has a medic?"

"Unlikely. But maybe they'll let us out so we can get one." I wink.

Marilynn's lips part.

"It was a joke. I'm really funny and make them sometimes." *Hello? Have you heard of sarcasm?* She's so stiff. I'm going to have to pay her back for this pain relief by teaching her how to have a sense of humor.

"Yeah." Her cheeks blossom in color. Dark red spreads down her neck, reaching her ears and collarbone. "That was funny." Though her soft face remains untouched by humor or any sign of a positive reaction.

I nod. It was funny.

Her small hands work my foot with precision. I wonder what happens when she lets go. Will the pain come back? Will it hit me like a rogue wave? I decide it's best to distract myself, just in case this doesn't last. It would suck if I wasted this time thinking about the pain instead of enjoying it.

"You were engaged to Aurick," I prompt, studying her immediate reaction to his name.

Marilynn recoils but recovers quickly. "Yes."

"Wow. That sounds...*sickening.*"

I don't think I will ever forgive The Demechnefs. Aurick's father tortured and killed mine. And made me believe he was a monster. A predator to his own son. I ended up in the asylum because of it. I ended up being hosed down by Belinda like an animal in a cage.

But Charles never gave in. He loved me. He fought for me.

My heart pumps acid to my arteries. I could vomit just thinking about this if there was any food in my stomach to turn over.

"But you ran away from him," I add.

"I did."

"Do you still love him?" I can imagine Chekiss smacking me upside the head right now. I'm invasive. I *know*. Okay, but my mouth has a mind of its own. It just blurts out anything.

"I think a part of me will always love him a little." Her chest moves up and down with slow, uneven breaths. "But it isn't the kind of love that's written about in fairy tales. It's the kind that hurts you in the end. The kind that cuts deeply and doesn't quite heal right."

"I understand." Now she's speaking my language. I know love. It was my only anchor in this sick world. It was the only shining beacon leading me back to shore.

"What about you?" She pinches the spot on my foot harder. "Have you found your fairy tale love?"

I don't know why, but that question makes me want to sob into my hands like a little boy. It's what I've always wanted. What I've dreamed of my entire life. A soul mate. A lover to grow old with. I can see it when I watch Skylenna with Dessin or Kane. The way her whole world shifts, slows down, pauses just to see him smile.

I want that desperately.

Probably more than anyone here.

But there are times I feel unworthy. As if I'm fated to die alone like some cosmic irony.

"No. I have never been loved, nor have I ever been in love." The words taste like ash and hopelessness on my tongue.

"That makes you sad."

"Of course, it does," I snap with a sharp tone. "Love is the most beautiful thing in the world. It would be a tragedy if I died here without ever experiencing it."

"You're not going to die here, Niles." Marilynn grimaces. Those plump, cherry-red lips turning downward.

I laugh quietly. "It's looking pretty grim."

We remain quiet for a few minutes while she continues to massage my foot. I'd feel guilty that she's staying up late to do this for me if it wasn't relieving so much pain. I'm so fucking grateful; I wish I could give her a hug.

"Thank you for being kind to me," I say sleepily.

She wakes up from a deep thought, looking me over with those wide, ocean-blue eyes.

"I get teased a lot. I don't mind that at all, because I wield my humor like a sword. I love to laugh and to make others laugh. But sometimes it's nice to be seen and respected."

Rambling. I always ramble. It's bad enough that this poor girl is rubbing my foot to keep me from waking up the prison with my screams. Now I'm talking her ear off.

"I see."

Marilynn leans her forehead against a bar, steering her contemplative expression away from me as she reflects.

"I think you're a good man," she adds in a whisper. "When you go to sleep tonight, maybe you'll dream of your soul mate instead of having a nightmare."

I smile sadly. "Maybe."

# 7. Blood

## Skylenna

I nearly panic when my eyes peel open to see the charcoal ceiling and crooked bars over my head. I have a flashback to Albatross and his wicked ways of tormenting me. I remember the hardness of Absinthe's hand cracking over my cheekbone. It turns my stomach upside down, releases a cold sweat across my neck, and constricts my lungs from expanding to bring in more air.

But I feel him beside me.

Feel the beating of his heart sending a ripple through the air that only I can sense.

Feel him slowly wake up. Open his eyes. Blink. And to think, there was a time when I thought I'd never see him blink again.

I turn my head to watch him adjust to our temporary home. And my entire body seems to sigh at the sight of him. His furrowed brow. Clenched jaw. Warm tan skin. And those dark-mahogany eyes.

He sits up against the bars, rubs a hand over his face, and I can see his mind working. A constant, well-oiled machine that is trying to get us out of this mess. But he won't do it alone. I swear on everything…Dessin will not do this alone.

My stomach gurgles loudly, and Dessin shudders, eyeing my waist like it just said something highly offensive.

"It's fine," I say with an embarrassed laugh.

"No, it's not."

Bad mood Dessin. He's cranky. Hungry. And murderous.

Look out, Vexamen Prison.

The doors to each cell open simultaneously. Metal clanks and feet shuffle. Like last time, we wait for the crowd of prisoners to head to the showers first. Once they're out of sight, we exit together.

"Before anyone asks, no, I did not masturbate last night. So, if any one of you had wet dreams, it wasn't because of me. I was a good boy." Niles stretches, smiling with tired eyes.

"Nobody, I repeat, *nobody* asked." Ruth shakes her head and tries to fight back a smile.

"*Okay*. Let's pretend like you weren't all thinking it. Picturing it. Probably couldn't sleep because you were hoping to hear it," Niles says smugly.

He clearly got a good sleep last night. I was worried his burns would keep him up, especially since we don't have his special cream.

Warrose rolls his eyes, making an effort to completely ignore the sound of Niles's voice.

The group starts moving, but Dessin puts one hand on my chest and starts walking me into my cell. A hungry, insidious look in his eyes. Determination to do whatever is on his mind.

"Dessin?"

He looks back at Warrose. "We'll be right behind you."

Warrose snorts and nods, ushering Ruth to keep walking.

"What's going on?" I ask.

He backs me against the bars, breathing heavily, inhaling through his nose to smell my neck, my collarbone, my cleavage.

My breath comes out in a stuttering rush against his face. And it's as though my body understands what he needs. What he's so desperate for. A release from the stress of this. A moment away from it all.

"You want to do this right here?" I ask, my voice low and breathy. Sentinels follow our friends to the showers, but there is one who

72

remains close to our cage, watching us with predatory eyes.

Dessin nods like the animal in him is unable to form words. Only rough, needy actions.

With one quick motion, he pinches my nipples through the thin material covering them. Then he yanks them hard toward his chest. "Mine," he growls. It's practically inhumane. Territorial. Deep and rugged. And he looks over his shoulder, daring that armed guard to do anything other than watch. Normally, he wouldn't allow anyone to see me indecent, but we don't have many options here, do we?

"*Ah,*" I hiss at the sharp sting that radiates within my breasts. But that pain shoots a current of heat through my entire body. "Yours," I whisper.

Dessin hikes up my legs, pressing his hard erection against my wet apex. His weight nails me against the cage bars, grinding into my tailbone, strong enough to leave bruises. But I don't care. There's nothing important to me other than the way he's grinding against my clit.

"We can't," I exhale. *But why not?* I know we're supposed to hide our affection for each other. But he needs a release, and so do I.

Dessin's chest grumbles against my hardened nipples.

We need this. Just once.

"It has to be quick." I reach my hand down to his growing length. My vision blurs. My mouth waters.

He keeps his eyes level with mine as I yank down his pants, letting his large cock free. The head is shiny with precum, but Dessin doesn't seem to notice. He's lifting my hips higher, angling my center just right. I move the material to the side for him, gritting my teeth as he rubs the head through my wetness.

I see the sentinel shifting on his feet, trying to get a better look at my exposed areas. But Dessin shields me with his body, hiding us in the shadows.

"Oh," I moan, writhing in his arms. Dessin's jaw clenches, and his cock pulses more precum over my clit. "Only a little."

Even with his eyes glazed over, he nods once, understanding what I mean. He pushes the tip of his large dick inside of me. Nudging me to open for him.

I gasp against his lips as a spasm undulates right above my pelvic bone, opening my channel for him. God, I want him to shove it inside of me until I'm unable to form words. I want him to take me roughly. I want him to slam into the hilt.

But this little bit ignites the flame of our arousal. It starts a frenzy.

"Do you think you can come like this?" I ask him. I know I can. It'll just take a little pressure on a certain spot.

Dessin makes an attempt to say yes, but instead, he rests his forehead against mine and uses his thumb to rub circles over my throbbing clit.

"*Dessin*," I groan loudly.

"Fuck, Skylenna," he breathes. "The amount of restraint I'm using to not bury myself inside your pretty pink cunt is going to kill me."

My pussy clenches in a jerky reaction to the dark depths of his voice. I feel an overwhelming amount of liquid pooling around the tip of his cock, dripping down his shaft and down my cheeks.

And with that, he pushes a little more, hitting that spot, causing my spine to arch, my toes to curl, my head to lull back. I cling to his back and neck like a parasite, grinding like I've lost my mind, pulsing against the head of his cock to chase that rush.

"I'm almost—"

"No." He grabs me by the neck, pulling my face a centimeter from his. "You don't come until I say you can."

This makes me that much closer to bursting into flames. His breath emits heat into my mouth, and I open a little wider, giving him access to dip his tongue past my lips. The wet warmth swirls around, touching the back of my throat with vigorous intent to claim, to dominate. I cry out against his plush lips.

"You are mine in this prison. *Mine*."

Fury pinches his brow, darkens his gaze. And I know it's because, deep down, he's scared to lose me here. Scared of what this place might do to us.

Dessin snatches my lips between his teeth and bites down until we both taste blood. I yelp, tingling with pain and pleasure in the pit of my belly. Something in his face goes wild and ravenous, needing more of me, making him insane with hunger. With one hand, he slides his fingers over my aching clit and around the wetness that coats the inside of my channel, all without removing his tip.

He brings those fingers to his nose and breathes me in.

"Smells fucking delicious," he grates. "Makes me want to eat you in here until our friends come looking for us."

My eyes flutter closed as I imagine him feasting on me in the shadows of this cage, taking his time as he laps me up in a lazy, careless rhythm.

"Mine," he growls again, licking his fingers clean.

"Then mark me," I challenge, running my tongue over the blood that has dripped from my lips to his. "Cover me in you. I want it to drip down my thighs."

I see it in his jaw first. The way he bites down, tilts his head, sucks in a sharp breath. Then grunts into my open mouth, raw and gravelly. The vibration and feel of his hot breath send me tumbling into a wave of my own pleasure. The muscles in his tightly coiled abdomen flex and jolt as he roars against my mouth. A white rope shoots out over my clit, gushing over my pussy.

To my surprise, Dessin uses his tip to push some inside me.

I smile against his mouth. "Getting a head start?"

He doesn't return my smile. Only stares for a short moment.

"I love you, baby. I can't show it enough. Even in a place like this. Nothing can stop me from worshipping the ground you fucking walk on. Understand?"

As my feet hit the floor, I wrap my arms around his neck, pulling his broad chest against me for a hug. The small movement reminds me of the first time we hugged in the abandoned Demechnef building. He hesitated then, like he was unsure of how to respond to an act of affection.

He doesn't hesitate now. His arms circle my waist, clutching me to the hard planes of his body like he's desperate to mold me into him. My heart fills to the brim with warmth and butterflies.

"Do you remember hugging me when we were just friends?"

He holds me tighter. "Yes."

"Why did you always wait so long to hug me back?"

Dessin sighs into my hair. "I was afraid to get too close to you. I was the one who was supposed to carry out your plan. And when you pressed your body to mine...I felt things I've never felt before."

It's amazing. Even in this prison, we're able to make special moments. I hold it close to my heart and tuck it away in a safe place.

"Did you get hard?" I blurt out. *Oh god.* I pulled a Niles. I ruined the moment with an inappropriate response. "Ignore that. I've spent too much time around Niles."

"Extremely hard. It was often painful to be around you." He smiles. "And we've all spent too much time around Niles. He has the kind of personality you can only take in small doses."

We both laugh, and as we turn to leave my cage, the sentinel is still here. Dessin dwarfs him in every way, breathing through his nostrils like a dragon. I bump him with my elbow, urging him to lay low and move along.

But the suicidal sentinel challenges Dessin with a single look, smug and taunting.

"Don't take the bait," I whisper.

He lifts an eyebrow, exhales with a slight grumble, and turns to walk. The guard follows us, occasionally jabbing Dessin in the back with a baton. Quick, cruel pokes that are followed by his sneering chuckles. I grit my own teeth before I make the decision to lash out for him, twisting my body to attack with—

Dessin tugs me by the arm, lowering his lips to my ear. "Don't take the bait."

I blow out a breath, simmering and quivering on the inside.

*We'll get through this.*
*We'll get through this.*
*We'll get through this.*

THE SHOWERS ARE FILLED WITH screams, loud thuds, and the sounds of someone choking.

Dessin and I push our way through the crowd of naked prisoners. Water and soap sloshes at my ankles, mixed with a thin stream of blood. And then we hear Ruth scream.

"Move!" Dessin begins bulldozing through anyone who stands in our way. I follow his every step, my heart knocking painfully in my chest, my breath running ragged through my lungs.

*Please, not Ruth.*

If anything happens to that sweet girl, I'll never forgive myself. These screams will haunt me until my last breath. Tears spring from my eyes. My fists clench in a fierce preparation to fight. To kill.

We make it to the center of the showers, where the broken pipe is hosing down the crowd watching the incident.

Ruth stands unharmed next to Niles and Marilynn, covering her breasts and pelvic area. Her face is tomato red, tears glisten over her bronze eyes.

"Stop it, Warrose!" she screams again.

I follow her eyes to a very naked Warrose. His tattooed back is to us, and he's holding a short man by the throat, lifting him in the air with one arm as if he doesn't weigh more than a sack of feathers.

The naked man is pale, yet every inch of skin is an embarrassing shade of pink like he's been slapped all over. Veins protrude into his forehead, and his blond beard dangles over Warrose's wrist.

Ah, he's the man we encountered yesterday.

"I don't care that you were jerking yourself to the sight of her. All I'm saying is that your tiny excuse for a penis *offends* me. For no reason in particular," Warrose says casually.

I look down at the half-erect dick on the blond-bearded man. It loses its firmness with each second that Warrose chokes the man out.

Dessin cracks up, dropping his fighting stance and laughing as he realizes the reason behind this outburst. The sound causes me to flinch, then smack Dessin on the arm.

"Tell him to stop!" Ruth begs us.

"No, Warrose." Pause. "Stop that." Pause. "Put the nice man down," Dessin says in a monotone, half-assed attempt. He shrugs as if to say *I tried*.

I bite back a smile. "Back off, Warrose."

With one last look at the petite, shivering man, he tosses him to the floor with a splashing wet thud.

"Little guy was masturbating at the sight of Ruth." Niles pops up behind me with a smile. "I know, that's obviously not funny. Duh. But I'm not going to lie, when Ruthie had to squint to see the man's little erection, it was hard not to laugh."

"You're such a psychopath!" Ruth stomps her foot in a puddle, doing her best to cover her naked body. "We're supposed to be laying low!"

Warrose takes one big step toward her, small drops of water splashing off his broad chest down to her scowling face. I never realized how much bigger than her he is. At least a foot and a few inches taller. Her narrow, bony shoulder span is half the width of his. His presence nearly swallowing her whole.

"Have I offended you?"

"Yes!"

"And the insect of a man trying to reach completion while staring at your ass *didn't*?"

"He didn't touch me, did he?" She narrows her eyes.

"Would you rather me kill the bee after it stings you?"

"How about we table this conversation until we're in private?" I signal to the crowd still watching us. "Let's go find out if we're being fed today!"

I look over at Dessin for backup, but he's still pressing his fist to his mouth, stifling a laugh.

Warrose's dilated eyes flash to Dessin, and he cracks a small smirk.

"Tell me you wouldn't have done the same."

"I'd have ripped it off his body."

"You'd need a pair of tweezers and a magnifying glass to find it," Warrose deadpans, and they both burst out into deep, throaty laughter.

Changing out my wet uniform for a dry one, I give Ruth a quick hug.

"I heard you scream and thought something bad happened to you," I whisper.

"Something bad *did* happen to me. The chicken coward tried to defend my honor and probably put a target on my back," she seethes.

I roll my eyes. "I thought you were hurt. I got scared."

Ruth wrings out her wet, curly hair, studying me with pitying eyes.

"My safety isn't a burden you need to carry, okay? You have enough on your plate trying to get us out of here."

I do have a lot on my plate. Dessin has a lot on his plate. But we wouldn't have a plate without them. No matter what she says, the fear of losing her in this place won't go away. I won't be able to truly be at peace until I know my family is safe.

But I nod anyway.

We walk into the dining area with caution, stiffening our spines and drying our mouths. Will they feed us today? Will they forget about our confrontation yesterday?

We don't make it three steps in before the serving staff slowly, intentionally turns their backs to us. Shunning. Making a statement.

Dessin and I stop walking. It takes a sudden surge of self-control not to reach for his hand, seek his warmth.

"Fuck this," Dessin growls, taking a damning step forward to confront the assembly line of prisoners.

I snatch his elbow before he takes another step.

"*Don't.* Remember the three-strike rule." I keep my face neutral. Keep my chin high. "We're valuable to Vexamen. They won't kill us this way. They're just playing with us."

If we mess up now, the consequences could be astronomical.

Dessin huffs through his nose, eyes still burning a hole through the prisoners serving food. Hands tighten around air, veins pulsing over his forearms. He takes one look back at Warrose, silently communicating his bloodlust.

"*Shit*," Warrose scoffs, stomping to an empty table.

"I lost my appetite in this disease-infested toilet bowl anyway." Niles pinches his nose. The smell is rank. Today it's a mix of onions, body odor, and rotting meat.

But I can't stop my stomach from begging for a scrap of food. It twists and ties itself into an aching knot. I haven't eaten since we left Demechnef. How many days has it been? We're lucky we've been drinking the water that dumps down on us from the broken pipe in the showers. Otherwise, dehydration would have been the silent killer.

"I'm going to get us food," Dessin promises as we get settled in our cold seats.

"Don't worry about it, Dess. Fasts are good for detoxing our bodies!" Ruth chimes, running a small hand through her mess of damp curls.

I frown, somehow her eagerness to see the bright side in such a dismal situation just makes me more upset. But it also makes me love her more. I understand her views on food. That city trained us to see eating as the enemy. To see every bright side to weight loss and vanity. I still have that unhealthy mindset flaring up, checking my waistline, observing the size of my arms and thighs. It's hard to get rid of. I hope we can work on it together.

"I don't like nicknames," Dessin deadpans.

Warrose raises a dark eyebrow at me. A taunt gleaming in his weary eyes.

"You sure about that?" he asks with a mischievous smile curling his lips.

"Don't," Dessin says flatly.

"Not even the time you named yourself the...*Dess-Aster*?"

We collectively gasp.

"I was seven."

"Or *Dess-Truction*?"

Dessin sighs. We finally break, cracking up at the idea of Dessin nicknaming himself.

"Awe," I coo, patting his thigh.

"Sounds a little...*Dess-Perate*." Niles grins widely, clearly proud of his own wit.

Dessin slices his glare to Niles, pinning him in his seat silently. Niles drops his gaze to his lap.

"You had to ruin it," Warrose says.

Our laughter fades as we notice a shadow hovering over our table. An old woman with brassy gray hair and a scarred-up face sets a plate with a fancy cover on our table. She does a polite bow and utters something in old Alkadonian.

"She said *compliments of the chef*," Ruth translates skeptically.

The room's chatter fizzles out.

I hold my breath while Dessin reaches out his hand, plucking the silver cover off the plate. Niles immediately gags.

A steaming pile of fresh...*shit*.

Human feces.

My face burns as I quickly look away, meeting the eyes of prisoners that are insidiously tickled. Silent chuckling. Parted mouths in pleasant surprise.

I want to bury them all.

"Now they've done it," Warrose mutters.

I blow out a frustrated breath, ready to tell Dessin to cover the damn plate. But I realize Warrose is shaking his head at Dessin's reaction. And

I'm a fool if I thought he could submit to anyone, even if it means laying low until we figure out what's going on.

Dessin stares at the plate. Dead behind the eyes. A storm of ice and fire clashing in his mind. May God save their souls, because Dessin certainly won't.

"Dessi" I don't get to finish saying his name with firm caution. He's up. Towering over the old woman. And there is only a brief moment before he stares down at me with that familiar glint in his deep, hickory eyes. It's the same look he gave me before he snapped the man's neck in the abandoned Demechnef building.

He swipes one of six forks from the plate. And they're all mindless idiots if they thought he couldn't use a fucking fork as a weapon. With one jab, he blinds the old woman. Like stabbing a toothpick into an olive. She shrieks, falling to her brittle knees and clutching her hands to her face.

"Well, fuck," Warrose chuffs out a laugh.

Dessin throws the next two forks like a dart. They soar over tables until they meet their targets. Two elderly men in the serving line. They get hit in the shoulder and collarbone. Not fatal, but they howl like dying animals.

Before he grabs the next fork, a bladed chain whips through the air, latching onto his bare chest. It sticks to him like a magnet for three seconds before the sentinel yanks his arm back, ripping the chain from Dessin's chest, removing chunks of flesh in the process.

"*Veetewz!*" the sentinel bellows.

I rise from my seat. To help. To fight. To—

Copper. The scent is horrible and unforgettable. It's entwined with the smell of the sea, salt, and fish. The briny air. The crashing waves.

I'm on the beach, yet I'm still here. Sand fills my boots. Smoke stains my skin.

And there's blood. He's bleeding. It drizzles down his wounded chest. I reach out to help him, but it covers my hands, my arms, my clothes. Hot and dripping off my elbows.

"No," I breathe.

"Skylenna?" I hear Niles, but my vision is tunneled. I taste the sea. I taste tears.

I look down at my bloody hands again. It's everywhere. The blood is everywhere. I am covered in Dessin's blood. In Kane's blood. Greystone. Aquarus.

"Dessin," I utter with a cracking voice and quivering lip. "*Blood. There's so much blood!*"

Dessin looks down at his slashed chest, then back at me with his face loosening in surprise. A strange emotion flickering in his alert gaze.

"I'm fine. It's just a scratch," he says hesitantly.

I shake my head. It's the sickle. The sharp, curved blade. It's cracked through his ribs and severed a lung. It's killing him. He's dying.

*Blood. Oh, god, there's so much blood.*

My hands.

My arms.

My entire world goes up in flames as I watch it happen, *feel* it happen all over again.

"Someone—help him," I whisper, unable to breathe, to speak, to understand what's happening. My heart explodes in my chest, my entire body trembles like an earthquake.

Blood. It's everywhere. It covers the tables and chairs. It gushes down my legs. And I hear the waves roll onto the shore.

*He's dying.*

"Skylenna…"

"No." That girl is dead. She drowned in the asylum. "*No!*"

The cold, striking rage gives no warning. It possesses me like a demon seeping into every pore of my soul. It mutes my logic and blinds my reason.

I begin attacking with my bare hands. My body is flung through the air in a screaming, thrashing fit. With one painful tug, the bladed chain is out of the sentinel's hands. I wrap it around his throat and break his neck. *Snap!*

"*Skylenna!*" Muffled voices. Distorted screams.

I can't stop myself. The thirst is unquenchable as I lay into the prisoners charging me. My throat burns from the cries of a banshee leaving my lungs. My knuckles crack into cheekbones. My teeth pierce salty flesh.

And that monster soars within me. Lighting up every sensible part of my mind in white-hot flames. I attack as if I have no beginning or end. No possibility for death. No limitations in sight. It's all a furious blur of faces and blood.

"Down you go." A familiar voice. Dessin's voice.

My vision blurs and I'm swaying, stumbling; my face smacks against hard stone. My stomach dips like I'm drunk, and even though I know I'm lying on the ground, the entire prison spins.

"*Ugh*," I groan. The taste of blood and someone else's skin.

A pair of fingers swipe across my lips. *Dessin. What happened?*

"And here I thought the beautiful blonde would be the least of my problems." My eyes widen despite the tilting world and deepening nausea.

Dessin's voice, but it's scarred and detached. Light and cynical.

Kaspias.

"Keep those fucking hands off her," Dessin grunts.

I search for him through the sheet of blurry tears. He's on all fours, trying to keep himself steady. The thing in his ear is keeping him from standing against his brother.

"Killing a sentinel is a serious offense. The punishment is grave," Kaspias announces, and his stern glare bounces between Dessin and me. It's almost…pained. Like he desperately wishes he didn't have to do this.

The dizziness could kill as my stomach rolls over.

"Let her go!" Dessin shouts, slamming his fists on the jagged floor. "Skylenna!"

The world swoops out from under me, arms hook under my knees and back, and the thumping of footsteps vibrate up my body.

Kaspias leans closer to the man I love so only we can hear him. "Dessin, I promise—I won't hurt her."

I try to slither away, but he only grips me tighter. I'm panting with nausea, making me go limp in his arms, breathing heavily against his chest. He smells of rust and the execution block.

"I can walk," I try to say, but it comes out in a long slur.

"Please, don't be difficult right now."

Bile creeps up my throat.

"You killed a sentinel in front of a room full of witnesses. Just go with it, alright?"

I swallow down the acid, trying to relax my body against the survival instinct to fight. Could it be that he doesn't hate us? That maybe he wants to help?

The chatter from the commissary dims as we move further down a hallway in the prison. I wait to speak until I'm sure we're alone. Maybe this is my chance to get through to him. Figure out why he isn't being cruel, especially for a commander of the Vexamen army. I got through to Dessin in the asylum. What's to say I can't get through to this man, too?

"Did you mean what you said to your brother back there?" I ask in a quiet voice.

"About not hurting you?"

"Yes."

Anticipation tightens a knot in my belly.

"I meant it."

My shoulders sag, and I try not to let my mind blossom with hope and relief.

"But weren't you raised to be this ruthless killer? A brutal commander?" *I want to believe you. I want you to be on our side. For Kane. For everything he's been through.*

Kaspias looks down at me, his face finally clearing from the dizziness warping my vision. His brows knit together, forming a thick crease. He seems to hold his silence to study my face with a contemplative curiosity. His lower lash line is rimmed with black paint, casting an ominous cloud around his gaze. Aside from the scars, piercings, and beard…he looks just like my Dessin. My Kane. There's a tangible connection forming with the seconds that pass, the look he's giving me.

"My brother was raised to be a killer, too, wasn't he?"

"That's right."

"People are capable of holding on to their humanity." The corners of his eyes wrinkle. And he almost looks desperate, needing me to agree, to confirm that he in fact still has his humanity unbroken.

I eye him skeptically. "You didn't seem this way when you first introduced yourself to us. Why reveal this to me now?"

Kaspias grunts his acknowledgment to a passing sentinel. In this silence, I look down at my hands covered in blood and strips of skin. My body still shivers from the dissipating adrenaline. And I still feel the heartache of being back on that beach. Dessin must be out of his mind with confusion and panic. They'll all be wondering why I acted like a feral animal being cornered.

"I can't always show my true colors," he admits.

"Maybe you can prove it then? Help us get out of here."

"Why did you kill a sentinel?" he inquires, moving on as if he didn't hear my proposal. "You appeared to be in a frenzy when I showed up."

The muscles in my back shudder. *There was so much blood.* I dissociate from the memory before it pulls me under like a riptide.

"Something brought me back to a memory I'd rather never relive."

"What triggered it?"

"Blood."

"Blood?"

"Dessin's blood."

He raises his chin.

"I thought I had moved past it, I guess. But it's as if I was back at that place all over again…" I shake my head, burying the thought, the memory, deep, deep, deep in the well of my mind. I shouldn't even be discussing this with him. Not until I know his true intent.

"Is there anything I can do to help?" he asks innocently.

My eyes shrink to small slits.

"You still don't trust me."

I stare without blinking as we turn another corner in this endless hallway.

"No," I answer truthfully.

"Tell me." He pulls my damp body closer to his armored chest. "Do you want to marry my brother one day?"

The intimacy of that question throws me off.

"I do."

"Then one day, I'm to be your brother-in-law, right?"

I nod while swallowing down my discomfort.

"Family?"

I nod again.

"Then we should trust each other."

I look up at him until he redirects his attention to my face, tightening his jaw as he waits for my reply.

"I want nothing more than for that to be the case," I finally say through a pent-up exhale.

Kaspias's blackened eyes glimmer in the strange red and yellow lights overhead. And I can see a future with him in it. One where Kane spends time with him, making new memories that they were robbed of as children. It warms my heart to be able to assist in making this happen for them.

"All I've ever wanted was a family," he says quietly.

And with that, we come to a stop. His arms disappear from around my body. Air cradles me, tossing my hair around my face as I fall. The floor crashes into the back of my head, hard and fast. I groan before turning my head to vomit. It spills over my chapped lips, all stomach acid and bile.

"Did that hurt?" A sickening smile colors his tone.

Momentary shock and betrayal scourge their way between my breasts. Between the fall and his sudden twisted change in ego, the nerves in my spine are set on fire. *What the fuck is this?*

"I *said*...did—that—hurt?" He overly enunciates as if he's speaking to a child.

Every single drop of my blood drains to the south of my body. The silence that follows his condescending voice is suffocating, eerily agitating, like listening to a fork scrape over a plate. And my heart, my poor, stupid heart. How could I have fallen for this? What was I thinking?

Duplicity clogs my veins. I can hardly breathe while I'm filled to the brim with anger.

My fingernails dig into my palms. "*Nope.*"

"Pity. Now get up and walk, future sister-in-law." He kicks me in the back with the tip of his boot. I hiss but scramble to my feet, determined not to show him weakness.

"You have one strike out of three. Do you want to hear your punishment?"

I grind my teeth until I give myself a headache. It's unnerving to hear the man I love in his voice. To see his face covered in a beard and piercings. I want to cover my ears and squeeze my eyes shut. But I just keep looking forward at the dark hallway illuminated by the circus lighting. *Fool me once.*

"It's called *The Hunt.*"

*Goodie.*

I take a quick glance at my arms. Specks of blood. Numbly, I pat my fingers over my chin, throat, and face. Wet. Drizzling. Blood.

"Did you think I'd pity you for that sad excuse of your tantrum?"

My heart gives a vicious thump.

How could I have believed that act?

"Can we get on with this game?" I ask with boredom drooping my eyes.

I roll my shoulder back, force myself to my feet, and drill my focus on the task he's given me.

*The Hunt.*

# 8. Hear Me

## Skylenna

At the end of the hall, we stand in front of a wide brass door. It's old, rusted, and covered in claw marks. Kaspias steps around me, unlatching the door and tugging it open. A fog creeps out, carrying the stench of gunk from the inside of a drainpipe and bad breath.

"I heard you aren't fond of dark, enclosed spaces," Kaspias purrs, keeping his back to me.

I gulp, and my hands tingle with anticipation. Leaning forward, I try to get a better look inside. There is no floor. Only brimstone walls, and a black, endless drop.

I step back, ready to fight him on this. I'm half his size, half his brawn. But I know how to fight, and unfortunately, he probably does, too. Getting a good look at him, he's tanner than Dessin. Arms and chest have more hair. And he looks like he's scarred from head to toe.

He smirks. A lip ring glinting in the dim light. "You think you can fight your way out of this?"

"I think I could slit both your wrists before you had a chance to blink," I say calmly. If I wanted to, I could reach into his mind. I could pull his least favorite memories to the surface. I could make him *drown*. But he's Kane's twin brother. He's Kaspias Valdawell. Taken as a baby. Forced to train before Kane was ever taken by Demechnef.

Despite his previous trick, the ease with which he could betray me without remorse, I have to give him the chance to show me he has the same heart, the same blood, as Sophia. There must be a soul deep down.

"I'm going to enjoy hearing you cry. Can I get one tear before you lose your footing?" He has this expression that I can't help but find annoying. A childlike taunting. An immature inflation of self-esteem.

"I'd never cry for you," I whisper, feeling my vision start to blur. "But by the time I leave this prison, I'll watch you weep like a child."

"Such a sweet sister-in-law," he says as I sway right into his arms. The room tumbles around my head, making me hold my stomach and pray I don't vomit again. "Have a nice timeout."

I'm pushed forward. My head hits the brimstone wall first, scraping into my hairline. I fall into foggy darkness, cold like the winds of the North Sapphrine forest. It stings my skin, slaps against my hair, and I don't have a moment to scream before smashing into the shallow water. Pain explodes up my spine, boiling into my limbs.

My back, arms, and legs hit a gravelly bottom. The chunky, polluted water only cushioning my fall enough not to knock me out. It's as if I've been tossed down the pit of a half-empty well. I cough out the splash I accidentally inhaled on impact. It tastes like dirt and decay.

*Shit. Dessin is going to lose his mind.*

I look up at the flickering slit of light above my head, feeling Kaspias's presence as he waits for me to cry. To scream. To beg for release.

But I've conquered this fear already. I've learned to deal with it. I remember reaching up for Young Kane's hands as he pulled me from the darkness. I remember that the basement can't hurt me. It never did.

Groaning quietly, I pick out the piece of brimstone jabbed under my scalp. It slides out like a thorn with blood trickling from my hairline.

I have to get out of here. Dessin might get himself killed trying to get to me. And Warrose will help him. But what will that mean for Ruth and Niles? We have too much to lose if anyone steps out of line. Kind of like we did today. *Ugh!* Dessin will blame himself for this. For losing his temper. For attacking the serving staff.

I slap my hand down in the ankle-deep water I'm lying in.

"I'll be around when you're ready to cry on my metaphorical shoulder. You know, since *I'm* up here, and *you're* down there." Kaspias snickers before slamming the door shut. A teeth-rattling boom echoes down the well.

"Fuck you," I breathe.

After a moment, I reach my hands around, searching for a dry space where I can sit. But it's all water and bumpy walls. And it's fucking freezing down here. A windless chill like the temperature in Aurick's ice chest. I rub my hands up and down the backs of my arms to get some friction, create heat. But I'm shivering. Sucking in stuttering breaths.

Is he trying to give me hypothermia? I'll die down here before he can get me out.

With a deep grunt, I stand, holding on to the slimy walls to keep balanced. I just have to climb up the wall and put my toes and fingers into the crevices until I'm hoisted to the top. When I reach the door, I can kick it open. I can find a way out.

I latch on easily, then begin climbing.

It's sad, really, how quickly I fall back into the disgusting well of water. My fingers and arms dig into the rocky wall as I come down, scraping into them like knives through tissue paper. I howl as my tailbone collides with a sharp rock, cutting into the thin material of my uniform. Broken fingernails. Gashes the length of my thumb. A bruised ass.

I try thirteen more times. But I'm weak, shaking, hungry, thirsty, sliced up, exhausted.

Slumping against the wall, I close my eyes, trying so hard to block out the heavy stench of sewage. And although my body is tired, harmed, begging for comfort—my mind is stronger than ever.

I touch the perimeter of the void. Feel its luring presence imploring me to step within its boundaries. It's like a soft rain during the fall weather. A swift wind of red leaves and a cold mist falling from the sky. I take a deep breath and let myself sink into the abyss.

My arms wade through the night, searching for that memory that wants to reveal itself. But amid the peace, there's a pull in a different direction. A sound that breaks the glass of silence, a noise that is so familiar, I could name it if I could just get a little closer.

Swimming through the dusk of the void, I follow that song like a beacon, guiding me, singing my name. A tune only I can hear from a great distance. And I'm flying out of the void, over the Vex Mountains, across the Midnight Sea, and back to the Dementia. The wind gusts over my face, drying my skin, sifting through my tangled hair. And that soft tune turns into a roar.

A mighty thunder from a great beast.

On the shoreline of one of the seven forests, I'm pulled downward, tumbling through the air and clouds until I see him.

Our friend.

Our protector.

DaiSzek.

His powerful stance of black fur and russet feet brace into the sand as he howls. A devastating cry for his family. For me.

"DaiSzek!" I scream from a great height above his head.

DaiSzek looks up, meeting my floating figure in the sky.

Oh, how I've longed to see those great cinnamon eyes again. My heart dips and soars at the sight of him. At the sight of Knightingale creeping out of the forest line behind him, wiggling her butt and perking her tall ears. She can see me, too!

I land in the sand with a silent thump. Without a moment of hesitation, I throw myself around his thick neck, gripping him like I might never get this chance again.

"Oh, baby boy!" I sob, scratching his back, kissing the top of his head. "Can you hear me? See me?"

DaiSzek chuffs in response.

I kneel in front of him, signaling for Knightingale to come closer. She greets me by nudging her nose aggressively under my hand to give her pets, too.

"I need you to get help," I tell DaiSzek.

He lifts his giant head a little higher in sudden alarm. He understands me.

"We're in the Vexamen Prison. And I think we're on the precipice of war. I need you to find the Stormsage Keep. Lead them to the other colonies. I'm hoping they'll understand that I've sent you. That I need their help. If their prophecy is accurate, they'll know where we are."

DaiSzek sighs loudly and presses his head against mine. Those beautiful eyes close. And I want nothing more than to stay with him. Tears sting the backs of my eyes.

"Don't come to Vexamen, okay? It's too dangerous for either you or Knightingale to get caught." But DaiSzek straightens his back and stares into my soul with an utter look of defiance. "Please," I beg.

He releases a long, devastating howl and takes off in the forest with Knightingale tailing right behind him.

Something cold and sharp latches onto me, yanking me back into the void by force, a delirious motion of nothingness that rushes past me until I'm back. I'm sitting in my own body being reeled upward toward a dim light.

"You still alive?" Kaspias calls down with a smile.

I rub the backs of my arms, trembling so hard my bones start to ache. My wet hair only makes the biting chill that much worse. I long to be wrapped in a blanket, sitting in front of a fire in the forest with Kane. I summon the memory of when we were children. When he would keep me warm at night under the twinkling stars.

"I hope your legs still work. It's either run or die."

# 9. The Hunt

## Dessin

My mind is a war of slaughter and hellfire.

"Tell. Me." I'm in Helga Bee's round, red-cheeked face. Holding my temper back with a string.

We're in the eerie, circus-themed stadium. Ruth is trying to clean the wounds on my chest. Warrose is pacing the length of the stage. Marilynn is helping Ruth get clean cloths and alcohol. Niles hasn't moved from his seated position, staring blankly at the floor.

"How should I know, Beetle Brain? There are tons of punishments for killing a sentinel!"

Punishments.

Kaspias is going to punish my girl.

*Sorry, Kane. I'm going to have to break your brother's neck.*

Kane lingers in the front, swarming my head with guilt and panic. He's right to feel this way. It was my fucking fault for losing my temper. If I had just kept calm, Skylenna wouldn't have had that breakdown. What was that about? She was fine one moment…

*I'm inclined to agree with you,* Kane sighs.

"Kaspias seems to have a soft spot for Skylenna. Maybe he'll protect her from the punishment?" Ruth asks as she dabs the gashes on my chest. I look down at her wearily. She's so small, so innocent, and so fucking naïve.

"You bought his little performance, huh?" I grit through my teeth.

She quickly looks away. "I don't know. He could have a little crush on her." The light shrugging of her shoulders pisses me off. The thought of Kaspias Fucking Valdawell having eyes for Skylenna, my Skylenna, makes me want to rip the skin off of his bones slowly, with a smile.

"Name the punishments," I direct back to Helga Bee.

The tall, burly woman purses her thin lips. Thinks with an overexaggerated *hmm* sound. Thrums her stubby fingers over a chin covered in acne.

"There's the Black Widow Room, Winter's Well, Scarecrow Show, and The Hunt."

I crack my neck, forcing myself to get it under control. The names set me on edge, and this woman talks so damn slow. It's a recipe to set me on a murderous streak.

"Explain. Each. One."

Helga Bee snorts. "Yeah, yeah, yeah. Keep your knickers on! I'm getting to it." She picks something out of her crooked teeth. "Black Widow Room is a place in the prison where a female inmate is given malrose grass to put them in the *mood.* They're laid out on a table in front of a group of soldiers. The grass gets them so wet and wrangled that they tickle their fancy just to relieve the crazed horniness!"

My brain stops working. "Excuse me?"

"Not a bad time to scurry your furry! Amiright, Gerta?" She bumps her large grandma elbow into Gerta's side. Gerta blushes, winking at Niles. He doesn't even look up.

Warrose stops his pacing to look at me, one eyebrow raised, mouth parting slowly.

"Hell no!" He stomps up to Helga Bee, putting both hands on his head. "Tell me that's the least likely of scenarios. Something like that happens, and you can pretty much guarantee this man will burn this prison to the ground with all of us inside it."

"Relax, Donut Boy. The Commander isn't of the perverted type in the Breed. He likes a good show. Likes a good beating."

That doesn't make me feel any better.

"Donut Boy?" Warrose narrows his eyes.

"What punishment would he generally lean toward then?" I ask.

Helga Bee shrugs. "I'd say either Winter's Well or The Hunt. And if he's in a real bad mood, maybe both."

"I really don't think so!" Ruth chimes in. "He really looked like he wanted to help her."

I open my mouth to bite her head off for being this stupid; anger burns the pit of my stomach, but Kane stops me.

*Not a word to her, man. She's family. Focus.*

I pinch the bridge of my nose. "Explain Winter's Well."

She groans like a child. "Why? It's going to happen anyway. No use in fussin'!"

"Listen—"

Someone's shoulder bumps into me, a quick shove. I dart my eyes to the intruder, seeing golden hair and scarred-over skin that has been licked by vicious flames.

Niles gets in Helga Bee's face, wearing an expression I have never seen before on him.

"Answer the fucking questions. That's my sister you're talking about. And we don't leave family behind." There is no humor, no playful smirk. Only eternal fire raging behind his unhinged gaze.

Helga Bee takes a small step back, blinking in surprise.

"It's a well. Cold as shit, with a little bit of nasty old pipe water at the very bottom. Prisoners are left to freeze down there until they're near frostbite stages." She cocks her head away from Niles, but he doesn't move.

"And The Hunt?"

"You see those prisoners with cages on their heads and no ears? Big as ogres?"

I nod, exchanging a look with Warrose. The same one that trudged along at night, curious about Ruth in her cage.

"They're actually the vile product of generational brother-sister fuckin'! Called Blood Mammoths. Deep in the West Vexello Mountains, they're bred and taught to hunt, kill, and abduct Vexamen Breed soldiers for sport. They're bloodthirsty as fuck! When they're imprisoned by The Commander and his special team of elite, they cut off their ears, put a cage on their heads so they can't bite anyone. Side note, the bacteria on their teeth is deadly if they take a chomp out of your neck."

I look up at the high ceilings, covered in cobwebs, stained with black smoke. Could this get any worse?

"The inmate that's on the chopping block gets thrown into the prison at night, stripped down to their birthday suit, and forced to run from the Blood Mammoths until sunrise. Once those dumb ogres get the scent of their skin, hair, or blood, they become enraged with finding 'em."

Niles and I don't breathe. We wait for Helga Bee to tell us the good news.

"The prisoner gets blindfolded and placed somewhere in the prison to find their cage, like a rat in a maze. They don't ever make it, though. Beaten until they're bloody and dead."

I release a slow, poisonous breath.

"Skylenna isn't like the other prisoners," Niles says, detached and exhausted. "She'll make it."

# Skylenna

I WANT TO SHOW HIM MY inner strength, but my teeth deceive me. They chatter endlessly. My muscles rumble under my skin from the biting frost. And I'm tightly hugging my arms to my waist, a feeble attempt to gather any heat at all.

"I bet my brother swoons at this sight of you. All wet and helpless." Kaspias makes a fake attempt to hold back his laughter. He inspects every inch of me. Not with any sexual intent, but scientifically. Medically. The way an intellectual would study an anomaly.

Suddenly, a pair of rough hands grip my sopping wet uniform, tugging downward until fabric stretches and rips. I flinch at the gust of air sweeping over my nipples. My hands fly to my private parts, shielding them from his eyes.

He's quiet for several seconds. Just staring at my naked, quivering body.

"You *are* pretty. And your curves are supple despite the way they starve their women in your country." Kaspias lifts his chin with a pitying smirk, and it's so similar to Dessin, I force myself to turn away. "I bet he thinks himself a real king for claiming you, hmm? *Yet*…you don't do it for me."

"Then why are you staring at me like every other man with an erection?" Provoking him is probably the single dumbest thing I can do in the face of a Vexamen Prison punishment. But I'm too cold to care. Too annoyed at his demeaning words to think this through.

Kaspias snatches the back of my head, fingers curling around a wet bunch of hair like he might yank it out by the root. "Do you have any idea who you're talking to? I'm the fucking Commander of the Vexamen Breed! I've gutted men for less. I've beheaded mothers for defending their children. I've terrorized small villages on a whim. I could scalp you for the slightest bit of disrespect!"

Perhaps I've gone mad. Perhaps I've been mad this entire time. But I grin in his face, proud, taunting, and vicious. "So do it, little boy."

For a single heartbeat, fear hangs over my gut. There's a twinkle in his eyes made of coal and frost, an impulsive thought that tells him to prove a point. To scalp me right here. To parade my bleeding head around the prison. To make a spectacle, even though he's supposed to keep me alive.

Instead, reason and logic win that silent debate. And that royally pisses him off. He settles for something less effective. I feel the world explode before I even catch a glimpse of his fist. Bone smashes into my jaw and mouth, and it blasts through my nostrils, eyes, skull, and spine like a shockwave. The quick punch makes me clamp down on my tongue, a slice through thick meat, and blood spills over my chin.

Kaspias laughs.

The void wants to bring me back to the moment Aurick hit me in his bedroom. How I crawled away from him, shielded myself from another beating. Cried and cried and cried. As the blood trickles past my lips, as the splitting headache zaps behind my eyes, I mourn her. I silently hold her in my arms, and tell her she doesn't have to be afraid anymore.

Because unfortunately for Kaspias, that little girl is dead.

I move faster than the magnet in my ear can send me into a whirlpool of distorted gravity. Leaping into his arms, I use my last bit of strength to chomp down on his ear, aiming for that piece of metal, the dull earring. The room spins, piercing through my sense of balance, and as I fall from his shoulders, I yank, clamping down on that earring until I hear a tear.

Kaspias grunts as my back hits the floor and the walls tilt around me. I can't focus on his movements, can't even seem to think straight. But the feel of his boot slamming into my ribs is how I know I've made him *hurt*.

"You'll pay for that!" he bellows as he continues to kick and bruise and knock the air from my lungs.

But through the gnawing pain, I smile up at him. With bloody teeth and tears gushing from my eyes.

I smile.

# Ruth

DESSIN PACES THE LENGTH OF his small cage, hands flexing at his sides, jaw working as his mind caves in on itself.

"He's no brother of yours," he growls to himselfor to someone in his head.

We've never seen him talk out loud before. It always seems like he has those conversations silently. Even Warrose watches him with concern pinching his brow.

"We have to do something," Niles begs from his cage, face pressed between the bars.

Dessin gives him a quick, agitated glance. "No."

*No?* Isn't he the infamous Patient Thirteen? The man who would take down armies just to get to Skylenna? He'd never let anyone hurt her. Especially not Kaspias.

"Are you kidding? Now you decide to be a pacifist?" Niles exclaims.

"My girl has leaned on me like a crutch for too long." Dessin stops pacing. "She's so fucking powerful. I must let her grow into that power. I can't stunt her growth by slaying her monsters again, not when she can so easily do it herself." Even as he says these words, I can see how much he's trying to convince himself of them. How much he wants to break through this cage, how much he wants to hold her in his arms and tell her that she's safe.

"She can handle this." I nod. "After everything she's been through, she can handle anything."

My words hit a nerve because Dessin closes his eyes slowly, hanging his head.

It's hard to hear, but true, nevertheless. We all watched as she held his dying body in her arms, trying to stop the blood. And when his heart stopped beating, her screams stretched on across the Midnight Sea, breaking us with the agonizing sound of her despair. She died right there with him.

This isn't the same Skylenna.

She's something stronger.

Something far more resilient.

I wish I were more like her. Because if the roles were reversed, this family would be risking their lives to save me.

"We're going to be here for her when she returns," Warrose says, hazel eyes firmly on Dessin. He steps closer to the bars that separate him from Skylenna's empty cage, looking down absently at the floor she's slept on. "We need to figure out a way around this ear magnet thing."

Dessin blows out a humorless laugh. "That's Skylenna's job."

"It is?"

Dessin nods.

"What's your job?" He cocks an eyebrow. "What's *my* job?"

"To come up with an escape plan. It's just something we decided to split responsibilities."

Warrose sighs, lowering himself to the floor. "Did that make her happy?"

Dessin's chest moves up and down. His jaw tightens. Gaze planted on the rocky ground.

"Yes."

"Seems like she's wanted that for a long time."

"She's always wanted to be a part of my plans," Dessin says quietly.

"Yeah? They're not all butterflies and roses." A flash of resentment tightens the muscles in Warrose's back.

Dessin finally looks down at him. "I know we haven't talked about it yet."

The plan to fake his death. The plan Warrose had to bear the truth of alone. The plan to pray for Dessin's revival, to watch Skylenna spiral, to standby unable to give her solace.

"Fine by me." Warrose crosses his thick arms over his chest. "I thoroughly enjoy staying mad at you."

Dessin's mouth tics.

I instantly became aware of heavy breathing beside me. Rotating my head to the left, I see Niles watching the conversation play out with radiant glee. His face pressed between the bars, mouth open in a slight smile, and round eyes bouncing from Warrose to Dessin.

Marilynn keeps her eyes on her lap to at least give the illusion that she isn't eavesdropping.

"*Niles!*" I whisper, snickering.

His invasive stare slides to mine. "Best part about prison? No privacy."

Warrose and Dessin turn to us, ready to insult Niles for being a pest. But something shrill cracks through the hallway. A piercing sound echoing from another wing.

We freeze, waiting through a beat of silence.

The sound grows louder, defining in range and tone. A sound we've all heard at least once before. A woeful pitch to our ears that reminds me of sand, sea salt air, and blood.

Skylenna screams.

# Skylenna

"I DIDN'T KICK YOU *THAT* hard. Get up!" Kaspias looks down at me with genuine confusion. Those mahogany, black-lined eyes follow the string of bloody saliva that hangs from my mouth.

As I struggle to stand, Kaspias groans and hooks his hands under my arms, lifting me with ease to stand upright. I try to control my breathing, but it's shallow, labored, painful to move my ribs. I make a solid effort not to wince.

Naively, I hope that this was it. This beating from his short fuse temper. Maybe I can go back to my cage now.

"It's almost midnight. The rules are, there *are* no rules, other than having your hands—here, like this," he hooks a rusty chain from the collar around my neck to shackles around my wrists behind my back "and completely without your sight." He wraps a thick cloth around my head, cloaking my eyes in complete darkness. An object grazes my hair before I hear a click, then a sting knifed into my temples. I whimper at the piercing of a needle in my scalp.

"There. It's stapled to your scalp. No chance of it falling off."

I retract two steps, blinking repeatedly to adjust.

I don't like this. This prison is completely foreign to my knowledge. It's a maze. And now I'm blind. What will he have me do next? Will I be able to make it back to my family?

"This is the punishment?" I ask cautiously. He wants me to wander around naked? Blindfolded? It's almost midnight, meaning I'm in no real danger because everyone is already in their cages.

"Have you met the Blood Mammoths yet?" His mouth is close to the side of my head. He's leaning in to make me uncomfortable.

"The what?"

"The giant, beastly men with cages on their heads? The ones that wander the halls at night? Did you really sleep through it?"

I school my features. He won't see the fear that is crawling up my gut and into my throat.

"Obviously." *I would have remembered something like that.*

I can feel the mocking energy of his smile. "Pity. Well, you're on the other side of the prison, as far from your cage as you can get. I'm going to set you free. Then, I'll let the Blood Mammoths get a sniff of the blood you've left on the floor. They'll chase you down like rabid dogs hunting for their last meal."

*Fuck.*

"What are my chances?" Do I really want to know? It won't matter.

I'm making it back to my family. I'm making it back to Dessin. If only I could mute the trickle of panic tingling through my limbs.

"I've only seen two prisoners make it back out of one hundred."

*So, not impossible then.*

"Too bad they were missing major limbs."

*That won't be me. That won't be me. That won't be me.*

My stomach twists, and my mouth goes dry. I'm filled with nervous energy yet throbbing everywhere. I've been thrown down a cold well, left to freeze, then beaten. How will I make it back? How will I outrun these bloodthirsty men?

A voice sings past my mental walls, weaving itself into my thoughts.

*"The woman who once brought compassion to the Emerald Prison will one day bring fire. And with her new reckoning, the enemy is doomed to fail."*

Judas's recitation of the prophecy given to the Crimson Kres. For once, that damned prophecy gives me a spike of hope, a surge of adrenaline. I'm meant to make a difference. I'm meant to overcome the enemy.

"When do I start?" I ask calmly.

Kaspias grinds his teeth. "Now."

He shoves me forward until I'm tumbling to my knees, scraping them against the sharp-edged ground. The torn skin stings my kneecaps, forcing a grunt from behind my bared teeth.

But I don't wait to recover. I'm up, jumping forward as if I have all the energy in the world. My bare feet shoot out in front of me, leaping into the air to break out into a sprint. Immediately, the blindness makes me angry. I can't throw my hands up with caution, preparing to run into something, someone, a set of metal bars, a stone wall.

But I remember the hallway in front of me is long and wide. I should get a decent amount of distance between Kaspias and me if I just run in a perfectly straight line.

He said I was at the farthest end of the prison. How do I know which way to go? I know I need to take a moment to think, to find a way to map my escape. But my blood is rushing like a waterfall to my ears. My breath is ragged and frantic. And my mind is spiraling, thinking of my last words to Dessin, Ruth's face, Niles's hugs.

I have to make it back.

DaiSzek needs me.

Chekiss is all alone.

As I glide down the hall, I'm not sure how much distance I have left to cover before there's a fork in the road, before I

Stone. Unmovable. Unfazed by my face smacking into its cold, uneven surface. I gasp as the impact shoots up my nose, rattling my brain. Blood spurts from my nostrils. Tears run down my cheeks. And the pain stabs its teeth into every nerve above my collarbone.

"Fuck!" I choke, wincing at the tenderness across my nose, hoping nothing is broken.

The sound of rustling chains, heavy footsteps, and guttural grunting sets my spine pin straight. The Blood Mammoths must be gathering behind me to catch my scent like Kaspias said. I won't wait around to find out. I've never heard of these beasts, never had the chance to learn their strengths. How fast they run. How efficient at tracking they are.

I'm blind.

But my legs still work, so I follow the feel of the hallway, veering right and keeping the side of my foot against the wall to keep myself from slamming into anything else.

I want to call out to Dessin to find out how far I am from my cage. But that might get me caught sooner.

*Think, Skylenna.*

There's a frenzy behind me. They sound more like wild animals than actual human beings. Based on the vibrations through the ground, I can tell they've started running. Heavy, thumping footsteps. It sends a jolt of fear through my stomach. Another dose of adrenaline.

I have to run faster. I have to figure out where I'm going. But those footsteps grow louder, rumbling the metal cages with each stomp.

*Shit, they're fast.* Longer legs, maybe? Longer strides.

The war drums of my demise pound in my ears. *Focus, Skylenna!*

Only, I can't. A large, bumpy hand grabs my wrist. A death grip. It tries to heave me backward, followed by a demonic, gurgling snarl. I act on instinct. Every move Kane taught me in the Red Oaks. Every maneuver. They flood my mind with possibilities.

My leg kicks back, bucking out and upward like an angry horse. The bottom of my raw foot makes contact with a groin, I think. The mangled *oomph* is the only indication that the Blood Mammoth is down.

They're on my heels, no matter how fast I try to run. My ribs scream with each breath I take. My nostrils are swollen shut. I'm in bad shape.

But the void nudges me, brushing up against my skin the way a cat would rub against its owner. I hesitate. I can't go in there right now. What if I stop running? What if my body goes limp, and the Blood Mammoths devour me on the spot?

With a sharp breath, I don't go in, but I do expose myself to it. Allowing that vast openness to find me.

*"Take a sharp left...now!"*

The voice is bold yet feminine. It's a whisper so close to my ear, I can practically feel her breath skimming my cheek.

My feet do as they're told. I pivot to the left, wishing I could reach my hands out to make sure I don't run into the cages along my side.

*"Who are you?"* I ask within the safe barriers of my own thoughts.

Something sharp and hard hits my back; the sting is shocking enough to make me trip and stumble. *Ugh!* Are they throwing rocks?

*"You wouldn't believe me if I told you,"* she says with wisdom buried deep in her tone.

I cough, fighting to breathe past the pain and the blood running from my nose down my throat. *"You'd be surprised!"*

*"No, actually I would not."* She pauses, as if waiting for something. *"Duck!"*

I bow my upper body to waist level, keeping my pace in a hunched form. What sounds like stone crashing into stone bangs against the ground in front of me.

*"Leap over it now!"*

I jump over whatever it is they tried throwing at me.

*"How far are we?"* I ask her.

*"We are almost to the stairs."*

*Stairs?!* I don't dare ask how many flights there are. It'll sicken me to find out. One step at a time. One challenge at a time. I can do this. I have help now. And that notion warms my heart. Behind this blindfold, within this darkness, there's a woman who is helping me.

And somehow, I trust her more than words can describe.

*"Slow your pace. There's a door coming up directly in front of you. Turn your back to it and reach for a long, metal latch."*

I spin halfway, reaching my shackled hands in a grabby motion, desperate to feel it entering my palm. Coldness touches my skin.

*"There!"* she exclaims. *"Pull upward, and open the door."*

The door scrapes against the floor, creaking on its hinges as I drag it open.

*"Good, Skylenna. Now slam it shut, and push the latch down to lock it!"*

Relief floods every limb, every organ of my body as I complete her task backward.

She directs me up the stairs, each step one at a time until I'm able to run without tripping. But sprinting uphill is so much harder than running through a long hallway. I'm wheezing, gasping like a fish out of water.

*"Fuck!"* It's had to be at least seven flights by now.

*"Two more!"*

*"No."* I shake my head, doubling over to relieve the sharp pain in my sides and the fire in my lungs. *"I can't."*

*"Skylenna, you are the Fallen Saint. You burned the Emerald Lake Asylum to the ground. Avenged every death and freed the patients held prisoner. You've endured Mind Phantoms and the death of your true love. You. Must. Keep. Going."*

The Blood Mammoths manage to kick the door down several floors below us. But they're roaring like hungry lions. And I'm filled to the brim with a black flame, a smokeless fire gifted to me by this woman. This being that is guiding me.

I nod my head, brushing my forearms against the serrated railing as I continue to sprint upward. The stairs are pounded by footsteps below. And I can imagine they're skipping steps, covering more ground.

*"One more!"*

With bleeding feet and quivering legs, I pivot backward, swinging open the door on the last flight of stairs, and take off.

*"Don't panic."* Her voice is calm, but her words are lethal. *"There are more on this floor looking for you. You know how to fight. You must maneuver your body exactly as I say. Understand?"*

"Yes," I whisper out loud.

*"Good, now run!"*

Her terminology is that of a fighter, because she instructs me effortlessly. I swing my legs in the right direction, making contact with soft underbellies and groins, and sweeping my feet out to knock giant bodies off their feet.

*"Wait, Skylenna, no!"* The panic in her voice is quickly answered by my body being thrown into a set of bars. My forehead bangs against metal first, then I fall to the ground like a sack of potatoes.

My coughing fit is interrupted by nails as sharp as claws biting into my arm, grating down my flesh.

"Argh!"

*"Fight! You're surrounded!"*

They've got me. By the sound of their labored breathing and the smell of their rancid breath, there must be more than four. A pair of fists slam down on my body like a primate beating down on another animal. The air is knocked from my lungs. Another fist is thrown down across my face, hard enough to send blood spraying from my mouth.

The woman's voice is screaming for me, but as the Blood Mammoths start to yank on my limbs in a violent attempt to pull them from my body, I know what I must do.

The void greets me like an old friend. And I find their minds, collectively, reaching my hands into their collective subconsciousness as one.

*"Skylenna, don't!"*

But it's too late. I graze their minds like I'm stepping into their world. And I know how to pull them into the prison void, but it's not right. It's grotesque and insidious. In a repetitive flash, I see who they are. I see what they've done.

Organs. Entrails. Cannibalism. Deep in the West Vexello Mountains, they'd hunt something other than animals. They'd hunt children.

I let out a scream that crosses land and water. A scream that I feel connect with one beast, one monster. He can hear me through the howling wind, through the sounds of the forest, through a bond that only we share.

And nothing on this earth can stop DaiSzek from crossing oceans to find me. I feel it in his bones—the determination, the fury, the destruction waiting to be set free.

*Please, find me, my boy.*

*"They've let go! Run, Skylenna, Run!"*

My brief visit into their minds threw them off of me, if only for a moment. I choke on a sob as I jump over their scrambling bodies, throwing my full weight into a race back to my cage. It's close. My family is close.

"Skylenna!" Dessin's voice.

"There she is!" Ruth.

"Run! You're almost here!"

"Oh, god, what have they done to her?" Warrose.

Their gasps at my appearance are audible. Wetness drips down my neck and nude chest. I must be covered in blood. But all I can feel is relief wash over my entire body like a hot shower.

I want to call out to them. I want to scream their names. But my breath is coming from weak, thin lungs. All I can do is cry as their shouting grows louder. Their words get closer.

*I'm here! I've come home!*

*"Throw your leg back. Eleven o'clock!"* the voice yells, sounding as urgent and excited as I am to get back to my cage in one piece.

I oblige, stopping my run to twist, jab my leg back, make contact with a kneecap. The beast wails like a baby, yet the sound is deeper than any man's voice I've heard. Two hands wrap around my ankle, tugging me backward.

*"You're facing him now. Block his blows, two o' clock. Yes, good. Now again."* The blows nearly send me flying, but I hold my ground. *"To the knee again! He's wounded there."*

I kick as hard as I can, using every bit of energy left to make him bleed. My friends scream for me, cheer me on, tell me more are coming, more are here. I have to run, have to make it a few more steps.

I turn, slamming into a hard, sweaty chest.

Multiple hands, fists, and feet begin wailing on me. They beat into my flesh like a slab of dough to be kneaded. My body is jerked side to side until I'm knocked to the ground, the back of my head cracking on the brimstone. Everything goes fuzzy behind my blindfold.

I can't focus on one area of pain. My nerves light up in red, flashing alarms from head to toe. I'm sobbing, hiccuping, trying to hear that voice, trying to stop screaming.

"Get off her! I'll rip your fucking heads off!" Dessin is louder, angrier, and more unhinged than I've ever heard him. Niles tries to encourage me, Ruth begs for my release, but Warrose's voice stands out like a shining beacon.

"Find your strength. Go into the darkness, and don't come back until you find that light."

Another fist punches the side of my face, swiping the blindfold from my eyes, yanking out those staples puncturing my scalp. I blink in surprise, clearing out the fuzziness, the tears, adjusting to the red and yellow circus bulbs. And as I focus on the Blood Mammoths towering over my beaten, bruised, feeble body, I can't help but scream.

Their hair is black, hanging down to the floor, and eyes small, like tiny charcoal. Their skin is waxy, shiny, and covered in oozing boils. That rusted metal on their heads is in the shape of a birdcage. They smile down at me with only three or four teeth and large, rotting gums.

Before the next foot comes down on me, I let the void drape over them like a body bag. I follow them into the darkness as their consciousnesses tumbles, ignoring the grotesque images I saw before. We whiz past that.

And now they're mine. Now they're in my kingdom, suffering the same fate they've just made me suffer. Being chased naked, beaten, scared, screaming.

"This is who you are now." My voice comes out like that of a god. Laced in echoes, in an otherworldly, thunderous presence. "Scared. Small. *Powerless.*"

I hover above them, like the devil over his pit of writhing souls. And my words are their gospel, their command, their only way of existence. I can feel their fear set in. A feeling foreign to them, never before felt. My words rewire the essence of their very beings. Because here in this prison void, I am the creator. The god. The devil.

And they are my dolls to play with.

*I've fixed them.*

With the sound of whooshing wind and my stomach dipping, I fall to the ground by the cages of my family. A loud thud. Looking up, the Blood Mammoth's eyes are leaking tears of blood.

And they scattered like cockroaches.

# 10. The Side Effects

## Skylenna

One cage automatically opens.
I'm unaware of the person above me as I get scooped up, carried, and held in someone's lap.

"She's cold as ice. What do I do?" Warrose asks in a quiet panic.

I breathe in through my nose. He smells of a winter storm, of dark spice. I try to focus on that as I tremble ferociously as if I'm seizing. Ice coats my bones, splinters through my veins.

"Mm-ake it st-op," I stutter through chattering teeth.

This is much worse than last time. When I took Aurick to the prison void, I was cold for a few long moments, but it passed. This feels different. It's as if I've been tossed into a blizzard without an inch of clothing. It's as if I've been frozen at the core of an iceberg.

It's agony.

"Her lips are blue," Warrose says to someone. "Why is this happening?"

"She went to the prison void again," Marilynn suggests.

"Take your pants off, Warrose. She needs body heat." Dessin. His voice is hoarse, strained, broken. I want to reach out to him. I want to tell him I made it. I made it back to him.

Warrose sets me down. Moves quickly. I hear pants hit the floor.

"I'm sorry. I have to," he tells me in a rush, then hisses. "Christ, her skin is ice."

But his is fire, and damn, it feels good. I'm held, squeezed, and secured tightly in his naked lap. He puts my face in the crook of his neck, wraps his large arms around my body, rubs up and down until the friction builds warmth.

"Bring her closer to my bars," Ruth begs.

Warrose doesn't object. He swivels to the left, bringing our naked bodies closer until a pair of arms are holding my legs.

"Tell Dessin—I made it," I whisper to Warrose. My breathing is low, but I need him to hear it. I need him to know I'd do it again to be with him. I can't imagine the stress, the anguish, he went through worrying about me.

Warrose nods, sighing. His head tilts away from me to look at Dessin.

"She wants me to tell you that she made it."

Dessin's cage is silent. No response. No good job. No faint laugh. Only utter quiet from his space within those bars.

I peel my eyes open despite how swollen and raw my face is. Through the tiny slits, I see Dessin is crouched in the corner of his cage, face in hands, shoulders quivering slightly.

*Oh, Dessin.* How it must kill him not to be able to hold me right now. It's unlike him not to break every rule to come rescue me. But he can't do that anymore, not in the way he used to. I must be given the freedom to stretch my wings and fly over men, just like Asena once told me.

"Why does this happen when she goes into the prison void?" Ruth breaks the silence.

Tingling is brought back to my toes, seeping its way up my feet. She massages my legs softly, then brings my hands to her lips, blowing hot air on them, dropping quick kisses on the knuckles. I smile into Warrose's neck.

"I think it's because she exerts too much energy into that place. It's easy for her to go there alone now that she's had time to explore it, but not for her to bring someone along." Marilynn's voice is like a smooth glass of wine. Refined and silky as it touches my ears.

"Skylenna, did you bring any of those monsters to the prison void?" Niles asks.

I nod. "All of them."

The group makes an "*oooh*" sound.

"What did you do to them?" Warrose's breath grazes the top of my head.

"Made them scared."

"Huh. Not super creative, but I'll take it!" Niles says.

I roll my eyes, but wince at how badly that hurts. Two heavy marbles pressing against my tender sockets. I can't breathe through my nose, can't wrinkle my brow, can't even swallow right. As the adrenaline wears off, the aching sets in. My arms burn from where they scratched me. My stomach has its own pulse, a steady beat of poison running through each bruised organ.

It rushes over me like a tsunami.

"*Fuckkkkkkkk*," I groan.

"What?"

"It hurts. Everything hurts." I can barely speak. My jaw is hardened to one open position. I wonder if any bones are broken. I guess I have no way of finding out until the swelling goes down. God, I'd give anything for a drink with Aquarus in a hot bath.

"We have to get her cleaned up," Ruth whispers to Warrose. "I don't even know where most of this blood is coming from."

Is there a lot of it? Is it bad that I don't even care? Sleep is my only escape, my only way out of this constant throbbing. And I'm so damn tired. My eyes droop, my breath grows heavy, and I want to float away now.

"We will tomorrow. She's been through too much to move her now."

"Warrose?" I mutter sleepily.

"Hmm?"

"Will you—tell Dessin something else—before I fall asleep?"

A small movement tells me he nodded.

"Tell him I love him. Tell him I'm gonna dream of that castle he promised me."

Warrose's chest moves up and down. He places a soft kiss on my head.

"I'll tell him."

# 11. Surviving The Night

## Niles

Warrose and Skylenna fall asleep almost immediately after I assist with picking the lock of her shackles through careful instruction. And Ruth follows shortly after, never letting go of Skylenna's hand.

I try not to wake anyone up as I cry into my hands.

That was excruciating to watch. Hearing her scream, seeing her naked body sprint through the dim halls, watching the blood drip and gush over her skin. I can't rid the images from my mind.

And the way they beat her. My shoulders shudder violently. Heaven have mercy…I'm surprised she survived.

Ruth and I held hands the entire time. Praying. Hoping. Screaming for those bags of rotten meat to let her go, leave her alone, stop hurting our sister. I held my cries in for Ruth. How could I break apart when she is always so strong?

But now that everyone is sleeping peacefully, I can let it all go. The tears stream down my neck and onto my bare chest. I've learned a thing or two about crying silently. When I was a small lad, I used to cry after lessons at the child brothel. I used to sob so loudly that they'd have to beat me for it.

An older girl named Edna taught me how to cry without making a sound. She taught me how to hold myself together until I was alone. She showed me the ropes, made me strong, helped me cope with my fate. That same year, Edna ran away, only to be found and drowned in a river by her uncle.

"Niles?"

I sniffle before I turn to face Marilynn.

She's scowling, like she doesn't want to care to ask, but does. "Are you in pain?"

I shake my head, quickly wiping my wet face.

"Worried about Skylenna?" she asks again.

"Yeah." *Damn, I need a tissue.* "That was just…a lot to see."

She waits a few moments with that nearly permanent grimace, watching me clean myself up. "You really love her, don't you?"

I sigh. "So fucking much."

"Have you told her how you feel about her?" she asks hesitantly.

"I mean, she knows—wait." I choke on a laugh. "I'm not *in* love with her. She's my family. Like my little sister."

Marilynn blinks in surprise. "Oh. Sorry. I didn't mean to assume. They are both such beautiful women, Ruth and Skylenna."

"And *they'd* be the ones falling for *me*. Not the other way around." Sure, they're pretty and all. But look at me.

She smirks. "I see." But something clouds over her eyes.

What an odd woman. How can someone frown and smirk at the same time? She always has her arms crossed, standing away from us in an off-putting stance. Like she doesn't want to stand near our family. Doesn't exactly want to be associated.

"What's wrong?"

"Nothing. Well,"—she pulls her long, red hair to one side—"I'm so hungry. My stomach is eating itself."

I know the feeling. It's been two days without a meal. How long will this last?

"I haven't followed the lady-doll regimen in years. I've always hated this kind of fasting."

"Really?"

"Yeah. Look at me. I love good food, and it shows." She wafts her hands over her curves. And fuck me, because my eyes linger way too long on her heavy breasts and soft thighs.

"You look goo—nice." I dart my eyes away. "Very good and nice."

"Thanks." She almost laughs. The sound is strained and weird, and some might say it was a cough. But it was definitely, almost, probably, kind of a laugh!

"I have a new respect for the women in our city, forced to do the lady-doll regimen. This is brutal. And yet they'd go through this hunger every day."

Marilynn nods, deep in brooding thought. "Unfortunately, most of them aren't forced anymore. Not like they were during the first years of settlement. They're deeply brainwashed. It would take a lot to change that society."

Before I can think of a response, Skylenna lets out a childlike whimper.

We whip around, turning to face her still nuzzled in Warrose's arms. But something shifts in the last cage. Dessin shifts, watching her stiffly.

"Have you been awake this whole time?" I ask him.

Dessin gives me a look that could kill. It's insufferable, full of exhaustion and nervous energy. So, that's clearly a *yes, and also, fuck you, Niles.*

Skylenna sucks in a sharp breath before she wakes herself up in a crying fit. Holding her arms up, defending herself from air, from nothing. Tears well over her swollen cheekbones. And her throat is hoarse, scratchy as she pants.

Dessin and I are on our feet, gripping the bars of our cage, powerless to help her. The thrashing wakes Warrose up abruptly.

"Help her," Dessin barks.

"I got it," Warrose says, trying to hold Skylenna still. "Shhh, it's going to be okay."

But her arms stay up to protect herself, and she isn't calming down.

"Tell her she's safe."

Warrose glances at Dessin, then back to Skylenna's wincing face. "You're safe, Skylenna."

"Keep saying it."

It takes several times, chanting that phrase that Dessin seems so sure of. He rocks her back and forth, wipes her tears away with the pad of his thumb. And through his gentle voice and soothing presence, I decide I respect him a hell of a lot more. Warrose doesn't know Skylenna as well as Dessin, Ruth, and me. He's Dessin's friend. Yet he's working so hard to take care of her, to help her sleep peacefully, to assure her that she's no longer in danger.

"I'm safe," Skylenna finally mutters back in a disoriented haze.

Dessin sighs, sliding down to the ground.

"Good." Warrose releases a breath. "Now, sleep, kid."

I relax my shoulders and take my seat. From this angle, I study the bars on Dessin's cage. *No...that can't be right.* I lean forward to get a better look. Two bars are bent away from each other. As if someone was trying to pull them apart.

My gawking stare flicks to Dessin, arms crossed, brow furrowed as he watches Skylenna like a hawk.

He almost succeeded in prying his cage apart just to save her from the Blood Mammoths. My eyes gloss over with tears, and my throat becomes thick. He really would do anything for this girl.

He'd bend iron with his bare hands.

"Wow," Marilynn utters next to me.

I peek over at her.

She nods at Dessin's cage. "Only one explanation for that."

"Which is?"

"Soul mates."

# Ruth

LEAVES SLAP ACROSS MY face as I sprint through the Emerald Forest. The earthy air is layered with fog, and the soil is damp but soft, sticking to the bottoms of my bare feet.

I feel like I'm flying.

My body is learning to move faster, the muscles in my legs looking defined.

I can be useful.

"*Shit.*"

A gurgling sound echoes through the trees, the stones, the mountains. Then, coughing. Loud, wet heaving. I stop running and look up to the sky.

"*Flip her over!*"

I jerk upright in my cage, blinking away the sleep as I try to make out what I'm seeing. Warrose turns Skylenna on her side, lightly patting her back to get her to cough.

The phlegm in her chest is thick, sticky as it clings to her throat. She squeezes her eyes shut as her body convulses, clenching and contracting to get out whatever is lacing her lungs.

"You're doing great, just clear it out," Warrose says soothingly.

I stroke her arm through the cage, covered in dried blood and sweat. "Does she have a fever?" I ask.

Warrose shakes his head. "The opposite. She's still cold."

Hands bang against bars. Once. Twice.

I stare at Dessin with wide eyes. He looks like he's seconds away from having a full meltdown.

"She definitely has a broken rib." Warrose presses lightly on her side.

Skylenna spits to the side as she clears whatever was in her throat.

"She's going to be alright," I tell Dessin, trying to calm him down. "We just have to get through the night." Although my heart doesn't believe it. I ache everywhere for her. My soul sister. She looks moments away from being swept up by the angel of death. I blink away the tears gathering in my eyes.

Skylenna lets out an agonized groan. Dessin grips the bars, flexing every muscle in his upper body.

"Want me to sing you to sleep?" Warrose whispers.

She tries to nod. But it's barely a movement. I want to kiss her cheeks. Tell her she's so brave. Tell her how I look up to her, admire her strength, and want to be just like her.

*Wait, sing? Warrose can sing?*

He pulls her to his chest again, cradles her softly until his chin rests on the top of her head.

I can't help but start to cringe as I imagine his rough, deep voice breaking out into a song. There's no way he's talented in this area. His natural pitch is a growl, ragged, and baritone.

"*Hidden in the red, it's said he's made of storm.*" The words are edged and flowy, sinking to the pit of my stomach. My mouth falls open.

"*Spun of thunder, built of lightning, of a god is how he was born.*"

Niles sits up next to me. My skin prickles with goose bumps. That voice. So full of soul. Of emotion. It makes my lungs empty of air.

"*He cannot be seen beneath the darkened skies. Can only be felt in a time so dire. Not a dragon that soars the clouds, but an angel that brings fire.*"

"Christ," Niles mutters.

"*In the darkness, in the shadow, all alone he will wait. For the RottWeilen belong with a family of fate.*"

I gasp with Niles. This song is about

"DaiSzek." Skylenna smiles with her eyes closed. "My boy."

Warrose continues singing, lulling her to sleep with his husky, soft words. A tune that nudges my heart, chips it right down the middle.

She snores lightly against his chest. We're all silent as we listen.

"That was beautiful, Warrose," Niles says.

Warrose glimpses over my head, raising his eyebrows at Niles in acknowledgment.

"Did you make that up?" I ask him quietly, careful not to wake Skylenna.

"No."

"Where did you learn it?"

"It was just a song I learned as a kid. Some people in the Bear Traps had legends of RottWeilen, of ancient spirits, hidden villages, time travelers. Old wives' tales."

I smile. "They thought he was a bedtime story."

Warrose nods.

I watch him from the corner of my eye, studying the way he holds Skylenna like a small child. And she does look small in his massive arms against his brawny chest. I've never seen him so gentle, so sweet. He took care of Niles, Chekiss, and me when we were following Skylenna through her journey to learn about her past, but he was so grumpy then.

Now... he looks like he's afraid to hurt her by moving. Afraid to wake her up. Afraid to go to sleep. Like a father taking care of a baby.

I guess I've never seen him in this light.

"I didn't know you could sing."

He exhales slowly. "I used to sing Kane to sleep when he was little."

Something about that statement tugs at my heart, wrapping it in a death grip. When they were subjects, no, *prisoners* of Demechnef. That's how he would care for Kane.

"When did you learn you had a beautiful voice?"

"I wouldn't say beautiful." He chuckles, looking away in thought. "But when I was three, I decided I wanted to practice and get really good. I wanted to perform at the theater in Chandelier City. I wanted to be the star of their plays."

"Did you ever get the chance?"

"No. I didn't."

Turning my head, I hide the frown pulling at my cheeks. I feel awful for growing up so privileged. And for some reason, I need to know everything. Need to know how he grew up. Need to know if he was happy.

"Can I ask you something personal?"

"Sure."

"Do you know why you were taken? How old were you?"

To my left, Niles and Marilynn whisper back and forth. It looks like we aren't the only ones who are having trouble sleeping. But Dessin is worse. He's slumped in the dark corner of his cage, brooding, seething, waiting for the morning to come.

"I was six. One winter, I got lost in the North Saphrine Forest trying to hunt while my father was sick. My parents found me in a cave, snuggled by White Venom wolves. They're native to the Stormsages. Anyway, they're known for being vicious hunters. *Especially* in winter. But they saved me, kept me warm, and fed me until my parents found me."

I blow out a breath. "That's so sweet."

"After that, I started venturing out to the forests more often. I'd make friends with a lot of the animals. Talk to them because I didn't have any friends. And just grew fascinated with them, I guess." He moves a lock of hair away from Skylenna's face. "Long and sad story short, my parents were very religious and thought I was some kind of devil. They sold me to Demechnef."

"For being around the animals?" I balk.

"For talking to them."

"Could they talk back?"

He laughs. "No. But sometimes they understood me."

"Then why would Demechnef buy you?"

"Because they're afraid of the forests. Afraid of the undiscovered species. They saw an opportunity to train me, make a weapon that could control these beasts. Some gentle, some malicious."

"That must have been horrible for someone who loved those creatures so much." I sigh, leaning against the bars that separate us. My arm brushes his. "They were your friends."

"It was. But Dessin eventually broke us out, and I was able to go rogue."

His back straightens enough to tell me he isn't exactly happy talking about this part of his life. I don't blame him. If my parents sold me, I wouldn't be able to talk about it with anyone. The memory would be too painful to revisit.

We spend several minutes listening to the eerie circus music that runs in a never ending, glitchy loop. Cringing as it breaks apart with white noise.

I can't stop sneaking peeks of Warrose taking care of Skylenna. Why does he have to have this soft side? Why couldn't he continue to be that graceless brute?

"Are there any animals you don't like? Any you're afraid of?" I ask, feeling this tugging need to know more about him.

"Only one, though I'm not sure if it's a myth or actually exists." He scratches the facial hair lining his jaw. "A Dralutheran. They're these ginormous reptilian leviathans. Like mutated basilisks and dragons. They only hunt apex predators but have never actually been seen in combat. Always isolated. But said to be indestructible, the most feared of all beasts."

I picture the giant monster in my head. "I bet DaiSzek wouldn't be afraid of it."

"No, I don't suppose he's afraid of much." Warrose nods in agreement. "But based on mythology, that might be the only being in the world that could truly challenge him *and* win."

I go eerily quiet at the idea of DaiSzek losing a battle. Chills prickle over my bare skin. I wish he never said that. It's a gift to believe DaiSzek is unmatched in every way. I hope he never shares this theory to Dessin or Skylenna.

"Please don't ever pull the shit she pulled today," Warrose says under his breath, changing the subject.

"Pull what?"

"Anything out of line. This could have easily been you."

"It could have been any of us." I narrow my eyes. "But thank you for pointing out again how much of a weak link I am." And there's the tactless moron I know.

He grunts. "That's not what I'm saying—Skylenna got lucky she figured out how to pull them all into that prison place. We can't do that. *You* can't do that."

"What's your point, War-Man?"

"If this was you, bloody and beaten in my arms, I'd never fucking forgive you. Okay?" Anger simmers off his skin like a steady puff of steam.

I scoff. "Fine by me! I'd be unconscious or probably too dead to notice."

He whips his head in my direction, glaring with brilliant seafoam eyes. His lips part to say something. They shut almost immediately. Open again, then he growls as he turns away.

"Cat got your tongue?" I mock.

He grinds his teeth, looking straight ahead. "You're so fucking oblivious."

"Yeah? What else?"

"Annoying."

"Mhm."

"Stubborn."

"Certainly."

"Entitled."

"Definitely that."

"Stunning."

I open my mouth, but this time I'm the one to slam it shut. My head pivots to look straight ahead. *Stunning?* I'm almost pissed at the way my stomach flops forward. The way my chest tingles.

*Stunning.*

"Cat got your tongue?" he asks with a knowing smile in his tone.

"I should try to get some sleep," I tell him with a fake yawn. Truth is, there's no way I can sleep with Skylenna like this. I can feel the aches, the throbbing in her bones, the chill resting under her skin from here.

"Good night."

"Warrose?"

"Yes?"

I sigh, closing my eyes. "You have a beautiful voice."

Peeking up at him from beneath my lashes, he smiles to himself.

"Thank you, little rebel."

# 12. Family First

## Dessin

Skylenna wrinkles her nose as she starts to wake up.

It's her tell. It's that little sign I wake up early to see. That adorable movement that makes my ice-cold heart begin to thaw.

"*How is she?*" Kane rushes to the front, burning my thoughts with crippling stress and guilt.

"*She survived the night.*"

We both sigh heavily.

I thought I lost her. The gurgling sound in her chest. It could have meant a lot of things. A broken rib puncturing her lung, causing a collapse. Or the space between her chest wall and lungs filling with blood.

She was kicked, stomped on, scratched, thrown, and beaten as if by a cluster of apes.

My fists clench and shake at the memory. She tried to protect her vital organs, but they came from every angle. That strength couldn't have been matched. And she was blind to it all.

Last night was hell to live through without a moment of sleep.

I glance over at her again with uncontained anguish swelling in my gut. She stirs in Warrose's arms, taking shallow gasps, feeble whimpers, and furrowing her brow.

*"How will she be able to walk through the prison with you all?"* Greystone asks with an uncharacteristic tenderness to his tone.

*"She can't. I won't let her."*

The lack of sleep and food is causing my system of alters to suffer. The anxiety, panic, and creeping fear are worse than the asylum. Because now we have to keep them all safe. Keep them all fed. Keep them all from dying a gruesome death.

Watching Skylenna touch the brink of death, hearing her scream, and now seeing the aftereffects of her beating made me violently sick. I vomited hot bile in my cage. Heaved until nothing could come up. My thoughts raced on building the escape plan. But I've been so distracted, so tired, so hungry.

I'm at a breaking point.

We need food.

"What happens when the cages open?" Warrose asks me.

I don't take my eyes off my girl. "I'm staying here with her."

"We all will," Ruth adds, looking almost as tired as I am.

I can't deny her this. Any of them. They love her, too.

I nod once.

"I can see if there are any supplies to clean her up. Maybe take away the pain," Niles offers with wide, naïve eyes coloring with desperation to be useful here. Even though it's not a bad idea, I can't let him go out there on his own.

"I'll go with him," Marilynn says reluctantly.

I study her. The bags under her deep blue eyes, the dryness of her freckled skin, the way she holds her stomach to fight the hunger pains.

"Fine," I grumble.

"Try and find alcohol so we can disinfect these wounds. Bandaging, capsaicinwhich is found in chili peppers for the painwater to get her hydrated, and fuck, if you can find a blanketshe's still so cold." Warrose adjusts her in his arms.

I have to remember to thank him for this with my life. He stepped up for her last night. I wanted it to be my cage that opened, obviously, but I was just happy she made it back. That someone was able to take care of her.

"We'll find Helga Bee. That one prisoner had his hand chopped off. They were disinfecting it with alcohol, remember? I bet she knows where we can find medical aid." Niles paces his cage, waiting for those bars to open.

I'm itching to be let out, too. The second these cages open, I'm running to her. My chest feels broken, cracked open like an egg, my heart gushing out of me.

"Maybe I can ask Kaspias for some food for her? Just this once," Ruth suggests hesitantly.

The last string of patience I had snaps loud enough to ring in my ears.

"Do you have fucking brain damage? He's the one who did this to her! He's the one who is relishing in making us suffer. Look at her face!" I'm standing now, gripping the bars with every ounce of strength I have left.

Ruth drops her wide eyes to Skylenna. We both scan the blackening bruises on her face, the forming scabs, the drying blood, the swelling forming in stiff lumps. It makes me want to obliterate all of humanity.

"*That's* what he did! You need to drop this fantasy of that man being a hidden saint. He's not one of us, Ruth! He's *not* my brother!" My voice echoes through the halls of this prison wing. It booms across the brimstone floors, waking every last prisoner who was still asleep.

A rumbling of groans and voices bounce back to us.

"Back off, Dess!" Warrose growls. "Just because her instincts aren't the same as yours doesn't mean she's wrong."

I glare at him through lowered lids.

"Don't give me that look. We're going through hell together, alright? Doesn't give you a pass to take this on alone. To be a dick and shut us out."

My fury rises to the surface. He thinks he knows what's going on in our head? He thinks me being a dick is what matters right now?

"The woman I love is lying bloody and broken in your arms! You really want to pull this card right now?!" Blood rushes to my face. Heat prickles under my skin.

"Yeah. I do. Because I had to watch *you* lying bloody and broken in *her* arms!" Warrose's voice breaks at the word *her*. "I had to watch her go up in flames, beg you to come back, kiss your lifeless body, and ask someone to save you!"

It's as if he's swinging that sickle through my chest all over again.

"And I couldn't say a goddamn thing to comfort her! I couldn't tell her I was going to try to bring you back to life. I couldn't tell her this was all a part of a grand plan. I made a promise to my best friend. My brother. It was literally your dying fucking wish." He fights to gain control of his tone, his hoarseness. But the tears come anyway. Those hazel eyes well with pent-up grief, and he tries to blink it away.

"I had to look at your corpse and attempt to give you that crazy ass spring water, which had a pretty good chance of not working. And then at your funeral? Seeing your casket? She lost it, Dess. She fucking shattered into a million tiny pieces. And all I could do was watch."

That thick wall of ice starts to melt.

"I love her, too, brother. So, no. You don't get to be a bastard to us. Because I love her, too!" Tears drizzle down his cheeks. And I have to break the burning eye contact. I can't stand to see him cry. It was only a few times in my life that it happened.

"You're right." I take a deep breath, reeling in my temper. "I'm sorry."

He grinds his teeth. "And?"

My gaze meets Ruth, who is rubbing her hands over the backs of her arms.

I sigh. "I'm sorry, Ruth. You were just trying to help."

Ruth flashes me a sad smile, gulping down her discomfort from the weight of my stare. She doesn't deserve my outbursts, I know. But I'm teetering on the edge of a full-on outrage, a disastrous breakdown. And with this amount of stress, there might be another alter who splits.

"I'm so thirsty," Skylenna finally says, trying to peek up at Warrose through swollen eyelids.

My heart beat picks up, kicking a hole through my breastbone at the sound of her voice.

"We're getting water for you just as soon as"

"Dessin?" she utters, that sweet voice sounding like she tried to gargle glass.

"Yes, baby?" I practically collapse.

"Your cage..." She tries to open her eyes wider, looking past me. "The bars..."

At this, the entire group shifts awkwardly, looking at my confinement with the same question they've all been dying to ask.

"It's sturdier than I thought," I answer.

She pauses. "Show me your hands."

I release a low grumble in the base of my throat, flexing my fingers as I hold my palms out to her.

The group sucks in a sharp breath. I'd love it if they had the decency to pretend to be busy. But here we are, way too involved in each other's private moments.

Skylenna frowns at the plum purple bruising on the inside of my hands. But I don't care. I would have broken my bones to break through that metal.

*"I love you,"* she mouths to me.

The cage doors swing open.

"Go now!" I urge Niles and Marilynn. "Beat the crowd."

They nod eagerly, racing down the hallway without another word. And I bolt right after them, turning on my heels to join Skylenna in Warrose's cage. I get down on my knees in front of them, holding my arms out.

"I've got her," I tell Warrose. "Thank you for taking care of her."

He gives me a tight nod, passing her over to me as if she only weighs the same as a puppy. My chest collapses on itself as I smell the coppery, dried blood covering her body. Feel the iciness of her skin. She's so fucking fragile it kills me.

And to twist the knife in my heart, she smiles despite the swelling in her jaw. She coos at the sight of me. I could cry like a newborn baby at that smile.

Warrose stands up, naked, and in my face. Thankfully, Ruth hands him his pants.

"Why?" I ask Skylenna.

"Hmm?"

"Why did you do it?" I kiss the bruises on her collarbone. Kiss the wounds on her cheekbones. "Why did you freak out, baby? Why did you kill that sentinel? I had it handled."

She shakes her head, frowning like it's too painful to say.

"I'm not mad, Skylenna. I swear, I just want to understand."

"The blood was everywhere," she croaks.

Ruth takes a seat next to Warrose, stroking Skylenna's sliced up feet.

"On my chest? Look, see? I'm fine now. They barely got me."

"It was spilling on my lap. It covered my hands." She holds her arms up to show me, fingers shaking at the effort. "It gushed over your chin as you tried to breathe." Her small voice breaks, and hot tears leak over her swollen lids, streaming through the dried blood.

I suddenly wish I could reverse time, taking back my stupid fucking question. Taking back my faked death. Taking back her grief.

"Oh…" is all I can manage.

"And you stopped blinking. You stopped *breathing*." Her cries turn hysterical. She chokes on snot and hiccups. "Oh, god, Dessin! I saw it happen again! I was there! You were—dying in my arms!"

Ruth reaches out to hold Skylenna's hand, holding back her tears.

"Shhh, *fuck*, I'm so sorry. It's my fault. It's all my fault. I should have realized—"

"I begged you to come back, and—DaiSzek, he cried for you—and you were—so cold!"

The urge to cry with her builds like lava in my throat. Her entire body trembles in my lap, and I can feel the devastation fall from her in waves.

"I'm an idiot, baby. Look what I've done to you." I panic, breathing erratically as I watch her drown. She's like this because of me. I gave her irreversible scars. Wounds that can never be healed. That was the price we both paid.

And Kane's guilt rising to the front is more than overwhelming, it's cataclysmic.

"He's safe," Ruth says, grabbing Skylenna's hand and plastering it to my bare chest. "You feel that? That's Dessin's heartbeat. He's safe. He's alive."

I fail to stifle my shock as I watch Ruth.

"Say it, Skylenna. He's safe with you."

And just like that, Skylenna's breathing slows, and she blinks away her tears with determination pinching her brow.

"He's safe with me."

Ruth smiles. "That's right. You're both safe."

Skylenna leans her ear against my chest to listen to the steady rhythm. Sniffling, fighting to control her sobs.

I reach my hand out to grab Ruth's thin fingers. I don't think I've ever held her hand before, but it feels right. "*Thank you*," I mouth.

I'm ashamed for snapping at her. Especially when her heart is this big. She didn't need to come on this mission with us. She's lived a sheltered life, never experiencing true terror like this prison presents. But she's here. And she just made my girl feel better.

"You're welcome," Ruth whispers.

I rock Skylenna back and forth, savoring the way she clings to me. That even though she's this powerful creature now, I'm still her rock. Nothing in the world is a better feeling than that.

"Dess? We'll give you two some time alone. Ruth and I will get a shower and bring back some towels."

I can hardly nod my head. It feels so damn good to hold her, to finally relax in this hell hole. But I'm grateful for the time alone. For the moments of peace with just the two of us.

"I'm sorry, Dessin. I fucked up," Skylenna whimpers in my shoulder.

"No, you didn't." I kiss her hair several times. "Nothing matters now. It's just you and me."

"I missed you."

My cock throbs against her bare ass in my lap. I groan at the bad timing, but I love her so much. Hearing her say these things just undoes every bit of restraint I have.

"It was agony not being able to hold you last night."

She nods. "I know."

"So, Warrose didn't get a hard-on last night, did he?" *Say no.*

She laughs against my chest, then winces as the pain shoots through her ribs.

"Of course not."

The fact that I shouldn't make her laugh is its own kind of torture.

"I guess that's good."

"Jealous?"

"I was too fucking out of my mind scared for you to be jealous." I breathe in the scent of her hair, closing my eyes as that slight whiff of lily and rainwater make it into my senses. "But also, yeah. Kinda."

She groans. "Don't make me laugh."

"I'm sorry."

My breathing grows heavy as I finally can relax enough to drift close to sleep for the first time since being in this place. Our bodies meld around each other. And I let her soak in every last drop of heat I can give.

"He gave his body to keep me warm," she comments.

"He did."

"But no one on this earth is as warm as you. You're my blanket in a blizzard."

Male pride fills my chest. "That right there makes the entire night without you worth it."

"Will you be here when I wake up?" she asks sleepily.

The truth of the answer bites into my heart like an apple.

"As long as you promise to wake up."

# Niles

"THIS PLACE SMELLS LIKE an actual asshole," I whisper to Marilynn as we jog into the stadium area.

"I'm inclined to agree with you." She cringes inwardly.

We spot Helga Bee and Gerta at the same time, waving them down.

"Hey there, golden pup!" Helga Bee greets, losing her breath from doing squats, jumping, and throwing punches in the air.

"Is that my new nickname?" I grimace as Gerta leans her damp arm against me, batting her eyelashes, and stinging my burns with salty sweat.

"Sure is. You're cute and cuddly, like a golden puppy! Gerta says so."

Gerta nods.

"We actually don't have time to chat," Marilynn says grumpily, stepping forward and reaching a hand to loosen Gerta's grip on my arm. "That hurts him. But you can hold his hand."

Gerta blinks her surprise, then blushes while she grabs my left hand.

I ogle at Marilynn in wide-eyed disbelief. She generally looks too pissy to be this observant. Yet she knew Gerta was hurting my burns.

"Skylenna was hurt badly in The Hunt. Where can we find supplies?" I ask.

"Where is she?" Helga Bee stops her exercising to look around.

"Not here. We had to keep her in our cages." *And it killed me to leave them. But she needs help.*

"You're supposed to bring your wounded here, ya know. That's probably gonna cost you tonight, dumb pup!"

"What do you mean?"

Helga Bee uses her skimpy uniform to wipe the sweat dripping down her splotchy brow. Then attempts to dab the rest of her skin dry.

"It's Fun House Night!" She wafts her hands around the giant room. "I told you all about Fun House Night!"

*Fuck us right up the ass.*

"Oh, shit."

"Yep. 'Tis a real doozy! We're all going to be entertaining those dick-jerking, bloodthirsty, mommy-killin' sissies!"

"But Skylenna should be exempt, right? She was nearly beaten to death last night," Marilynn grits.

"Nope. Even those who have lost a limb still have to join the festivities."

I kick the side of the stage. "Fuck this. Can you help us get supplies then?"

She fake coughs, pointing her thumb behind the stage. "Take what you need, grumpy puppy. The next wave of prisoners will flood through those doors in about a minute. You can slip back to the cages that way."

# Ruth

I HATE TO SAY IT, but I feel remarkably safer with Warrose guiding us to the showers.

"There are buckets in the corner. I'll grab that if you can grab a few towels," Warrose whispers, his facial hair grazing the side of my ear. I hide my shudder by scratching my nose with the back of my hand.

We strip off our clothes without looking at each other and rush into the blazing cold water. He walks us into a corner, where no one can watch me scrub down. I don't object because, honestly, I'm not in the mood to see another little man beating his thing off to me in front of everyone. I just want to help Skylenna.

"You about done?" he asks with his back to me.

"Yes." I finish rinsing out the suds from my hair.

We quickly disperse to dry off and get what we came for. After slipping on another uniform, I grab an armful of towels. Warrose signals me over, but something down the hall, toward the prison commissary, grabs my attention.

Kaspias leans against a wall, hands casually hooked in his pant pockets, looking out at the inmates eating.

Maybe I am delusional. Maybe Dessin is right. I'm naïve and ignorant.

I offer Warrose an apologetic look before dashing down the hall, arms holding the stack of towels, chin up, and jaw set.

Kaspias meets my eyes as I race down the hall, raising an eyebrow.

"Hi," I pant, clutching the towels to my chest like they might protect me.

"Hello."

Up close, Kaspias is identical to Dessin. Same height, sharp jawline, same close-set brown eyes. But the differences make him another creature entirely. His lip and ears are pierced with spiked silver jewelry. Those frigid eyes are lined with black paint, and he has a well-kept beard.

I'm suddenly at a loss for words. Unable to remember why I approached him.

"Is that all?" he asks with grating annoyance.

I shake my head. Gulp. Study the charcoal plated armor on his shoulders.

*Focus. Skylenna is hurt. You can do this, Ruth. You can be helpful.*

"You can gawk at me from a distance. Get the fuck out of my face before I drown you at the Fun House tonight," he barks.

*There's a Fun House tonight?*

"Kaspias," I breathe, blinking the panic away from my thoughts. "I need your help."

This washes the aggravation from his features immediately. Something like hilarity hooks the corner of his mouth and twinkles in those empty eyes.

"Go on…" His head turns to the side, the same way Dessin's does when he's about to play a game.

"Skylenna…she's hurt badly. And the kitchen staff is starving us out. I-I just need a small amount of food for her. Anything to help her get some strength back."

The dark intensity of Kaspias's stare burns a hole through my skull. I suddenly want to run away, break the connection that makes me feel empty, lost, hopeless.

"And what makes you think I want her to regain even an ounce of strength back? I'm the one who put her in that condition."

"But—"

"Would you like to suffer the same fate, Ruth?"

"If it gets you to fulfill my request, yes," I answer without a moment to think about it. I'd probably drop dead. I wouldn't be able to use the special gifts that Skylenna has. I would be beaten to a lifeless pulp. "Yes," I say again.

Kaspias narrows his eyes. "Yes?"

I nod. Warrose may kill me first. This is beyond idiotic.

"You would likely not even make it ten yards before my mammoths crushed you," he muses without breaking eye contact.

"She needs food. Not much. And something for the pain and swelling."

"Why?"

"Because she's been in and out of hypothermic levels all night. She hasn't had a meal in three days. If she's going to last another day, she needs help."

"No, I mean, why would you sacrifice your own life so that she may have a bite of food?"

I glare at him as if the answer is obvious. "That's what family does."

Kaspias blinks but doesn't say anything.

"Dessin is *your* family. You weren't raised together. And you've both been victims of cruel, heartless governments. But he's *your* brother, Kaspias. And this is the woman he loves." My eyes well with tears, and my throat aches to cry.

His eyebrows pull together with a look that almost edges close to sympathy. But after a second, he grins and breaks out into laughter.

"Look at this!" He swipes his thumbs over my eyes. I squeeze them shut against his calloused skin, jerking away from his hands gripping my head. "Tears? Have you really gotten this attached? You think the words *family* or *brother* mean anything to me?" He laughs harder, tasting my tears from the pads of his thumbs.

"Ruth," Warrose calls from a few paces back.

I hold my hand up for him to stay put.

"If you want Skylenna to survive a Fun House Night, if you want to keep your head from being chopped off by the Mazonist Brothers, then you'll make sure she survives this!"

His smile falls away. "My brother would never let her die."

"Maybe not. But he certainly would die trying to keep her alive. Then you have one of their bodies on your hands before they can be of any use to this country."

I feel Warrose's heavy presence at my back. But I don't break my furious gaze from Kaspias. From his unfeeling expression.

He gives me a once-over look, then cracks his neck. "Wait here."

I turn to Warrose after Kaspias heads into the kitchen. He looks down at me with confusion, waiting for an explanation.

"Dessin was right," I say with a shrug. "He doesn't care about any of us, but he does care about himself. And he would be in trouble if Skylenna doesn't survive tonight."

Without a word, Warrose pulls me against his chest, wrapping his arms around my exposed body. He's so warm. So strong. I fight the urge to melt into him.

"That was clever, kid."

"You're not mad?"

"I definitely was at first, but the fact that you proved Dessin wrong feels like Christmas Day," he rasps against my hair.

I smile.

# Skylenna

MY ARM SCREAMS IN PAIN as if I'm being skinned alive.

"Hold her still."

"She's so wiggly."

"It's okay, Skylenna. We're just cleaning your wounds," Marilynn grumbles near me.

I squint through the watery blur coating my eyes. Two heads hover around me, moving, bickering, and messing with my limbs.

"*Ow!*" I hiss, trying to yank my feet away from a glowing golden head.

"They're trying to keep your wounds from getting infected, baby." I'm still snuggled in Dessin's arms. Held tight against his chest.

The sting subsides, replaced by cold water cleaning my skin.

My vision clears, and I look right at Niles wrapping up my feet.

"Nurse Niles at your service!" He grins, placing a kiss on top of my foot. "See? Boo-boo all better."

I roll my eyes, smiling against the swelling in my cheeks.

"Drink this," Marilynn says, passing a cup of water to Dessin. He holds it to my lips, tipping it upward for me to drink.

The sensation running down my throat is a blast of endorphins tingling through my bloodstream. Cold water soothing my dry mouth, my tight esophagus. I moan at the relief.

"You think that's erotic? Just wait until I rub this pain-relieving ointment on you!" Niles chirps, waving a jar of brown cream in my face.

"Niles," Dessin grunts.

I tap Dessin's arm. "Deal with it," I mutter into my cup. "I need his quirkiness right now."

He sighs, nuzzling his nose in my hair.

"You heard her, Muscles. Only one of us is endlessly hilarious, and it's certainly not—*you!*" Niles taps Dessin on the nose with his index finger, making a *boop* sound. Then instantly retreating like Dessin may try to bite it off.

"*Skylenna*," Dessin warns.

But I just laugh, cringing at the way my ribs light up in a lightning storm of pain.

"I'm sorry, Sissy. This ointment only helps with open wounds. Not so much fractured bones."

I sigh. "It's okay."

"I may have something that can help." Ruth and Warrose stand in the entryway of this cage, holding a tray, towels, and a bucket of water.

"No way," Marilynn says under her breath.

"It's soup. Smells terrible. But it's better than nothing. And there's this drink that the soldiers take when they're severely wounded. It remedies that pain during recovery so they can continue fighting." Ruth kneels down in front of me. "Do you want to eat first or drink the cup of black goo?"

I look down at the bowl of steaming broth and a metal cup filled to the brim with black liquid.

"How did you get this?" Dessin asks.

"Kaspias," Ruth and Warrose say in unison.

Dessin stiffens beneath me.

"He didn't want to help. But I made him understand that his life would be on the line if anything happened to either of you at tonight's Fun House," Ruth explains as she stirs the bowl of soup.

"What's the catch?" I try to sit up, but my body groans like an old ship about to sink.

"You have to participate in tonight's Fun House."

"Fuck no." Dessin holds me closer.

"We don't have a choice," Niles adds. "Everyone goes in. Even the injured."

The group falls silent as we all watch the old spoon spin through the steaming soup. The aroma isn't great, but it makes my stomach grumble just the same.

"Here." Warrose covers me in towels from the shower area, distributing them over my nakedness. "How's her temperature?"

"Better," Dessin says.

"She looks a little better now that you two have cleaned her up a bit." Warrose studies me like a doctor would a patient. "Any more broken bones?"

Dessin shakes his head. "Just a dislocated shoulder. But I popped it back into place while she was sleeping."

"Eat," Ruth urges, holding the spoon out to me.

Eat? When the rest of my family is still being starved out? Just because I was beaten doesn't make me any more deserving than them.

I shake my head.

"Are you nauseous?" Marilynn asks.

"No."

"Skylenna," Dessin grumbles, trying to get a better look at my face. He knows me well enough to find the answers written there.

"I won't eat unless you all do, too."

They hesitate before arguing with that logic.

"I'll take a bite, after each of you do first." My word is final, and they can hear it in my tone. Either we all eat, or I suffer right along with them.

Ruth takes the first spoonful before passing it to Niles.

"Damn, how can something taste so good and so rancid at the same time?" He rubs his tummy like that one spoonful was enough to fill him up.

One by one, we finish off the bowl of soup. Ruth has me drink the black sludge, helping me force it down without puking. Niles finishes applying the ointment. Marilynn washes the blood out of my hair. And Warrose sings to me as Dessin rocks me back and forth.

I smile up at them as the pain drifts far below the surface. Muted. Colorless. And I realize, it doesn't matter where we are. An asylum. Demechnef Headquarters. A savage prison.

We are home if we're together.

# 13. Fun House Night

## Skylenna

*"Join the fun! Run, run, run! Our soldiers wait! Run, run, run! The Ringmaster calls! Run, run, run! Only corpses are late!"*

Dessin keeps a hand on my lower back as we follow the prisoners back to the circus stage. The speakers blast a child's creepy song that, I suppose, is meant to get everyone in the mood to participate in Fun House Night.

I want to cover my ears.

"It feels like I'm walking to my own funeral," Niles deadpans.

"We find Helga Bee first. She can at least give us some insight on what to expect," Dessin instructs us calmly.

We file toward another entry to the stadium. The doorways are open enough to see the glimmer of golden light and hear the unsettling music, a combination of trumpets, violins, and an old organ. But worst of all, the muffled chatter of more human beings than I have ever heard before in one central setting.

"Do you think anyone dies from these little shows?" Warrose leans close to Dessin's ear so the others can't hear him.

"Maybe."

I have to hold out hope that we're far too useful for the Mazonist Brothers to dispose of us in a cheap, gory circus. We're weapons. Why would they be so careless with us?

"I think they're trying to scare us into submission," Dessin mutters under his breath.

"Hmm?"

"The Mazonist Brothers. Think about it. What better way to ensure our loyalty? Make the alternative to their plans for us seem so much worse. Keep us in this deranged slice of hell long enough, and we'd do anything for them to stay out of it." Dessin strokes my back as he whispers in my ear.

"I was literally just thinking about the Mazonist Brothers and why they would risk our safety like this," I muse, savoring the way his lips graze my hair. "Can you read minds now?"

"We're back to that theory, huh?"

I shrug.

"It seems we've been together long enough to think on the same frequency," he adds.

Something about that idea puts my mind at ease. We're growing closer in ways neither of us understand. It feels like he covers my weaknesses, and I cover his. Where one of us ends, the other begins.

"You think they'll be watching this Fun House Night?" I ask.

He nods, watching the line file through those grand double doors into the blinding light. Nerves prickle over my bruised arms, twisting my stomach like a ribbon into a bow. Theoretically, we may be safe from dying here, but not from suffering. And what about the others? Ruth and Niles would mean nothing to our captors. In fact, they may act as further incentive to do their bidding.

*"Focus on getting through tonight."* The voice is back, so real I can feel the tingle of her breath on my cheek.

*"You still aren't going to tell me who you are?"* I ask in the stillness of my own thoughts.

*"No. At least, not until you need that answer desperately."*

I arch my eyebrow. What's that supposed to mean?

142

*"Will you help me keep them alive?"* Even in my mind, my question is shaky and rimmed with alarm. We're two steps away from walking through those doors. Into an arena of Vexamen soldiers waiting to be entertained.

With an edge of old wisdom, she answers, *"Always."*

Dessin squeezes my hand once before we take our first steps into the giant room of chaos, beaming golden bulbs and a darker shade of red, like dried blood, coloring every surface.

An announcer's voice blasts through the stadium of people, echoing across the high ceilings, zinging from wall to wall. I follow the sound to a tall, lanky man standing on a raised stage, surrounded by a ring of fire.

*"That's the Ringmaster."*

I nod, waiting to share that bit of information with Dessin.

The Ringmaster is dressed in a glamorized military uniform. Dark red tailcoat with gold trim, a glittering sequined vest, golden chains, leather gloves, and an obnoxious top hat.

*"Tevezuíez dulesev nad pöxex ra sïs hogrsás? Bixex nuei bäship Demechnef qeinx ta hues mäh?"* His tone reaches the audience, and they laugh, then boo.

Ruth moves close to us to translate. "But shall I switch to the new language of our sister country? That way our little Demechnef guests may understand me?"

Dessin rolls his eyes. "I'm going to guess not."

The Ringmaster makes another joke, pulling another laugh from the stadium.

"Best to leave them in suspense then," Ruth deciphers, gawking out at the crowd unnerved.

"Does anyone see Helga Bee?" Dessin asks us.

I search the lines of prisoners filing around the stage, looking up at the ceiling with dread. No sign of her round, blushing face. *Come on, Helga Bee. We need you.*

We follow our lineup of prisoners toward the edge of the back end of the stage. The crowd throws things at us, not the other prisoners, but us specifically. Handfuls of popcorn. Rotting fruit. And some kind of sludge. They scream at us in outrage. The name Demechnef pops up multiple times.

"I'm not going to repeat any of what I'm hearing." Ruth lowers her head.

"Don't make eye contact with them." Dessin turns to us quickly, jaw set in authority. "We don't know how interactive they can be."

I blow out a breath. I want to be strong for my family, I do. But my body is still so stiff from the swelling and bruises. The black sludge Ruth brought me helped with the pain, but I'm still aching and unable to move swiftly.

The Ringmaster yells something final, the beaming lights flash, the music shrieks to its highest volume, and the stadium ignites in wild energy to cheer on the show.

"He says, '*you know the rules. Deserters will be thrown in the Vex-Reaping! Behold, the Swinging Pit!*'"

"But we don't know the rules." This may be one of the first times I've heard fear in Niles's voice. He doesn't usually show negative emotion. Merely covers it up with humor. But that golden face is missing its charming smile. He stays close to the group the way a child would cling to its mother's leg.

"Did you think they'd give us a manual?" Marilynn snaps at him, irritated and overwhelmed.

"Everyone watch what the prisoners in front of us do. We'll learn the rules that way." Dessin scans the stage, studying it thoroughly.

But we need more than to watch. I have to keep us all alive. Dessin and I are safe due to our value to this country. Our family isn't.

A forty-foot ladder rises from openings in the stage floor, stretching to the glowing ceiling. My eyes follow its length, searching its surrounding area for a purpose.

"Look at the bars," Dessin says, pointing upward. "They look like swings."

A stomach-wrenching terror swells and expands in my core. *Heights.* It has something to do with being at least forty feet above the stage.

One by one, inmates climb to the very top, as if it's routine, a regular occurrence in their week. The first five hesitate, looking down as if waiting for something to appear.

The stage floor unlatches mechanically, parting right down the middle. It looks like a large pool. Dark water. And for the view of the stadium, it has a glass outer wall so the audience can see inside. A rumble of boots stomping on floors erupts through the crowd. They roar with anticipation. Shout words I don't understand.

And the five inmates jump away from their ladders, spreading their arms out to latch on to the brass swings six feet in front of them.

My stomach drops as a heavier prisoner slips, plummeting toward the water with a garbled cry. But it's strangely quiet as he breaks the surface of the water. I lean forward to see his body floating. No struggle. No attempt to tread water, paddle his way to the edge of the stage, or scream for help. Instead, for a few long seconds, he looks like he's enjoying himself.

Dessin nudges me to look back up at the other prisoners holding onto their swinging bars. It looks harder than it should be. They're slipping, gasping, making an impressive effort to wrap their fingers around the bars.

"I think they're trying to swing to the next set of poles, but they're fighting to hold on," Dessin whispers to the group.

Jolting my body upright, the man in the pool lets out a childlike cry. A feeble sob. He thrashes through the water like it's made of mud. His words come slurring past his lips in a rushed attempt to call for help.

"He's calling out for his mother," Ruth tells us cautiously. "He keeps saying, '*you're not a pet. Don't obey them.*'"

"Alright, what the fuck is going on?" Warrose growls from behind us.

But Dessin and I are at a loss for words. I'm only sprinkled with an ounce of relief when two prisoners swing to the next bar and fumble to the ladder at the end of the stage. They whoop as they descend, flipping off the crowd of Vexamen soldiers.

"So that's the goal? Make it to the next set of bars, then to the last ladder?" I ask.

*"That's the goal,"* the woman in my head answers.

I balk at the sudden intrusion, forgetting she is still here.

"I'm more concerned with the pool at the bottom." Dessin watches two more prisoners plummet to the water, having the same reaction as the first.

*"Tell your friends it's an oil from their Raven Bone Mines. It seeps into your skin and pulls you into your worst nightmares."*

145

I blink, process the faceless, nameless thought. They're going to think I'm insane.

I repeat her words exactly, pausing at the end to wait for the questions that are bound to surface.

Dessin turns to face me with an even expression. "How," he ponders in disapproval, eyes tracing over my face. "Skylenna, we just got your body temperature back to normal. You can't go into the void now."

I shake my head. "I'm not."

He narrows his eyes, looking back at Warrose.

"She has another card to play, doesn't she?"

It's silly, the way a fire in my chest flickers to life with pride. I was never the one with impressive traits to show off. I was the one to cower behind Dessin. To watch his work in admiration.

"I heard a voice when the Blood Mammoths hunted me through the prison. It knew things. Guided me while I was blind. And now it's back, helping me to make it through tonight." It sounds…*nuts*. Off the wall, feverish, out of my mind, in la la land crazy.

But Dessin lifts his chin, a triumphant gleam in his eye. "Incredible," he whispers.

"This may be the only time in my life I will blindly follow someone who hears voices in their head," Warrose states.

"Wrong." Dessin steps forward in line without looking back.

Warrose purses his lips. "Forgot you were here."

The pool is now crowded with flailing inmates. Some of them are swallowing the oil and sinking to the bottom. Some of them are trying to reach for an edge.

I raise my eyes to the stadium of soldiers. They wear their plates of matte black armor, some with helmets, others with half their heads shaved in intricate designs. I follow the crowd to an organized row at the highest perch in the stadium. It's hard to see that far away, but their faces are painted. Clowns and skeletons. Beasts and reapers.

*"Those are the commanders and highest-ranking officers."*

"Does that mean Kaspias is up there?" I ask out loud.

Dessin follows my line of sight.

*"Yes,"* she says calmly. *"Female inmates have the option to leave the Fun House and service the higher ranks in private rooms."*

146

I decide it's best to keep that nugget to myself.

Dessin is next in line, looking up at the prisoner climbing above his head. A sentinel waits to give him the go ahead. My stomach coils painfully in a tight ball.

*"Tell them the swings are greased. It's easy to fall when you jump to grab on,"* the woman whispers urgently.

"The swings are greased!" I yank Dessin's arm, curling my fingers around his taut muscle. "Be careful. Please."

Dessin stares into my eyes for what feels like an entire minute. I soften under his gaze, the one that sinks to the bottom of my soul like an old ship. It's in this look that says all we need to communicate. He loves me. I love him. In the moments where we couldn't deny our attraction in the asylum. In the days when only I was allowed to enter the thirteenth room. In the nights we'd spend under the stars. Not even death could keep us apart.

"Everyone hear that? The swings are greased. Don't let go of it. We *all* make it to the other side." And he's climbing up the ladder now, taking my heart with him.

The sentinel makes me wait as he scales the ladder with speed and precision. His eyes are locked on that swing, watching inmates fall with screaming terror echoing in the stadium like a symphony of death.

Ruth squeezes my hand as he reaches the top, balancing on the balls of his feet, watching the swing move forward and back, timing it just right. His movements are methodical, perfect even. With a sudden stillness, the swing comes back toward him, and he leaps for it. A stellar presentation of his accuracy, so much so that the crowd goes silent. His technique is to jump high enough to secure his hands around the ropes of the swing that aren't covered in grease. I pass that information on to the others.

Warrose squeezes my shoulder as I start my climb. Nerves bundle together in my chest at the soreness in my limbs. Even with that concoction I drank earlier, my joints are screeching in misery. Muscle cramps in my thighs, but even worse, the shoulder that was dislocated is swelling, throbbing, growing weak from the exertion.

And I'm only climbing a tall ladder.

*Fuck.*

"Breathe."

Dessin makes it to the second swing but doesn't fling himself to the end. He waits, hanging from the ropes as I step up to the top.

His gaze insists that he's not moving until he knows I've made it to him.

The crowd fusses over this, shouting and throwing things. But I fight to tune it all out. I have to jump at the right moment. I have to place my hands on the rope instead of the bar.

My heart dances under my chest, stomping around with building anticipation. The swing falls away, then comes back.

I squat low, then explode upward toward its brass bar. The stadium is muted around me as I soar through the warm air. My hands stretch out, aiming for those ropes. Dessin's voice blasts through the wall of my concentration.

"Hold on!"

But the moment my hands lock around the swing, gravity pulls me down, pounding into my wounded shoulder like a hammer. That sharp spike of torment makes me shriek, flattening my lungs. Tears crowd my eyes. And the distress comes in sporadic waves. I lose all control over my hands, only caring about making that paralyzing sensation disappear. It blisters under my skin, crackles along my bones. And I must let go, I have to—

Defeat alone forces a cry of frustration from my lips as I watch the stadium move around me in a blur of reds and glowing light. Cheers and loud music spiral back into my ears, briefly distracting me before I see the sheen on the surface of the dark oil pool below me.

It's cold, thick, and heavy. I sink to the bottom with the cruel gravity that drags me down. I spin around, wafting my hands through the syrupy goo, unsure of which way is up and which way is down.

*I've failed! I couldn't even hold on for two fucking seconds!*

A whoosh of oil rushes over my body, and suddenly there are hands gripping my waist. Strong arms lift me, pushing me up above his own body. Why am I surprised he would dive into this unknown pond of poison? Why am I elated by the idea that he'd give up certain safety to be with me?

Breaking the surface, I wipe my mouth and nose first, frantic to suck in air.

"Swim, baby! We have to get to the edge before—"

It's the Raven Bones Mine oil. It works so fast we don't have time to escape it. My nerve endings tingle, my brain fills with a misty fog, and it's as if I'm plunging from a cliff or a mountain top. My stomach dips. And Dessin grabs onto me, his strength bruising me in an effort to not let this separate us.

I blink away the solid layer of oil, shake my head from the hit to my equilibrium. But I'm no longer in the stadium. No longer in the prison.

I'm on that fucking beach.

My toes sink into the sand.

My arms prickle with goose bumps against the briny ocean breeze.

"No!" I scream.

I can't go back to this day. I won't.

The beach erupts in a battle of clashing swords and the grunting of grown men. I can't escape what appears right in front of me, Dessin holding those two babies. Locking eyes with me.

"Dessin, behind you!" I bellow. Not again. *This can't happen again!*

The tip of the sickle rips through his flesh, breaking the bone in his chest. Once silver, now glossy with blood. I howl at the sight.

And it happens all over again. He crashes to his knees. I fall to him, bracing his full weight in my arms. I can't rid the burning scent of coppery blood and sea salt from my nostrils.

This show of utter horror can't get any worse. I just have to survive what I've already done once before. *He's mine, God! Please, don't take him away from me!*

"Let me help!" Ruth begs, rushing to my side.

This isn't right. This isn't how it happened.

She drops to a knee in front of me, pressing her small hands to Dessin's wound to help stop the bleeding. Those soft brown eyes peer up at me, shining with fresh tears.

"Ruth, no!" Warrose roars from several yards away.

Her head slides off her body, thumping to the sand as her frame sways for a moment.

"Oh god!" I screech. "Ruth!"

Thick ropes of blood spew from her gaping neck. And then she simply falls forward, landing on my leg. Her head is facing me. Eyes open. Mouth parted.

My Ruth.

My soul sister.

Gone, without a moment to say goodbye.

In a frenzy, I try to gather her head in my hands, and try to piece her back together. I wail as the tears spring from my eyes. *Not dead. Not dead. Not dead.*

Dessin chokes and gargles on his own blood in my lap.

"Somebody help us!" I blubber, holding them to me the best I can.

"Skylenna!" Niles shouts from behind me. "We have to get him out!"

*No. Not Niles.*

I turn in time to see the fire consume every inch of his skin. His screams pierce my ears, surging through my body until his pain is my own. But he doesn't put the fire out. The flames grow bigger, higher, sending smoke signals to the clouds.

And DaiSzek is caught between the burning stakes, he's

*"Can you see me now?"* A voice made of iron, silk, and old wisdom breaks through the storm of my trepidation. I look up through my tears, searching through the battle raging on before me.

*"Focus, Skylenna,"* she purrs.

I blink the tears away, squinting to see past the blood.

*"In the trees."*

*There.* A tall, lean woman. Glowing bronze skin, long coffee-colored hair, and white paint drawn in beautiful streaks across her face. She nearly blends in with the trees with her red leather attire, corset, gold buckles, and belted straps from her neck to her ankles.

"Are you—the voice in my head?" I ask between sobs.

She nods once.

I'm suddenly made aware that nothing here can hurt me as long as I know it isn't real. A cool shower of respite coats my skin.

*"You can pull Dessin and your friends out of this through the sound of your voice. Be their anchor. Find the light in this darkness."*

I exhale slowly. I think of the warm memories. The bright beacons of light that have guided me through hard times before.

I remember the day Kane took me to the Red Oaks on the hottest day of the year. We swam in the lagoon, ate fruit on the bank. I was nine and he was twelve. It was the first time he kissed my hand. I felt the thrill of freefalling into a pool of pure, uncorrupted happiness. After blushing and turning away, I brought the top of my hand back to my own lips and kissed the same spot.

His eyes widened.

And I said, "It's like we actually kissed!"

Kane threw his head back and laughed. "When we finally have our first kiss, it won't be through your hand, Skylittle!"

I thought about that moment every day until I lost my memory.

Through hazy clouds and slow motor functions, I have the sensation of my mouth back. Only now, instead of the beach, I'm sitting in the Red Oaks.

"Dessin? Can you hear me?" I call out to the soothing winds.

His arms still hold me in the oily pool. We tread the thick liquid together, blind and stuck in our own minds.

He doesn't answer.

*"Reach him with your light,"* the woman says.

"Remember when we first met in the asylum? Everyone told me to be afraid of you. They warned me countlessly. Even Niles and Chekiss. But when I looked into your beautiful brown eyes, I was almost embarrassed at how far from fear I strayed. I felt lightning pass through me when I shook your hand."

I hesitate before I continue. We're swimming in oil. And Dessin is making no attempt to respond to my call. Is there a chance this is…Aquarus?

After a long pause, I say, "I've been waiting to see you again since our time in the bathtub. You saw me at my worst, Aquarus. I'm sorry for that. But do you remember how we drank, and you told me all about your time in the inner world?" I feel silly speaking to the empty forest of red oak trees. There's a chance it's not even

"Little siren?" His husky, deep voice seeps into the wind around me.

"I'm here. Follow my voice," I say with a smile.

"I'm confused."

"I know. But as I speak, I want you to feel me in your heart, okay?" I don't wait for his confirmation to continue. "When we were in that tub, I flirted with you."

"With your foot," he drawls.

151

"Yes." I grin. "I liked you."

His presence seems to move closer somehow. "Do you still?"

"I do. You were there for me, comforted me, even though I'm only a human to you. Even though you hardly knew me."

A large man steps out from behind a cluster of trees, pushing the red leaves away from his face. He's over six foot seven, broader and more muscular than any man I've ever seen. His hair is long and golden, tied in a few braids down his back. Arms and chest covered in a beautiful art of blue tattoos.

"Aquarus?" I step forward.

He nods, studying the length of my body with cerulean eyes.

"We're in the Vexamen Prison, fell into a pool of drugged oil, and are pretty much hallucinating right now. I'm not exactly sure how we're sharing a hallucination, though," I breathe out.

"I don't need an explanation to have time alone with you," he says, low and twisted in the northern accent. "And I'm not surprised we've found ourselves in another human lodging of imprisonment."

I laugh, blushing as he takes another step closer.

"I think we need to have positive thoughts in order to get out of here. I'm worried our friends would have jumped in after Dessin and me."

He lifts his chin in understanding. "I see."

"What are your happy thoughts, Aquarus?"

"The sunset glimmering off the ocean surface."

"And?"

"Coral reefs at dawn."

"Go on."

"The way a shipwreck ages beautifully over time."

I watch him, imagining all the magical sights he's visited in the inner world.

"The bathtub," he says finally.

"The bathtub," I repeat.

He nods, unblinking as he doesn't take his eyes from me.

"Have you given much thought to it?" I ask casually, kicking my foot in the dirt.

"For the first time, I've been eager to come to the front again. Because of the bathtub."

The wind, carrying the scent of cedar and rain, brushes his long hair over one shoulder. And if possible, he looks even more ethereal than he did before. His stance, those calm, watchful eyes. I'm drawn in like a moth to a flame.

With two cautious steps, I reach my hand out to touch his face. That square jaw and coarse stubble. A large, iron hand seizes my palm, plucking it between two of his fingers. He examines it carefully, like he's never seen a woman's hand up close before. My wrist rotates slowly in his grasp, and his cool fingers snake up my skin, caressing me like he's never felt anything so soft.

I can't help but gasp as he pulls me forward, gently placing my open hand over his cheek. Aquarus exhales, like he's waited a lifetime to be trapped here, against my palm.

"You're so warm, little siren," he rasps.

My stomach swarms with rabid butterflies. His cool skin tingles my nerve endings, sending a rush of adrenaline down to my lower belly.

In the distance, a murky hole opens to us. Flickers of light, brief roars of a cheering audience. Aquarus barely glances at it.

I narrow my eyes through the opening, catching a glimpse of Warrose holding Ruth in the sheen of the pool of oil.

"Warrose!" I scream, trying to break through his drugged haze. "You have to think of happy memories. You have to pull Ruth out of the hallucinations with positive thoughts!"

I don't know if he hears me, but we need to try to get back.

"Aquarus, if we don't make it back in time, we might drown."

Even though he doesn't believe he can drown, he shifts anyway, kissing the palm of my hand before entwining his fingers with mine, and running toward our way back to reality.

# Warrose

THE OIL DOESN'T WORK ON me the way it does the others.

Maybe it isn't only native to Vexamen. I used to have to trudge through oil in a cave to get to the Nyx-Neruvian Bats. They used to suck me into horrendous hallucinations, but after fifteen or so forced trips from Demechnef, I grew a tolerance. But that's only half the battle. It numbs the part of your brain that can take action. That motor function where you can command your body to swim your way out of it. All I can do is hook my arms under Ruth's and hold her to my chest while I kick my legs to keep us afloat.

"You have to think of happy memories. You have to pull Ruth out of the hallucinations with positive thoughts!" Skylenna screams at me in a slur.

Hope spikes through my chest, flipping my heart upside down. I wasn't sure how long I could hear Ruth scream, feel her shudder in horror at whatever she's seeing behind her lids.

"Ruth," I say calmly, even though I want to shout, curse, beg, grovel. Anything to make her feel better. "It's Warrose. I'm here."

She continues to thrash in my arms, sloshing the oil around in greasy waves.

The crowd cheers as another inmate sinks to the bottom, drowning in what I can only imagine is an excruciating death.

Happy memories. Do we have any of those? I don't know much about her past. And we don't have great ones together.

*Uhh, okay, let's try this.* "Think of the time you yanked me in that river, remember? I was pissed, you were stubborn. I yelled at you. You yelled back."

She cries out in pain, and it feels like someone jabbed a knife in my back.

*Fuck.*

I suck ass at this. I've never been great with my words. With trying to make someone feel better. When Kane cried after training, I would pat him on the back and say, "There, there."

*You have a beautiful voice, Warrose.*

The idea sizzles to the surface of my brain. The room is so loud with people drowning, soldiers chanting, no one else would hear me.

I start to hum the beginning of a song. A tune my father used to sing to my mother about the queens of Alkadon. It's originally about one blue-eyed, blonde queen who ruled beside four kings. But I change one small detail.

154

*"The queen of kings, only one, must she be if there were none. Born in forest, filled with stars, her beauty radiates through her scars."* My voice vibrates my chest into her tense back. She whimpers at my words, stirring slightly.

*"Her blood is to rule, her heart is to fight. But when men bring darkness, her* brown *eyes bring light."*

*Find your way back, Ruth.*

*"My queen is ruby, shining in red, but did you know how hard she tries not to lose her head? Kings are cruel, conjuring war, drawing blood, and craving more. But our* brown-*eyed queen will outlive the sun, for her reign of peace has only just begun."*

My father said five hundred years ago, she was the only ruler who outlived the other four kings. They tried time after time to behead her, but the people's love protected her.

"Warrose," Ruth croaks, her hands tightening around my wrists.

"I've got you," I say huskily in her ear. "I'm not letting you go."

"I shouldn't have jumped in," she groans, letting her head fall back against my shoulder.

I'm just thankful Niles and Marilynn made it across. I know Dessin would have a heart attack if he had to worry about saving everyone. The moment Ruth saw Skylenna fall, she scrambled up that ladder so damn fast. She wasn't thinking clearly. But fuck, it was brave. Fierce. And kind of funny that she thought she could be of any help to them in here.

"I can see again."

*Thank God.*

"Good, I'll swim us out of here the moment my brain is able to speak to my body again," I grunt. It's getting harder and harder to keep us above the pool of oil, but I won't let her drown. I don't care if that means letting her use my body as a human floating device.

"You followed me in," she states with a heavy tone. "You didn't have to jump in after me."

"I did."

She sighs, and it almost looks like her eyes are glossing over with tears.

"I fucked up."

"I know."

"I thought that I'd be able to swim fast, help Skylenna before the oil could mess with my head. I-I messed up, Warrose." Her voice is a shell of a whisper, weak, gentle. Filled with embarrassment.

I don't say anything. But my arms pull her closer to my chest, hugging her in my only form of comfort.

"I shouldn't be here," she sniffles, tightening her grip around my wrists.

"I'm dead weight for the group. I'm going to get someone killed. I'm usel—"

"Don't finish that statement," I growl.

"It's true."

Fuck, she's trying so hard not to cry. The knot in her throat thickens, straining her words.

"Look how much you've helped. We'd be sitting ducks without someone to translate. We wouldn't have gotten that bowl of soup from Kaspias without you."

The pool of oil sloshes around us in waves, slapping upward against the backs of our heads, splashing over our chins.

"You want to know what the audience thinks?" she asks me with a mocking tone.

Not even a little bit.

"They're yelling at me to join the higher-ranking officers in private rooms. It's the only way a female inmate can escape the Fun House Nights. By servicing a commander with our bodies…"

I spit out a trickle of oil that slips past my lips. "Fuck that idea right up the ass."

"Maybe I should take the offer. That way, none of you have to worry about keeping me alive." She says it like it's an option, but I know the notion is making her cringe.

A slow, creeping rage blisters under my skin.

"I could—"

"Ruth, my little rebel, if you offer another horrible fucking idea while we're in here, I'm going to drown myself." But the damage is done. I can't get the goddamned image out of my mind. Ruth (wearing her pathetic excuse for a uniform) in a private room, with wild Vexamen soldiers. No. *Fuck no.* Christ, why would she think that's any better than this? I'd rather save her ass here than imagine her small, delicate frame under a demented member of this country's armed forces.

"You're growling," she comments.

*Am I?* My chest expands as I take a steadying breath.

A man next to us howls like a dog, sobbing as his eyes gaze vacantly at the ceiling. The crowd rumbles, stomps, waves their arms in the stadium at something the announcer says.

"Please keep that thought as far away from your brain and mouth as it can get, okay?" I try not to sound too demanding. But if I come across as a dick? So be it. She'll never make good on that dumb ass suggestion.

"You're not the boss of me."

I roll my eyes as her body shifts backward, and before I can adjust, her ass is pressed firmly to my groin. My teeth grind to the point of pain.

"Aren't I, though? It'll do you some good to have someone tell you what to do," I whisper in her ear. My cock throbs as she shivers against me.

"Should I call you daddy, too?"

Heat, blood, and energy completely abandon my brain to rush to my crotch. What the fuck is happening? Did that turn me on? Yes. *Fuck*, it really did.

"You can." The words are sticky in my throat. We're in front of a stadium filled with sadistic monsters, and I'm sporting a hard-on at the word *Daddy*.

"And I suppose you'll have me bend over when I'm bad, too?"

*Fuckkkkkk Ruthhhhhhhh.*

Without thinking, I push my hips forward, nudging my erection against her ass, then like a psychopath, I wrap my hand around her narrow throat. She goes completely still, breath hitching in her lungs, goose bumps rising on the back of her neck. And to my surprise, she arches her back and ass against my hard cock. I lose all control of my body. I groan into her ear.

"Thank God, you two are alright!" Skylenna's head pops up to the right of me, shocking my balls back into my body.

"Shit!" Ruth's body jerks in my arms, but still, neither of us can move.

"Aquarus can swim now, he'll get us out," Skylenna explains, hair coated in oil, face glistening with sweat.

I feel completely emasculated as Aquarus drags us through the oil, heaving each of us on the stage with little effort.

Marilynn and Niles rush to our sides with towels to dry off the oil. My skin tingles and twitches as my motor functions start to work again. Without making eye contact, I slap Aquarus on the back and say, "Thanks, man."

He nods, eyes clouding over as they dissociate.

"Niles and Marilynn are okay?" Skylenna asks, unable to see that they're standing close by with the oil clouding her vision.

"Okay, look everyone, I was definitely going to jump—I mean, obviously, right? But then I had an irrational fear of the oil lighting up in flames and I froze." Niles kneels beside Ruth, who is making disgusted faces as she wrings the oil out of her hair.

"And I told him we would only add to your plate if we jumped in, too," Marilynn adds irritably.

Ruth rolls her eyes, feeling bad enough for thinking she could help.

The Ringmaster yells out an announcement, his words causing the soldiers to jump up in celebration. Behind me, the stage floors close over the pool. Sealing the prisoners inside who haven't drowned yet.

I look up at Aquarus. "Looks like you got us out just in time."

"What did he do?" The alter blinks in slight confusion, looking from me to the closing stage, trying to figure it out.

"Aquarus was able to swim through the oil before any of us could. He got us all out," Skylenna says, stroking the back of his arm.

"Dess?" I narrow my eyes at him.

He nods once, looking up at the Ringmaster, who has begun a new speech.

"Ruth?" Skylenna raises her eyebrows for that very helpful translation.

"He says it's time for the Vex-Reaping. And he's explaining how this time, they won't run out of oil..." Ruth's eyes widen as she whips her head back to the stage. "Niles, close your eyes!"

# 14. Vex-Candles

## Marilynn

Three stakes appear in the center of the platform, they've been soaked in oil. Sentinels walk the selected inmates out to stand in front of the designated stakes.

It hits me like a heart attack.

"Niles, close your eyes!"

I turn to Niles with fright jittering up my spine. He looks confused, squinting to understand what he shouldn't be seeing. I don't wait to see if he'll be able to handle it. My hand finds his eyes, gently shielding them from what we're about to witness.

Skylenna and Ruth nod their thanks to me as the color drains from their faces.

These prisoners are going to be burned alive.

"I guess my fear wasn't so irrational," Niles murmurs, making no attempt to release my hand from his face.

No, it wasn't.

"He's saying these prisoners got caught trying to jump from the top of the tower. If they had succeeded, their deaths would have been painless. This punishment is for failing." Ruth looks back at Skylenna with a wrinkled brow. "So, they tried to…"

"They're suicide jumpers," Dessin clarifies grimly.

I swallow the lump forming in my throat. I wonder who these prisoners are really. Are any of these people dangerous? Evil? Or are they victims of this cruel society the same way asylum patients were?

The two men and one woman start resisting as they're tied to the stakes. The woman cries out something in another language, screaming, spitting, and fighting to break free.

"She's begging to see her child," Ruth whispers, tears glistening in her brown eyes. "He's a soldier here. He's watching from somewhere in the stadium."

We all look around curiously, but no one is stepping forward. The soldiers laugh, throw their drinks, applaud for the punishment to continue.

The woman with long sandy hair, a face full of premature wrinkles, and scars covering her body yells something between sobs. She looks out to the audience, searching through her thick tears.

"*Josen!*" she screams. "*Josen, Mamen ez hieeź!*"

"She's explaining that she has loved him since he was in her belly. That she tried running away to keep him from Vexamen. But they captured her, only used her for the milk she could provide. It killed her to be his pet."

No one claims to be her son. No one raises their hand. No one races forward.

If he is out there, this speech doesn't move him to speak up.

The sentinels light the stakes from the bottom, and I'm surprised to see how slowly the fire catches. How it simmers at the bottom like it's taking its time.

"I can smell it," Niles comments, his Adam's apple bobbing along his throat.

I take a step toward him, catching the scent of woodsmoke and the bitter mix of the oil. The soldiers chant, stomping one foot as the flames lick the base of the wood.

"They're really going to make us watch this," Warrose grumbles in disbelief.

My mind has always been a special fortress. No one taught me to be this way. No one showed me how to protect those tender, intimate spaces of my soul. It's simply a knee-jerk reaction now. I shut myself off to the man in front of me, blinding myself to his needs, fears, and gentle heart. I become a cold, immovable mountain. No one can hurt me. No one is strong enough to make me crumble.

Then why must my impassive glower stretch down to Niles's scars? To the muscle in his forearm flexing and relaxing as if in a special rhythm.

*Stop, Niles. Fucking be a man.*

I pull my shoulders back and lift my chin in defiance of this hurricane being violently contained in my stomach. I know of Niles's history, and the idea of him seeing what's happening right now…to hear it. To *smell* the burning flesh all over again. Nerves tighten around my chest like a noose. I can't imagine what's going on in his head.

The room is ignited with screams of agony as the flames eat at their feet.

Niles turns to stone, but his breathing becomes erratic. Sweat forms over his brow, and he's suddenly bracing my hand over his eyes like it's his only anchor to sanity. I nearly slink away from his touch, alarms going off in my head to detach, disengage, *walk away!*

"I don't want to be here," he gasps.

That fortress inside me wants to ignore him. Or maybe be a little cruel in response.

"I know, Niles." *What am I doing? Let one of his friends comfort him.* "It'll be over soon."

His entire body is quivering like a newly sprouted tree in a sandstorm. The smoke fills the space around us, slipping into our nostrils, infused with the stench of scorching flesh. The prisoners wail in agony, bucking against the restraints that bind them.

"Please, make it stop." Niles can hardly breathe. He's wheezing as sweat drips down his chest, and he squeezes my hand over his eyes like it may stop the flashbacks. It may put an end to the psychological torment he's reliving.

Skylenna looks back at me, her eyes flickering darkly to Niles. She takes a step toward him, but I stop her. What am I doing? She clearly knows him better. Knows how to comfort him. But I'd be lying to all of them if I said I didn't know Niles at all.

"I'm—going to lose it." My chest grazes his stomach as he leans into me. And I feel that little girl inside me begin to break free. The one that wants him to know her.

"I've heard stories about you since I was a little girl," I whisper, standing up on my tippy toes to bring my mouth and words closer. "My parents used to read Judas and I the prophecies that all the ancient colonies passed down from generation to generation. It was said that you were the patient with a heart of gold. The man who would sacrifice all he had to protect those he loves." Tears burn hot as they line my eyes like a second skin. His story has always weighed on my heart like a medal of honor.

*Reel it in. Don't let it get to you.*

"There were stories about me?" he asks, fighting to keep his breath under control.

"Yes." Although the stories of Patient Thirteen and The Fallen Saint were a fascinating, epic love tale…nothing compared to my favorite character.

His mouth parts in surprise. It's as if the entire stadium goes silent for us.

"I used to ask my mother to tell me the story about your valor in the Battle of Hangman's Beach. I cried every time she told my brother and I of your bravery, your undying effort to free DaiSzek."

"You did?"

I nod, even though he can't see me. "You were my favorite bedtime story. The Niles I learned about…he is strong in the face of terror."

He swallows, goose bumps forming on his arms.

*Don't say it…*

"You are a *hero* to me, Niles." The tears swell over my lashes, and I can't keep the passion from leaking into my wavering voice. Anger is a ship wrecking into the iceberg of my soul. Why am I doing this? Why can't I just steer clear? Why did my cell have to be right next to his?

As the stakes roar with flames, the stadium ruptures in animated chaos. But Niles lifts my hand from his eyes. He gazes down, meeting my eyes with a look of seriousness I have yet to encounter from his humorous manner.

He's...so beautiful.

Niles parts his lips to speak, but for once, can't find the words. He watches the tears trickling down my cheeks and uses a thumb to catch the next tear before it can fall. He smiles with both pain and warmth as he stares at that tear on his thumb. And before I can speak again, he pulls me against his body, wrapping his strong arms around me. My face presses against the center of his chest, inhaling his scent of oak, sunshine, and the soap from our showers. Never in my life have I received a hug with such tenderness, such affection.

It's a Niles hug.

My arms curl around his waist to embrace him back, feeling the detail of his muscles, his scars, his soft skin. And it's the way he runs his hand through my long red hair that sends chills prickling over every inch of my skin.

My thoughts are a war of screaming and begging. I'm walking a dangerous line by letting myself *feel* this.

As I open my eyes, Skylenna stands in my line of sight, watching our embrace with an emotion I can't identify clouding her eyes. She's thoroughly examining my posture, body language, and the tears running trails of pent-up emotion down my freckled cheeks. *You can back down, Fallen Saint. I'll keep my distance from your golden boy.*

After a long moment, everyone is standing around us. Ruth puts a hand on Niles's shoulder. "It's time to head back."

But he doesn't move. Doesn't acknowledge that they're all waiting for us. He takes in a deep, soothing breath, and kisses the top of my head.

"This family loves to ruin a good hug, huh?" he jokes, returning back to his humorous state of being.

Walking back to our cages, I replay that hug.

Over and over again.

# 15. Slow To Anger And Great In Power

## Skylenna

It's been nearly two weeks since Fun House Night.

Nearly two weeks without food.

The kitchen delivered dead rats on a platter. Dessin kept his cool. Niles woke up howling in pain from his burns or from a nightmare about the fire. He stopped abruptly due to Marilynn somehow soothing him back to sleep. Warrose got into another fight in the showers. Ruth chewed him out for an hour about making things worse.

And my body has been healing.

Slowly.

But it's hard without food.

Dessin has been grilling Helga Bee about everything she knows regarding the layout of the prison. About the security measures they must take to keep prisoners inside. She only knows about the exterior from seeing it herself, and some rumors she's heard about the security. The prison is the tallest landmark in Vexamen. Three connecting towers. The only way up or down is by rock climbing. Soldiers that arrive every week for Fun House Nights have special equipment, a pulley system, that allows them to easily scale the length until they reach an entrance. But those platforms are crawling with sentinels.

Helga Bee says all possible exits are guarded by swamp dawpers. Cousins of night dawpers. Gangly creatures that can sniff out hot organs a mile away. They devour their prey down to the bone, one lick of their tongues, and their saliva eats right through your skin.

But without a way to remove the device in our ears, we're sitting ducks.

"I really hate to say anything nice about Demechnef, but shit, I really miss their feather beds!" Niles sighs dramatically, leaning his head against his cage as we get settled in to go to sleep.

"Me, too," Ruth groans.

Dessin nudges me through the bars that separate us. The circles under his eyes are like smoky bruises, deep and shadowed. I reach out to touch them, running my fingers across his prominent cheekbones.

"You're not sleeping," I say sadly. It's not a question. I know how his system works. When he's in a high-stress environment, his entire way of existing, as well as that of the other alters, is thrown into a whirlwind of survival mode. Meaning insomnia, migraines, vomiting, depression. I can see it all on his face, no matter how hard he tries to hide it from me.

"I'm okay."

"Dessin…"

"Baby, I survived the asylum for four years. I'm fine." But his warm mahogany eyes are so tired, so weak. My heart cracks down the middle.

"What can I do?" I whisper.

He reaches his brawny arm through the bars, his hand cupping the side of my face. I lean into his heat, and my eyes close on instinct.

"This," he murmurs, fingers massaging the side of my head. "I'm dying to touch you."

His deep voice chases away the chill in my bones, drawing heat from my center. I open my mouth to suck more oxygen into my lungs.

"If I slip my fingers between your legs, will you clench around me? Just once?" he asks with dark arousal glazing over his eyes.

I bite my tongue to keep from moaning. We have zero privacy here. But God, the sexual tension has been building like a shaken bottle of champagne.

I nod eagerly. Just one touch, quietly, discreetly.

Dessin sits up quickly, suddenly wide awake. He angles his hand between my legs, grazing the back of his finger along my soaking wet slit. I squirm at the contact, and he flexes his jaw, closing his eyes in silent euphoria.

"I should be fucking you every day," he utters, pulling his finger away to see how it glistens in the glowing light of the flickering bulbs.

"Yes."

"You should be sitting on my face to wake me up every morning," he adds, blacking out at the thought.

I let out a quiet hum. Low enough to avoid our friends hearing me.

The corners of his mouth tick upward. He prods my entrance with two fingers, unable to fit them both in. We exhale in unison.

"Aquarus told me about your moment with him."

I look up at his brooding face, clenched jaw, and dilated pupils.

"And?" I inquire.

"I got jealous."

I blink in surprise. My first night with Greystone, Dessin told me he wouldn't get jealous. That it was different being with alters.

"It made my dick so hard," he whispers, then begins circling the ring of my ass with another finger. "I wanted to fuck the thought of him right out of you."

"But you said—"

"I know what I said." He uses the arousal from my throbbing pussy to lubricate my ass. "And I know I'm contradicting myself. But now I want to claim you. Show him you're *mine*."

I choke on a gasp as he eases his fingers inside both of my holes. A pulse runs rampant in my core, building a single flame of desire into a beastly inferno.

"I'd give anything to taste you right now, baby." He sinks his middle finger in my ass and his thumb in my quivering pussy. My back is facing our friends, and it's like we're all alone, hiding in the shadows of our cage.

My head falls back at the way his fingers hook.

"I love when you fill all of my holes."

Dessin's eyes shudder with fire and madness. "*Careful*," he grits through clenched teeth.

"Or what?"

"Or I'll traumatize our friends by fucking you through these bars."

My eyes roll back in my head, my cunt flutters with insatiable need, and I'm close to seeing stars. How can we have such an attraction through all of this hell? It's like a magic curse between us. An invisible bond that can't be broken.

Our friends bicker loudly behind us, cackling like little hens. It's the perfect amount of noise for what I feel is rising in my lower belly.

"Dessin?"

"Yes, baby?" He saws his large fingers inside me, curving his movements to hit the perfect spot. My mouth falls open as I arch against the bars. I'm tingling, throbbing, undulating against the bars for more of him. Crazed. Feral. An addict for the hard lines of his abdomen, the mountain of muscle in his arms and chest. My mouth waters at the idea of pleasing him like an obedient, good girl.

"If I come right now, will you keep me quiet?" I ask, breathy and unstable.

Dessin drops his head with an anguished exhale, like my words have officially defeated him. He nods, unable to give me verbal confirmation.

"Do you love me, Dessin?" I ask, barely a whisper, barely a sound at all.

"*Yes*," he mouths, his breath continuing to huff over me. "I love you so much, it's fucking painful to be separated by these bars."

I'm careful not to move to tip the others off, but I want to grind against his hand so bad that my thighs twitch.

"Are you going to marry me one day?"

His stormy expression lightens a little. "Yes. I'll marry you."

"And—"

"And I'll fill you full of my come until it's dripping down your thighs for days," he growls, moving his fingers faster, harder, bruising me with pleasure. "Until there's a baby in your belly."

My climax explodes around me. An idyllic blast in my lower half. A sense of floating, dreaming, *flying*. Dessin's hand flies over my mouth to silence any sound that comes close to bursting from my lips. As the jolts of my desire subside, I look down at the long bulge in his pants.

"My turn," I purr. But a noisy splash of liquid hitting the floor pivots our attention away from each other.

"Are you alright?" Niles asks in alarm.

Another splash, and I'm standing up to see what's going on.

Marilynn is hunched over, wiping her mouth on the back of her hand. A puddle of bile spreads across her cage, surrounding her. She leans back against her bars with a thud, wincing as she coughs.

"Hey, talk to me," Niles pleads.

But she doesn't respond, only closes her eyes and lightly dabs at the sweat beading across her pale brow.

We're all standing now.

"Marilynn?" Ruth asks.

"Give me a damn minute," Marilynn groans quietly. "I'm just—*processing.*"

It's been too long since we've eaten. We're all weak and sickly. Is this the beginning of the symptoms you get before death?

"It's because she hasn't eaten," Dessin finally clarifies. "If we don't get some form of food in us, we're all going to start having terminal indicators until we starve to death."

Marilynn shakes her head.

"Tomorrow, we have to—"

"You're all about to trust me a lot less," Marilynn announces, her silky voice resounding over Dessin's.

"Huh?" Niles cocks his head back. "What's going on?"

"I'm late." Her eyes are glassy, tired, heavy.

Late...*Late!* "Do you mean..."

"I've missed a period."

"That could be a result of starvation," Dessin says, though his eyes are narrowing suspiciously.

"It's not from starvation. I had sex with Aurick before we left."

"Come again?" Niles blurts out.

My jaw hangs from my face like a decaying branch on a tree. I knew it. I fucking knew we couldn't trust her. If she slept with Aurick...well, what does that even mean? Is she in love with him? Did he send her to spy on us?

169

"Why?" Warrose asks in disgust.

"She was engaged to him at one point…" Ruth points out.

So she *is* still in love with him.

"I've heard the stories," she declares in a frigid tone. Cold edges, like she's trying to reign in her frustration. "We grew up hearing about the adventures you all have had."

*Her point?*

I look over my shoulder at Dessin. He's stiff, watching her like a predator gathering intel on his prey.

"And I've—I've only heard of myself mentioned in the prophecies a couple of times. *This* is one of them. It's something I had to do." Her honeyed voice wavers, tapering off as she tries to tie her emotions down.

"Hold on a second," I interrupt with a disbelieving laugh. "You're telling me it was in a prophecy that you fuck Aurick once after returning and get pregnant?"

*Is anyone buying this?*

"That's exactly what I'm telling you," she breathes, meeting my eyes with venom and resentment.

I bristle with anger. "The man who hit me. Who tricked me into his home. Who—"

"*I know who he is!* I know what he's done!" Her voice blasts through the prison in a fit of indignation. "You think you were his only victim? I lived under the roof of Vlademur Demechnef! I suffered through their games, their hot tempers, their distaste of strong women. All for a fucking *bedtime* story told to me since I was a small child. You think I wanted this? To live my life as a spy? Never understanding who I really am? All for an epic tale that may or may not come true?"

I'm not sure where to look. I have a wandering gaze that won't settle. We haven't known Marilynn long, but she's hardly seemed like the type to raise her voice. And here she is, wiping snot and tears from her face. That pale complexion now rosy from her outburst.

Niles breaks the silence by clearing his throat. "Why did the prophecy say for you to sleep with him? What was the reason?"

"If I say it out loud, it may never happen. And then I'll have done it for nothing."

"Not nothing." Ruth kneels to be at eye level with Marilynn. "Regardless of the reason, you're having a baby. Now eating for two!"

Ruth's harmless statements sends a surge of devastation through us all. The air shifts as we all realize…it's not just us anymore that's being starved.

It's a baby, too.

The group breaks out in a storm of horror.

"We'll get you something to eat!"

"Should we do a kitchen heist?"

"Maybe I should talk to Kaspias again…"

My mouth is dry and cottony, and I can't seem to think of a logical way around this. It's true, no matter the cost, we need to find a way to get Marilynn food. But how are we going to manage that without getting strikes to a sentence? The goal is to feed her and her baby. The cost could be a Vex-Reaping for one of us.

I rotate on my heels to see Dessin brooding in the shadows, arms crossed, and an unreadable expression on his face. It's not common anymore for me to have trouble reading him. But right now, I have no idea what he's thinking.

"Dessin?"

His eyes are like death warmed up as they glide to me. It's in the tendrils of smoke that wrap around his irises, the corruption that bubbles like lava, that I take a step back, allowing him to process whatever is working itself out in his mind.

"Let's sleep on it," I suggest loud enough to break up their subtle rise in volume. "We're all exhausted and hungry, and now we have a big problem to solve. Tomorrow we'll figure it out."

They seem to agree, getting settled in. Niles has lost all of the gilded color in his face, though I'm not sure if that's due to the recent news or his weakening state. He stares off into the dim lighting of the hallway, getting lost in his thoughts.

*"Help us,"* I ask the woman that lingers in my mind.

After several seconds, I twist my fingers together, worrying she might be gone forever.

*"I don't think I need to,"* she replies coolly, as if she's woken from a long sleep.

*"I think now more than ever you do! It's not just consenting adults anymore. There's a baby we must look after."*

She's silent again. I come close to losing my patience.

*"You're forgetting who you're sleeping next to,"* she finally says, that dreamy octave like a lullaby. *"His thoughts are loud. Tortured. Violent."*

*"You can hear him?"*

*"Yes. But he cannot hear me."*

*"What's he thinking?"* I try not to look over at him. Although, I'm not sure I even need to. I can feel the heat simmering from his stoic frame.

*"His mind is hard to follow. An intricate web of plans. Moves and countermoves. It's unlike any mind of any living human."* She pauses, considering something. *"Apart from yours, of course."*

*"Should I be worried?"*

*"Sweet dreams, Skylenna."*

# Skylenna

WE TAKE OUR SHOWERS IN complete silence. No one looks at each other. No one says a word.

It's sad how quickly we adjust to the freezing cold showers. How we stand naked in front of each other like animals being hosed down. How we just sort of *exist* here, lifelessly letting the water drip down our faces, bleeding into our eyes, seeping past our lips.

We stopped laughing. Stopped making jokes. Stopped the fun, witty banter. Even Niles seems suspended in a careless daze. It breaks my heart, stomps a boot in my gut. We can't go on like this. It's not fair.

"What's the plan when we get to the commissary?" Warrose bumps elbows with Dessin as we dry off.

"Sit down."

"That's it?"

Dessin's eyes are two swords that shoot to Warrose's throat.

"Do nothing."

Warrose glances at me with raised eyebrows. I shrug. Dessin isn't one to give up, but I honestly have no clue what he's planning.

We follow the assembly line of prisoners to the commissary. Being cruelly poked, shoved, and bruised by the sentinels that have nothing better to do. It's difficult not to feel defeated. I've thought about ways to get Marilynn food. Ways to sneak into the kitchen. But even Helga Bee won't risk getting starved out. They watch us like hawks. Only Kaspias was able to slip us some soup. And I don't think we'll get that lucky twice.

I turn to Ruth. "Do you think you can talk to Kaspias again?"

She shrugs. "I can try."

Screams fill the commissary as the front of the line enters through the high-arch doorways. Long strings of words jumble together, fast phrases we can't understand.

The assembly line speeds up, curious to see the ruckus. Stumbling around each other, shoving, throwing elbows. Our group huddles together. Dessin, Niles, and Warrose form a circle around us. A male instinct to keep us close, safe from the stampede of interested prisoners. Immediately, Ruth and I hold Marilynn close, protecting her from the chaos of violence breaking out around us. She eyes our hands with prickly skepticism.

We keep our steady pace, entering the commissary along with the wave of inmates gasping, shouting, laughing. I search through the crowd, straining my eyes to peer through their jostling bodies.

My feet stop dead in their tracks.

Muscles lock in place.

A familiar awfulness twists around my organs, gripping my throat like a demon that's broken loose from hell, wreaking havoc on this prison.

A burly woman lies naked on the center table. Apple in her mouth. Ankles and wrists tied together. Dead and roasted like a pig. And to top off the image of pure savagery, her leathery, cooked body is on a patch of lettuce, potatoes, cheese, onions, carrots, and squash.

The table is set like a feast for a king.

"It's…the head cook," Ruth translates through a disgusted gasp.

"Dear God," Niles chokes.

The smell travels through the room like a plague. Each of us gags, winces, or plugs our nose at the sour, burned stink.

I revolve to my left slowly, our friends following my cautious movements. Dessin stares at the aftermath of a rather *creative* murder. His expression is a show of dark clouds and thunder powerful enough to rumble the earth.

"It was you, wasn't it?" I say with a vigor of chills that shell my skin, burrowing under it for good measure. Bile splashes against the back of my throat, burning the roof of my mouth. Though I'm grateful for this power move, I'm still human. And a dead body is still a dead body.

His dilated, chocolate eyes dart to me, and the heat sweltering through our connection is molten hot. A phoenix of flames. He winks, drawing a throaty, shocked laugh from Warrose.

"No fucking way. *Christ*, you're a goddamned artist." Warrose places his hands on the back of his head, chuckling at the confused faces surrounding the crime. Even with his dark humor, it's obvious that he's disturbed by Dessin's choice of death for the cook.

Dessin takes a step toward the kitchen staff. The same individuals who have deprived us of food for weeks. They frantically glance at their head cook with confusion, fear, and repulsion. With his unrelenting presence in front of them, the crowd backs away, giving him the floor.

Whispers die out. The foreign gossip slows to a stop.

All eyes on the once infamous Patient Thirteen.

"*Ahyë quòvex na müoi këx,*" Dessin growls in a flawless accent.

*He knows Old Alkadonian?!*

"Holy shit," Ruth barks out a laugh that is entwined with a deep cringe followed by a gagging sound.

I grab her elbow impatiently, shaking her for a quick translation.

"He says, *I'll take my meal now.*"

We gawk back at the kitchen staff, jaws dropping, eyes tracing over his large, muscular stance. A silent question if he could really have pulled this off. A prisoner can't escape their cage. A prisoner couldn't have possibly been able to overcome the special, fucked-up magnets in our ears. *Right?*

Dessin smirks, like he knows the doubt that they might have. And with a quick kick of the feast table, the head cook's naked body rolls to the side, revealing a bloody carving on her belly that says:

174

## Patient Thirteen's Puppet

A tremor of déjà vu invades my thoughts. Albatross. Dessin's temper.

"He's *back*," I say, shaking my head. Am I surprised? No. Am I perplexed as to how the hell he pulled this off? Absolutely, yes.

The kitchen staff race back to their places behind the assembly counter. Rushing in the endeavor to curate a tray. Dessin nods to us, walking to the front of the line.

After receiving our shitty trays with their disgusting excuse for food, we walk back to our table, ignoring the gaping eyes and blur of whispers.

"You're a son of a bitch," Warrose says as he spoons in a mouthful of whatever stew concoction they served us.

Dessin watches Marilynn hum in delight, shoveling the goopy brown substance into her mouth. She peeks up from her hunched position over her food, feeling the dominating weight of Dessin's eyes on her. The corner of her mouth moves up a millimeter. It's not even enough to be deciphered as a smile. But I'm going to count it as one.

"I haven't seen a Dessin magic trick in a while," I remark, peeling off a piece of bread. "I do hate that they forced his hand. Made him resort to doing something this...*disturbing*."

"A Dessin magic trick?" he repeats.

"Yeah, a magic trick from *hell*," Ruth adds theatrically. "Remember Meridei's dining party? Oh my god, you guys should have been there!"

"What'd he do?" Niles's voice echoes from inside his metal bowl.

"He blackmailed every conformist and orderly with private photographs of their family. Then poisoned them with the champagne. It was a fireworks show of puke," I explain.

"Why?" Warrose asks, even though he's grinning like he doesn't need a good reason.

"Because they were harassing Skylenna," Dessin says flatly.

"Did it work?" Warrose bites off a chunk of his stale bread.

"Obviously."

Niles laughs from inside his bowl. He's slurping that stew up like a dog.

My spoon bobs on the edge of my index finger, probing the air in restless circles as my impatience pulsates between Dessin and me. And he, being the man who can usually sense my impending questions, tilts his face an inch in my direction, though he doesn't meet my eyes yet. Waiting for him to look at me is as thrilling as seeing the sun on a moonless night.

"Are you going to tell us how you pulled this off?"

The table's chatter tapers off into a fuzzy quiet as they turn to Dessin in anticipation. The question is the only one that matters right now. We have no way of getting out of these cages. He was secure in his confinement when I woke up this morning.

"What do you think I've been doing for the last two weeks?" Dessin takes a sip of his water, pointing at his seat that's facing the kitchen staff. "Every time we've sat in this commissary, I sit here. Why? Because I get to watch how they work. I figured out who the head cook was, saw that she was the one calling the shots. Learned she gets here before the rest of the staff at dawn to prep the food."

We stare at him like children listening to a fascinating bedtime story.

Dessin glances around at our faces and shrugs like that should be enough explanation to piece together.

"But how did you get *out* of your cage?" Niles demands with childlike wonder.

Dessin signals with his chin to his shoulder. I gasp as I lean closer, seeing now that it's swollen and out of place. He signals to Warrose, nodding for him to come over.

Warrose rises from his seat, blowing out a breath as he examines Dessin's arm on the way over. "Shit, I can't believe I didn't notice it was dislocated."

With a slow rotation of his forearm, Warrose snaps his shoulder back in place. Dessin doesn't even flinch. My insides are gutted at the wet, crackling sounds that come from his shoulder and Warrose's precise movements. How did *I* not notice?!

"I had to rearrange my body a little bit to get out of the dent I made in my cage," he explains briefly, like it's no big deal. He dislocated his own damn arm, and it's *no big deal*.

"You mean the small space you made when you pulled your bars apart that time Skylenna was being attacked?" Ruth says with a hanging jaw.

Dessin snarls at the mention of me being harmed.

"And you roasted the head cook with a wounded shoulder," I deadpan.

He blinks like that shouldn't be a surprise.

I shake my head with a smile, continuing to eat my hot meal like it's the best damn thing I've ever tasted. And it kind of is. This small victory is delicious. It put a smile on all of our faces. It fed Marilynn and her baby. It squeezed a few new jokes out of Niles. It gave Dessin dominance again, even if it's only over the kitchen staff.

"Oh God, is that Skylenna humming while she eats again?" Niles licks his lips and leans back with a full belly and satisfied smile.

I open my mouth to bite back, but a rough knuckle grazes my cheek. Warm and electric. Dessin's gaze descends into my eyes like an anchor being dropped in an ocean.

"Fuck off, Niles. That's the sweetest sound in the world to me right now."

# Warrose

I CLEAN MY BOWL.

Literally.

I polish it, savor it, maybe even cradle it to my chest.

We all do.

But not the little rebel.

I glance down at her half-eaten stew with genuine offense taken at the sight. She's really going to pull this again? We've been starved for how long, and she's going to politely leave half her food to show us that she's taking proper care of her weight?

We've been *starved!*

"Hell. No." I huff out sharply through my nostrils.

177

Ruth points her stubborn, stony face in my direction, challenging me with tendrils of resentment coiling around her throat.

"Speak. Full. Sentences." She injects the command with unfeeling iron.

This condescending tone pulls the same reaction out of me that I used to get with Absinthe in our Demechnef training. Irrational anger. An explosive approach.

"Full sentences, huh? Eat your goddamned food like an adult. You're beautiful no matter how many calories you eat. There. Better? Was that full enough for you?" My chest tightens at the way her spine snaps straight and her face flinches in an effort to not show any reactionary emotions.

Clearly, I hear the insensitivity of my words.

But it's too late. They're out there. I've said them.

"I'm no longer hungry." Ruth pushes her bowl away an inch.

But wait…are her round, doe eyes glistening? She stares into the vastness of the commissary with the graceful posture of royalty. Deciding I'm not worth her time to even look at.

Skylenna moves like a shadow around the table until she's kneeling on Ruth's left side, placing thin fingers on her wrist. Ruth keeps her head forward, but glances down with her brown eyes.

"I know it isn't easy, but I'm so proud of you," she says warmly. "This was good." She taps a finger on the half-eaten bowl with pride and encouragement.

Ruth's eyes are no longer glistening. They're watering excessively.

My lips roll in, trying to conjure back every harsh, judgmental word I said.

"We can finish it together if that's something you'd want. Like the bathtubs, remember?" Skylenna's gentle approach causes pangs in my stomach, clamping closed around my heart.

*Stupid, stupid, stupid.* I see what she's doing. I see how my approach was *fucked.*

"Okay," Ruth finally mutters in a low, undetectable volume. And thankfully, Niles is babbling away about the menu for the week and what he's excited to eat next. Therefore, it's giving the illusion that this is a private moment.

Skylenna's glowing emerald eyes flash with silent victory. She hooks a finger around the edge of the bowl, dragging it toward them as she talks about a night when they snuck food into a bedroom. They eat one spoonful of the stew at a time as they gossip, snickering about other unrelated topics. It's a kind, clever tactic on Skylenna's end. She's distracting her with positive emotions as they eat socially. No pressure. No judgment.

I scan the table to see if anyone else witnessed my assholery.

My eyes collide with Dessin. And he's not doing a *great* job at holding back the judging scowl on his own face.

I purse my lips. *"I—fucked—up,"* I mouth with a poorly contained cringe.

He pauses. *"I'm—not—going—to—disagree—with—you—on—that."*

*"And—now—you're—the—expert—on—manners?"*

His lips twitch as he reads mine.

As the group rises to leave, Skylenna tugs on my elbow to stay behind. Waiting quietly until Ruth files out behind Niles in a line to the stadium.

"I know," I sigh in defeat.

"No. I don't think you do."

My head and shoulders droop forward. *I'm a fuckup. I know.* Might as well call me Niles, the family pariah. The village idiot.

"Warrose?" Skylenna grazes the hair on my arms with her fingertips.

I raise my eyes to meet hers.

"You are not a woman. You have never been forced to starve yourself as a part of the lady-doll regimen."

*Thank God almighty.*

"It's okay that you don't understand what that does to a woman's mental health. But I'm going to educate you so that you can appropriately respond to her as she recovers from this trauma without…"

"Without sounding like an ignorant bastard."

Her laugh greases the air around us. The soothing sound helps some of the anxiety exit my chest cavity. "Yes. *That.*"

I reach behind my head to tighten the tie holding my hair up in a ponytail.

"I don't mean to be such a dick when I see her doing that...I'm angry at what the city did to her. And I guess I take it out on her in the moment."

"Which isn't fair because she's the victim."

"Right," I say with a cloud of self-loathing hovering over the word.

Skylenna's stare loses focus as she thinks about a solution. Her complexion had a beautiful golden glow, much like Niles's, before we entered this place. Now, she's gone a little pale. Clammy. Her honeyed hair has lost its shine. And she looks several pounds lighter around the waist and hips. I worry about her, too, the way I'd look out for a sister. We bonded that night I had to share my body heat. Or even when I helped carry her away from Dessin's lifeless body.

I guess I haven't taken much time to acknowledge my fondness for her.

"Can I give you a few responses for the next time she rejects her food?"

I nod hopefully.

"Telling her you're here to listen if she ever wants to talk about it. This is important because the road to recovery is long, and if she feels comfortable enough to open up and be vulnerable...it makes self-awareness that much easier for her to confront the hard stuff." Skylenna absently keeps her fingertips on my forearm as she continues her list. "Let her know that you're proud of her for eating the amount she did. Offer to eat a little more with her. Never give advice or criticism. Help her understand that she is not to blame for this hardship."

Guilt pierces my chest and twists like a rusted dagger. I feel like a fucking fool for talking to her with such insensitivity all this time.

"I'm sorry, Skylenna."

"You didn't know. I know you were just frustrated because you want her to see how beautiful you think she is without these extreme tactics," she offers with a sympathetic smile.

My Adam's apple jumps. I do think she's beautiful. Is it that obvious?

"Now that you understand a little better, will you please be more considerate of her feelings?" Skylenna squeezes my arm to bring my focus back down to her.

"Of course. Thank you, Skylenna."

# 16. Bunny Moon Tag

### Ruth

"I hear it's time to celebrate, Beetle Brain!" Helga Bee does a cute, jiggly dance around him.

Dessin sighs. Skylenna laughs.

"Saw you had to hack off the grimy old kitchen hag! I thought y'all would have settled for sucking some dick to get food again!"

Warrose scoffs with an eye roll.

"No dick sucking necessary." I snicker at the unamused expressions between Dessin and Warrose. "Not when we have old grumpy Dad to filet our enemies." I slap Dessin on the shoulder.

"Don't call me Dad," Dessin grumbles.

"Daddy Dessin!" Niles slaps his knee. "*Haha!*"

We sit on the stage during the regale hours. Prisoners nurse their wounds, exercise, or nap in the stadium seating. The glowing red light makes Helga Bee's face look rounder than normal. Her giant blue eyes shine with a tint of pink.

"Impressive. But how are we going to party?" Helga Bee searches our faces for an answer.

Party? We're in *prison*.

"No one is partying." Skylenna chuckles. "We're just happy to have food in our systems."

"Nonsense! You're a family, aren't you? A pack? A squad? A sneaky little sixsome?"

"Don't say sixsome." Warrose grimaces.

"What about Bunny Moon Tag? You must refuel your pack culture! Your family spirit! How do you expect to keep the squad morale alive?" She ruffles Niles's perfectly coiffed hair. He curls back his lip in annoyance.

"What's Bunny Moon Tag?" Marilynn asks.

"*What's Bunny Moon Tag* she asks." Helga Bee snorts, elbowing Gerta in the bicep like it's an inside joke. "It's only the most iconic game us East Vexello Mountaineers play after a hard-hitting battle!"

"How do you play?"

"Simple! We wait until a full moon and spread out to find a white spearheaded bunny. Whoever finds it gets to chase after the other players until they pummel them into the dirt! Then they hand over the bunny, and it's that person's turn to chase!"

Warrose arches an eyebrow. "Why does it have to be a full moon?"

"And why the bunny?" Skylenna adds.

"Dunno! It's just tradition!"

We all stare at her blankly, then, in one giant rumble of sound, burst into contagious laughter. Helga Bee and Gerta flinch at our hilarity but grin widely as if they told a joke on purpose.

"And you want us to find a bunny and play this moon game?" Niles stretches his arms, smiling as he yawns.

"No! Do you knuckleheads think I'm nuts?"

Dessin stares without blinking.

"Have a fun day together! Play a game! Must I spell it out for the supposed geniuses?"

"Only one genius, actually." Warrose nods his head to Dessin.

Skylenna coughs out a laugh. "Thanks for the suggestion. But—"

"Helga Bee, can those swings be lowered a bit?" Dessin asks with a change in tone, pointing to the trapeze bars forty feet in the air.

"Sure can!"

"What's going on?" Skylenna asks.

"One person swings at a time, the rest lock arms on the stage and catch the swinger as they come down. The most creative way of swinging and falling wins." Dessin huddles us together.

"Did the fumes of the dead body you just cooked kill your fucking brain cells?" Warrose lets out a breath of nervous laughter.

"I'm with Warrose on this one." My eyes meet the piercing hazel stare across from me. He narrows them in suspicion, like what could he have done to win my agreement on something.

I'm over the snide remarks he made in the commissary. I get it. He's an oblivious idiot who has no way of understanding the pressure to maintain a specific body type. It's fine. It's not as though we're friends anyway. We're sort of stuck together like stepsiblings. Family, out of pure coincidence and lack of freedom.

"As reluctant as I am to say this, I agree with Helga Bee. We need something just for us. A fun day. Let's make some good memories in this shitshow, yes?" Dessin rubs the back of Skylenna's neck as she grins up at him.

"Really?" she squeaks, practically levitating with excitement.

"Yeah. I'm not a grumpy asshole all the time."

"Only like ninety-nine-point-eleven percent!" Niles chirps.

We lock eyes like children. Niles grabs my hands as we start bouncing around with glee. He yanks me toward the ladder, looking up at the swings lowering halfway to the ground.

"Ruthie should go first since she only weighs four and a half pounds!"

"Never comment on a woman's weight, Niles," Marilynn tsks.

"Right. Sorry. Ruthie should go first since she has the worst attitude!" he corrects himself.

I snicker, slapping the unharmed skin on his arm. He assists me on my first step up the ladder like the unrefined, prickly (almost) gentleman he is.

"The cost of failing is being a little loser, Ruthie!" Niles shouts up at me with a self-satisfied giggle.

He skips over to the others where I hear Skylenna say, "Since Chekiss isn't here..." *Pop!* She swats him on the back of the head. The group cracks up.

As I reach the swing, I look down at my friends linking arms, forming a human net. Now that I'm up here, this feels stupid for no damn reason. Nerves bubble under my skin, making me laugh loudly to release the building elation. I bounce on my heels, grinning like an idiot down at them. They peer back up at me, mirroring my exact expression. Except Dessin, which makes me grin harder.

"This is so stupid!" I yell down with another laugh. "What if I break both my legs?"

"You could also break your neck!" Warrose adds with a deviously handsome smile.

"But she's worried about her legs because she thinks she's a fast runner, you see," Niles explains in what he believes is an appropriate volume. "Run around a tree a few times, and she's suddenly a speedy gazelle!"

*Dickhead.* "Skylenna..."

"I'm on it!" she hollers back. *Pop!* I throw my head back to cackle.

"We're ready for you, Ruth!" Dessin shouts, adjusting his footing near the others.

I squeal, tapping my feet simultaneously on the ladder. Adrenaline, jittering anticipation, and youthful happiness flooding my veins. *"Ahhh!"* I screech, jumping forward, and latching onto the swing with success!

"Yeah!" I cheer, swinging my legs back and forth to get some momentum.

The stadium blurs into a smear of glowing red and charcoal black. I laugh again, kicking my legs around like a toddler.

"Promise you'll catch me?" I screech.

"It's certainly a possibility!" Niles shoots back.

"We'll catch you! And I'll smack Niles again when I have a free hand!" Skylenna promises.

"I'm not going to let you fall." I can't look down, but I know the texture of that low, rugged voice. His statement makes my toes curl. It's enough to make me let go.

With a yelp like that of a small animal, I drop through the cool air, hair flying wildly around my face. And like the chicken coward *I* am, my eyes squeeze shut. Just as my stomach dips, taking a dive into my throat, a firm web of arms breaks my fall. Breath whooshes out of me as Niles groans dramatically.

"You didn't break your legs!" Warrose whistles, helping me stand upright.

"There wasn't an ounce of pizzazz in that performance, Ruthie! Watch the master take a whack at it." Niles lets go of the leg he caught and struts up to the ladder.

"Anyone wanna have some fun with Asshole Niles for this round?" Dessin asks us with raised eyebrows.

We answer in *yeps, mm-hms, and say more.*

"That's what I thought." He smirks with menacing thoughts swirling behind his eyes. "When we catch him, everyone needs to make noise like he's the heaviest fucking human you've ever encountered, then bend your knees to cushion his fall and collapse onto the stage."

"So, catch him, then flatten like a house of cards." Warrose grins, and I'm ogling his stunning face with a huge smile back. He blinks as his intense, fiery eyes cross paths with mine. And something about how he won't break eye contact, how he holds my stare like he's trying to figure something out, like he's digging into the earth of my soul. *Something* about it drops into the pit of my stomach.

"Are you peasants ready for my godly descent to the mortal world?!" Niles spreads his arms wide at an invisible sun that's shining down on his overinflated ego.

Regardless of his idiocy, Skylenna and I snigger.

"Oh, we're ready," Dessin mutters to just us.

I'm not sure if I've ever seen so much merriment on his face. He's not exactly smiling. But that stain of a permanent scowl isn't present either. The pronounced brooding that makes him so unapproachable is lessened. His features are somewhat lighter. And I'm sure it has to do with the fact that he keeps stealing glances at a tittering Skylenna, her cheeks bright red from sporting a constant grin.

"You got this, Niles! The worst that can happen is a broken neck!" Warrose taunts with a falsely supportive tone.

"And there's certainly a possibility that we'll catch you!" I mock.

We all sag forward and chortle obnoxiously.

"Ha, ha, *ha!*" Niles drops into a squat, positioning his arms outward, and leaps like a cute little frog. "Wheeeeeee!"

He sticks the landing, whooping breathlessly.

"If anyone gets wet or hard from having to touch my body, don't be embarrassed! It's totally normal!" Niles calls out.

"Pfft," Skylenna chuffs.

Dessin closes his eyes to suppress an eye roll.

"He's certainly confident," Marilynn says, watching him swing back and forth over our heads.

"Here I come, little losers!" Niles twists his body sideways, spinning in the air like a ballerina attached to a music box.

"House of cards," Dessin reminds us.

The second he hits our interlocked arms, I wince at how much heavier he is than I would have imagined. We beam like drunk fools as we groan boisterously, swaying under his weight.

And Warrose just can't help himself as he says, fighting a groan, "What's the status of your current weight, Niles?" And we flatten to the stage like a house of cards.

Niles squirms on top of us, gasping and trying to form words. He rolls to his side to peer down at us with shock and disapproval. "Are you kidding me? Where'd all your showy muscles go? And we call ourselves an elite unit? The fuck happened?!"

"No one calls us an elite unit," Dessin says.

"Niles, you're crushing my arms," Skylenna grunts.

Warrose and I have tears forming from laughing our asses off. My belly is clenched so hard, I'm in physical pain. Seeing Niles's astonishment at our failure was one of the greatest rewards in life.

"You guys have all lost my trust," Niles barks.

"We'll live, fat ass," Warrose counters.

Our perfect symphony of laughter is interrupted by a foreboding shadow shifting over us. His hulking posture is as chiseled as Dessin's. But those scars covering his face and neck, those piercings, that beard. They couldn't be farther from each other.

"Don't stop on my account," Kaspias purrs.

# 17. The Invitation

## Dessin

I'm on my feet in a heartbeat.

The fun we created with the game has been drowned out by this... *dead* man. A maelstrom of emotions swirl like a cyclone inside my chest, feeding my clenching heart, pounding into my clenched fists and into my legs as I lunge toward him.

*I'll remove his head for what he's done.*

The world spins but not fast enough.

This action has replayed in my thoughts since Skylenna arrived in front of our cages, broken and soaked in her own blood. This violent idea has blossomed, twisted, morphed into its own obsession since she told me Kaspias beat her.

Kaspias beat *my* girl.

The territorial energy of a lion revs up my chest, curling back my lip, grumbling in my throat.

*I'm going to fucking kill him.*

My equilibrium tilts like a ship in a hurricane. But the action was already in place. The thought too powerful to intercede.

The hard knuckles along my fist make perfect contact, sharp and full of loaded aggression. They crack into something that makes a popping sound; I'm unable to see where along his face my hit landed due to the screen of blurriness casting across my vision.

"*Argh!*" A spray of ruby liquid shoots from his face.

And I'm falling, rolling across the ground in a gnawing pit of nausea.

*Worth it.*

A pair of cool, soft hands are stroking my back and arms. Golden hair tickles my face. Lilies and rainwater brush past my nose. She growls something, the words lost to me as I consider vomiting as far away from my girl as I can get.

"That *wasn't* nice," Kaspias grunts slowly, spitting out blood.

I blink with frustration, trying so hard to clear my brain of the fuzziness.

"You're lucky he can't do worse right now," Skylenna says through her teeth.

"And to think I came here to extend a polite invitation."

Bullshit. I watch through cloudy eyes as he spits blood out again. A smirk nearly touches my cheeks, but not quite. I won't be smiling until I can beat him the way he beat Skylenna.

*I want to talk to him*, Kane says.

*No.*

*He's our brother.*

*I don't fucking care.*

"Well extend it then! Don't let the fact that Dessin knocked two teeth out stop you," Warrose taunts with a cruel laugh.

Did I knock his teeth out? *Brilliant.*

"The Mazonist Brothers would like to dine with you tonight." Kaspias stares coldly at the group, like he hates the idea of it but is forced to say something. "All of you."

"Will you be there?" Skylenna inquires cautiously.

"Yes."

"Then no."

I cough out a laugh. Fuck, I love her.

"Do you know what the word mandatory means, little girl?" He

188

smiles down at her like a raging psychopath.

I tap Skylenna's arm to let her know I'm ready to stand up.

"I do. It means I don't give a good goddamn, and I'll do as I please," she responds like she isn't a prisoner at all. Like she isn't at anyone's mercy. Like she's a god among men.

And that does it. Her tone, her wrath, her blatant disrespect for authority makes my dick rock hard. I rise to my feet with her, clenching her waist like I might rip that uniform off if I'm not careful.

"Is that right?" He takes a step closer to us, breathing through his nose like steam may start coming out of it. "Because my brother already has two strikes. Did you know that? One for starting the fight in the commissary, and two for roasting my precious cook in her own oven. You must know what happens if he gets a third…"

Well, shit.

Skylenna's shoulders slump a little next to me.

"Let's stop with the pissing contest," Niles interjects. "We'll go, alright?"

"Beautiful." Kaspias massages his jaw, studying our friends as he lands on what he's looking for. "Until next time, *Ruth*."

There's a tense beat of silence before Warrose slams his hand down on the stage floor.

"What the fuck is that supposed to mean?"

# 18. The Not-So-Fantastical Dining Party

## Skylenna

"**C**alm down, okay?" I whisper as I walk behind Dessin.

The iron collars on our necks are now chained to each other, forming us in a straight line as we follow Kaspias down the long hallway at the top of the prison. We're jabbed, kicked, taunted, and degraded in another language by the many sentinels we pass along the way.

Dessin releases a low, hardly audible growl deep in his chest. I know he's teetering on how much self-control he has around Kaspias. I almost wish I never told him about the beating before sending the Blood Mammoths on The Hunt.

"We can't know what game they're playing until we can see the whole board," I add on.

He looks over his shoulder at me, huffing a surprised laugh.

"That sounds like something I would say."

"Mmm, nope. Definitely something *I* would say."

He chuckles again. "Fine, you coined it."

I reach my hand to his back against the pulls of my chains, stroking a finger down his spine. My smile falls as I examine the scars covering his tan skin. Remembering the day I went back to that horrible memory. To Kane racing in to save me from the fire. How he tried to go back for Scarlett's body and was burned from the house caving in on itself.

He walked through fire for me.

And Dessin had to suffer the pain of it for months.

Alone.

In the Emerald Lake Asylum.

*God, I'm glad I burned that place to the ground.*

I can't help but tug on the memories that color in the obscure spaces of my mind. There were so many years where I've lived without his warm memory. The vacancy that was in my heart for so long.

If I'm not mistaken, the hallway expands into its own wing, growing in size and grandeur. Torches hang on the charcoal walls, roaring in orange flames. Iron pillars. Stone gargoyles with glowing red coals for eyes. It's the carbon copy of an evil, black castle. A dark-aged dining hall with a gaudy grandfather clock ticking away, grating against the silence. The rich smell of roast beef, melted butter, and something sugary pours from the giant double doors outlined with glimmering firelight.

"Best behavior, captives. I'd hate for anyone to earn another strike," Kaspias calls, shoving the double doors open like he's arrived home from a long day at work.

I'm blasted with a gust of cozy, warm air. The kind that carries that slight whiff of a burning log in a fireplace. We pause at the entrance, watching Dessin lift his chin, take a predatory glance around the room, then step inside like his demented presence has swallowed the place in its daunting shadow.

Following behind his steps, the table decorated with a lavish feast steals my attention first. It's a smooth, onyx, rectangular table. The unpolished metal platters hold roasted animals I can't identify. Their legs are tied together, and they're on beds of garnish. I'm instantly aware that we're all reminded of the head cook Dessin torched as Niles groans behind me.

"Welcome," an old voice rasps at the end of the table.

My eyes, alert and wide, dart to the source. Two old men. Black matte armor, numerous medals of honor decorating their chests, lush fur collars, and black paint smudged around their eyes. It's hard to tell in this candle-lit room, but the rumors are true. They're twins.

The Mazonist Brothers.

The leaders of Vexamen. The outcast royals of Alkadon. The navy twins who believed in a superior militia, a government that could pluck babies from their mother's arms and turn them into humans without empathy, without the gentle touch of a parent.

And they're like… a hundred years old.

"It feels like we already know you," the one on the right says. "I am Malcolm. This is my brother Maxwell."

Their voices aren't loud and commanding. They're soft and rusty, like their vocal cords are tainted by years of smoking a pipe.

"We've heard a lot about you from where we come from as well," I say with cold venom, grasping the chain connected to my collar. "Interesting how you treat your guests."

"All great and terrible things, I'm sure." Maxwell chuckles. "My apologies for our manners, but the vicious rumors and legends of the two of you are quite the story. We would be old fools to let you roam before us without some form of security."

Dessin tilts his chin down, looking at the brothers with something violent and unforgiving. "Nothing great or terrible. Simply…*unimpressive*."

Malcolm and Maxwell stiffen, narrowing their eyes and raising an offended eyebrow. Leaving a small crack in that well-crafted image that they are sovereign leaders, kind and just.

They are men with fragile egos.

"Is that a fact?" Malcolm asks carefully, as if he's trying not to lose his temper.

"And what about our history makes us *unimpressive*?"

Kaspias plops down in a stone seat beside Maxwell, stretching his arms in boredom, kicking his heavy boots on top of the table.

"Are you going to ask us to sit?" Ruth's small voice practically echoes across the high ceilings.

The brothers turn their heads eerily slowly, and they look Ruth over, assessing her posture, her sharply pointed shoulders, her curly brown hair. It feels like an entire minute passes us.

"She looks—"

"—familiar, I know. How very odd. Kind of makes you think—"

"But that's absurd. That would mean…" Malcolm trails off.

"Not that we're not enjoying the show of a slow descent into a shared delusion, but can we get to the point of this invitation?" Dessin stares at them, unblinking.

"Please." Maxwell gestures to the table of open seats. "*Ruth* was right. We should have asked our guests to sit."

I cock my head to peek at Ruth. She looks entirely freaked out and just as confused as the rest of us.

Servants appear behind us, dressed in giant cloaks with hoods that completely shadow their faces. Like tall, silent grim reapers. They sit us down, unlatch our chains from each other's necks, and reposition the chain to a hook on the table in front of us. I'm sitting directly across from Dessin, nearly touching shoulders with Kaspias. Warrose is on my left, with Ruth sitting across from him. Niles is next to Ruth, facing Marilynn.

"Isn't this nice? So civil of two warring countries to sit down for a nice meal. Now, what were you saying about our unimpressiveness, Dessin?" Maxwell purrs softly, eyes fixed on the meat in front of him.

"You may call me Patient Thirteen," Dessin says without a sliver of emotion. "It's who the dead refer to me as in Dementia. And it's who the soon-to-be-dead will refer to me as here."

I hold my breath. *Straight to the point.*

Malcolm opens his wrinkled, old mouth to retaliate but is swiftly cut off.

"And by unimpressive, I mean, two brothers were exiled for their extremist views from Alkadon, the greatest country in the world. They were forced to leave their riches, status, their names blacked out from history, and their power and lineage extinguished. And what have they become from this shame? Rulers of a country of desert and infertile land. Leaders that torture babies, animals, and mothers. Tyrants that resemble toddlers stomping their feet and crying out to the rest of the world that they're somehow bigger and better for being too cowardly to pick on someone their own size. How am I doing so far?"

Warrose lets out a breath of surprised laughter. And I can't help but grin, open-mouthed and suppressing my own laugh.

"Well, shit," Niles utters.

"You hear that, Maxwell? He knows it all. The young man believes in the information his captors told him. Believes in false history like an arrogant little puppet!" The old man rises from his seat to lean toward Dessin, elbows shaking as he supports his weight.

"Am I wrong? Then educate me," Dessin challenges.

"Would it make a difference? You are clearly a passionate patriot of Demechnef."

Dessin smiles, though it doesn't touch his eyes. "Quite the opposite. I think both countries are shit."

Each servant leans around us to supply our plates with food, pouring us wine, and adjusting our napkins across our laps. Their spindly fingers are covered in thin, translucent skin and blue, protruding veins.

Niles reaches his hand out to lift his fork, but Dessin cuts him a glare that could stop anyone dead in their tracks.

"*No one eats*," Dessin mouths.

The Mazonist Brothers exchange a charmed look. "We wouldn't poison our guests. It's perfectly safe."

Is it? I consider going into the void to check. Tracing back over their previous actions.

"Then why can I smell black rose of the well? You tried to cover it up with…" He cocks his head forward to get a better whiff of the steam. "Cilantro and onion. You didn't think you'd get away with it, did you?"

"What's black rose of the well?" I ask.

"We've done no such thing," Malcolm says in offense, placing a hand over his chest.

"A plant that extracts the truth when ingested," Dessin replies without looking away from the Mazonist Brothers.

*Damn.* And who's to say they didn't add anything else to our meal? Maybe something that can't be detected by scent?

Maxwell catches my eye with his slumped, casual posture. Fingers steepled together. A smug curve of his withered lips. He taps his brother on the shoulder, tossing a handful of shredded meat into his mouth like a heathen.

"Whether we did or did not is irrelevant. Either you eat dinner with us willingly, or we force feed you the way we do to some of our children in the breed." His mouth is sloppy, and he is making smacking sounds as he talks.

Force feeding? *No.* The throbbing memory of Absinthe whooshes across my vision. The cold bathtub. The hard crack of her knuckles to my cheek. The tube that drained raw egg into my stomach.

No. Just, no.

"I'd like to see you fucking try," Warrose growls, fists in tight balls by his silverware.

"Remember that little thing in your ear?" Kaspias barks out a laugh. "You're all nothing but sheep now."

He's right. We're sitting ducks. Refusing is futile. But maybe if I just slipped into the void, took the Mazonist Brothers to my own special prison, we could win the war before it even starts. We can protect our secrets.

Dessin's dark, rigid eyes slam into me, locking me in his dooming stare. He knows exactly what I'm thinking somehow. The knowledge of it hardens his jaw, stops his chest from moving. He shakes his head twice. A look that says, *Don't you fucking dare try it right now.*

*"Not yet. You'll need your energy for something far more dire than this."* The woman reappears like a sweet puff of smoke in my mind.

My shoulders slump forward. *"But the truth is dangerous. They can use so many things against us in here."*

*"You and Dessin are special, Skylenna. Your minds are capable of power that exceeds the makings of black rose of the well."*

*"What am I supposed to do?"*

*"Let your instincts take over. Dessin has already crafted his plan."*

"We'll eat," Dessin states without breaking eye contact.

"We will?" Niles blurts out.

In a show of good faith, Dessin takes a bite of a seasoned animal leg. Despite the knowledge of it being laced with black rose of the well, my mouth waters as the steaming juice drips on his plate. We've been starved for so long. And even though we finally got to eat today, let's be honest, it was sewage goop.

Maxwell stuffs another handful of shredded meat into his slobbery mouth, grinning with rotting teeth as we all follow suit.

I reach for the same type of roasted leg that Dessin bit into. My stomach twists with both salivating hunger and fear of what will happen when our bodies react to the truth spilling from our tightly locked lips.

Is there anything I should hide from them? Anything of vital importance?

*Let your instincts take over.*

Releasing a quiet sigh, I bite into the succulent, hot meat, scraping my teeth across the bone. *Fuckkkkk, it's like a drug.* The rosemary seasoning, savory juices, tender substance. The bliss. The endorphins. The blast of dopamine!

"Oh, ride my face. I want to hate it. I do. But I'm practically coming," Niles groans loud enough to make the brothers laugh.

I roll my eyes, digging into the pile of weirdly colorful vegetables. They're sweet like cream with a slight crunch. I melt into my seat, reminded of the time Aurick planned a final feast for me. Or what about the night Ruth and I raided his kitchen, ate sweets and drank wine, and gossiped in the bath!

"Skylenna, this reminds me of the time at Aurick's house! Remember the wine and baths?" Ruth exclaims, taking a long swig of her wine. "That was so good! But the food wasn't nearly as tasty as this!"

"I remember!" I laugh, mirroring her actions and sipping my wine as well.

Wow, like smooth grape juice. It's silky as it runs down my throat.

"My mother used to give Judas and me cinnamon cookies and milk when we were little," Marilynn explains with a full mouth. "That's when she used to tell us the stories of the Fallen Saint!"

Fallen Saint? Me. The prophecy. Wait, aren't we not supposed to know about it? But wouldn't it be far more important that the leaders of Vexamen aren't privy to that knowledge either? *Fuck, it's the truth plant!*

"I was a vegetarian for years," Warrose grumbles through big bites of his meat. "Can't remember why now."

My wide eyes jump to Dessin, who is eating in deafening silence. He makes no show of how good the food is. Doesn't spill any secrets. Doesn't even let his features show how much he's enjoying the meal.

Dessin, Kane, Greystone, Dai, Aquarus, Kalidus, Foxem, and Syfer.

*Syfer is a mute alter. He split when Demechnef trained me to be able to withstand torture without spilling secrets to an enemy interrogator.*

I've never met this alter before. I suppose there would never be a cause for it, unless for this very reason. The brothers are trying to extract information from us. But this is exactly what Demechnef has trained him for.

Syfer is...*empty.* Features slack, hollow of any emotion. I stare at him through my ravenous chewing, reading his body language with cautious intrigue. With a slow blink, his echoing stare shifts to me.

It's the first time I've ever felt an unpleasant knot in my gut from this body's gaze. It's like looking at an ocean's horizon at midnight, feeling the vastness look back at you, creeping into the crevices of your soul. A great power, yet not a single drop of humanity. No color, no light, no sound, only a lingering dread. A heavy loneliness.

"I worked as a child. I never talk about it, never even think about it." Niles takes a long, wet gulp of wine. "It's twisted, isn't? The underground transactions that go on in the Chandelier City with children? Were any of you a part of it? I don't suppose so. I felt alone for a long time. Never had any friends like what I have now."

It's like water fills my chest, and I forget how to breathe.

I bite off a chunk of bread, *chew, chew, chew.*

He never talks about his childhood, not after that day he shared his demons with me in the asylum. It's been an unspoken vow between us. Those memories make him feel sick, make him feel ashamed.

"That's terrible, Niles. What other tragedies go on within Demechnef's borders?" Malcolm purrs without touching his food.

The table falls into a movement of more chomping, slurping, snagging other foods scattered throughout the feast.

I turn my head to Syfer. He eats mechanically, moving his fork to his lips at an unhurried pace. I snag his attention by clearing my throat, holding his gaze filled with nothing but smoke and air. My instincts on what to do next are clear.

"I'm sorry to leave you, especially since we haven't been introduced yet." The urge to spit out more bits of truth claws at my insides. "But I've decided they won't get what they want tonight. The Mazonist Brothers have yet to grasp the limits our minds can exceed."

It's the first sliver of emotion crossing Syfer's brow, a twitch of a muscle. Maxwell growls something beside me. A warning. A question.

But the voices around me sound like water droplets hitting the glassy surface of a warm pond. A whisper down a long tunnel.

And DaiSzek is by my side, bowing for me to climb on his back for him to take me far away.

To the Ambrose Oasis.

*I SHOULDN'T BE EATING THIS MUCH. I shouldn't be eating this much. I shouldn't be eating this much. I shouldn't be eating this much. I shouldn't be eating this much. I shouldn't be eating this much.*

*I shouldn't be eating this much. I shouldn't be eating this much. I shouldn't be eating this much. I shouldn't be eating this much. I shouldn't be eating this much. I shouldn't be eating this much.*

*I shouldn't be eating this much. I shouldn't be eating this much. I shouldn't be eating this much. I shouldn't be eating this much. I shouldn't be eating this much. I shouldn't be eating this much.*

Potato soup drips down my chin. I can't seem to eat this all fast enough. My hands are shaking, my mind is rabid, my heart is pumping blood into my limbs to get me to move faster.

I want it all. It's not going to be enough. Will they have more food? Could I ask for more when I'm done with all of this?

"Slow down, Miss Ruth. Did they not feed you well in Demechnef?" one of the brothers calls from down the table.

I shake my head, forcing myself to swallow. *Be polite, use your napkin to wipe your mouth. Be a lady.*

"We followed a lady-doll regimen. It kept our figures intact, and our skin smooth and flawless." The words tumble out of my mouth without any filter to consider what I'm saying.

Malcolm tsks. "That must have been dreadful."

"I was hungry a lot," I agree, trying to ignore how my mouth salivates for more food. "But at least I always looked my best."

I start shoveling the cheesy noodles into my mouth, nearly blacking out at how euphoric the taste is. I never want to leave. I'll stay here forever, eating, drinking, eating, drinking.

"And how close are all of you? Friends? Traveling companions? Family?"

"Family!" Niles beams, then looks at Marilynn. "She's a little new to our group, but fitting right in!"

Should we be telling them this? I don't know. I can't think past the sugar, the hot bread, the chunky soup.

"And do you plan on being in their family for long, Marilynn?" Maxwell says after he swallows a spoonful of soup.

"I do. One day I am destined to—" Marilynn slaps her hand over her red lips, staring at us in shock, like she's just figured something out.

"To what, dear?"

Her pale cheeks bloom with color. And it's as fast as the time I take to blink. Marilynn throws herself forward, slamming her forehead down on the iron table over and over again.

I scream through the delirious haze.

Niles jumps to his feet, being choked back down by his collar. Warrose and I turn to Dessin and Skylenna, looking to them for a reaction, for an appropriate response. Dessin continues eating without so much as a concerned glance. Skylenna stares vacantly at her plate, eyes glazed over.

"What the fuck is going on?" Warrose barks.

Marilynn's face flops into her plate of food as she falls unconscious. A sharp pang of warning slams into my gut. Something's wrong. Something's not right.

"Ignore her," a brother coos. "It's just us now."

But adrenaline zings under my skin, begging for me to move, to run.

"*Eat*. The food is still hot."

I respond like my mind is made of putty. Forks clank against plates. And I'm suddenly filled to the brim with pleasure radiating through every nerve after each bite.

"So, family, hmm? These are your brothers, Ruth?"

Family. Brothers. Are they?

"No," I answer as I lick my spoon. *So good. So good.* My tongue tingles. My low belly burns. "Warrose is not my brother."

"Oh?"

200

I fist my hands into a heap of more food, getting sweet potatoes all over my fingers. I run my tongue along my knuckles. *So sweet. So tasty.* But how many calories? Will I see this as new layers of fat on my hips? Along my ribs?

"He's not my brother," I reiterate.

"What is he?"

"I don't know."

I can sense Warrose eating slower, listening to my words through his own captivating indulgence.

"Why don't you know? I thought you said you all were family." Malcolm pushes with gentle patience.

"I want to suck his cock." The sentence falls from my lips without any thought. And now that I'm really thinking about it, my mouth is watering for another reason, my inner walls are clenching around air.

Warrose looks up from his food, his stare burning into me like molten lava. It warms my center, licking between my legs.

"I see." Someone chuckles from the other end of the table. "You could take a small break from eating, Ruth."

*What does he mean?*

I can't look away from those glittering hazel eyes. They're the glass on the seafloor, green and blue, unearthing my secrets and arousal.

"Go on, Ruth. You have our permission to taste him."

A servant unlatches my collar, guiding me to Warrose's side of the table. My legs are wobbly, my mind covered in thick fog. But I'm burning all over, tingling with the feverish need to do exactly as they say. *Touch him. Taste him. Look at his length. Hold it in my hands.*

"Where would you like her, Warrose?" Maxwell's voice is eager, menacing.

I look up at Warrose's lofty height, his shadow enveloping me. His tattooed chest is moving like a wild animal out of breath. And that only makes my hardened nipples chafe against my uniform.

"On her knees," Warrose says in a deep, rusted tone.

I'm guided by primal need and instinct. There's a pounding ache between my thighs, meandering through my insides. I drop to my knees, looking up at his dilated pupils and clenching fists. And my entire body jerks with a downpour of rigorous arousal.

*Touch me, oh god, Warrose. Please touch me.*

I'm squirming below him, worried I might start drooling at the sight of his growing crotch.

"Are you attracted to him, dear?"

I nod like a pet waiting for a treat. Heart thrumming as Warrose has to adjust his pants. He's so handsome, so beautiful. That dusting of dark hair running in a trail under his navel. How would it feel against my tongue? Would he moan at my touch?

Taut lines form across his brow, and I almost weep with pure joy as he runs his fingers through my hair. That calloused skin grazes my scalp, and I pinch my thighs together to ease the throbbing agony.

"Are you hard for Ruth? Should she touch you to find out?" These voices are demented, filled with the wrong kind of lust. But I can't find room in my brain to care.

Warrose nods like he doesn't remember how to shape words.

Nervous flutters fill my stomach as my hand reaches out to him. I press my palm against his thick, pulsating cock covered by his breeches. We both groan in a symphony of bottled pleasure. He's hard for me, ready to have my mouth, my tongue.

His large hand covers mine, adding pressure to his stiff length. I hiss at the contact, my hand lighting on fire. He pilots me, using our hands to stroke him.

"Pull it out for her. Let's see how much of you she can take." It's Kaspias's voice that pierces the layer of lust. I almost forgot he was here.

I'm practically bouncing up and down as Warrose fists himself under his waistband

Chains rattle behind me. Gasps. Brisk movement. And a tan hand lands over Warrose's heart. I follow the arm to see Dessin standing next to me.

"Not today, kids." He nods over his shoulder, and Skylenna grins, wide and disturbing. She kicks the table over, sending the feast crashing to the ground. Metal clanking against the floor. Niles curses as he tries to get in a last bite, falling over with it.

Skylenna leaps over the mess, bare feet landing on the arms of Malcolm's chair. She's crouched in front of him, knife to his wrinkled throat.

Kaspias is on his feet, ready to pounce.

"Go ahead," she taunts. "See if you or this earpiece can move faster than a flick of my wrist."

Through the heavy daze and insatiable hunger, I've never been prouder of my soul sister.

Dessin helps me to my feet, signaling for Warrose to check on Marilynn, who is still unconscious.

"We'll be going back to our cages now. Thank you for a wonderful evening." Skylenna hops off Malcolm's chair, tossing the knife at the hoard of wasted food.

Niles and Warrose lift Marilynn from the messy floor, but Niles waves him off, insisting he can carry her himself.

"Fine," Maxwell says as he waves Kaspias to stand down. "We learned enough for one night. Sleep well, children."

Dessin slings my arm over his shoulder as he helps me walk back to where we came from. I want to beg to stay with the food, with Warrose. Why did they interrupt? I'm so confused I can hardly make sense of anything right now.

"Whatever's going on in your head will pass shortly," Dessin tells me in a hushed tone.

"I'm hungry."

Skylenna appears on my other side, throwing my other arm over her shoulder.

"Hey, that was pretty cool what you did in there," I gush, my face way too close to hers.

She laughs. "Thanks, Ruth."

"I almost gave Warrose a blow job."

Skylenna exchanges a look with Dessin. "I know."

"In front of Niles…of all people," I add to Dessin.

He purses his lips as if to say, *Yeah, that makes it worse.*

"You almost gave me a blow job?!" Niles hisses behind us, carrying Marilynn with ease.

"No!" Skylenna and I snap at the same time.

"Good because that's incest!" He pauses for a long moment. "I've never been attracted to little Ruthie."

"Good to know." I roll my eyes.

"I was talking to Marilynn."

I glance back at her unconscious body hanging in Niles's arms. Her forehead is bloody and swollen. Why did she do that? What even happened tonight?

"Niles, please shut the fuck up. I have a migraine." Warrose. He's tailing us. *Warrose.* I almost...

"I wasn't going to actually do it!" I blurt out, gripping Skylenna's shoulder in a panic. "I swear! They must have drugged my food with ecstasy! Right? I would never have actually done it!"

"Is that fucking right?" Warrose shoots back.

"Dessin!" I shake his upper body. "Tell me the food was drugged with ecstasy!"

He looks at me with narrowing eyes, then shifts his focus to Skylenna on my right. He opens his mouth, then closes it. Opens again.

"Is lying to a friend in this situation acceptable?"

I groan in the back of my throat. Letting my entire body go limp so my friends will carry me. They chuckle as they lift me off the ground, watching as I drape my hand over my eyes dramatically.

"I'm still hungry!" Niles complains.

"The plant will dissolve from your system in a minute or two," Dessin says.

After several seconds, my stomach protrudes, my gut feels swollen, sore, stretched to its limit. I let out a faint whimper, frowning as my head lulls back.

"I want to puke!"

The rush of endorphins is gone. Vanished in the pit of misery my stomach has curled into. Sweat trickles down my lower back. And my mouth salivates for an entirely different reason.

We make it back to inside our cages, and as I'm placed on the cold floor, that dreadful aroma of buttered popcorn, candy, and burned skin makes my insides wither. I want a warm blanket. A silk pillow. I want to fall asleep with oils in my hair, body butter layered over every inch of my skin.

Niles sits in Marilynn's cage, holding her head in his lap. He caresses her merlot hair absently.

"Is she going to be okay?" I ask.

Niles lifts his head, blinking at me like he forgot anyone else was here. Breath releases from his chest, and he shrugs tiredly.

"She was really determined to keep that prophecy away from

them."

I nod. "It's for the best." *Especially if we aren't even allowed to hear it.*

But he's done talking tonight. With a soft sigh, he lies down, pulling Marilynn to his chest. I roll away, turning to my side to see Warrose staring at the rocky ceiling.

"We're not talking about it," I bite.

He chuffs. "Don't flatter yourself. There's nothing to talk about."

*Oof.* I keep my features schooled as that sting stabs through my chest, making it hard to breathe. Confusion ripples through me, leaving a bad taste in my mouth. Nothing to talk about? I almost...*we* almost...in front of everyone.

"You're right," I agree. But the rejection swells in my throat. How could he think that? I've never been more turned on in my life. His soft touch in my hair did more for me than the three times I actually had sex.

"Good."

I clench my teeth together.

A thought crosses my mind. I'm the one that taught Skylenna the art of flirting, right? Shouldn't I be able to test if he means what he says?

"We won't talk about it ever," I add.

"Fine."

"About how I got on my knees for you," I say slowly, leveling my eyes at his silhouette.

He hesitates. "Right."

"Or how I ran my palm up the shaft of your cock."

His entire body stiffens. Those lips part, then close, then part again. No words come out.

"Or about what would have happened if Dessin didn't stop us..."

He glances at me from the corner of his eyes. "What would have happened?"

*Okay, here goes nothing. Brace yourself, War-Man.*

"You would have pulled your hard length out, and I would have held it in my small hands." I pinch my thighs together at the thought. *Hell, I'm turning myself on.*

His breath hitches.

"Or how I would have stuck my tongue out so you could tap your tip against it."

Warrose drops his head against the ground, pinching the bridge of his nose. The muscles in his arms tighten as he lets out a faint growl. "*Christ.*"

"Good night, Warrose."

I grin in victory as I roll over, coming face to face with a wide-awake golden boy. Niles meets my eyes. He's beaming. Cheeks pinks. Eyes round.

"I'm one proud papa, Ruthie!"

# 19. Targeting The Weak

## Marilynn

The rancid steam of sausage and pus-colored grease coming off the breakfast makes me vomit in front of everyone.

Niles pats my back as I get it all out. Too many people sitting at nearby tables stop their loud conversation, watching me get sick.

"You shouldn't have hurt yourself last night," Skylenna comments.

"I know." *Pregnant. Aurick's baby. Prophecy.*

"Was it really that important that the Mazonist Brothers didn't hear any bits of the prophecy?" she asks.

I wipe my mouth. "You have no idea."

"How're you feeling?" Niles asks as he examines my sore forehead. Why does he have to be so nice? So caring?

"Splitting headache. Nausea. Tender breasts."

He raises his eyebrows. Looks down at my boobs. Back up to my face. "Ah."

The table laughs. But I can't shake the prickle of nerves rising on the back of my neck. The feeling of someone watching me. A wave of unease. A stare burning a hole in the back of my head. I turn around to peer over my shoulder, scanning the sea of beat down faces, inspecting whether anyone is setting their focus on me.

We follow the single-file line to the regale hour in the stadium. I follow behind our group at the end, holding my forehead to ease the sickening throb from knocking myself out last night. I can't even bring myself to laugh as Warrose makes a joke about Niles having baby arms. Or Niles flexing to show the group his muscles.

Everything hurts, and I feel paranoid.

We enter the stadium, but as I step forward to follow my group inside, several pairs of arms wrap around my stomach, chest, throat, and legs. I try to scream, though some kind of cloth is shoved into my mouth. A hand secures itself there to keep me from making any noise.

I know how to fight back. I know how I should manipulate my body to break free. But they have me in a tight grip, too many of them are holding me down. And my head is fucking pounding. I squirm, buck, thrash around, but I've gotten nowhere. We're ushered down a private hallway, into a dark, secluded room.

The five men and two women start yelling at me in Old Alkadonian. I try to tell them I can't understand but am unable to speak through the ball of cloth.

*What if they try to hurt my belly?*

Panic triggers my adrenaline. I'm tingling from head to toe. Ready to fight. Waiting to see what they plan on doing with me.

I'm slammed on a table, held down as a skinny blond man holds a tool in front of me, small like a pair of scissors without sharp blades. He waves it around with a taunting smile. Blond beard. Thin, measly limbs. It's the same man who tried to masturbate to Ruth.

*Damn it.*

I try to ask what he wants, but it comes out in a muffled slur of vowels.

Without so much as an explanation, my hand is held out toward him, and he hovers the metal tip of the tool toward my index finger.

*Wait...*

My maneuver to swivel off the table is seamless. Judas always used to describe my stealth and fight as like a feral cat. Hitting the floor, they all reach for me, but my legs hook their ankles. A few drop. Hands latch around my throat. When did my wrists get chained together?

I'm defenseless as my vision fogs up.

With a thud, someone tosses me back on the table. I gasp into the cloth, heaving as I try to gain my bearings. Did I pass out? Ankles are chained to the table now. I sway and shift with the dizziness from being strangled.

"*Holonasecoon!!!!*" I try to tug my hand away, but they have me pinned to the point of dried cement, chained, and outnumbered.

"*Pahhhleeese!*" Do I tell them I'm pregnant? Would they care? Could they even understand me if it weren't for this cloth in my mouth?

The skinny man smiles with his rotting, brown teeth. And with one swift squeeze, he clamps the tool around the tip of my nail. My eyes bulge from their sockets. I gasp as he rips it clean off the meat of my fingertip.

"*Ahhhhhggg!!!*"

The pain swoops in like an apocalyptic forest fire. Searing through my hand, winding up my arm. I howl against the rag, choke on my own screams as he does it again and again and again. The awful sound of nails peeling off raw, exposed flesh.

*Why are they doing this to me? What have I done?*

My thoughts rot in my brain, turning into a sour mush. My eyes go blurry and blind through the thick coating of tears. I'm shaking, suffocating, unable to make sense of the beginning or ending of my anguish.

The dark, decaying room spins, and I turn my head to the side. Vomit floods my mouth, being blocked by the gag and a hand. It has nowhere to go, nowhere to exit. I try to swallow it back down, the chunky, sour substance, but it just keeps purging back up. I convulse forward, gargle on it, fight not to breathe it in.

"*Vezënzx dou naz éxvz!*"

Someone dislodges the cloth from my gaping mouth, allowing me to tip my head to the side and heave.

I wince against the white-hot flames devouring my fingertips, my shaking hands. Bile burns the back of my throat, tears drip endlessly from the corners of my eyes, and I can't catch my breath.

Did the others not notice my absence? Are they even my friends?

The shrimpy little man holds my fingers up to my face, showcasing their bloody ends where he ripped off my nails. I gag and cry out at the sight.

"*Demechnef bïuzetx!*"

"You're making a mistake," I whisper through unhinged panting, attempting to lick my cracked lips.

"*Demechnef bïuzetx!*" they chant together.

"My friends have—bad tempers," I explain, knowing full well they can't understand me.

I just have to get back to them. I know they don't see me as one of their own yet. I know I'm new, and they don't trust me very much. But the truth is...I've loved them my whole life. I've been distancing myself, trying to protect my own heart.

After I'm struck across the face, blood drizzles from my nose to my lips. They unlatch my chains and flee the room before my vision can clear.

With lethargic, sickly steps, I make my way back to the stadium. I can't stop the tears from falling, can't keep my legs and arms from shaking. I'm humiliated. Deeply ashamed. I told them I could protect myself. I told them I was an asset. But I was caught off guard and didn't react fast enough. Maybe it's because of a concussion? Maybe it's because I was afraid they'd kill my child if I fought back?

I step into the circus lighting of the stadium, wobbling forward, one painful step at a time. I can't seem to focus on anything; my mind pushes me to zone out, escape reality, get lost somewhere deep in the uninhabited passages of my own mind.

Shock.

*I'm in shock.*

Inmates move out of my way. Tears slip between the crevice of my lips. And my fingers are in agony. It's as if every nerve ending is screaming, ripping to pieces, buzzing with violent electricity.

I hear my name. One glance up, and they're running to me. Niles. Ruth. Skylenna. Warrose. And Dessin leading the way.

I bring two fingers to my upper lip, touching the wetness I feel there. Pulling my hand away, I see that I'm still bleeding from my nose. *How did this happen? What did I do?*

"Her fingers," Ruth croaks.

"Who fucking did it?" Dessin growls, examining my face with a look of mass murder flaring within his pupils. "Point them out."

Niles stares at me in shock, blinking repeatedly like he's trying to clear his thoughts of a traumatizing image.

"You didn't know I was gone," I say through a dry mouth. "No one—came looking for me."

Guilt clouds Skylenna's forest green eyes. She looks to Dessin with determination and shame.

My eyes are stinging with fresh tears. I never cry. Why can't I keep this under control? They just keep coming, swelling over my lids, washing down my cheeks. I taste blood, salt, and the remnants of bile.

"I'm sorry," I mutter bleakly. "I'm sorry. I'm sorry. I'm sorry. I'm sorry. I'm—"

Someone grabs the caps of my shoulders. They say something, but I can't hear past my own apologies. They spill past my lips, unburying themselves from a life with Aurick. A life living under Vlademur Demechnef's thumb. A life of the lady-doll regimen. A life of starvation and vanity. Bleeding was a reason to apologize. Being an inconvenience was a reason to say you're sorry.

"She's in shock," Dessin states coldly. "We need ice water, bandages, and some kind of ointment."

"It hurts," I say absently. But my body is numb. *Numb. Numb. Numb.*

"Marilynn. I need you to tell me who did this to you." Niles places his thumb and index finger on my chin. His touch is velvety, cool, soothing. His other hand traces the trail of my tears, wiping them away with the utmost gentleness.

I unlatch my gaze from his and look around the stadium seating. *There.* The six of them have their views from the sixth row, watching the show with pride.

Dessin follows my sight, glances at Warrose and Skylenna only once. It's the silent communication between soldiers, the kind of unspoken language right before battle.

"Wait…" But the three of them break out into a confident power walk.

Niles is suddenly behind me, wrapping his arms around my waist, pulling me flush to his strong body, and resting his chin on my shoulder.

"Niles," I say in alarm, watching Dessin, Warrose, and Skylenna race up the stairs of the stadium. The terrorizing group of six anticipating a fight with great pleasure.

"I'm not letting you go until they make them suffer," Niles replies.

I relax against him, sobbing at how wonderful his embrace feels. His special aroma of oak, sunshine, and soap. He holds me so tightly, matching the pace of his breath with mine. There is nothing in the world like a Niles hug. No prophecy could have ever predicted it.

I didn't realize until now that Ruth had left, racing around the stadium to find the supplies Dessin requested.

"I'm going to take care of you," Niles promises.

I close my eyes at his sweet voice, sniffling as I hear chaos break out in the sixth row of seats. I'm still unsure if they see me as one of their own or if they just care about the safety of my baby. Either way, I'm angry, grateful, confused, timid, and terrified of getting close.

My life has been a long road of being alone. Of pretending to be someone I'm not. Of hiding out after I faked my death. I was not hugged often.

Sentinels watch from their posts as Warrose and Dessin drag bodies down from the seats, dropping them at my feet. Groans and wheezing. Blood. Disheveled hair.

"Is this the one that led the attack?" Skylenna asks, showing me the scrawny man's face and yellow beard.

I nod.

"What would make you feel better, Marilynn? Should I remove his nails, too? Or is that too merciful? Perhaps his teeth. Or maybe leave him to walk around without a scalp." Dessin is calm, yet something under his surface absolutely terrifies me.

I open my mouth to speak.

"Let me do it," Niles says sternly, letting me go to stand in Ruth's care.

"Niles," Skylenna warns.

But Niles detaches a sharp metal rod from beneath the stage, walking to my attacker with a callous, disconnected look in his eyes. Dessin watches him, lifting his chin as his stare quickly darts from me to Niles. He nods, holding the grunting man down while Niles uses the shiv to saw off the man's scalp.

Ruth hisses, shielding her eyes from the gory mess.

But I watch. Listen to the guttural screams of a grown (or *half-grown*) man. I follow the gushing of crimson liquid streaming over the front of his pinched face. Stinging his eyes. Splattering across Niles's bare chest.

The madness implodes around me. Warrose and Skylenna harm the others. Making a point to avenge the way I was harmed. Ripping off their nails, bashing their heads to the floor. And Dessin watches Niles as he rips off the last piece of the scrawny man's scalp. Something of concealed admiration glinting in his close-set brown eyes.

"You'll die of hepatitis from this rusted metal before you can ever lay a hand on a member of my family again. I hope you suffer," Niles grits, spitting in the man's face before rising to his full height.

Dessin drops the man to the floor, narrowing his eyes on Niles.

"Niles," Dessin says in a husky voice.

Niles wipes the blood from his face with a quivering hand, sliding his weary stare toward Dessin.

"You've met your monster." Dessin puts a hand on his shoulder. "And that monster protected your family. Do not reprimand it for that."

It's as if he could see the war flashing through Niles's mind. The self-deprecating thoughts for maiming another man.

Niles gives him a tight nod and turns to me. "We need to get her cleaned up."

Ruth is already dipping my fingers in bowls of ice water, assembling bandages on the stage beside me.

"It'll take about ten days for the nail beds to heal. And four to six months before the nails grow back," Dessin tells me, to which I shrug against the well of pain. My fingers might as well have been cut off.

My muscles shiver uncontrollably. Each bone aches like it's being pounded by sledgehammers, every nerve pulses painfully, and I can't seem to get warm.

"She's in shock," Warrose says, pulling my hair out of my face.

"That's probably a good thing. Ripping nails out is a form of torture for a reason," Dessin replies.

Skylenna is suddenly at my feet, kneeling in front of me. "I'm so sorry we didn't realize you were gone. I'm sorry we didn't come for you." She holds my hands in hers and squeezes. "You are family, Marilynn. One of us. We won't leave you behind again."

My heart swells in my chest. *Family. One of us.*
"Promise?"
Niles kisses me on the head.
"We promise."

"**F**uck the Chandelier City, it hurts like a bitch!" Marilynn howls, gritting her teeth against the tears.

There isn't much we can do. Dessin said that harming fingernails is a form of torture because they're the source of so many nerve endings.

"Is that a phrase now? *Fuck the Chandelier City*?" Warrose smirks down at Marilynn. "Can we make multiple variations of that? Fuck the Emerald Lake Asylum. Fuck the Slaughter Circus. Fuck the Mazonist Brothers."

"We can determine how much pain we're in or how pissed off we are based on which noun we're feeling," I add, trying so hard to make Marilynn smile.

"Alright, fair. So, what's the rating for each?"

I tap my chin, thinking. Failing not to look at Marilynn's forehead wrinkling as she bears down against the pain.

"Chandelier City is mildly hurt or pissed. The Mazonist Brothers are tolerable but still painful. Slaughter Circus is '*I'm about to explode*'. Emerald Lake Asylum is an apocalypse." Dessin sits across from us in a dark corner of the stadium seating

We're huddled away from the other prisoners, sitting on the floor, tending to Marilynn. I don't know if I've ever been this mad at myself. I didn't notice she was gone, didn't even look behind me to make sure she was still by my side. She's just so quiet. But of course, that's no excuse. We bantered here by the stage while she had her fingernails ripped out by that psychopath.

I still taste the blood of that bastard's scalp in my mouth.

It'll probably give me nightmares for years. I'm not like Skylenna or Dessin. My brain doesn't protect itself that way. I scalped a man in front of my family and nearly blacked out. The only thing keeping me moving was the adrenaline, the image rotting in my brain of her bloody fingers.

It crushed me to hear her say that no one came looking for her. Because, if I'm being honest with myself, we would have noticed Skylenna's absence immediately. Dessin would have found her before her nails were touched.

"Fuck the Slaughter Circus," Marilynn clarifies her statement.

We all blow out a breath.

"We need something to dull the pain," Skylenna says with a frown.

"Like *this* big bitch?"

I look straight up from my seated position to see Helga Bee and Gerta hovering over me, carrying a huge tin bottle.

"What is it?" Dessin asks.

"*What is it*, Beetle Brain asks?" Helga Bee elbows Gerta with a cocky chuckle.

Dessin sighs with lowered lids. Skylenna grins next to him.

"It's Mother Nature's cure to depression! It's God's apology for making life so shitty! It's—"

"We get it. Alcohol," I say.

"Give it," Marilynn begs with red-rimmed eyes. "Oh wait…I can't have it." She looks like she's about to sob all over again.

"Not alcohol, you nincompoop! Honey of Sweet Nectar Valley! It makes you feel good and relieves pain! Even safe for the kiddies!"

Ruth boops my nose with a wry smile. "Nincompoop."

"Give it to her!" I snatch the bottle from Helga Bee's stubby fingers, practically diving in front of Marilynn to help her drink it.

She covers the lid with her red, swollen lips. And it looks like…my cock twitches, pulsing with pressure as I watch her gulp down the, uh, sweet valley stuff.

Damnit. I dart my eyes away as she meets them. Twin sapphires. Deep blue lagoons. They contrast with her freckled skin and vibrant hair. And those plump lips…I wonder what they would look like wrapped around my hard—

"What happened to her anyway?" Helga Bee asks.

"She got jumped when we weren't looking. They ripped out her nails," Skylenna says, still seething.

"*Ah*. That's a gang territory marking ritual. It's a way to show other males in a group that they want your females. They were challenging you boys to a good ole' fight to claim your women!"

Dessin looks like he might have an aneurysm.

"So it could have been Skylenna or me targeted, too?" Ruth asks.

"Yeppers! It's just a pecking order. Nothin' personal."

"It's pretty damn personal." I grimace at her to stop talking now. Fuck this place. Fuck these inmates.

"You want to tell us a story, Marilynn? Get your mind off the pain?" Ruth rubs a hand in circles over her back.

"The only stories I can tell you, I'm not allowed to tell you." Her eyes lose focus for a split second, and she shudders. That pearly white, freckled face converts back into her usual grouchy scowl.

Hmm. What other stories does she have on me?

"Do you know the story of DaiSzek and Knightingale?" Skylenna asks with hopeful eyes.

Marilynn's lips twitch into something close to a smile. "I do. The whole story. Not the watered down one they put in a child's bedtime story."

"Aren't DaiSzek and Knightingale the two scruffy mutts back at home? How do they already have stories?" I ask.

"They were the fae and elven warriors from a long time ago! They ended a war and saved their people," Skylenna explains with fondness. "Can you tell us the story, Marilynn?"

"Gerta loves a good story time! We have some good ones, too.

Remember the mountain orgy four winters ago?"

"Oh, god," Dessin grumbles.

"Tell us, Marilynn!" I beg with panicked eyes.

Ruth and Warrose nod with wide, *help-me* eyes as well.

Marilynn takes another swig from the tin bottle, which helps her hands tremble a little less. She licks her lips, blinks sleepily, and nods with a relief-filled sigh.

"DaiSzek wasn't always a warrior king. Didn't always have special abilities. At the start of his journey, he was only a stonemason's son. He lived in a country across the world called Neslanox. A civilization of honest, hardworking farmers." Marilynn pauses to lean her head back, getting comfortable. "Knightingale was the daughter of a war chief in Dementia. One afternoon during training, she hit her head on a rock and said an archangel came to visit her. The angel showed her a vision of DaiSzek cutting stone and told her that the two of them were very special…"

"Ohhhh, I like this story! This is good. Would be better with a couple orgies, but I'm here for it!" Helga Bee bursts, making us all jump.

*Am I that annoying when I'm inappropriate?*

"The archangel told her that when there is battle of great evil, God sends two warrior angels. These angels are born with the truest forms of love, friendship, and pain. When under pressure, they don't turn to dust. They turn to diamonds."

"Wow," Skylenna breathes, eyes glistening in the sunny circus lights.

"These angels were created by God to wield ethereal power that emerges from strife, from heartbreak, from hardship. They were cut from the same cloth, beings of a twin flame, a star split down the middle. Warrior soul mates that can find each other across time and space. And Knightingale knew she had to find DaiSzek. From the mere glimpse of a vision the archangel gave her, she knew her heart belonged to the stonemason's son. The humble fae that was kind to his neighbor, gentle to his flock, and had no idea the burden that sat on his shoulders."

And fuck, now I'm tearing up. It's beautiful.

Marilynn takes a few shallow breaths, glancing down at her raw fingertips.

"In the time it took Knightingale to sail to Neslanox, she was abducted by pirates, sold into slavery, beaten, tortured, and starved. DaiSzek watched a plague overtake his country. He nursed his family and friends as they all died slow deaths. He was the only one immune. In search to find more fae who had survived, he took a boat and sailed to the nearby country of Rouzella. He was treated like a king for being fae, given his own legion of servants to care for him. Elven servants. In Rouzella, the elven race was hated and forced to serve in order to stay alive.

"DaiSzek made many enemies by freeing those in bondage. One day, he was captured and brought to the public executioner's block. Moments before the blade was swung, an elven servant emerged from the shadows and unleashed a scream so powerful, it woke the ocean. A tsunami drowned every fae servant master, carrying them out to sea.

"Knightingale told DaiSzek of her vision from the archangel, shared her knowledge of the war that was going to erupt between the many species across the world. Fae, elf, Druid, shades, beasts, dwarves, trolls. They left with the small army of loyalists they gathered along the way, setting sail for Dementia, the country where the fighting was the thickest. Seven divided races. All out to destroy each other. Over the years, DaiSzek learned of his own divine abilities. Portals to transport him through great distances. And when Knightingale was in trouble, threatened or harmed, he could shift the skies, bring darkness to the land, and call upon a dragon so magnificent, so devastating in war, it's unclear if its existence was real or a metaphor, and its final resting place is still not known."

I turn to glance at Skylenna and Dessin. They steal each other's gaze multiple times. Silently communicating. Questioning. Admiring.

"On quiet nights sailing to Dementia, they would make plans to return to Neslanox after the war was over, living their life together in solitude, growing old in peace until they could return to heaven together. But the war had grown out of control. The seven races were threatening to destroy this world with the combat between light and dark magic. It was because of their different forms of magic that this world was imploding, turning them against each other. The archangel had returned to Knightingale to tell her of a world where the seven races could live in harmony. Where their separate natures wouldn't be the cause of their fighting, where their magic could be at peace without rebellion."

"What happened?" Ruth asks, leaning forward.

"DaiSzek and Knightingale arrived at the peak of the war, where their magic had spun out of control. They learned of a way to open an interdimensional portal together, giving each race a choice. Stay and live at odds with their magic, or go back to a world that would accept them. A world without humans." Marilynn takes a shaky breath, blowing a shiny red strand of hair from her eyes. "It's said they gave their lives so their people could return to their own world. They never made it to their own private island. Never got to grow old together."

Something like fear and desperation flashes across Skylenna's sharp features. Is she worried that'll happen at the end of this road for them? That they'll give their lives for this prophecy? This war? She's always been so selfless. Always puts us before herself. I can't imagine a world without her, without Dessin (even though he can be a dickhead). They're my family.

"That's so sad," Ruth murmurs. Just like me, she looks at Dessin and Skylenna. We all do. Assessing their reaction to this story. Adjusting to the way they perceive it. But we're all thinking the same thing. This story, in a way, sounds like a mythical version of what they've been through. Their traumatic pasts, hardships to end up together, and the way they literally would summon a dragon to save each other.

Their lives mirror one another.

Beautiful and tragic.

Hopeless and romantic.

My heart winds itself together in a spool of barbed wire.

"You'll have your happy ending," I announce, watching the way Skylenna and Dessin's eyes return to reality and shift to me. "Unlike DaiSzek and Knightingale, you'll make it to your Neslanox."

To my surprise, Dessin's eyes brighten. He smiles. He actually fucking *smiles*.

"To growing old together." Dessin raises an imaginary glass.

Our group mimics his motion, holding our hands up as we say, "To growing old together."

# 21. Induced Frenzy

## Skylenna

**D**essin has a plan.

He doesn't dare breathe the details out loud. Why? Because an artist doesn't reveal their painting until it's complete. But no words need to be spoken for me to catch on to his shift in demeanor. I don't miss how his attention roams each room we're in. How he studies the timing, the schedule, the body language of each sentinel changing shifts. There is a good chance he already has the inner workings of this place down to a science.

But I don't ask him about it yet.

"What's on the agenda today?" I ask Ruth as we hear the announcer through the iron doors.

She narrows her eyes as she sorts through his fast, dramatic way of talking to the crowd. Her dark eyebrows pull together in confusion. The Ringmaster takes a long pause, then shouts something to which the crowd explodes.

"Oh god." Her eyes widen, and she looks from Dessin to me in uncertainty. "He said…he said…"

"Spit it out, little rebel." Warrose leans against the door with a bored expression.

"Ecstasy Dance." She stares back at him coldly.

"What's that mean?"

It sounds sexual. And that can't be good for my situation. I'm with Dessin. He'd cut the hands off of any man who would touch me.

"I'm listening for an explanation."

We wait around her, watching the subtle changes in her expression as if it will tell us anything.

"Something about a gas…"

Dessin turns to me, face stoic, chin raised. And although he'd never show it, he's concerned. "You stay by my side the entire time."

"Yes."

"What do you think it means?" Warrose asks, though it seems he's already put it together.

"I think they're going to pump a concoction of drugs into the air. Methamphetamine, synthetic cathinone, cocaine. Opioids to stimulants," Dessin explains, still studying Ruth's reactions.

"Why?"

"To increase dopamine and serotonin levels."

"Dumb it down for me," Warrose deadpans.

"To spread sexual urges and arousal."

Ruth blinks out of her concentrated trance, soft brown eyes darting between Dessin and me. "It looks like Helga Bee is going to get another orgy story."

"What now?" Niles steps forward.

"Look, I don't know how this is going to work. I don't know how strong the gas will be. But it's a fucked up, perverted way to entertain the goddamned soldi—"

Dessin stops abruptly, realization springing in his dark-mahogany eyes.

"What?" I ask, placing a hand on his shoulder.

"I'm going to fucking kill him."

"Who?" I struggle to follow his line of thought, but it only takes a moment to narrow down the *he* referenced. "Kaspias?"

"He's going to watch whatever happens on that stage. He'll probably…" Dessin trails off with a clenching jaw and a string of curse words.

"We can worry about that later," Warrose interrupts. "What's the plan for this one?"

His forehead beads with sweat, and he avoids looking at Ruth altogether. I wonder if it's been awkward for them to be around each

222

other after what happened at the dinner party.

"Our inhibitions will be lowered, but I don't know if we'll be able to resist the drugs. Either way, we have to stick together so no other prisoner gets their hands on our girls. Got it?" He's staring at Niles and Warrose now, eyes firm with the command of an alpha.

They agree quietly. And I feel terrible at how uncomfortable this must be for them. Dessin and I are mates. If something sexual happens…it's okay. Weird to have an audience, but it's consensual.

"Ruth? Marilynn?" Dessin urges us to huddle closer before the doors open. "I don't know what your sexual preferences are. I don't know how reserved you are. Normally, I wouldn't need to. But please know, we would never fucking touch you without consent in our right minds. I might have an alter that will emerge to resist this drug. But that's up to Skylenna. As for both of you, I need to know if you feel safe with us."

Ruth and Marilynn peer at each other for a second, then look to Niles, Warrose, and Dessin.

"Whatever happens, we're in this together. Just… please don't let another prisoner have me," Ruth says with a quivering voice. "I consent."

"Over my dead body," Warrose promises.

"I…agree," Marilynn breathes out in agitation. "Just please, don't leave me behind." Marilynn's words puncture a small hole in my heart. She won't be forgotten again. No matter what happens.

"I won't take my eyes off you," Niles says quietly.

And the doors open.

Cheers of drunk men, blinding red and yellow light, bursts of fire, and the giant stadium exploding with violent, lustful energy. The heated atmosphere is sticky and humid from the frantic gathering of exhausted bodies, hungry for an escape but hungrier for pleasure.

It's harsh on the senses, looking around at the restless soldiers bouncing in their seats, the dark carnival, the insidious zoo of criminals, the mad house of torture and entertainment.

With each step, the air swells with dust, stale body odor, dried blood, and a bouquet of alcohol-infused breath. It balloons to stomach-churning levels around me.

Dessin caresses the back of my hand with his knuckle. The lightest of touches that zaps a charge through the terror that gushes out of me. I take a breath, focus on the roughness of that knuckle. Focus on something else that will distract me from the nerves curling around my stomach.

"Remember the first time we walked into the tavern of the Nightamous Horde?" Dessin asks in that low baritone, somehow knowing I needed to hear his deep, rugged voice.

"I do. Thinking about the time I had to straddle you?"

"Yes." Desire forms like thick webs over his voice. It's smooth like butter melting on top of a juicy steak.

"Me, too."

The Ringmaster pivots on his platform, looking down at the herd of human cattle he is welcoming to the stage. I flinch at the paint on his long face. Red lips that make his smile appear wide and unnatural. Black smudges around his eyes. White, like baby powder, covering his skin and ending under his chin.

The rest of the sea of faces come into view, the soldiers hollering, also decorated as...

"Clowns," Niles gasps behind me. "I hate clowns!"

"Don't look at them," Dessin commands.

I avert my eyes and blow out a breath. They're everywhere—crazy, colorful, disturbing faces that are anxious for the show to begin.

"This is so fucked up," Warrose growls.

We're shoved onto the platform, holding onto each other as the mob of inmates grows anxious, pushing, knocking elbows, and whispering in Old Alkadonian.

The Ringmaster makes a final statement, throwing his arms in the air as a veil of smoke floats from the ceiling, draping over the stage like a blanket of haze.

"He told them to secure their masks and enjoy the Ecstasy Dance!" Ruth shouts over the screams.

My eyes flash back to the clown faces. It's not paint. Not makeup. They're wearing masks!

"Skylenna!" Dessin yells, reaching for me through the sudden chaos of hysterical bodies moving through us like a channel of water.

Warrose and Niles attempt to hold on to Ruth and Marilynn, but the current is too strong. The screams of men and women fighting to find the person they want to stay close to overpowers our voices. And I'm stunned into silence, emotion cluttering my throat, dread biting into my lungs. We can't be separated! What if I'm assaulted? What if the drug is so powerful I let it happen?

"Dessin!" I shriek, pummeling my way through sweaty bodies.

But my voice is drowned out. It's a theater of panic. A display of crying women. Some are happy about it, searching for a partner or multiple inmates to couple with. Some already have a crazed look in their eyes.

And the fog is falling, almost here, almost encapsulating us in its thick curtain of drugs.

"Oh, god! *Dessin!*" Helplessness ricochets over my limbs.

I hold my breath against the initial contact, resist the urge to suck in the cloudy mist that sprinkles over my skin. Prisoners have already begun to inhale, letting their heads lull back, eyes rolling, pupils dilating. I pinch my nose, bustling through another group of people. The more my muscles work, my limbs move, the more I need oxygen.

It happens after a moment of heart-hammering silence. I take a deep breath in. It tastes of burning plastic, bitter and salty on my tongue. The world of fire, flashing lights, and frantic bodies…*softens*. A sweet, sugary atmosphere takes its place.

*Why was I so upset? It's so nice here, so thrilling, so…*

My thighs pinch together as I watch two women kiss, deeply, passionately, like no one else exists around them. A couple on my right gives each other oral.

The rapid movement of uniforms being tossed to the side licks my skin with its immodest presence. My heart beats at the pace of a jack rabbit. A hungry sensation buzzes in my lower belly, like crawling bugs, like warm honey drizzling between my legs.

I need to be touched.

Spinning in circles, I search the multitude, rubbing my hands across my prickling skin, breathing like I've just hiked up the side of a mountain.

My eyes lock with a man pumping himself into his fist. And, although my flesh is humming, my clit throbbing, something feels *wrong*. Like taking a bite of a dessert that isn't sweet, it's bitter and sour. I take a step away, unsure of how to avoid this confrontation. *Wrong, wrong, wrong.*

He says something in words that don't make sense. A language I can't decipher.

Another step back.

*Wrong.*

He leaps for me, arms circling around my waist, ensnaring me against his hairy chest. I yelp at the contact, at the way my body responds yet rejects the arousal. His half-salute erection bumps against my thigh, searching for a hole. Pubic hair scratches and pokes, causing my molars to smash together at the uninviting texture.

Not what I want. Not welcome. Not what I need. Not *who* I need.

The prisoner leans over my face, puckering his thin lips, but is ripped from our embrace like a tree being uprooted by a storm. His body jerks back headfirst, flying into a group of strangers groping on the floor.

"What did I wake up to, darling?" The voice with the accent that curls my toes, lined with silk and liquid gold. Soft yet graceful. Even through the thick haze, I recognize the alter almost instantly.

"Greystone," I breathe with a weak whine. His name alone corrodes like melting metal through my core.

His lofty stance is leaner in a way, confident, carnal. Those charcoal eyes, pupils expanding to saucers, are a blow to my lungs. They harden my nipples, scorch my flesh, melt me to a pathetic puddle on the floor.

"I don't understand." He adjusts his hard cock in his pants, fighting the greedy need to stroke himself.

"You don't need to," I explain with trembling hands. "Do you trust me?"

Greystone looks out at the crowd, at the mounds of naked inmates, the clowns veering from the stands in an eerie quiet they usually don't display.

His weighty gaze slides back to me. "Yes."

Greystone closes the distance, strong hands cradling my head, full lips crashing over my mouth with heat, vigor, and deafening pleasure.

My core lights up in a show of fireworks. His hot tongue dips into my mouth, slipping over mine. He sucks on my bottom lip, moaning into my lungs like he's trying to reign in his irrepressible arousal.

"I usually take my time, sweetheart," Greystone explains past my lips.

I nod. "This time will be a little different."

"Yes, it will." He rips off my uniform, holding the weight of my breasts in his palms. "Will you forgive me for fucking you like an animal?"

I whimper in response.

"Good girl," he exhales in a rush, pulling his veiny cock from his pants, fully engorged and standing straight up. With a quick bend of his knees, he lifts me to wrap my legs around his waist. "I have no wall to push you against, so I'll have to settle for a human, won't I?"

No logic. No moral high ground. My pussy clenches around air over and over again. My legs twitch around his hips from my spasming core. Desire hangs low in my belly, twisting tighter and tighter, screaming for a release. I itch for his calloused hands to touch me, for him to suck on my skin, my tongue, my lips.

Greystone turns my head to a woman behind me, standing tall on one leg and the other draped over the shoulder of a muscular back. The inmate on his knees squeezes her thigh as he laps between her legs.

"There," Greystone whispers. He walks us toward her until the bare skin on my back is flush against hers. It's electric. Steaming. Gratification boiling under my surface.

The woman throws her head back, lulling on my shoulder. Eyes closed, mouth open, high-pitched whining as the man devours her clit. Flames spike through my core, and my arousal is dripping down my inner thigh.

"Oh my god," I moan.

"Stay still, sweetheart. I don't want to come yet." His eyes shudder as he lines up the tip of his length with my hot, wet center. "Filthy girl, you'd let me stick it inside you against the back of a woman getting her pussy eaten?"

"Oh, yes." Static lines the edges of my vision.

"Would you like me to ease it in?"

I shake my head.

"That wasn't an answer. Do I need to start calling you names in order for you to be good for me?"

Names? Do I want that? Every fiber in my body squeals yes. A rogue wave of wanton energy makes me nod my head. Words. Can't form words.

"Are you a slut?" he asks with clouding eyes. An inch. He pushes it in an inch.

"Y-yes."

"You *are* a slut, Skylenna." He sucks on my nipple, hard, aggressive, unlike his usual style. "You'll let me fuck you however I want, won't you? Filthy, little girl."

"P-please."

With one powerful thrust, his full size slams inside me. I howl against the overwhelming pressure, trying to adjust as fast as possible. The woman behind me turns her head and kisses my neck. It only adds bliss to this experience, loosening my walls, slickening his entryway until I'm undulating against him.

"Fuck, I've never wanted to come so fast, my good, little slut."

His voice spears through me, sending a flood of wetness to my center again. The symphony of soaking, slapping sounds only adds to our ecstasy dance.

"If I come on your pink, exposed cunt, will it drip down to the ass of the woman who is—kissing your neck?" He almost can't get the words out.

My inner walls spasm at the notion, sending an unexpected climax rolling through me like a demonic possession. I scream his name, latching onto him as I ride the waves.

"That's my good girl." And he's coming now, pulling out just in time to shoot a long white rope over my exposed clit. He's right. It drips down like a mess of drool, ending on the woman at my back.

To our surprise, he's rock-hard again. So quickly. Like the last orgasm never happened. This drug sends a new blast of horny energy.

We continue fucking as if this night of euphoria will never end.

# Warrose

MY LIP IS SLICED AND bloody from fighting someone off of Ruth.

On our corner of the stage, the prisoners are ravenous, violent, desperate to get their hands on her. I end up shielding her body with my own.

*And that was my first mistake.*

"Warrose!" she screams, face pressed against the stage floor as three other prisoners pummel their fists down on my back like an angry pack of primates.

I flex every muscle across my shoulder blades, bracing as their punches undoubtedly leave bruises. They eventually grow tired, scurry off, and find mates of their own.

"I'm here," I exhale into her ear, my lips grazing her curly hair. She smells so…angelic. Like honey and vanilla. Like an afternoon in a library drinking rose chamomile tea.

Blood and heat rush to my groin.

"Warrose…" And she doesn't sound so scared anymore. Her voice has lost its edge, tilting in a curious angle.

I know I shouldn't…the drugs permeate my brain like a fast-acting poison. *Resist, Warrose.* She's beautiful, yes. Gorgeous. Small enough to spin her entire body on my dick. Fuck, yes. *No!* Control. Discipline. This isn't how I want her. In fact, I don't want her at all. She has a bad attitude, is rude, arrogant, and has a sharp tongue. *I want to make her choke on my…*

I bury my nose in her hair, inhaling deeply, like an animal in mating season. Those fucking pheromones nearly blind me.

And to my horror, Ruth moans lightly, followed by a small gasp. Like that small noise embarrassed her beyond repair.

"Don't do that. *Please* don't fucking do that." I don't recognize my own voice. It's rougher than gravel. Darker than midnight in hell.

"I'm sorry. We can fight this, right? We must."

I nod, though I'm still breathing in her scent like it's the only drug I'm on. My mouth parts against the edge of her ear, and I can't control myself. I can't stop the hot breath that whooshes out of me. Can't fight the way the wet inside of my lip catches on her skin.

*That is my second mistake.*

Her back arches abruptly as if I've pushed the right button. As if I've pulled the right string. She delicately grinds against my throbbing length, and it's gentle, slow. She's trying to go unnoticed.

It ignites the base of my spine. I hold my breath. Go completely still.

Ruth rocks her narrow hips back once more, and that does it. My lower body jerks forward, pinning the center of her ass with my hard cock.

"You have—an erection," she observes under her breath.

"I'm aware."

"Well, get rid of it."

I blow out a laugh. "It doesn't exactly want to leave. And you're not helping by arching for me."

Neither of us move an inch.

"I don't want to be here either, okay?" I snap. This is the worst-case scenario. She doesn't want this. I'm a monster for holding her down with my aching erection. She'll never forgive me if it goes any further than this. She'll never be able to go near me again.

"You don't?" Offended. She sounds *offended*. "Not even when I do this?"

Ruth takes my hand in a smooth, calculated motion, and...*fuck*, she places it around her throat. My fingers react without my command, curling around her skin with added pressure.

This will be how I end. Death by exploding erection. Death by blue balls.

"*Ruth*," I warn, growling against her hair.

"Yes?" Her tone is taunting, dripping with seduction.

"I can't do this to you. Not like this."

"Like what?"

Reminding us where we are, someone falls in front of us, being fucked in missionary.

"I wouldn't be able to forgive myself."

But the smoke around us is irresistible, rearranging my values, my morals, my inhibitions. The man I know is losing to this beast that wants her. Needs her. Is desperate to choke her while I fuck her.

"Then don't have *all* of me. Just, I need" Ruth wiggles her ass underneath me "*release*. Please, don't make me beg."

*Beg.*

That word.

It fucks with my head.

It undoes my last feeble string of restraint.

"You want me to give you release, my little rebel?"

"Yes."

I tighten my grip on her throat.

"Should I take what I want?"

Her nod is hesitant. Enough to tell me exactly what I should do.

"Arch for me." My command is almost degrading. An abrupt order. A baritone husk in her ear. "Yes, like that."

She's limber, flexible, tight as a rod. The pleasure of seeing her ass in the air stabs right through my balls. I rock my pelvis against her, growing harder at the little sigh she makes.

"How much have you done with a man, Ruth?"

"Enough."

"Be specific."

It's hard to ignore the display of nakedness in the stadium. The clown faces. The screams. The moans. It's a concert of madness.

"Penetration. Lasted like a minute." She sounds insecure.

I smirk to myself.

"Do I have your permission to do something you've never done before?" I ask, gripping her hips like I'm claiming her, bringing her in as close as I can get. My hips rotate, jerking against her to relieve the swelling in my groin. The dry grinding is both erotic and driving us both further into madness.

"Depends," she gasps.

"I want your ass, Ruth. I won't penetrate you. I won't take your lips. I won't take your cunt."

She inhales sharply, turning back to look at me with crazed, dark eyes and a gaping mouth. "You want my—why? How?"

I run a finger between her tight cheeks, adding pressure through her thin uniform until she gulps, maintaining fierce eye contact with me.

Nothing in the world would make me happier than to bury myself inside her, lift one leg over my shoulder, kiss her leg, her foot, her toes. I'd make her eyes roll back; I'd keep one finger in her ass the whole time.

But I'm not all beast. I'm a man who holds more power. More strength. I won't ruin something that could be romantic for her...

"Do it," she pants.

I give her one last buck of my hips, rubbing my hot erection between her legs. The ecstasy in there grows thicker, a tangible fog in my lungs, blurring my vision, brightening colors. The animal in me can't be contained any longer. With both hands on her hips, I jerk her ass toward my face, pulling that skimpy uniform to the side.

The humid air kisses her bare, glistening flesh. And like an uncivilized creature, I lean into her pink cunt, breathing in through my nose and taking in her heady, sweet musk. It sends a furious pulse of desire straight to my cock.

"Goddamnit, I want to taste you." I shudder, hands pulling her cheeks apart as I gaze at her nudity. She's fucking beautiful everywhere.

"Oh, please," she pants against the floor. "Please, taste me."

I shake my head. "Not until you ask me when you're sober."

"Please, Warrose!"

I reach around to snatch her chin, tilting her face to look back at me. Those gorgeous brown eyes are fevered, hungry, venomous.

"I want you to make a mess on my face when we're far away from here. You understand?"

That rational sliver of her conscience seems to understand me. She nods.

"Good. Now tell me how this feels." I lick my thumb, then probe the tight ring of her ass hole, pulsing against it gently.

Ruth clenches, gasping shyly.

My dick aches, and I can't wait any longer. *I wish I could take this slow, Ruth. I really do.*

She yelps as I yank her backward, spreading her cheeks wide and running my tongue over her puckered hole. She's mad with nervous energy, writhing against my mouth, arching like she's about to break her spine in half.

*That's it. She's done for.*

The beast inside me snaps the head of the man with self-control. I devour her ass, lapping, sucking, eating her wildly. And to my utter, profound pleasure, she grinds against my mouth, moaning loud enough to send an echo through the stadium.

I fist my cock, now painfully hard in my pants, stroking myself at her eagerness to feel my tongue probing that tense ring.

"Oh...oh my..."

"Is your cunt wet for me, baby girl?" I kiss her ass cheek, eliciting goose bumps to rise on her thighs.

She looks back at me, eyes hooded and bloodshot. "Say that again."

I raise my eyebrows in question.

"Call me that again."

The urge to ejaculate is paralyzing. "Baby girl."

"*Ah*, yes." She turns back, reaching between our legs until she's gripping my aching cock.

"Fuck," I growl, jolting into her hand.

"I want you to…"

"What?" I ask, unable to think clearly with her hand wrapped around me.

"I want you to—make love to me."

God is testing me. I'm going to fail. *Please, don't let me fail.*

"No," I grunt as her hand squeezes. "You want to come. And I'm going to make that happen in front of all these perverted soldiers."

I tangle my hand in her curly hair and tug sharply, angling her face to look up at the stadium.

"You see those clowns, baby girl? They're going to watch your face while I make you come, okay?"

She whimpers, doing her best to nod against my strict hold on her.

I clamp my hands on her inner thighs, squeezing the soft skin and guiding her back to my tongue. I lap at her relentlessly, tempted by the devil himself to run a finger between her dripping folds. But I promised. I shouldn't. She's probably so warm inside that wet center, so sinfully delicious.

I growl into her ass, feeling the claws of insanity pull me under, hold me down, threaten to rip my conscience apart.

"Promise me this won't end when we leave here," she gasps, clamping down every muscle.

"Is that what you want?" I lick her hole, lovingly this time, sending a shiver up her delicate spine.

"It's what I want."

I hesitate, massaging my fingers against her scalp. My brows wrinkle together as I frown. Is that really what she wants? Or is the ecstasy controlling her speech? Giving her impulsive thoughts?

"Okay," I breathe. "I promise." *On my end, at least.*

Keeping my tongue against her, I push the tip of my index finger inside, pulsating as I lick. Her surprised moans fill the stadium, louder, breathier, an aphrodisiac. She gyrates her hips against me, drawing out a guttural groan from deep in my chest.

*Fuck, I'm not going to last.*

232

"Do you see them looking at you, Ruth?" It comes out in a rough whisper.

"Yes," she moans.

"Show them the inside of your mouth for me."

She clenches around my finger. "Oh my god, I'm going to…"

"Yes, baby girl? Tell me what you want so you can come."

"I want my pussy to hug the thickness of your cock," she gasps, her breath getting stuck in her throat, and then she jolts, crying out to the stadium. Her orgasm practically vibrates against my finger, chasing the chill from my bones.

And I almost miss it.

Almost don't look up to check.

Kaspias removes his clown mask and stares down at her.

# 22. Bedtime Stories

## Marilynn

"There you are!" Niles shouts, shoving past a group of naked inmates. "I'm sorry, the crowd pushed me away from you."

I've been in the fetal position for the last several minutes. It's not that I'm afraid, not that I'm weak, not that I'm incapable of defending myself.

It's that I don't want to. The electric charge of this smoke is damning.

And I'm having flashbacks.

Brief images of Vlademur Demechnef sneaking into my room at night. Blurs of the next morning, sobbing on the kitchen floor as I told Aurick. It's confusing. These memories. The awful way my body is reacting in this setting.

But seeing Niles, it dulls the pain in my heart.

"Thank God," I breathe.

"Did anyone touch you?" He kneels down to me, cradling my face in his warm hands.

I shake my head.

"Good. They wouldn't be breathing right now if they had." He pauses, lifting his brow in the way he does before he tells a joke. "And by that, I mean I would have run to Daddy Dessin to beat him up for me."

I snort. "Daddy Dessin takes care of everything."

Niles is quiet for a moment, doing his best to keep his hooded eyes clear of the lust that is pumping viciously through the air. "I'm not going to hurt you."

His voice curves around my spine, pours into my heart like warm honey. I want to touch him, feel the sharpness of that jawline. Feel the silkiness of his golden hair.

"But will you touch me?"

His Adam's apple bobs. "I don't have to."

"Why not?"

"The gas isn't as strong on me as it might be for you." He waves a hand around the stadium. "It's been used on me enough *before*...enough to build a tolerance."

My skin is hot and tingly. I run my hands over my body, unable to fight the jittery feelings swarming my gut like a colony of ants.

"You..." *Think clearly, Marilynn.* "You and I have similar backgrounds."

"Oh?"

I pinch my thighs together. *Stop looking at his crotch.*

"Aurick's father. He hurt me. He *assaulted* me. I didn't get a say in what happened to my body." I wish I could stop the fluttering in my lower belly. This topic is hard, serious. And it's certainly not the time to get turned on.

Niles lifts his chin. "I'm so sorry, Marilynn."

He's touching me. He's touching me. My vision lights up in a show of shooting stars.

"You know the feeling?"

He nods with tight lips.

The world roars around us in a blur, painting smudges of color in my periphery. Fire. Flesh. Clown faces. But it's muted as I look up at him, descending into his kind eyes.

"I don't want to make you feel obligated to touch me," I say, making a strained noise. "Just, please ignore me while I"

Releasing a soft sigh, I rub a hand between my legs, graze my fingers over a nipple. The flush of warmth and the compulsion to stroke my sensitive skin are torture to ignore. It's almost painful, like failing to scratch an itch that drives you completely mad after several moments of letting the tension build.

Niles's eyes flash to my hands, watching them wander, watching them tease my breasts, my warm center.

"I don't think I can ignore it," he finally states without looking away from my hands.

That sentence, simple and straightforward, is like a deep, sensual massage over my entire body. I can't tell if it's the drug or just my own heart that yearns for him to say more things like that.

"But I thought you weren't as affected by the drug as I am?" I'm squirming.

"I'm not."

"You're not," I repeat.

"I'm affected by you."

He plants those four words in my heart like seeds in a rose garden. They blossom in my chest, filling me with color and a floral aroma. That feeling of falling in my sleep makes my stomach dip.

"*Oh.*" It comes out as more of an exasperated breath than anything else.

He's affected by me. *Me.* Marilynn. The woman who lived under the roof of the leader that ruined his life. The girl that still lives inside me, the small one that used to beg her mama for stories about Niles Offborth, the man full of love and a heart of gold.

*Get a hold of yourself.*

With slow, intentional movements, his hands slide up my neck to my cheeks. And those stormy, oceanic eyes are squared solely on me.

"Have I really been your hero?" he asks.

"Yes."

Surprise washes forward like a morning ocean wave across his face. Even though he knew the answer, there's that piece of him that lacks the confidence to believe it. A small slice of self-deprecating thoughts.

"I've never been a hero to anyone."

He'll never know how sad that makes my heart, withering like a rose without the sun.

*Distance. Distance. Distance.*

Niles leans forward, placing a kiss on my cheek, gentle and cautious. I nearly faint at his soft lips hovering over my jaw. His breath tickling my face still trapped between his hands. I, on the other hand, can't breathe at all. My brain has commanded my body to stop functioning. To halt all progress. Every nerve ending puckers at his closeness.

"Please, Niles," I exhale, a mix between a moan and a whimper.

He brushes the tip of his nose over the corner of my mouth, lovingly, adoringly, like he's mesmerizing the smooth surface of my skin. And my eyes flutter close, blacking out the hysterical sounds drumming against my ears, the sweaty bodies riding through the high of the gas in the air.

His scent of sunshine has dimmed, the misery of this hell dampening his special fragrance. But as his nose brushes against my own, I catch the special aroma that is strictly Niles. Still there. Still sweet.

My clit throbs at the way he teases the closeness of our lips, the way he breathes cool air into my parted mouth, the way he rests his forehead against my own. I'm sucked into his atmosphere like a meteor plummeting to earth.

"Please," I say again.

He hisses as I press my breasts against his chest, grating against my erect nipples. A spark of glittering electricity travels the length of my spine.

"Ask me to do it." He places a light kiss on the corner of my mouth.

The self-control I have to not rip my uniform off is award-winning behavior. He traces his bottom lip over mine, so subtle I'm not even sure if we made contact.

The words spring from my mouth earnestly. "Kiss me."

Niles expels a breath of release as he dips his head down, capturing me in a kiss I've only seen in my dreams. It encircles me like a hurricane. He's everywhere. Hands on either side of my face. Hard edges of his body flattened against the soft planes of mine.

"Marilynn," he whispers against my lips.

And I open for him, tasting his air, the swift dip of his tongue. He kisses like it's an art, a graceful, elegant dance between partners. A conductor of a symphony. Every time he moves, I move. Head tilts, mine follows. Passion ignites my limbs, screaming through my bloodstream with pure excitement.

*He's kissing me. He's kissing me.*

It feels too good. Too right. Yet I know I'm supposed to pull away, to resist, to keep my distance. I don't like it. Not at all. Right?

He hooks his arm around my waist, swallowing me in his embrace.

And I'm going to tell him. That he is the greatest bedtime story. The sweetest dream. But a black smoke fills the air, and someone screams.

# 23. The People Of Vexamen

## Skylenna

Dessin blinks back to the front at the sudden shriek that stabs through the air. The dissociation takes longer this time. Zoning in and out. Through the drugs and scenery, he's colossally disoriented.

With a grunt, he pulls his cock out of me, inhaling that black dust because we have no choice. No time to run. No time to think.

It acts as a whirlpool, suctioning out the drugs that glazed over my brain, slowed my logical thoughts. An anti-ecstasy fog. A cure to the mindless sexual frenzy.

The scream pierces the stage again, causing another outbreak of panic. Prisoners grab their uniforms, running in every direction.

Dessin looks over my naked body before his thunderous eyes land on mine. He grips my waist, tugging me to him.

"I'm not getting separated from you again," he growls, heaving my body up and over his shoulder.

I don't protest as he covers my naked rear with his large hand.

Sprinting us off the stage with the rest of the bewildered inmates. Although hanging upside down, I still search for our friends. I can't imagine how horrified they must be by recent events.

"There you are!" Ruth pokes her head around Dessin's back to come face-to-face with me. Her face lights up with amusement. "Skylenna, you're naked!"

"Gag! Cover her up!" Niles pops up behind Ruth.

"I like when she's naked." Dessin's back rumbles as he speaks, and my cheeks flush.

"Put me down." I tap his lower back impatiently.

"*Mmm*. Nope."

"Fine, keep me on display for Kane's *brother*."

He sets me down immediately. Warrose laughs. And I scramble to pull my uniform back onto my body.

The Ringmaster appears on his special raised platform, surrounded by fire scorching the moist air. His speech is brief as a teenage boy dressed in a soldier's matte black armor, chains, and piercings steps onto the stage with a stoic look of confidence. His left arm is extended behind him, pulling a leather rope irritably.

I step forward with raised eyebrows. *What the hell?*

It's not just a leather rope. It's a leash. And it's pulling a woman in her late thirties across the stage. She crawls behind him with bruised, brittle knees, stained rags for clothing, and matted hair that hasn't seen a comb in months.

"Is this another weird sex thing?" Niles whispers.

God, I hope not. The look on her face says it wouldn't be consensual. She's gawking up at the crowd, tears collecting at the corners of her eyes, and stumbling to keep up as her leash is jerked forward. She chokes and gasps while falling to the ground, scrambling to crawl again behind the teenage soldier.

The teenage boy ties her leash to a wooden post in the center of the stage, ripping off her rags to expose her scarred, gnarled back.

The crowd cheers for the boy, and he grins up at the masses with a victorious fist in the air.

The Ringmaster starts shouting again, throwing his hands up, pointing at the leashed woman with menace glinting in his beady eyes.

"Ruth?" I look back at her watching the Ringmaster intently.

"The boy has been in training his whole life, keeping his mother as a pet to...*abuse*."

We whip our heads back to the mother. She's been abused by her own son? A pet on a leash? *What the fuck is wrong with this country?*

"That's fucked," Warrose grunts.

"This is his test before he can make it to the finals. He must degrade, humiliate, and whip his mother in front of the legions. If he shows any sign of sympathy, any hesitation, he'll be thrown into this prison as a faulty product, shamed for being incapable of joining the Vexamen Breed." Ruth circles her hand around my wrist, looking up at me with pleading eyes. "That poor woman."

There are female inmates sobbing around us, holding their dirty hands over their mouths to stifle the noise. It's the first time I stop to think. What were they convicted for? Are these prisoners here for failing to conform? Is this place like the Emerald Lake Asylum? Victims of a deranged patriarchy?

I bite down on my lip, looking up at Dessin, seeing the same dreadful contemplation hardening his jaw.

The woman begs in another language, trying to get her son's attention as he unravels a whip. The edges are laced with small blades. The handle is shaped in the head of a wolf, brass and aged.

"She's trying to remind him of the moments she held him in her belly, how she loved him before meeting him, how she'll forgive him no matter what," Ruth translates with a trembling voice.

Dessin clenches his fists so hard, they turn stark white. It's been a while since the veil of the void nudged at my mind, coaxing me to see what it has to offer. Looking at the hard lines on Dessin's face, I know the void is luring me to a moment only Dessin can see.

I mentally step close to the void, pressing my ear against the soft plasma of its border.

"*It's okay, sweet boy,*" Sophia says softly. "*You and Arthur are going to make it without me. I'll always be with you.*"

I remember the night by the lagoon. The night Dessin told me the start of their trauma. How Sophia told him everything would be okay. A mother's love in the face of certain death.

Dessin's eyes are red and murderous, glaring at the scene spinning out of control.

"I'll always love you, my son." Ruth chokes as her eyes fill with tears.

"No." I shake my head. "Stop…"

My feet move without conscious demand. And it's as if we are one soul, the way Dessin moves with me. Falling in step as I stride toward the wooden post, setting my focus on the quivering mother.

"No!" I shout, shoving past other inmates, leaping onto the stage as the teenage boy winds his arm back.

The mother's body bears down as the whip slices through the air, and—

Dessin's hand snatches the teenage boy's wrist mid-swing. The crowd gasps and stands at the sudden intrusion. The boy soldier appears genuinely shocked that anyone would disrupt this sacred ritual. His golden eyes stare into Dessin's with a thousand questions, yet no sound passes his lips.

"*Zasquátz nës Demechnef!*" the Ringmaster roars with a gaping smile.

I stand in front of the woman bowed to her knees, naked and terrified. With my chin held high, my eyes trace over the unusually quiet audience, meeting a few narrowing stares. Some taken aback in surprise. Others taunting, daring me to get myself into trouble. I find Kaspias in the top row with the other higher ranked soldiers. He slides his mask off, watching me with a blank stare.

"Pathetic," I shout loud enough to reach each corner of the stadium.

The Ringmaster raises his pointy chin.

"Maybe some of you can understand me. Maybe not. But for those who do, translate to your friends the carefully selected word: *pathetic.*"

The Ringmaster seems to translate, as well as many soldiers conversing in the stands.

"Pathetic because you think it makes you all-powerful to prey on those who are weaker. A mother. A child." I don't move an inch as I watch their faces, listening to those who can translate. "But maybe you can prove me wrong! You know who I am. You know the great and terrible Patient Thirteen. And yet we've taken down leagues of your own men. Not so all-powerful if you ask me."

"If you're so powerful, why are you nothing but a dirty prisoner in our country?" the Ringmaster asks me from his platform, accent twisted and thick, loud enough for others to hear.

I stare back at him, tempted by the void that grazes my skin.

"What makes you think we aren't exactly where we want to be?" Dessin's voice booms across the stage, deep enough to make the Ringmaster flinch.

The Ringmaster pauses before he releases a cruel, throaty laugh.

"You think you are so special, don't you? Then why don't you both take the mother's place at the whipping post!"

The crowd roars in agreement.

Dessin and I don't hesitate. We walk confidently to the post, unlatching the woman's bound wrists. She looks at us through heavy tears and confusion. I only nod, helping her back into her rags, shielding her naked body from her son.

The sentinels strap us to the post with rough movements. My hand is so close to Dessin's, I caress the back of his knuckles with the pad of my index finger. He looks at me from under his thick lashes, speculating about my expression to try and understand what I'm thinking. I smile up at him, nodding my head once.

There's a tangible connection that radiates between us. Like it's this right here. *This* is what we were sent here for. An empowering shiver races over every inch of me, filling my veins with explosions of adrenaline.

Dessin grabs my hand, entrapping it within his warmth, within the safety of his embrace. And neither of us fear the pain, fear the humiliation. Because this is our choice. And we make a decision in this moment to not to flee to the Ambrose Oasis. Not to let another alter take over. We'll feel it all.

"How strong are you now?!" The Ringmaster roars right as we hear something whistling through the air. Dessin's upper body barely flinches. Only a subtle jerk at first contact.

It whistles again, carving into my skin, feeling as though someone has dragged a dagger down my spine. I could scream. I want to. It's a way to relieve the pent-up agony forming in my lungs. But my eyes remain locked with Dessin's. It kills him to watch me suffer, but we both know I am no longer that shy girl he met in the asylum. I have released my dragon.

I can breathe fire.

"Watch the Demechnef heroes bleed!"

The stadium of belligerent soldiers drum their feet against the floor, creating the vicious beat of a war drum. They howl with murderous rage, desperate to see me cry, hear him beg.

I grip Dessin's hand harder as the lashes come fast, burning a hole through my back, into my ribs. I'm flexing every muscle, clenching down as the white-hot pain shoots through every cluster of nerves. Tears gather over my eyes, and I swallow them down. The stubbornness to show my strength overpowers the need to weep on this post.

"Stay with me," Dessin grunts under his breath.

"I'm with you." The words scrape from my throat, carrying the weight of my need to scream out.

The teenage soldier huffs and curses as he throws all of his youthful strength into each lashing. It's clear his only goal now is to show the world how weak we are. He won't stop until he hears us fall apart.

But that won't happen.

We've made our decision.

We are prepared to lose every scrap of skin on our backs. We are prepared to prove a point.

And the whipping goes on for what feels like another sixty minutes. My back is numb and lifeless. I'm hanging like a broken doll from my chains on this post. But I have not made a sound. Have not shed a tear.

The teenage boy is panting like a rabid animal, wheezing as he coughs from the excessive exertion. Something clatters and splats on the stage floor, and his footsteps storm our way.

My hand is sweaty and shaking in Dessin's grasp, but he never lets go. Never tears his eyes from mine.

The boy snatches me by my long hair, yanking my head back until I'm looking up at his glistening face, sweat dripping down his nose. With labored breathing, he screams something in my face, spitting as he over accentuates certain letters.

"Wait," Dessin breathes.

But the fist knocks straight into my bottom lip, then again into my cheekbone. I taste the bitter iron flavor.

Dessin thrashes against his restraints, firing off a string of profanities at the boy.

But my ears are ringing. My vision blurs. My head is slammed against the post, banging my brain around in my skull. I dangle from my chains in a delirious, throbbing heap.

The boy rears his arm back again, balling his fist, from which I'm guessing his goal is to knock me unconscious. He jerks forward, throwing his weight into his punch.

Dessin catches his fist, and the stadium falls quiet.

His knuckles turn white, gripping the boy's hand with a volcanic rage rising to the surface. Unsurprisingly, Dessin has managed to break free of his shackles. The notorious Patient Thirteen. The dangerous escape artist. And he is as agile as a mountain cat as he twists the boy's wrist backward, making a loud snap. The boy screams, falling to his knees.

"I'd like to watch her break your bones herself. But I'm not that selfless," Dessin growls in the boy's exhausted face.

But his sense of balance is tampered with too quickly. Dessin sways before hitting the floor, eyes glazing over as he stares up at the ceiling. Panic floods my lungs, stabbing me in the heart.

The boy uses his other hand to beat Dessin. Pounding his face with one clenched fist. Attacking a defenseless man into a bloody pulp. My bloodshot stare darts to our friends waiting on the sidelines. Warrose is about to lunge, hands gripping the edge of the stage. I shake my head at him.

The teenage soldier moves back to me, smearing blood across my face, then spitting in my eyes, degrading me in front of his superiors.

And I know this won't end until I lean into the void. This won't stop until I discover that one weakness. I'm hit once more, knocking me into that pit of nothingness until I see it. I witness the source of what cripples the boy. Of what forces him to freeze, to solidify into a paralyzing state of panic.

*There*. I see it.

Through my throbbing face, swollen bottom lip, and blood coated mouth, I laugh.

It bubbles out of me, like seeing him in attack mode is the funniest damn thing in the world. And I sell it like my life depends on it. My laugh becomes a wild cackle, and the boy is stunned upright. His balled-up hand pauses over my face.

I grin through bloody teeth.

"Suck. My. Dick."

The crowd erupts in laughter and disapproving booing. They throw their drinks and food at the boy, yelling words that sound like there isn't anything more offensive in their language.

Humiliation. When his victim laughs through pain.

That's the weakness.

And he can't move past it. Unable to process why his methods of violence are having the opposite effect.

Sentinels drag the stunned boy away as he has failed this test. And as they undo my shackles, I race to Dessin's side on the floor. He grabs my hand, letting me help him to his feet. And we're both struggling to remain conscious. Our backs are dripping long trails of blood. Our nerves morph into poisoned daggers, piercing every inch of muscle. And though our shoulders droop forward, our chins remain high.

And something strange happens.

A prisoner, an old woman with weather-worn skin and cloudy eyes, drops down to one knee, placing a fist over her heart.

Slowly, another drops down, then another, and another. Our friends are the only ones still standing aside from the audience of soldiers. I hold on to Dessin, who looks just as confused as I feel. We search the staggered sea of kneeling men and women, old and young, all wearing the same expression. Respect. Hope. Allegiance.

The Ringmaster bursts through the silence in outrage, ending the Fun House Night with a red face and waving arms.

We don't see it right away. Not until she screams. Two sentinels drag the mother back to the stage and knock her to her knees. She looks up at us with a grimy face and missing teeth. Confused. Scared.

And they attack without warning. Long, rusty machetes gliding through the humid air, driving straight through the woman's chest. Cracking into bone. Plunging past muscle. I fumble back into Dessin's arms as the blood sprays across my face.

"No!" I scream, but Dessin holds me to his chest.

The mother falls in a wet, bloody heap. And they keep stabbing, as if the more marks they leave, the more cheers they'll receive.

Bile surges up my throat, at my pain, at Dessin's pain, and at this violent, awful murder playing out before my eyes.

"She's already gone," Dessin whispers in my ear.

Tears blur my vision, smearing the color of her skin with the rich red streaks spilling out across our bare feet. Her body *jerks*, *jerks*, *jerks*, and she stops breathing rather quickly.

But through the combustion of disapproval, sentinels whip us back in line, kicking elderly prisoners to the ground to keep moving…

Dessin and I look at each other. An ancient knowledge revealing itself to us. A clarity as pure and old as time.

DaiSzek and Knightingale.

Dessin and Skylenna.

One and the same.

Born to fight.

*When there is battle of great evil…*
*God sends two warrior angels.*

# 24. Switching Cages

## Marilynn

I can still taste the flavor of Niles's tongue.

But the yearning relaxing deep in my bones is quickly replaced with concern as a small whimper escapes Skylenna's mouth. Dessin watches her with anger brewing in his deep brown eyes. He's hurting, too, but it seems that seeing the wounds on Skylenna's back hurts more than his own.

"What can I do?" Dessin asks.

Skylenna thinks on this. "Got any juicy gossip to distract me?"

"I can't say I do."

"Wait!" Ruth cries, rushing to stand in front of her cage door. "We do need *girl* time."

Dessin looks slightly disgusted. "Why?"

"To discuss the small girth of your penises!" Ruth shoots back. "And we'll clean Skylenna's back and take care of her."

Skylenna chuckles, then winces, and I can't help but grin at the way Warrose narrows his eyes at her.

"Small?" Niles gasps with a hand on his chest.

"*Yeah*, so we need time to ourselves to chat," Ruth adds with a shrug.

"She really said small," Warrose comments to Dessin in disbelief.

"Beat it!" Ruth waves her hands so they can pick the cages furthest away from mine. "And no eavesdropping!"

The boys saunter over to the last three cages as we hear Niles mutter, "I have a huge penis, just so you both know."

Ruth waves us into my cage. "Hurry!"

We take a seat with enough room for Skylenna to lie on her stomach, giving us access to the lash marks. Long welts fill with fluid, blisters peel open and leak small trails of blood. Overall, it looks like a bear clawed at her soft, tan skin. I peer between the bars to see Dessin swat away Niles trying to tend to his back. I noticed the rectangular scars on his back the first day in prison. I doubt he's in as much pain as Skylenna, considering those kinds of scars usually damage the nerves.

"How's the pain?" I ask Skylenna.

She gives me a feeble thumbs up, face pressed uncomfortably to the rough floor. We dab at her wounds with a bowl of soap and water. After the number of injuries, we've decided it's best to keep supplies ready in case of emergencies.

"I thought some gossip might distract you from the pain," Ruth sighs with mischievous eyebrows.

"I'm guessing there's gossip to share after the ecstasy dance…" Skylenna mumbles.

A flutter tickles the inner lining of my stomach. I've never had girlfriends. Never gossiped. Always kept secrets. It's how we were raised. But this feels…exciting.

"Yeah…" Ruth tucks a loose curl behind her ear. "But I'm feeling shy. Someone else go!"

"I was with Greyst—"

"Alright, fine, I'll tell you!" Ruth whisper-yells. Skylenna laughs, and I pinch my lips together, doing my best to suppress my smile. "Okay, lately there's been some tension with Warrose."

"Oh?" Skylenna tries to hide a shudder as we clean the dirt from a rather deep wound.

"Yeah, okay, I know he's big, gruff, and stupid…but we just have this banter, this chemistry."

"He's not stupid," Skylenna snickers.

I apply ointment in delicate strokes, smearing it evenly. Skylenna's quiet, closing her eyes against my touch. She has so much strength for someone so young. Her life has consisted of suffering, heartache, and loss. I would love to tell her about her future. About the many secrets I know that could put her mind at ease.

"No, he is an oversized imbecile. But also, he has really pretty hazel eyes, right? And his muscles are sort of massive," Ruth says as she blushes.

"He is attractive," I agree.

"We did some *inappropriate* things tonight." Ruth purses her lips in embarrassment.

"We know," Skylenna and I respond at the same time.

"You do?!"

"You almost sucked his dick at that dinner! And there were no sexually enhancing drugs in that food!" Skylenna lifts her head to grin at her best friend.

"You're wounded and delirious." Ruth guides Skylenna's face back down to the floor.

"So, what happened?" I ask.

Silence.

"You had sex!" Skylenna gasps.

"Ew! No!"

Skylenna raises an eyebrow.

"He, well, he kissed me."

"That's sweet," I say, shivering at the memory of Niles breathing against my mouth, kissing my cheek, my jaw.

"Not on my lips."

Skylenna laughs, then groans at the sting of her lower back. "Go on..."

"It happened between my legs."

"Oh!"

"Not those lips either," Ruth clarifies, twisting her features in hesitation.

"But you said between your legs?" I narrow my eyes on her.

"More specifically, between my...*cheeks*."

My mouth falls open.

"Holy shit! Warrose ate ass tonight!" Niles explodes on the other side of the cages, face pressed between two bars so he can hear us better.

"I said no eavesdropping!" Ruth hisses.

"Christ, you have a big fucking mouth, Ruth," Warrose barks.

Skylenna and I fall into silent hysterics, trying to calm Ruth down but too amused to successfully stop her from throwing a small pebble at Niles's head. And… I'm laughing. I'm laughing. I promised myself I'd keep my distance. Not to bond. Not to get attached. I know too much. I've resented the prophecy since day one. *Stop laughing!*

"Well, how was it?" Skylenna settles back down, nestling her head on top of her folded arms.

"I had an orgasm."

"That's always a good sign," I say, reeling my smile in.

"Okay, it was crazy! Amazing!" she whispers into her hands. "But what does it mean? Were we just messed up by that gas? Or did he really want to do that?"

I have the same questions for Niles.

"Did you ask him that?"

She shakes her head at my question. I don't blame her. What would I even say to Niles? Do you want to be with me? Was our kissing a fluke? A side effect of our circumstances?

Skylenna sighs, reaching out her hand to grasp Ruth's fingers. "Do you care about him?"

"No."

"Ruth," Skylenna scolds. "Sisters don't lie to each other. How do you feel about him?"

Ruth looks down at her friend for a long moment, letting the question burrow into her thoughts. She wipes her hands on her uniform, then combs through Skylenna's hair with her fingers, caressing her like a loving mother.

"I don't know the answer to that."

Skylenna closes her eyes and smiles. "Yes, you do."

"We annoy each other constantly," Ruth mutters stubbornly.

"And?"

"And argue a lot."

Skylenna and I encourage her to keep going with our silence.

"He thinks I'm high maintenance. He doesn't understand the standards from the Chandelier City that I grew up with. He's dirty and rude." Her sharp features soften slightly, gazing off into the dark hallway. "But he has a big heart. He loves animals, believes women are as strong and important as men, and is a very loyal friend."

There it is. I hadn't paid much attention to Warrose and Ruth since meeting them, but I suppose I should have. Knowing everything I know. I *really* should have.

Skylenna smiles with closed eyes. "Was that so hard?"

"Yes. I'm physically ill."

We laugh, readjusting in our spots to get comfortable. I guess we're sleeping together. Like a girl's night. A sleepover. An empty feeling stabs through my sternum, giving me the urge to cry.

"What's your face doing?" Ruth asks me.

I shrug. "This is my first sleepover."

"Really?" Skylenna opens her eyes.

I nod.

Skylenna glances at Ruth with a knowing smile. "If it's going to be a true sleepover...you have to tell us your boy gossip. How did it go with Niles?"

"Unless it's super sexual and graphic." Ruth holds up her hands. "He's like our brother. So you may want to leave those details out."

"He *is* our brother," Skylenna corrects.

A giddy feeling swarms my stomach. "We kissed."

"On the mouth? Or between the cheeks like Ruth?" Skylenna raises her eyebrows, and we all laugh.

"On the mouth. It was really... special."

"You're blushing." Ruth points to my face. "Do you like Niles?"

I didn't realize it before, but my cheeks are warm to the touch as if I've fallen asleep by a roaring fireplace. My mouth opens, then closes.

"You don't have to tell us," Skylenna offers sleepily.

"The hell you don't! Marilynn, in order for this to be a successful girl's night, you must give us the naked truth." Ruth scoots closer, burning holes in my eyes with the intensity of her stare.

"Uh—promise you won't tell him?" I suddenly feel bare, exposed, nervous beyond reason.

They both nod.

"I get really nervous around him." *And that's a fraction of the truth.*

"Oh my god," Ruth gasps into her hand. "She has a crush on Niles!"

"I heard my name!" Niles whips his head to us.

My eyes bulge out of my face.

"No, you didn't!" Ruth fires back.

Skylenna snickers. "Warrose is right, Ruth. You do have a big fucking mouth."

"Has Niles said anything to you two about me?" I ask in a whisper. Do I even want to know? Will it make a difference? *It shouldn't. It shouldn't. It shouldn't.*

"We haven't had much time for girl talk with Niles," Skylenna explains quietly.

"But we can ask him! He has a big fucking mouth, too. I guarantee he'll spill his guts about the whole thing!" Ruth claps to herself, grinning ear to ear.

"No!" I half explode. "I don't want him to think I sent you two."

"He won't. Niles used to see himself as Cupid when I met him in the asylum. He loves conversations about love and relationships. We won't give anything away," Skylenna promises.

"Oh, this is going to be so much fun! Can you imagine? Our little Niles getting a girl?" Ruth swoons, grabbing my hand and doing a little happy dance.

I can't stop grinning. "I feel like I'm going to throw up."

"Marilynn? Can I ask you a question?" Skylenna asks through a long, pained wince.

"Sure."

"What do you know about the void? About what I can do?"

I scratch the back of my head, remembering the way my mother used to describe it.

"Uh…I can only tell you about what you can do now. Not about what you will do."

Her eyebrows shoot to the top of her head. "You mean I'll be able to do more?"

I nod. "The way I was told is your brain reaches higher levels of frequency through new trauma. With more heartbreak, you break through a glass ceiling, resembling your purest form as a spirit. Right now, you've broken through the dimension we can see, astral projecting into unseen worlds only traveled to by ethereal beings. And with this ability, you're able to travel to the places of memories and psychological locations in any person's mind."

Skylenna hums to herself, processing my explanation. "And the hypothermia?"

"Your body can't exactly compete with the strength of your soul. Though your spirit is immortal and radiating with endless power, your body depletes when you perform something that extraordinary. Like being a judge, jury, and executioner on someone's mind and actions."

"I'll admit, there is a part of me that enjoys controlling the fate of my enemies," Skylenna says thoughtfully.

"So do I." A familiar voice blasts through the shadows of this wing of the prison.

Our cages go silent as we all look up to see Kaspias stepping out of the darkness, into the dim light of the flickering circus bulbs.

"How are our little heroes after their sad performance? Have we switched from human experiments to desperate martyrs?"

Skylenna lies her head back down as if his presence doesn't deserve her attention. Dessin, on the other hand, is on his feet, gripping the bars of his cage.

"Jealous?" Dessin asks with a knowing smile.

Kaspias glances in his direction and laughs to himself.

"Am I? After watching your precious Skylenna with her legs spread and mouth open, I'd say—"

Dessin roars, slamming his hands against his bars hard enough to bruise his palms.

"She wasn't the only one you were watching," Warrose growls between gritted teeth.

Kaspias lifts an eyebrow innocently. "You mean Ruth? Yes, I do take a liking to the way she comes to climax."

Warrose spits on the floor in front of Kaspias's feet, shouting a list of profanities. His veins bulge from his arms and neck as he paces Dessin's cage like a hungry lion.

Ruth goes still, gawking at Kaspias as he winks at her.

"Did you need something, Kaspias?" Skylenna murmurs in a careless tone, still not bothering to look up.

Kaspias is unreadable. The only sign of annoyance is from the twitch his hands make, as if they desire to close into tight fists.

"I'm here to warn my dear brother," he finally replies with a smile that doesn't touch his eyes.

"You don't have a brother," Dessin says coldly.

"Keep the rebel act up, and I'll be forced to break your hearts."

Skylenna releases a cruel laugh.

"You don't think I will?" His black eyes shoot down to her careless position.

At this, Skylenna finally turns to face him, making an effort not to wince in pain. She shows her dazzling teeth in a menacing grin.

"I don't think you have the balls."

His jaw tics. "No? Then I suppose I'll leave you with this little nugget to chew on. How well do you trust the members of your sweet little family?"

We pause in silence, processing his intent.

"You never wondered how we knew you'd be on the ship that day? How we captured you so effortlessly?" Now Kaspias is smiling. "It never crossed your mind that we might have been tipped off?"

Heat simmers in my stomach, boiling bile up my throat. I can feel the wheels spinning in their minds. They all know each other well. *I'm* the odd man out.

"Something to think about. Hope you don't lose any sleep over it," Kaspias purrs smugly, making his exit.

My mouth goes dry as I watch their eyes turn to me.

"He's trying to break our trust," Niles says, clearing his throat. "We trust everyone here."

Ruth nods in agreement, but Skylenna and Dessin don't take their eyes off me. They aren't so convinced.

"I swear you can trust me," I state with a whisper of panic in my voice.

Skylenna takes in a deep breath, lying back down. "When my back is healed, I'm going into the void. I'm going to find out for myself if we can really trust you."

My skin prickles with anxiety, but I nod. She can't see the secrets of the prophecy that are in my head, but maybe if I can convince her to be selective…

# 25. Pleasure Through Pain

## Skylenna

The cold water runs through the open wounds on my back like chilled acid.

"Breathe through it," Dessin says softly.

We stand under the broken pipe in the community shower, surrounded by other naked inmates, including our friends. I woke up this morning in my own vomit, shivering, hungry, and thinking someone had dropped a burning torch on my back.

"It burns," I tell him through a strained breath.

"I wish I could make you feel better, baby."

"Like you did when Meridei whipped me?"

He pauses in a bubble of his own thoughts, then groans. "Yes."

The sound of the rumbling in his chest vibrates down to the base of my spine, right between my legs. I look up at him, squinting as droplets of water splash across my cheeks.

"Would you do it in front of all these people?" I taunt.

His pupils dilate to wide saucers. "I would."

"Jesus, fuck, Dessin. Put it away," Warrose grumbles in disgust, abruptly turning his back to us. My eyes dart down to see his thick erection nearly grazing my lower belly. The head is a light shade of pink with precum glistening at its entrance.

I blow out a breath, meeting those hooded, dark-mahogany eyes.

"You can blame Skylenna. She's painting a very vivid picture for me."

"Maybe art isn't her calling," Niles snickers to Ruth.

"I wish I could get on my knees for you right now and take care of that," I whisper, feeling my nipples grow hard, puckering toward him.

Dessin growls at the idea, looking around at the many bodies minding their own business. And as his gaze drags across the room back to me, I know this is going to be a terrible decision. Because his mind is made up. His chest rises faster, lips parting, and he takes a step toward me.

"Dessin…" I warn.

"Greystone got to fuck you last night. It wasn't me," he justifies.

"But…"

"Please?" His brow wrinkles inward, and he looks kind of desperate. I melt a little, smiling at the yearning clouding his gaze.

"Did you just ask *nicely*?" I gasp.

"I can be nice."

"I don't think I've ever heard you say please. I was confident you didn't know that word existed. In fact, I'm still unsure if you understand its meaning." My cheeks flood with heat as I smile, fighting the need to release the laughter in my chest.

"Skylenna…" Dessin lifts his chin, using the deepest baritone of his voice. "I am so fucking horny. Will you please let me run my tongue over your clit? Let me take care of my girl."

My pussy slickens instantly, clenching in an unsteady rhythm. I should say no, and Dessin would respect my decision. I mean, I was fucked in front of so many horny soldiers last night. I was fucked *against* a horny inmate.

The thought of doing this in public should make my stomach turn like it's digesting rotten food. Right? I shouldn't be getting wetter and warmer thinking about doing this…

"Our friends…" I utter.

"Warrose, Ruth, Niles, and Marilynn. Will you form a perimeter so I can get on my knees for my girl?" Dessin commands the backs of their heads calmly. Like his request is natural. Simple.

Niles is the first to laugh.

"My god," Ruth gasps with a giggle.

"Fuck, *really?*" Warrose grits.

"Anybody want to deny me this after we've just been whipped?" Dessin growls in irritation.

Our friends form a circle around us, but there are only four of them. There are large gaps that anyone can see through.

"Are we having an orgy?!" Helga Bee bustles toward us with her huge breasts and beaming red face. Gerta pops up beside Niles.

"Ah, damnit." Niles drops his head.

"Just turn your backs to them and pretend like you don't hear anything," Marilynn says.

"This is an assignment? Gerta and I are happy to serve!"

Dessin skims his hands down the sides of my thighs as he lowers himself to his knees, lustful brown eyes boring up at me. He's so dangerously attractive as he caresses his hands up and down the backs of my legs.

"Sling your leg over my shoulder," he orders in a low voice.

As I lift my foot, I catch a glimpse of his standing cock. He's loving this. Basking in the view of me bearing my pink opening to him.

"Just lick once," I whisper sternly.

He bows his eyes to me in acceptance. Though it's not hard to spot his defiance as he squeezes my inner thighs. There's a wickedness as he stares into my exposure. A potent, primal haze bludgeoning his self-control from every angle.

"Fuck, I can see it slickening your entrance, baby."

"Are you going to gawk at it all day?" I clench up, suddenly very aware of the honey of my arousal seeping out of me.

"I just might." But he leans into me, using two fingers to part my lips gently, breathing me in as his eyes fall shut. I'm quivering, zapped with bursts of euphoria under his fingers.

"Dessin," I whisper-moan.

"One lick."

He kisses my clit adoringly, nuzzling his mouth against my wet center, as if he's stalling, prolonging, and building himself up to savor that one lick.

But the tease is blazing under my skin, firing up my lower belly. Muscles wind up tight, roasting as I slam my molars together at the irrepressible surge of energy funneling through my bloodstream.

I hear our friends making loud conversation to tune us out, triggering a sense of urgency in me to move this along. The teasing is a form of torture he loves to wield at my expense and now, at our friends' expense.

"Dessin," I scold under my breath.

He kisses my wet lips again, exhaling a gust of hot air against my tender clit. A spasm ripples up my pelvic bone, and my thigh twitches on his shoulder. How have my legs not given out yet? How am I still standing?

As if drunk, Dessin moves slower than he's ever moved, running his tongue up my center, slipping over my hole. It clenches open and closed in a teetering violence. My mouth forms an "O," and I have to grip his hair so I don't fall over.

The vibrations of his groan buzz straight up my soaking channel. It's mind-melting. A fever dream. An incineration of endorphins and drugs.

His movements stop, and I can feel his resolve slipping along with my own.

"One more," he justifies in that rolling, growly tone.

I don't stop him. How can I? He licks again, this time faster, with a ravenous aggression. The way a starving animal would devour its first kill in a cold winter. And it doesn't stop at "one more." No, because Dessin's eyes turn a shade of bloodshot, hazed and hooded, as he laps up the honey of my arousal. Primal growls humming against my clit.

And as I edge toward my orgasm, Dessin's tongue spears inside me, fighting the way my hole clenches randomly. He's gripping me so hard against his mouth that his hands spread my cheeks as he lifts me higher above him. My feet actually dangle an inch above the wet floor.

"I'm going to—" My face pinches up, mouth gaping wide.

But Dessin nods at something on the other side of me. And suddenly a thin hand covers my mouth, blanketing the howl blazing out of my chest. My orgasm ripples along my inner walls, fluttering happily against his tongue still inside me.

As my feet touch the ground again, I sigh contentedly at the way that orgasm, even if it was only for a short while, took away the sting in my back.

Ruth lifts her hand from my mouth, smirking with raised eyebrows.

"My bad," I say with fire cooking my cheeks.

She snorts and turns around once more.

It takes my eyes a moment to adjust from their dilated state, but as they shift downward, I see how engorged Dessin's dick is.

"Hey," I say, reaching to help him stand.

"It'll go down."

I shake my head. "I don't want it to."

He's standing at his full height now, gripping his long shaft in his fist in an attempt to relieve the tension. Desire reignites in my chest, and my mouth waters as I imagine tasting his tip. Hot, feverish electricity ripples through my channel, still coated with his saliva and the wetness of my orgasm.

"One taste?" I ask quietly.

His brooding eyes flick to me through the shower mist. He has no self-control in front of my naked body. The way his half-crest gaze slides down my legs tells me he's trying to find the strength and failing.

"Yes."

I'm dizzy as I lower to the ground, knees touching the concrete. My eyes trail over the dusting of hair across Dessin's legs, the water droplets puddling around his feet. A finger hooks under my chin, lifting my face. The spray of cold water blurs my vision, but I can still make out the hard lines of his face.

"Show me the inside of your mouth, baby."

Something tight and needy grows inside me. A knotted, dirty form of pleasure. I open my mouth wide, sticking out my tongue.

"Wider. I want to see your throat."

I unhinge my jaw, finding it difficult to continue making eye contact with my mouth stretched to the point of discomfort.

"Good," he rasps, taking the base of his erection with his fist. "Lick up the shaft. Clean the length of it with your tongue."

The muttering conversations, trickle of water, and feet splashing through puddles fills the room around me. It's as if I'm on the drugged gas all over again. My eyes roll back in my head as I clean the precum off the head of his cock.

Dessin groans, deep and coarse, like he's in pain.

My hands knead his balls as I lap my tongue over every inch of his shaft, leaving shiny trails of saliva. I try to keep quiet, but the moans of frustration come out in a hurry. I bounce on my heels, shifting forward to take in more of him, savoring all of it. The taste. The scent. I'm alive and drenched in flames, consumed by the high, yet still sodden and boneless from my last orgasm.

"What do you need, Skylenna?" he asks.

I'm delirious as I answer, "I want you to fuck my mouth."

I know, I'm a *really* bad friend for doing this here. In front of them. But we need this to survive. Our love. Our touch. It ignites fuel inside our souls.

"Please," I beg.

Dessin's muscles bulge, and his dick pulses with pent-up energy. He lets his head fall back. "Yes. Fuck."

I don't give him time to adjust. In one quick maneuver, I take him in my mouth. I nearly gag as his impressive length bumps the back of my throat. Dessin's large hands twitch, then wind through my tangled, wet hair, pulling it in a death grip. My tender scalp screams at the pressure, but it all feels so good. The pleasure and pain, the tension, and the aggression.

In slow thrusts, Dessin fucks my mouth. I only gag twice, drawing out long strings of drool that hang from my lips to the tip of his cock.

"*Fuck*," he growls.

My arousal drips down my inner thighs at his baritone turning to gravel.

Dessin's fingers wrap around my chin again, forcing my gaze up. "Let me see your eyes water," he commands.

I squirm, hot and humiliated, as I catch wandering eyes landing on me between our friends' legs. My clit aches at how wrong this is. People know what we're doing. And there is no gas falling from the ceiling to dictate our actions.

With another firm thrust, tears are dripping down the sides of my face, swirling together with the cold water from the ceiling pipe. I taste the slimy precum at the back of my throat, moaning at how good he tastes. Trying so hard to swallow him down. Take more of his length.

"Baby, I'm going to come." His breathing is erratic, heavy, and labored. "My cock gets so hard when I see you with your mouth full."

"On my chest, please." I pull away, stroking his hardness in between both palms, slowly, sensually, without taking my eyes off him. My other hand slides up the beautifully carved muscles of his abdomen. The trail of dark hair. His erection tremors, growing hard as he jerks forward, and a long white rope shoots over my breasts.

Dessin does his best to silence the deep sounds that rumble up his throat. Without breaking our gaze, I wipe a hand across my nipple, gathering his cum and reaching between my legs to spread it on my clit.

"Jesus," Dessin exhales. "I fucking love you."

"I love you back," I whisper.

We quickly use the water to clean my breasts, so our friends won't see. *But that ship has kind of sailed, huh?*

"I might have nightmares about this," Niles warns as we get changed back into clean uniforms.

"Leave them alone." Marilynn uses her elbow to bump him. But I glare at her a moment too long. I can't help but revisit my suspicion of her.

I understand Kaspias was probably just trying to create a divide in our family. It was a clever tactic. Because we need each other, our trust, our loyalty to make it out of here. What he said, and when he said it, was strategic. But that doesn't make it false.

Marilynn is the only person here who isn't an open book. Dessin has known Warrose since he was a child. Ruth and Niles are my very best friends. I trust them with my life.

But Marilynn was Aurick's fiancée. She hated Vlademur Demechnef for how he treated her. What's to say she didn't switch sides to Vexamen? What's to say her arrival in our lives wasn't at the exact time she knew we would get captured?

I shake my head, wincing as the fiery sensation washes over my back again. Being intimate with Dessin really did a lot of good as a distraction. But it's still here, like an unwanted shadow, pain, a familiar acquaintance that keeps resurfacing in my life.

As we walk to the commissary, Ruth thumps her shoulder to mine. She beams at me with humor and fondness blushing her cheeks.

"What?" I ask.

"I think our friendship just got elevated to another level," she states with a sweet smile.

"What kind of level?"

"The one where I've heard what you sound like with a penis in your mouth."

"Oh, god." I drop my face into my hands. "Between you and Niles, I'll never live this one down."

Niles pokes his head in between us. "It's true. Even when you're on your deathbed, I'll whisper in your ear just before you pass and say, *'Remember that time you had a pee pee in your mouth, and Ruth and I slowly bled out from our ears?'*"

Ruth cracks up as I shove him. "I have no one to blame but myself."

"That is true," Niles says, not helping at all.

"Okay, but I'll say this. I'm happy you and Dessin have such a strong connection and a good sex life. The only experiences I've had in the past have made me question if sex is only for the man." Ruth gives me a once-over look. "But clearly that's not the case with you two."

That's not the case at all. Sometimes I question if I want it more than he does. But then he does something like this in the community shower, and that thought flies out the window.

"Hey, so do you think I should compliment Dessin on his dick size? Or is that weird?" Niles asks genuinely.

"It's weird," Dessin calls before stepping foot into the commissary.

"He's a fucking witch! An alien with exceptional hearing!" Niles gasps.

"No, you're just *really* loud." Ruth and I giggle.

Walking into the commissary is strange. It isn't the normal noise levels, with conversations we can't understand from table to table. Everyone is quiet, watching, standing.

I look to the assembly line waiting for food, and I blink as they shift out of our way, letting us move to the front of the line.

"What's going on?" Warrose asks.

"I think it's because of last night. The punishment Skylenna and I took for that woman," Dessin responds as he inspects the food being handed to us.

"*Teserëzex,*" one of the cooks says to him.

"*Teserëzex.*" They hand the last plate to Marilynn, smiling and nodding at us.

"What were they saying?" Dessin asks Ruth as we stride to our table.

"Thank you," Ruth translates in a whisper.

The large room comes back to life with conversation as we sit to eat our food. It appears to be brown mashed potatoes, a gray hard-boiled egg, and a slice of stale bread.

"Not bad," Niles chimes, digging in.

Sitting in this cold, hard chair, I'm trying to keep my face expressionless. But these wounds from each grating lash I got last night are biting into my flesh with a red-hot agony I can't ignore. The pain radiates down my spine, curling into my scalp, tightening the muscles in my shoulders.

"Baby?" Dessin stops eating to peek at my expression.

I sigh. He always knows. "It really hurts."

He nods once. "When we get to the Regale Hour, let's ask Helga Bee for more of that honey milk stuff that she gave to Marilynn."

I blow out a pent-up breath, closing my eyes against the blazing sting.

"Tell me something I don't know about you," I say.

Dessin places a hand on my inner thigh, drawing small circles with his thumb as he thinks about this. "Do you remember that time you hugged me in the abandoned Demechnef building?"

I open my eyes, look down at my food. The time he found that homeless man on top of me. He snapped his neck. He saved my life.

I smile at him weakly. "Yes."

"That was the first hug I've ever gotten," he admits. That dark brown gaze sweeps over my face and shoulders before returning to my eyes.

I blink in surprise. *His first hug?*

Dessin rolls his two vastly muscular shoulders back. It's a subtle tell for him. A hint that he just became the slightest bit embarrassed about this fact. I was his first hug. *Me.*

"Really?" A slow blush creeps up my neck.

"I'm not exactly a huggable person, Skylenna."

"You're the most huggable person I know." In fact, I'd hug him right now if it wasn't for the pain beating into my spine. "I feel safe when your arms are around me."

The corners of his mouth tilt into a smile.

"You know...that moment you pressed your body against mine, hugged me like I wasn't the most dangerous person you've ever met...that's the first moment I started falling in love with you."

I bite my lip to hold back my grin. Why is that the most amazing thing to hear? Knowing what he was thinking at that exact moment. Pairing that thought with my own memory of holding him close, thanking him for protecting me. It's blissful.

"And what was the second moment?"

"When you came into my room and fell apart after Aurick—*hit* you," he grits out the last part.

"Why?"

He runs a hand over his jaw. "You started to cry; it reminded Kane of the times you'd cry to him after Jack did something bad. And I realized hearing you cry was the first moment I'd felt real heartbreak. It nearly took me to my knees. I wanted to kill Aurick and take away your pain at the same time. I wanted to make you laugh. Hold you. Kiss you. Heal your bruises."

Dessin exhales slowly, trying to rein in his anger and hurt.

I remember that day well. Sliding my hand over his, I give it a gentle squeeze.

"I didn't get emotional about that incident all day. Not until I saw you, Dessin. Just seeing the concern flash across your face made me break. It was like I finally felt safe, finally felt I could stop pretending." Tears gloss over my eyes. Relief courses through my veins as I remember this, confessing how much of an effect he had on me.

"You are the love of my life, Skylenna." He brings my knuckles to his full lips, leaving soft kisses on my fingers. "I'll be madly in love with you until the day I die."

"And even then," I promise.

# 26. The Biblical Bond

## Skylenna

As we sit in the stadium, I sip on the honey of Sweet Nectar Valley. Gerta rubs a milky substance on my back, and Dessin refuses to be next in line. After a few minutes of arguing, he lets Warrose put the cream in his wounds. And of course, Warrose doesn't help the cause when he makes jokes about getting an erection from all the creamy lathering.

"You okay?" I ask Niles. He's been quiet for several minutes, which must be some kind of record for him. He's sitting right next to me, legs crossed, fiddling with the iron collar and chain around his neck.

"Not really," he answers.

"Let's talk about it."

He shrugs. "It makes me nervous about what Kaspias implied last night."

"Me, too."

I glance over at Marilynn stirring more of the milky concoction for Dessin's back. Her features are soft yet striking. Shiny red hair, plump cherry lips, a face of freckles, and sapphire blue eyes that seem to hold so much knowledge. I had a weird feeling about her when she joined us on this voyage. Maybe I should have trusted my instincts.

"She's a good person," he claims warily. "I'd stake my life on it."

"I'm not sure I would."

Marilynn tries not to glance over at Niles, but I can tell it's hard for her. If she is a traitor, could it be that her feelings for him are being faked? Is she acting?

"You know our first night here, I woke up in a blinding pain from my burns. Marilynn didn't sleep that night because she put pressure on certain parts of my foot, relieving the pain for me so I could sleep." His brow pinches, and he rubs his eyes with a rushed exhale.

My heart gives a violent thump, and I gawk at him in surprise.

"I—I didn't know she did that," I say breathily.

Why would she do that for someone she didn't know? Was that all a ploy to get us to trust her? But if so, why wouldn't she share what she did with the group? Why be modest and keep it to herself?

"I can't believe she's a traitor. Kaspias had to be lying."

"Okay." I pat his knee. "Kaspias was lying."

Niles nods with a sniffle, and I know there must be more to his mood.

"Is there something else that's bothering you?" I ask.

Niles's attention is fixed squarely on the dirty floor under his feet. There's a sudden weight of sadness that drapes over his eyes, carrying a thick sheen of unshed tears. It begs for the bittersweet, chest-opening release that comes from finally crying.

"I miss Chekiss," he whispers thickly.

Damnit. Hot tears well in my eyes, too. "Me, too."

"We're his kids, you know that, right? He's probably so scared, Skylenna. What if he thinks we're all dead?" A strained sob breaks free of his tight hold.

"No." I shake my head fiercely. "He knows we're alive. He has to."

Niles covers his eyes with one hand, silently crying to himself. "I just want to give him a hug."

The tears overpower my lids, streaming down my cheeks. The heartache is tangible, a dull and quiet pain in the pit of my stomach. I'm afraid if I stay here too long, thinking about falling into Chekiss's arms, the grief might swallow me whole.

"We're going to see him again," I mutter wetly.

"Yeah," Niles agrees.

A soft pressure appears on top of my head, and a pair of hands pull my long hair back over my shoulder. A subtle breeze carries his familiar scent of cedar, reminding me of our days under the Red Oaks. Our adventures traveling through the forests of Dementia.

A final tear slips from my left eye as he sits next to me, wiping that tear away with his thumb. I smile sadly at his gesture, sliding my hand into his as he studies the glistening tracks of tears that run down my cheeks.

"I'm not crying, I had something in my eye," Niles argues to literally no one.

"It's okay, Niles. I miss Chekiss, too," Dessin says softly. So soft, so kind, so gentle.

"You do?" Niles arches an eyebrow in suspicion.

"Yes. And you can cry in front of me. I'm not Dessin."

My head perks up, turning to the tall man sitting next to me with wide, glossy eyes. I study his easy posture, his tender eyes, his caring expression.

"No…" I gasp, my heart doing a dance of cartwheels in my chest.

"I missed you, honey," Kane says with the sweetest smile in the whole world.

A desperate whimper bursts from my lips as I throw my arms around Kane's neck, careful not to touch his wounded back. He hesitates, his arms hovering over my back, quickly realizing he can't hug me the way he wants to. Kane settles for placing his hands on the unharmed skin at my waist.

I cry against his shoulder like a small child. "What're you doing here?"

Our friends stop talking among themselves as they try to understand my sudden outburst.

"I heard you cry," he murmurs against my hair. The heaviness in his voice strikes a nerve deep in my bones. A memory that used to be thin as smoke, now cold iron in my hands.

When we were young, Kane hated hearing me cry. He never said as much, but there were times that I had a bloody nose or a broken arm, and he'd pull me from the basement. I'd throw my arms around his neck and burst into a flood of tears, bawling against him in both relief and devastation. He'd hold me fiercely, stroking my long hair, telling me that I was safe.

I thought he was as immovable as stone. A strong, unbendable force. But one day, he had to step inside the basement because I wouldn't leave the corner I was planted in. It was then that he held me, and he shivered. In the reflection of two mirrors, I saw that he was in tears. Shuddering as he soothed away my demons.

And it's in the storm brewing beneath those coffee-colored eyes, the way his massive shoulders slump forward, the damp heat permeating from his hands.

Kane still hates to hear me cry.

I weep harder, my tears dripping down his chest.

"I'm sorry I haven't been here," he rasps unevenly.

"It's okay," I whimper. "You're here now."

Kane pushes me an inch away from our embrace, cupping my face like I'm a breakable little doll. A fragile treasure he wants to keep safe from the rest of the world.

"I can't stay long." The long line of his throat ripples. "I told you I had a bad feeling before we left for the ship."

I take my hands off his shoulders to wipe my eyes, soothe the puffiness in my cheeks.

"You were right," I mutter sadly.

If we never came here, I wouldn't be separated from DaiSzek or Knightingale. Chekiss wouldn't be worrying himself sick. I'd get to see Kane all the time.

"I have another bad feeling, honey," he warns, planting a small tickle of uneasiness in my stomach.

"Really?"

"Mm-hmm. We need to get out of here." The cords in his neck pull taut, and as his jaw hardens, I can see he's grinding his teeth.

I let out an exasperated breath.

Kane takes a hesitant look around. "I can't stay long," he repeats.

Tears rush back to the surface as I comprehend saying goodbye right now. I feel like a little girl all over again, watching Young Kane close the secret basement door, shutting me back into the cold darkness.

I used to wave to him as I bawled loudly, hiccuping in uncontrollable gasps for air. I knew it broke his heart to leave me, too.

"Dance with me before I go?" he asks with his forehead pressed to mine.

"Okay," I sigh, rising to my feet, not caring if anyone thinks we're nuts for this.

Kane places a warm, large hand on my waist and reaches for my right hand. He rests his chin on the top of my head as I snuggle into his chest. We sway in silence.

"*As old as night, was it a star that was split from shining too bright?*"

I peek over Kane's shoulder to see Warrose closing his eyes, singing for us. A rugged harmony building into a haunting rhythm. Warmth that can only be summoned by the love of family spreads from my scalp to the tips of my toes.

"*Oh, heaven's sweetest answer. Oh, heaven's greatest treasure. Come to me, my soaring mate, for I have no wings to reach you. We were made to follow fate, not even the devil could undo.*" Warrose's voice carries, raspy, deep, and soulful. The notes shift through him, settling a lull over all of us.

I close my eyes against Kane's chest, breathing in sweet memories that radiate from his skin onto mine. Bathing in the Red Oaks lagoon. Climbing trees. Chasing DaiSzek. Sleeping under the stars.

"*Would two flames be born just to collide? Oh, oh, oh, come to me, my sinking mate, for I have no boat to reach you. We were made to swim with fate, not even the storm could undo.*"

"I love you, Skylitte," Kane whispers, slightly detached.

In a panic, I reach up to my tippy toes, desperate to kiss him before he leaves the front. Kane blinks in surprise at my brisk movement but closes his eyes to press his warm lips against mine. I sniffle as I open my mouth for him, feeling only a beautiful surge of love plow through my body.

In a blink of an eye, we're standing in Ambrose Oasis. But somehow, it's different. The sky is a soft shade of indigo, the stars twinkle through the misty clouds in the middle of the day, and everything is at peace.

I gasp, and it's like it never happened. We're back in the stadium.

We're standing in front of our friends, Niles and Ruth wiping tears and grinning up at us. And Warrose is still singing.

"Did you see that?" I ask, but the surprised look on his face tells me he did.

"What was that?"

A booming sound blasts through my ears, making my brain vibrate, my world tilts on its unstable axis. And I have to slam my hands over my ears to try to muffle the sound. It doesn't work. The sound roars through every fragment of my being. I fall to my knees in crippling shock.

"Skylenna?"

The sound crashes through me. A warning. An alarm. A horn of something almighty.

"What's wrong?" *Dessin.* It's Dessin kneeling in front of me, hands gripping my shoulders. Those dark irises pinning me down with concern.

"That noise!" I hiss. Don't they hear it?

"What do you hear?"

"It's so loud!" I stutter, gasping for air.

"Skylenna, focus. What is the noise?"

I shake my head. *I'm going to faint.*

"Visualize the sound, baby. Tell me what it is."

I squeeze my eyes shut. Letting the earthquake pull me under. It's enormous, great in power, like a…

"Lion," I choke out.

"A lion?"

"No," I say, letting the beast's roar form in my head to completion. "A RottWeilen."

"DaiSzek," Dessin exhales.

His colossal howl rumbles across an ocean to reach me. I can see the ripples of dominance his voice carries. I sway with dizziness, grasping at what he's trying to tell me. It's urgent. It's fierce. It's shining like a lighthouse in a storm, piercing through space and time.

"He's calling to me," I finally state, realizing everyone is huddled around me.

"Is he trying to tell you something?" Dessin pushes his question like it's life or death.

"Yes!" I lean into that beautiful, terrible sound, begging to understand his meaning. And it hits like a meteor shower. "He's coming for us!" I nearly scream. "Oh, Dessin! He's coming for us. He's not alone! *Oh my god!*"

Ruth is the first to jump to her feet with an squeal of excitement. The rest of our friends follow her lead. Warrose whoops with a fist in the air. Niles leaps with Marilynn in his arms. It's a combustion of happiness, relief, and love.

Dessin stares at me, breathing hard against my mouth.

"He's not alone?" he asks with joy and hesitation clouding his dark gaze.

I breathe in the RottWeilen's cosmic call, examining its depth, its range, its coded message.

"He has a great number at his back!" I remember what I told him when I visited Knightingale and him on the beach. "He did what I asked! He gathered the colonies." My voice breaks off at the end, twisting into a happy cry.

Dessin grins, kisses me feverishly, then pulls away in thought.

"Judas said there would be a war," he speculates.

I look away. "Six months." That was what our coded messages from him revealed. How long has it been since we were in that asylum?

"This has to be it." He runs his fingers through my hair. "We're going to make it out of here, baby. We can't let DaiSzek do all of the heavy lifting for us."

Electricity passes from my breath to his.

"It's time we made our move."

# 27. Buixezez

## Dessin

Skylenna sleeps in my cage tonight, lying across my lap as I apply cream to those gaping slices across her back. The blisters and welts have gone down, the bleeding has stopped, and my girl only winces a little against my thigh.

"How's that?" I ask her softly.

She groans in response.

"No more beatings when we get out of here, okay?" I lightly press cream into the longest lash mark down her spine, watching the fluid ooze out of her from the pressure. "When this is all over, we're going to only know comfort."

"Hmm," she coos with her eyes closed. "Where are we going to live?"

"I told you I'm going to build you a castle."

She nods. "That'll take time. Can we start with a cottage in the Red Oaks?"

I feel Kane sigh close to me, letting his eyes fall shut as he imagine the beauty of a life in peace. "I'd like that."

Everyone is blustering with excited conversation. The entire group took a sigh of relief the moment we were able to imagine DaiSzek striding in to save the day with an army at his back. Well, everyone but Niles. I watch him. He's lying on his side, brows scrunched together, trying to sleep.

Since when does Niles stay out of socializing?

"What is it?" Skylenna brings me back, following my eyes. "What's wrong with him?"

I shrug.

"Is he sick?" she asks again.

"Who cares? It's Niles," I reply coolly.

Skylenna doesn't respond with words, only a glare that snags my attention and pulls a defeated exhale from my lungs.

"I don't know," I say, using my thumb to smooth the worry lines from her forehead.

"Oh? I guess you've lost that special talent, huh?"

My eyebrow lifts. "What are you talking about?"

"The infamous Patient Thirteen who could study the body language of his victims, examine their strengths and weaknesses based on the way they walked, a spot they scratched. Right? I guess you've lost it." She shrugs, settling back down on my lap with a yawn.

I roll my eyes to the ceiling. "Well played."

She smiles against my leg.

Turning my focus back to Niles, I tune out the rest of the prison, carefully examining his small movements, heart rate, perspiration, muscle twitches, and the rhythm of his breathing.

"He's...upset," I say slowly.

"About escaping?"

"I can't read minds."

She laughs, and the sound reaches into my heart.

"No, he's not scared or anxious. More like his feelings are hurt," I clarify.

"Is that as much intel as your small brain can identify?" she taunts.

Greystone laughs close to the front, filling my thoughts with dirty intentions. Kalidus is near too, infecting my personality with cockiness.

I accept her challenge with a male eagerness to impress her.

My brain is a complex web of memories that I'm unable to forget. At least, the ones not including what other alters have experienced. I comb through the many obnoxious moments with Niles in the prison. I don't land on anything that would explain why he has his feelings hurt now. But maybe that's because I don't speak the theatrical language of Niles.

Skylenna taps her fingers against my kneecap impatiently.

I dig deeper. I sift through my memories of him in the asylum. I studied the other patients from their files. I didn't want to go into the intricate section without being completely prepared. I see his file opening in my hands in the dead of night, remember scouring his name and diagnosis. His file stood out to me because I could relate to his identity crisis.

The rest of the information is useless. Treatment plans. Notes of behavior. I almost close the file before the top right corner stands out to me. I blink in surprise.

"What is it?" Skylenna asks, watching my face diligently.

"What's today's date?" I muse, quickly counting back from the days since we arrived.

"Uh."

The dates connect, and the light goes off like fireworks in my mind. I chuckle, shaking my head.

Skylenna is sitting up now, eyes wide with curiosity. "*HA!* I knew you could figure it out."

"It's his birthday tomorrow." I shake my head. I don't remember when the last time any of my alters have celebrated a birthday. We have a lot of them.

Skylenna gasps, putting a hand over her mouth.

"He thinks no one is going to know, Dessin! His feelings are hurt!"

I smirk, imagining how entertaining it will be to watch him pout through the prison tomorrow. "Yeah."

She swats my arm. "Knock it off."

I stare at her in surprise. "This is prison. We aren't celebrating a fucking birthday. Especially not for Niles."

Her grimace is actually kind of scary. I pinch my lips together, leaning back an inch.

"We're celebrating my *brother's* birthday," she says, ice coating each syllable.

I glare back at her, unwilling to fight this fight. These desperate times call for desperate measures.

"Fuck," I breathe.

Skylenna grins, doing a little dance in her seated position.

"What's on the agenda, Captain? You want to bake him a cake and sing to the baby boy?" I roll my shoulders back, grimacing at the thought.

And fuck me, her big, emerald-green eyes light up.

"Dessin, we have to bake something!"

"No."

"Yes!"

"The only thing we're baking in these cages is irritable bowel syndrome from the food they've been killing us with," I deadpan.

She snorts. "Okay, funny guy. Seriously, get us out and to the kitchen. I know you can."

I can already sense the beginning stages of a massive migraine.

"What are we conspiring to do?" Warrose leans against his rusty bars, raising his thick brows at us.

"It's Niles's birthday tomorrow. We're breaking out to bake him something sweet!" Skylenna whisper-hisses.

"Oh." Warrose chuckles softly. "I'm out."

Skylenna narrows her eyes. It's both adorable and bone-chilling. "You're both pissing me off."

Warrose darts his confused hazel gaze to me, seeking answers to what we should do or say to weasel our way out of this one.

I lift a shoulder, chuffing out a laugh. "If I have to cater to Niles, then you certainly have to suffer with me, brother."

"Dessin, you're in charge of our escape to the kitchen. I'll be in charge of event coordination. And you'll be the lookout, Warrose!" Skylenna wiggles in her seat, beaming with excitement. Even if it is *Niles* of all people, how can I take this from her? She's so happy.

Warrose scoffs. "How am I reduced to lookout?!"

"Can you bake?" Skylenna crosses her arms.

"No."

"Then lookout it is!"

I smirk at my friend now pouting with his mouth open.

Niles is full-on snoring, out like a light, and we have about an hour until we need to break out of this cage. The first time I escaped to bake the cook in her own oven, I found a twisted piece of metal in her pocket. A makeshift key to the cages. To be on the safe side, I shoved it in a small gap between the floor and the wall at the back of my cage. I knew I'd need it when we finally figured out how to make a break for it.

Never would I imagine risking losing it to throw Niles a fucking birthday party.

I work out the fine details of making it past the sentinels on night guard, slipping into the kitchen, how long it will take to assemble ingredients, oven time, cool time, and how quickly we can make it back without anyone noticing.

The birth of Niles could add a strike closer to the executioner's block if we're caught. Is it worth it? *Mmm*, probably not.

But making my girl smile is.

"How long do we have until you're breaking us out?" Skylenna asks.

"Nineteen minutes now," I answer, then give her a side-eye. "How'd you know I already planned it out?"

She shrugs. "You had that look."

"What look?"

"The one where you've just worked out a problem."

I start to smile. "You know me that well?"

"Don't flatter yourself," Skylenna says with a small laugh. "I had to learn the language of your expressions when you kept so many secrets."

My face falls.

"*And* you have a handsome face. I watch you a lot," she adds with a shy smile.

*Good save.*

After the nineteen-minute mark passes, I fish the piece of metal out from its secure hole in the wall and thrust my hand around a bar at the front of my cage, jiggling it into the keyhole to unlock. My cage door clicks open, and I step out.

Warrose and Skylenna gape at me with wide eyes.

"How long have you been able to do that, you piece of shit!" Warrose yell-whispers.

"I'm getting flashbacks to the thirteenth room." Skylenna laughs.

I open both of their cages swiftly. We only have two minutes to get from here to the kitchen without being caught.

"Wait!"

I turn on my heel to see Marilynn waving at us. We walk to her cage, leaning in with raised brows.

"I know it's Niles's birthday. Can I help?" she begs.

I peer back at Skylenna. Her lips are pinched together. Those glowing green eyes suspicious. Unsure.

"I promise to stay quiet," she adds, licking her full lips.

"Can you bake?" Skylenna asks.

Marilynn nods with a glimmer of hope in her eyes. "I love to bake. It's all I did when I lived alone."

Skylenna sighs, glancing in my direction with a hurried nod.

"We have one minute and fifteen seconds," I announce in a hushed tone. Without letting the cage door screech, Marilynn slips out like a thief in the night.

We decide to leave Ruth sleeping next to Niles in case he wakes up. She won't be happy that we've left her out of the plan, but someone needed to stay here with him.

I account for the shift changes, the patterns of the Blood Mammoths that walk these halls. Over the weeks we've been captive, I've studied it all. Thankfully, those wretched creatures are fond of blind routines.

The lights are off in the commissary, so we're vigilant to slip around the tables and chairs, reaching our hands out to find our path in the dark. Warrose curses as he stubs his foot on a table leg. Skylenna snickers at his expense.

I have a countdown ticking in my head. There isn't time to do anything other than what I had planned, down to the second.

We flip on a few lights in the kitchen, searching through the ingredients to see what we have available to make.

"Not much to choose from," Marilynn comments, snagging what she can from the pantry.

"What are our options?" Skylenna asks.

"Pancakes…"

"Oh." Skylenna's shoulders droop. "Are you sure?"

Marilynn pauses, drumming her fingers against her bottom lip.

*Tick, tick, tick.*

"I think I can make a cake from the pancake batter and frosting from…ah, there it is." Marilynn fills her arms with ingredients, passing us jars to set out on the dirty table for her.

I'm relieved at how fast she mixes the ingredients with Skylenna's help. After the oven is heated, they slide in a metal container and clean up their mess.

"We have company!" Warrose races in the kitchen.

No. That's not within the perimeters of time we have. *Who is it?* Did they hear us?

"Lights off," I command. "Everyone under the table."

Everyone scrambles to crawl under the table. I flip the lights off, crouching low in a corner. The footsteps are light, and the pattern indicates it's a woman, around one hundred and forty pounds. The rhythm of her breath is slightly labored. She's older. Fifties perhaps.

My eyes grow wide as I notice a glowing light hovering closer, illuminating the doorway.

*I'm going to have to kill someone again.*

As the soft yellow light floods the kitchen, I lock eyes with the older woman. She's wearing a white hat. The new cook. Her sleepy facial expression doesn't change. No shift in the muscles of her forehead. No startled blinks. She isn't surprised to see us.

"*Canux é hoiex?*" she says, lifting her tone at the end, indicating a question.

*Help.* I recognize that word.

"*Buixezez,*" I respond, hoping I pronounced it right.

The older woman with a round face, olive skin, and fluffy brown hair, lifts her chin in understanding.

"*Canux yé dequexez tuex?*" I know that's not right. But I hope she pieces together what I'm trying to ask.

She nods twice and says a full sentence I can't translate for the life of me. I flip on the lights so we can finish. Skylenna gives me a few strange looks as she helps remove the cake from the oven and finishes the frosting. We rush out of the room, hoping the cook understood the assignment I gave her. Otherwise, this was all for nothing.

"Be honest, have you known how to speak Old Alkadonian all

along, or have you been learning while we've been here?" Skylenna finally asks as we jog back to our cages.

"I've been picking it up, committing Ruth's translations to memory."

Warrose laughs behind us. "Don't tell Ruth."

I wasn't planning on it. It's the one area she feels useful in. Plus, I'm not fluent in the slightest. It's a complex language with a lot of variations based on intent and circumstance. I'd need to see it written, to understand the grammatical practices.

We need Ruth, even if I can pick up on words and phrases.

We'll always need Ruth.

"What did she say?" Marilynn asks from my left.

"I think she asked if she could help or if we needed help."

"And your response?"

"I told her the word *birthday*. And asked if she could deliver it to our table." At least, I hope that's what was asked.

Ruth is awake by the time we return, looking pissed, confused, and like she's about to explode with questions. Loud ones. The kind that will wake Niles up.

"*Shhh.*" Warrose kneels next to her. "It's for Niles's birthday."

"Why wasn't *I* included?" Ruth hisses.

"Someone needed to stay with Niles," Skylenna answers, closing my cage and settling in.

"Great. So I was a prop in this adventure." She rolls her eyes, laying back down.

"I was a lookout. Join the club," Warrose grumbles.

Skylenna and I lay side by side on our stomachs, gazing into each other's sleepy eyes. She rests her thin hand over mine, stroking my knuckles.

"Promise you'll be nice to him tomorrow," Skylenna murmurs through a yawn.

"That is a tall order."

"Dessin…"

"He asks for it, baby." He does. He *really* does. Niles is a long list of adjectives that fall into the same category as annoying and obnoxious. Being nice to him for an entire day would cost me dearly.

"For me?" She flutters those long, wispy eyelashes.

I curse, surrendering to her request in quiet indignation. Skylenna grins at the look of defeat on my face, squeezing my hand twice. As her eyes go half-crest, I don't miss the signs of a concussion popping up one by one. She shielded her face from the light in the kitchen, as if it physically pained her. That boy at the whipping post bashed her head in during the beating. She vomited twice while she thought no one was looking.

I'll take care of her.

I'm sick to death of watching my girl hurt.

Before I drift off to sleep with her, I raise my head to look over at Ruth and Warrose, still awake, still talking.

"Ruth?" I whisper.

Her curly brunette head perks up, eyeing me over Warrose.

"Can you translate something I heard tonight?" I ask.

Ruth nods, waiting to hear it.

I relay the sentence the cook said to me in the best accent and pronunciation I can manage. Ruth's soft brown eyes glaze over as she listens, finding the right words in her head.

"It means… *'The mother you took the whipping for was my sister. I'll not forget your sacrifice.'*"

# 28. The Other Night

## Ruth

"You could have snuck me out to help," I argue.

Warrose rolls his eyes, crossing his heavy arms over that seemingly three-foot-wide chest. His shiny black hair fans out on the rocky stone floor around him.

"Don't give me shit," he grumbles. "You heard Skylenna. Plus, you were already dead asleep."

*Yeah, yeah, yeah.* I don't care. Niles is my best friend, too. I had no idea it was his birthday tomorrow. I want to be a part of whatever was planned. Seriously, Dessin doesn't even like Niles. Why did he get to help and not me?!

"You're grinding your teeth," Warrose adds.

My jaw stops moving, and I grimace in his direction.

"Mind your business," I shoot back.

The left side of Warrose's mouth quirks upward, curling in a reluctant smirk. I force myself to peel my eyes away from him as we lie in our cages in silence. Dessin and Skylenna have fallen back to sleep and Niles snores softly to my left. It's just the two of us.

After a few minutes, Warrose's eyes are closed, and his chest moves up and down in the heavy rhythm that usually means he's finally away from here, dreaming.

I rub my hands roughly against the backs of my arms, summoning heat as my skin prickles. It's so cold here. Always so cold. I shiver throughout the night, tossing and turning on the rough floor, scratching and cutting into my skin until I'm raw and sore. I'd give anything for a blanket, soft and warm. A thick comforter like the one Skylenna had on her bed in Aurick's mansion.

My bones shudder at the thought of being cocooned. I'd even settle for sleeping in the forest next to a fire that Warrose built for Chekiss, Niles, and me. That was nice. We'd listen to crickets, feel the simmering fire warm my toes, and when Warrose thought I was completely asleep, he'd pull my wool blanket to my chin.

He was gruff, rude, and anti-social. But there were moments I found sweet enough to make me look at him for long moments when I knew he wasn't paying attention.

"Ruth?"

I turn my head to see Warrose with his eyes still closed.

"Yes?"

"Are we ever going to talk about it?" he asks in a scratchy, sleepy voice.

"About what?" I *really* have the nerve to ask.

He glances at me from the corner of his eye, once, twice, stares at the ceiling without blinking. His left hand flexes against the charcoal ground, but it's so quick I barely catch it.

"The Ecstasy Dance," he says.

I release my breath slowly, so it isn't heard as a sigh. *The Ecstasy Dance.* Flashes resurface in my mind in a single blink. Being grabbed by multiple male inmates, tossed to the ground, hearing my name yelled in that husky baritone. Feeling Warrose's body shielding my own. Fireflies swarm my chest, leaving tingly eruptions in their wake.

I shift uncomfortably.

"What about it?"

At those three words, Warrose turns his head to face me abruptly.

"*What about it?*" he repeats, offended. "Are we still doing this?"

My gaze rips away from the sheer impact of his question. The bluntness of the topic he's trying to form into this conversation. And he doesn't avert his eyes at my sudden retreat. I can feel all of him burning his question into me through the bars.

"Say what you want to say, Warrose," I answer casually. "Be a man, and spit it out."

*Don't say it. Don't say it. Don't say it.*

"You asked me to promise you that what we were doing wouldn't end when we left that stage."

*He said it.*

I've been dreading this conversation every moment since it happened. What was I thinking, making him promise something like that with everything that was influencing us in the moment? What was wrong with me?

Embarrassment sets the nerves of my spine on fire. But I sound aloof as I say, "And?"

His gleaming hazel eyes just widen as his jaw tics.

"And I want to know how you feel about that." His nostrils flare wide.

"I was *drugged*." My words seem to spear through his chest. The impact of the way that sentence lands is almost visible as he flinches back.

"Then I'm sorry for the way I acted," he states, voice full of shame and regret. "I should have controlled myself better, Ruth."

I turn my head back to him, unable to blink away the astonishment tightening my expression. "Warroseyou don't have to be sorry. We were both under the influence of that gas. You did nothing wrong."

He shakes his head with that stubborn gaze. "No, I fucked up, Ruth. I could have stopped myself. I knew it was wrong." He closes his eyes for three seconds. "I fucked up."

I'm sitting up on my elbow now, shaking my head repeatedly. What is he saying? What have I done? I've made him feel like a predator for touching me. He wasn't. I wanted it. *Goddamn it.*

"Warrose, stop!" I reach for his arm through the cage, managing to grab hold of his wrist. "I begged you to touch me because I *wanted* you to."

His jaw flexes, but he remains silent.

"I wanted it. I'm sorry. I was embarrassed about what I said because I didn't know if you'd want it outside of that stage or not." My throat is a desert. I swallow dryly. "*I* fucked up."

Some strange emotion flickers in his brooding gaze, his rigid expression loosening for a single moment before icing over again.

"You don't need to try and justify my actions. I should have been stronger for you. I'm fucking pissed at myself."

No. We're not going to end the night like this. We can't.

I sit up, pressing myself against the bars. Warrose can't help but watch my hurried motion, his gaze switching from one of my eyes to the other. And I catch him off guard, reaching my arms into his cage to latch on to his wrist, dragging his hand up to meet my face.

"I was just scared you didn't want it, War." I gently place his calloused palm over my cheek. Absorbing his warmth falling from his skin in soothing waves.

Warrose stares at me with confusion and hesitation glimmering in his amber-and-sea-colored irises. His eyebrows scrunch together at an upward angle. And he doesn't seem to know what to do with his fingers.

"The gas helped me reach for what I wanted. That's all." I lean the weight of my head into his hand, closing my eyes. Tingles race under the area he's touching.

The muscles in Warrose's back and abdominals contract and bunch together as he sits up slowly, unable to tear his sharp, piercing gaze from mine. Like a dormant animal stirring awake.

"And what do you want?"

Even though I'm on my knees, he's sitting up now, towering over me, looking down at me with lowered lashes and parted lips.

"Not what," I breathe. Out of nowhere, tears swell over my eyes, blurring my vision of him. And I say it in a wet exhale, "Who."

Warrose shudders as he traps my face in his other hand, pulling me flush to the bars until his lips melt over mine. He...kisses me. Warrose actually *kisses* me.

Our faces bruise as we push ourselves so close, it's as if our kiss can bend iron. Command metal to shift. His thick fingers massage into my hair, against my scalp. And his kisses are both sweet and urgent, like we're under a limited amount of time to have this. To share energy and heat and the thoughts we've been feeling since we first met.

He presses his thumb to my chin, and I part my lips for him, opening my mouth so my breath can collide with his. He licks along the plumpness of my bottom lip, and I go weak in his hands, moaning my need to rip these bars from standing in our way. I wish we stayed in the same cage like Skylenna and Dessin. He could have me in his arms, lowering me to my back.

"My god, Ruth," he groans, smelling like an aged bottle of spiced rum and the fires he used to build us to stay warm in the woods.

The excitement that his voice sparks makes me want so much more. My tongue dips into his mouth slowly, hesitantly. And he pauses, only for half a second before his tongue meets mine, tasting and sensually caressing me with his kiss.

My poor heart. My weak, pounding heart.

But blood rushes other places, too. My legs wobble, my lower belly is scorched with tingles and desire. If possible, it's so much stronger than the night on that stage. My heart is in this. And we're not surrounded by stands of soldiers gawking.

It's only us.

# 29. The Best Day Of The Year

## Niles

I startle awake as the cages open automatically. A stampede of soldiers rush through the long hallway toward the showers, bare feet slapping against the stone floors, bodies of all shapes and sizes bump into each other in a haste to get to the front of the mob.

"Morning," Ruth says through a long yawn, stretching like a lazy cat.

I respond with an unenthusiastic smile.

As usual, we wait to exit our cages until everyone clears out, starting a walk behind Dessin to start our day. I look around at my friends, watching silently as they have their morning conversations. Dessin grumbles something I can't hear. Skylenna snickers, giving him a small shove. Warrose and Ruth don't say a word as they fall in step with each other.

There are far too many snide comments that flow through my head as those two awkwardly steal glances. Brown and hazel eyes clashing. *Did he catch you masturbating, Ruth? Or, no morning arguments? They must have fucked!* I don't say anything that comes to mind, pushing them aside so I can keep walking in silence.

Marilynn pats me on the shoulder. "You didn't wake up in pain last night. That's a good sign."

I guess. It still didn't stop the nightmares. I am grateful that the pain has lessened significantly, but the pity party I threw myself was agonizing enough.

"You okay?" she asks, trying to match my long strides.

I hesitate before answering. Would telling her that today is my birthday make me sound like a spoiled child? Maybe not, but it would make her feel bad. Think about it, we're in this disgusting, creepy-as-hell prison. What could she possibly do to wish me a happy birthday? What could any of them do?

It would be sad.

I would hang my head.

And everyone would feel so guilty.

It's my fault for even letting this get to me. A while back, Belinda hosed me down in the asylum and made me walk back to my room, wet and naked. It was my twenty-second birthday. She said it was a present. I was quite loud and obnoxious back then, so I claimed that when I got out of there, my friends would throw me a party.

Belinda spit in my face and said, *"What friends?"*

I vowed that if I ever had friends, we'd make a big deal out of birthdays. We'd eat sweets and dance and sing together, despite Belinda.

May her soul rest agonizingly in hell.

"I'm okay, thanks for asking," I reply with a clipped tone.

I'm still not quite sure about Marilynn. After getting to know her, I started developing sensations all over my body, like tiny insects crawling across my skin when she's around. My stomach dips as if the floor has fallen out from under my feet. I find myself watching her like she might disappear, run away, or die in front of me.

But Kaspias planted that doubt, and it's messing with my head.

Stupid twin brother of Kane. *Stupid, stupid, stupid.* I bet all members of that family are annoying and mean. I bet they eat bland toast without butter, hate puppies, and deface children's toys for fun.

Guilt brushes past me.

His family is dead.

*What's wrong with me?*

Oh yeah, I'm grumpy as shit. It's my birthday, no one knows, and I'm spending it wallowing in a fucking sadistic prison.

"Your jaw is tight, and your nostrils are flaring," Marilynn adds, stepping under the freezing water of the shitty shower, reeking of mildew and body odor. A shiver climbs up the base of my spine, and we dart our eyes away from each other's naked bodies.

It's obviously not easy. From my peripheral view, she's luscious in every sense of the word. Full, shiny red hair. And she's soft all over. Soft, tender thighs. Large, voluptuous breasts. A round ass that I want to squeeze so badly I'm driving myself up a wall.

"This place is just getting to me." But a thought occurs to me. "Are you keeping track of my body language?"

She pauses, rubbing soap through her hair. "Maybe."

That might be the only source of my smile this entire day.

After we're dressed, cold, and dried off, we head to the grimy commissary. With my head down like a dog that has just been kicked, I trudge through the assembly line, accepting my tray absently.

Is it bad that I'm a little pissed at the people closest to me for not noticing I'm upset? Other than Marilynn, of course. Skylenna and Dessin are so brainy, and for what? They can't even use their fat heads to pick up on my sour mood. How much do they care, *really?*

I pick at my food. Poke at my food. Stab at my food like it has committed a crime.

"Niles, you're bringing the energy down with your shitty mood. Cheer up." *Dessin.* Fucking Dessin says it.

Oh, so they *do* notice that I'm upset. They just don't care. Got it. Great. *Good!*

Skylenna tries to stifle her laugh with the back of her hand, nudging him with her elbow. And I scowl in her direction shamelessly. I wouldn't be surprised if smoke was puffing from my widening nostrils.

*Really, Skylenna? You're supposed to be my fucking sister!*

Someone approaches behind me, their wide shadow draping over my food. I can't find it in me to care, turn around, or look up.

"He's right, Niles," Skylenna says with a little too much volume to her voice.

My gaze snaps up to hers in a fierce grimace. I'm about to lash out, curse, and tell her that I'm very disappointed in her so-called special skills with the void. She should have been able to see it.

"The birthday boy shouldn't be wearing a frown."

My heart sinks to the bottom of my stomach. I blink. My mouth opens and closes repeatedly. The faces around me are beaming expectantly.

As if on cue, someone behind me lowers what looks like a brown pastry or a glazed cake to the center of our table. It has a melting white candle sticking out of the middle.

My eyes flick up to meet Skylenna. And suddenly, my vision isn't so clear. It's cloudy and warm. My heart melts into something gooey.

"Did you...?"

"We all did." She grins. My sister looks back at me with so much love, so much kindness. I want to crawl under the table and die for every horrible thought I just had toward her.

She cares. They all care!

"Marilynn made the cake," Skylenna adds.

A small hand pats my thigh twice. "Happy birthday, Niles."

Is it hot in here? Is it humid and misting?

I don't realize that I'm full-on crying until Marilynn wipes my cheeks.

"Make a wish before the candle wax ruins the cake!" Ruth pipes up.

I close my wet eyes, taking in a deep breath. I only have one wish that has always remained constant.

*I wish for a life filled with love.*

In a single huff, I blow out the candle and wait as Warrose cuts me a slice.

I dig in like it's my last meal. The shell of the glaze tastes like maple syrup. It's unique and tasty, and I've never loved a dessert so much in my life.

"How did you know?" I finally ask with a full mouth of sugary goodness.

Skylenna wipes her mouth, jerking her head in Dessin's direction.

"It was...*you?*" I ask in both horror and delight, meeting Dessin's dark brown irises.

"Don't cream your pants over it."

"But…you? Really?"

Dessin rolls his eyes, shoveling more food into his mouth.

I might cream my pants. I really might.

"How?" I lick my fork, watching Dessin intently.

"I went through your file in the asylum. When Skylenna noticed you were upset, I went through different scenarios until I landed on that one."

He went through my file. Wow, what a little creep.

"You stalked me?"

Skylenna laughs, but Dessin just stares at me. Blinks.

"Not funny?" I ask.

"No."

I SWING MY LEGS BACK and forth like a giddy child as we sit on the stage.

"What do you want for your birthday?" Skylenna asks, then pauses in thought. "Within reason, of course."

*Hmm.* Within reason. I sway back and forth in a little thinking dance. I'd ask to kiss Marilynn again, but come on, I'm no pervert.

What could they give me that would make this wonderful day that much better? What could—

Dessin crosses his arms over his chest. The movement steals my attention, roping me in until…I've got it! There is only one thing I want in the whole world. It will make this the best day of the year. We'll never forget it.

"I've got it." My eyes must look crazy. Excitement buzzes through me in a flash. My legs start shaking.

Dessin does a double take. Eyebrows crawling up his forehead.

"No," he says without hesitation.

"And you can't say no!" I blurt out in a panic.

"He's right, Dessin. It's Niles's birthday."

The urge to release an evil bout of laughter is more than tempting. But Dessin, for the first time since I've known him, looks genuinely nervous. His hands are fidgeting. *Fidgeting!*

"I want us to have a secret best friend handshake," I announce without breaking eye contact with him.

"All of us?" Ruth asks.

"No." I cross my arms, rising to my feet to mimic Dessin's posture. "Just me and Patient Thirteen."

Dessin glares at me for a long moment. He's not breathing. Not blinking. I giggle on the inside.

"Why?" The intimidating idiot has the nerve to ask.

"Because I want us to be best friends," I answer simply.

Skylenna coos, sweet little *oohs* and *awes*. Dessin's sigh sounds painful, as if an arrow is being extracted from his chest.

"Forever." I add the life sentence on with a final tone that implies negotiations are not on the table. This will be binding. Forever and ever. Amen.

"Fine."

"You're okay with that?" I push like a giant asshole.

"I said fine, didn't I?"

"Then why is your eye twitching?" I narrow my gaze on him.

Warrose throws his head back and lets out a laugh that is infectious. Everyone except for Dessin and me snickers at his expense.

"Let's get this over with." He practically growls each word.

"Yippy!" I leap, clicking my heels together.

Standing in front of the oversized meanie, I realize, maybe for the first time, that he's definitely taller than me. Not sure I like that, but what can you do? His creepy, dark gaze looks bored, but his jaw is clenched so tightly that I wouldn't be surprised if his bottom row of teeth was wired together with his top row.

I rub my hands together, levitating with sheer joy and sadistic satisfaction.

"Okay. First move, fist pump, like this…" I hold my fist out to tap his, only to be greeted with a semi-violent punch, making my knuckles yelp in pain. "*Ouchie*, yep. Good job, big guy."

Dessin's large eyes sweep over the perimeter for a moment, noticing how our friends are formed around us with big, dopey grins that turn their cheeks pink.

"Don't worry about them. It's just us. We're all that matters now," I tell him calmly, sweetly. It earns me that look. That dangerous, frightening, murderous look he gives those he's about to dissect or…*eat,* maybe. I'm not sure what kind of freak he is.

"Next move! Open your fist, now our hands slap, back of hand, then front of hand. Like they're in a fight. One of them cheated on the other, right? *Haha!*" I slap his knuckles with mine, then our palms collide. Damn, his hand is big. *Whew. Go, Skylenna!*

Ruth does a little clap after our second move is complete. My heart is racing. I can't believe we're going to have our own secret handshake. This is the best day ever!

"Third move—"

"And final move?" Dessin asks with a grimace.

I laugh, slapping him on the arm with my other hand. "Not even close!"

He looks at the space on his arm I slapped for a moment too long, making me instantly regret touching him. I giggle nervously, shooting wide, alert *"help me"* eyes to Skylenna.

"Third move! Our hands fought, now they have to make up. Pinch your fingers together—yep, like that. Then turn them side to side while touching them to my fingers. Kiss, kiss. *Muah, muah!*"

Dessin yanks his hand away as if he's just been burned by a stove.

"Niles," he warns.

But it's Skylenna's wheezing laughter that removes his attention from me, dragging it across the amused faces around us until his eyes land on her. She looks as giddy as I feel. Her face is the bright shade of a pomegranate, her eyes watery, and she's holding onto Warrose's bulky shoulder to steady herself.

The frustration scrunching Patient Thirteen's brows together loosens its grip on him. His taut shoulders relax. A brief smirk wavers over his full lips at the glimpse of my sister chuckling.

And I remember the moment I explained what a soulmate is to Skylenna in my room in the asylum. *Because once you find them, there is no life without them.*

It's true, isn't it? When he died in her arms, she lost all meaning in her own life. She wandered around those forests aimlessly. They really are soulmates. There was only one time before my life in the asylum that I knew I spotted a pair of soulmates. And trust me, I knew it in the depths of my spirit. It was a man and a woman I found arguing once.

The woman slapped him, stormed off, and…well, this is back when I had lost my mind.

Am I ashamed of what I put that couple through? Yes. Hell yes. It'll haunt me for the rest of my life. But I was so determined to prove true love existed. I was hellbent on healing the wounds I had from my father. And knowing what I know now about him, it was all for nothing.

I tried to prove they were soulmates by locking them in my basement. If I could just scare them enough, the man would try to protect the woman. And he did. It was a huge relief until the man said something to me. Maybe I was hallucinating from the psychotic break, maybe it was divine intervention. But I let them go.

"Niles?" Dessin asks with a raised brow.

"Sorry, okay, fourth move." I make Dessin memorize eleven more moves, which he does with ease and annoyance. The entire handshake includes kissy-hands, a hip bump, a mirrored-bicep flex, me miming catching him on a fishing rod and pulling him in, a catchphrase of *"Niles has a big…"* (showing size with a two-handed gesture), and ending in a nice brotherly hug.

By the end of it, I'm grinning ear to ear, and Dessin is rubbing his temples.

Warrose walks up to Dessin, slapping him on the back. "I'll commit this to memory for the rest of my life."

"I'd rather you didn't," Dessin replies.

Turning around, Skylenna and Ruth loop their arms through mine, walking us away from the group in a sneaky fashion.

"What's happening, ladies?" I ask.

"It's time for some girl talk," Ruth whispers.

"Oh! My favorite kind." I sit down with them in a few seats higher up in the stadium. They immediately go for it without any lube to smooth the entry.

"What's going on with you and Marilynn?" Skylenna asks.

I rub my jaw. Scratch my head. Ignore the way my heart stutters to a stop, then starts up again in my chest.

"I don't know." I shrug.

"Pfft, Niles! You of all men should know how to express your feelings!" Ruth bumps her knee to mine. "Throw us a bone!"

"There's something there," I admit, keeping my facial expressions to a minimum.

"What's wrong?" Skylenna leans in, looking suspicious. "Why're you so reserved?"

I shrug again.

"It's because of what Kaspias said, isn't it?"

I let out the breath I've been holding.

Ruth nudges me again. "Who cares? Let's pretend he never said it, okay? Tell us the truth."

"I might like her," I mutter, feeling bad for possibly having a thing for the potential traitor. "She's pretty."

She's more than pretty. Living in a fucked-up society where the women starve themselves…I've never seen a woman who hasn't. Her soft curves and appetite are beautiful. Stunning. I've become infatuated with her confidence, her shape, her disregard for the lady-doll regimen rules. And that's not even mentioning that radiant crimson hair. The smoldering depth of those sapphire blue eyes. What's not to like?

"We're your best friends, Niles. You can tell us everything," Skylenna says with a smile, giving me the push I needed to spill.

My emotions burst like a balloon in their faces. "We kissed at the Ecstasy Dance. Holy hell, it was amazing. Seriously. The kiss was a show of fireworks. A phenomenon made possible by the stars. I was immediately attracted to her, obviously. She's a beauty, right? But she's been telling me how I've been her favorite story in the prophecies she's heard about as a kid. It's the first time I've felt important. Special. Legendary."

I look down to see Ruth and Skylenna holding my hands, stroking my scarred skin with their thumbs.

"I feel good with her," I add shyly.

Skylenna releases a pent-up breath. "Kaspias better have been lying. I'm so happy for you, Niles."

I hope to God he was lying, too.

# 30. Missing

## Skylenna

"Line up for a headcount!" Helga Bee translates as we scramble to understand why everyone is running around.

The inmates form a line that stretches through the stairs of the stadium. Sentinels do a thorough walkthrough, counting, adding, and counting again.

"What's going on?" I ask, as we're allowed to disperse again once they're done.

Helga Bee shrugs casually. "Massacre."

"Come again?" Dessin narrows his eyes.

"There was an execution a league away from the prison, but everyone was slaughtered. No witnesses. No idea what happened, Beetle Brain. At least that's the rumor."

My head snaps over in Dessin and Warrose's direction. "Do you think…"

"It might be." Dessin nods.

"That does sound like something DaiSzek would do," Warrose agrees.

Hope and an everlasting love rumble through my bloodstream. They're coming for us.

We have to help them, break out of here early. Dessin seems to be thinking the same thing as his eyes shift from left to right, going over ideas, blueprints, a plan.

"I got separated from Ruth," Niles calls from behind me.

I scan the crowd of prisoners still parting. I search for that small, curly head of brunette hair. "Ruth!" I shout over the grumbling voices.

"Ruthie!" Niles yells with me.

Warrose is pushing past people, shoving grown men to the floor as he breaks out in a small panic. After what happened to Marilynn and her fingernails, we're not willing to let anyone out of our sight if we can help it.

"Ruth!" Dessin hollers, getting on the Ringmaster's platform to get a bird's eye view of the stadium. His alert gaze shoots down to me. "She's not in here."

Warrose hears that from across the stage. His head snapping up to Dessin. A thoughtful pause. He charges out of the giant room, bustling past anyone who stumbles in his way. His urgency heaves a formidable blast of doom that rings in my ears. *Shit. No, not Ruth.*

I race behind Dessin, feeling Niles and Marilynn falling in step behind me.

"Ruth!" My scream bleeds a downpour of terror.

Every horrible image flashes behind my eyes. Missing fingernails. A scalped head. Broken bones. I won't even let myself imagine a more permanent ending. It's *Ruth.* It's my soul sister. My best friend. *It's Ruth!*

We make it out of the stadium, into the dark, grimy hallway.

"Dessin," I whine, gripping his elbow.

"We'll find her, baby," he assures with a sick calmness to his tone. "I'll tear down this prison to do it."

But his confidence isn't enough for me. Ruth is the least equipped to defend herself here. If she's targeted, I don't know what could happen. Fuck, why wasn't I watching her? Why didn't I keep an eye on her?

The woman's voice in my head whispers to me. But it's too far away, too deep into the void to hear. My concussed head and back are in too much pain to focus on that dark, empty space. We can find her. We will find my best friend.

The Doll and the Domination

"Ruth!" Niles's voice echoes across the stone walls. And in one glance, I see how his hands tremble. We all know the cost of her not being able to defend herself.

Dessin holds out a hand to our group. Something to silence us. A signal as he cocks his head forward, closing his eyes to listen across a certain distance.

My heart is a wild stallion in my chest, bruising my lungs as it bucks and kicks. My body is already preparing to cry, clouding my vision with tears, quivering my bottom lip. I use all of my willpower to shut it down. Nothing has happened yet. This might be a misunderstanding.

And we all suddenly hear it.

Ruth.

A soft, pained whine.

Warrose reacts before I can even blink. Before I can even process. His large body barrels down the hallway with more grace and speed than someone his size should be capable of. And Dessin is on his tail. We flood the hallways, charging to our friend. Clearing the distance in long, leaping strides.

Rounding the corner, Warrose and Dessin halt. Digging their heels into the brimstone floor, bodies planting in front of us like an impenetrable wall.

I shove my way between their shoulders and choke on my own gasp.

Ruth's small body pins a man to the bars behind his back.

Ruth grips his face between her hands.

Ruth stretches up on her tiptoes.

Ruth kisses the man.

Ruth kisses…Kaspias.

# 31. "Woe to you, O destroyer"

## Skylenna

I search their frames pressed firmly together for any signs of a struggle. For any signs of a non-consenting powerplay.

Her legs tangle between his. And their kiss is…*intimate*. Slow. Passionate. Her thin hands wind up the length of his neck, one hand curling up into his hair, the other in his beard.

I have to restart my heart. Breathe again. Force oxygen into my bloodstream.

"Ruth…" I utter, broken, shocked, unable to process.

Her body rips from his in surprise, spinning with her hand over her mouth to face us. And I've never seen anyone look so completely caught off guard. We might as well have walked in on her mid-orgasm.

"*Shit,*" she breathes into her hand.

Dessin is the first of us to move. Taking a murderous step forward while I'm still here in the helpless form of a statue.

"Take your fucking hands off her." The careful steps forward are those of an apex predator creeping in on its prey.

Kaspias smirks at his brother, lifting his hands to show he is no threat to her whatsoever.

"Did he hurt you?" I finally find my voice.

The length of Ruth's throat ripples as she swallows deeply. Her soothing brown eyes search mine, and to both my relief and horror, she shakes her head.

"Ruth?" Warrose's voice cracks.

"Are you going to tell them, darling?" Kaspias purrs with smugness written all over his grin.

"Tell us what?" Dessin grits.

Ruth looks down at her bare feet, wipes her mouth with the pad of her thumb. She glances over at Kaspias, though not in fear or disgust. She looks at him for support.

The tall, edgy commander gives her an encouraging nod.

*What the fuck is happening right now?*

"The assignment I was given didn't seem hard at the time. But then, I didn't expect to love you all so much," Ruth says, releasing a shaky breath and pinning her meaningful gaze to me.

"What are you talking about?" I have no idea if I'm speaking or if it's Niles or Marilynn. I don't know what's going on. I feel like I've stepped into an alternate reality.

She bites her lip, twirling a curl around her index finger. "I was assigned to watch you all. To report back on everything I learned. It was an honor to receive these kinds of orders…but once I met you and went through everything we experienced together…"

Ruth's eyes fill with tears as the new reality sets in. It weighs me down like a house has collapsed on my shoulders. Sure, it's convincing. But I don't fucking buy it.

"No." I breathe through my nose to steady myself. "He can't force you to say these things, Ruth. We're soul sisters. I know it in my heart."

Ruth sighs miserably, looking back to Kaspias with an extended hand. He holds it in his, and at this, I take an offended step backward. *No.* NO.

Dessin's muscles flex, then go rigid beside me. He turns his head, staring at me like he's partially convinced.

*But it's a lie!*

"I love you, Skylenna. That wasn't a lie. I'm not some monster without feelings," she explains with watery eyes that look two seconds from spilling over. "But I was given an assignment that I had to carry out."

"Shut up!" I flinch, heat rising to my face like a vicious sunburn.

"You're good people! But this is how I was raised!" She's crying now, snot forming in her nose, which she repeatedly sniffles.

I flip my attention on Dessin. "Tell me she's lying. Look at her body language. Tell me she's been drugged or brainwashed."

Dessin's mouth parts like he wants to give me the honest answer that his instincts are telling him. But his dark chocolate eyes flick to my shaking hands, my twitching eye. He raises his chin at the challenge, examining her the way he would do to anyone who entered his room in the asylum. Patient Thirteen, the entity that could pick you apart, the being that could pull your secrets from your grasp like a loose thread.

Warrose steps forward, fists clenched, but face lacking any emotion.

"Tell me the truth. Is he forcing you to say this?"

She looks at Warrose with slumping shoulders. "I wish he was."

Kaspias lets out a laugh that lacks humor or kindness. It's mean. It's sour. It's meant to wound. "How do you think she's the only one able to speak Old Alkadonian? No one from Dementia can speak it."

Each word flies through my brain like a sword dipped in poison. *No.*

"Or who do you think told us that you were going to be on the ship? Did you really think Ruth just happened to meet you at Meridei's dining party? At the exact time when the two experiments met in the asylum? Coincidence? Fate for a special soul sister bond?" Kaspias laughs some more.

Ruth glares back at him and says, "Knock it off."

Each moment I've had with Ruth soars through me. How easily she accepted Dessin poisoning the staff. How quick she was to leave her life and family behind just to travel with us and outrun Demechnef.

Slowly, the pieces fit the narrative.

I peer back at Dessin with wide, pleading eyes.

And...he just *looks* at me. An expression that says a thousand words. Mostly apologies. But nevertheless, the truth is there.

My soul cracks right down the middle.

I'm instantly reminded of the moment I met the real leader of Demechnef. How I looked into Aurick's wintery blue eyes. He had no remorse. At least, not that he was willing to reveal in that encounter. The betrayal nearly knocked me to the floor.

But *this*…this is different.

This isn't just a betrayal.

This is the death of a character I have fallen in love with. Though my soul sister was fictional, she was still embedded in my heart like a birthmark. And she was never real. She's been a spy from day one.

Air whooshes out of my lungs, deflating me.

I take another step back, looking from Dessin to Warrose, and finally, my gaze lands on Niles. He looks exactly how I feel.

Gutted.

"Wow," I say with a bitter laugh, swiping a tear away with malice. "You played that part well, didn't you?"

Ruth places a hand over her stomach, pinching her eyes shut to release a few more tears.

"Stop crying!" I hiss, yanking my hand away from Dessin. "You can stop acting now! The show's over!"

My shoulders are quaking, and I'm going to vomit.

*She's not my best friend. She's not my best friend. She's not my best friend. She's not my best friend. She's not my best friend. She's not my best friend. She's not my best friend. She's not my best friend. She's not my best friend. She's not my best friend. She's not my best friend. She's not my best friend. She's not my best friend.*

"You must have had a good laugh all the times I bared my soul to you! You fooled me!" I'm yelling now, eyes wide, smile cruel. I can feel everyone's eyes on me now. But I can't stop the hate that's stinging my aching heart.

"And you?" I throw a sharp look at Kaspias. "Congratulations! You did it! In a single moment, you managed to rip us apart."

I applaud his efforts. Literally clapping my hands obnoxiously together.

He doesn't bother looking anything but pleased with himself. But that's the thing, I expected this of him. But Ruth? No. *Never.*

"How could you do this to us?" Niles's voice breaks, crumbling to his feet as he looks at our former friend with a broken heart.

Ruth opens her mouth to respond, but I beat her to it.

"Isn't it obvious, Niles? She's a sad girl with a sad life. And clearly, sad taste in men. She had nothing better to do!" Everything radiating from my clenching body is venomous. I'm like a wounded animal backed into a corner.

Warrose remains unmoving. Unyielding. A shadow among my uncontrollable flames.

"Was any of it real, Ruth?" He watches her carefully, like any small sign she could give him might disrupt this illusion she's painted for us.

I find myself leaning in, too. Desperate for some truth that might soften this blow.

Ruth doesn't look at him. Instead, she glances up at the ceiling with shame.

"Some of it was."

And Warrose winces. I, on the other hand, scoff loudly. The sound is wet and shrill.

"So, it's him then?" he pushes, the intent behind his question painfully clear to the rest of us.

In response, Ruth slides closer to Kaspias, enough so that he can wrap his thick arms around her upper body, molding her to his chest. And to make it so much worse, Kaspias rests his chin on top of her head, inhaling deeply with a condescending smirk.

Warrose turns away.

"Go then," I bark, thrusting my arm out in the opposite direction. "Ride off into the sunset with him. You've done your job."

"Actually," Kaspias interrupts. "She's still assigned to watch you. Cruel, isn't it? Ruth is still assigned to be your cage neighbor."

The hallway walls shrink, closing in on me until all I want to do is crush her. Remove his organs. Beat them to a pulp.

And before I can lunge, Dessin puts a hand on my shoulder.

"You've been with us long enough to know us, Ruth. And I'm sure you understand the consequences of your betrayal." He strides up to her until she can feel his breath on her face. "We will not leave this prison until you've paid for what you've done in blood."

# 32. Never The Same Again

## Warrose

I feel like I'm screaming underwater.

No one can hear me.

They're all above the surface.

And I'm forced to sit in the cage on her right. Hearing her sniffle. Peering at her from the corner of my eye to see her swollen face stream endlessly with tears.

The man in me who cares for the sassy, strong, argumentative Ruth wants to hold her hand. He wants to wipe away her tears. He wants to kiss her again.

That man is drowning, unable to take in a single breath as she cries.

How the fuck did life just turn upside down without any warning? How did I not catch on that this was all a performance? I can't even bring myself to think about every moment we've shared. Each sweet image is a paralytic being injected into my spine. A thousand different emotions course through my body in less than a second. Anger, devastation, white-hot fury, panic, humiliation, agony.

Ruth chose him. Maybe it was him all along. How long has that relationship been going on? The memory of his arms wrapping around her makes me want to bash my head against the bars, banging until my skull cracks wide open.

Kaspias fucking Valdawell.

She chose him. Right in front of me. Right after we shared that kiss. I couldn't sleep last night after I gave her small pecks all over her cheeks, her small nose, her long eyelashes. She giggled with pink-stained cheeks and starry eyes. My heart raced until everyone woke up.

And now this.

Ruth and Kaspias. I might throw up. I might break through the floor of my cage just to get away from her.

She's still crying.

Should I cover my ears? How is it that I can't stand the sound of her in so much pain, even after everything she's done?

"You've betrayed us all," Skylenna says in a low, detached voice.

I turn my head to look at her. She's leaning against her cage, eyes out of focus, face pale with a thin sheen of sweat, and she doesn't even look like Skylenna anymore.

She looks like a broken doll left to gather dust.

"No amount of fake tears will make us trust you again."

I can sense Ruth turning her head to my left, but she doesn't say anything. What is there to say? Skylenna is right. We've told her our secrets. Our plans. We'll never be able to talk to her about anything important again.

The finality of that makes me want to curl up and slowly die.

On the other side of Skylenna, Dessin is sitting in his own rageful silence. He's glaring at the rocky floor like it might hold answers. This must kill him as much as it does me. He's the one with the craft of knowing someone's deepest secrets. He can sense betrayal a mile away. How did he not see this one coming?

For at least an hour, we lie in silence, awake, alert. It's as though we're all bleeding out. Waiting for death to fall like a deep sleep over our eyes.

The wheezy sound of a man sobbing ruptures this bubble of grief we're all trapped in.

I sit up, catching Dessin do the same in my periphery.

Niles is hunched over, head between his knees, as his upper body shudders. The tan skin on his neck and shoulders turns red. His entire body seems to bear down like he's under attack.

Ruth clutches her hands to his bars, making a panicked whine at the sight of his abrupt breakdown. Marilynn reaches for him, too. But it doesn't matter, does it?

No one can fix the damage Ruth has done to this family.

"Niles," Ruth pleads, kneeling toward him. "Oh, Niles!"

The noises leaving his muffled face are heartbreaking, even to my stone heart. And it's astonishing to see and hear. Niles has always been this quirky, obnoxious, weird, inappropriate addition to our family. The kind of man who will crack a joke before he comments on his real feelings about a situation.

Yet here he is.

A grown man.

Sobbing hysterically.

*On his birthday.*

And it damn near kills us all.

# 33. Enough Is Enough

## Dessin

I glance over my shoulder to see Ruth sitting by herself in the commissary.

It's a similar sensation to my heart getting caught on a bush of thorns, and no matter how much I try to free it, only more damage is done to that soft tissue.

Why do I feel so fucking bad for her?

She should sit by herself.

She's a goddamn traitor. I've never seen my girl so numb, so completely shattered by this new truth. Then again, I didn't get to see her after I died.

"We're getting the fuck out of here," I announce quietly to the group.

Warrose barely lifts those hazel irises to me, picking at his food the way we all are. Unable to eat even if we really wanted to. There's a Fun House tonight that we should prepare for mentally and physically. But it's as though we've all taken a rigorous beating to the lungs.

"I've mapped it out. But there are a couple of holes that need clarity."

At this, Skylenna peers up at me through stormy green eyes, swollen and ice cold.

"The magnets in our ears," she says quietly.

"Yes. That, and I need to see blueprints for the outside of this prison. There aren't any windows. I have no clue what we would be running into as far as security goes."

She doesn't say it, but an idea flickers in those sad, emerald eyes.

"What?" I press.

Skylenna's focus bounces between both of my eyes. Back and forth. "What if a sentinel got us that information?"

I huff. "I don't see why they would."

Despite the desolation filling her veins, she smirks.

My eyebrows go up. "No."

"You don't even know what I'm going to say."

"Even *I* know what you were going to say," Warrose scoffs.

"If I can trick a priest into doing my bidding in the asylum, a sentinel will be no problem," she argues.

"A priest is easy, baby. Their religion and beliefs are their weaknesses. They'll do anything if you convince them that God has commanded it."

"A man with a penis is even easier. Especially when they're deprived in a prison."

My blood boils so violently, steam practically rises off my skin. Does she believe, even for a second, that I would be okay with this idiotic suggestion?

"*What* did you just say?" I can feel the fibers of my teeth scrape away as I grind my jaw back and forth.

"I'm going to seduce a guard." She's...*serious*. My stomach dips at the sight of her blank, stony face.

"Like hell you are!" I half explode, gripping the ends of the table.

"You don't think I can do it?" she asks with narrowing eyes.

"I—well, I…"

Of course, she can pull it off. She's long and lean. Her breasts are perfect and heavy in a man's hands. She has this glowing honey hair that I regularly envision balling in my fist as I thrust my cock into her from behind. Of course, she could seduce any man with a proclivity for beautiful women.

"I'm not spending any more time in this prison with her," she says coldly, daring me to disagree with her.

I study that sharp face for a moment. Trace the dark smudges under her eyes. Those bee-stung, swollen lips. She looks like death caught on fire. I don't have it in me to refuse her anything.

"Look," I sigh heavily. "Get the information from a sentinel. But please, don't take the Fun House offer given to women that would rather please a soldier."

"Why not?"

Well, for one, the image alone makes me light up in a jealous frenzy to cut someone to pieces for touching the woman I love.

"If I have to kill sentinels for this, I can't guarantee it won't result in me on the chopping block."

# 34. The Crafty Serpent

## Skylenna

"**D**istract him. I'll owe you," I tell Helga Bee and Gerta. Helga Bee gives Gerta a fervent high five, placing a hand on her round hip. Their excitement would normally make me laugh, but I have no laughter to give. It withered away in my soul, rotting at the grave I built for the Ruth I once knew, who is now gone forever.

"We're perfect for the job!" Helga Bee grins, her cheeks blemished with swatches of maroon.

And that settles it. Departing into the shrill stadium for Fun House Night, the plan is set. Dessin will likely go up in flames over my deceit, but enough is fucking enough. I want out of this torture chamber. I could handle the beatings. I could endure the starvation. But I cannot fathom staying in here any longer with the soul sister who betrayed me.

*I thought you sent her to me, Scarlett.*

Is her name even Ruth?

Was any of it true? How much of what she said was a lie?

It doesn't matter anymore. We're getting the hell out of here. Dessin has worked out a route of escape in that complex mind of his. I need to do my part.

Once we gather around the stage, listening to the Ringmaster introduce the night's events, I slip away to the exit designated for inmates who would rather save themselves the trouble of a Fun House Night and entertain the higher-ranking soldiers in another way.

The distance that separates Dessin and me is like the warmth being sucked out of my being. It's watching hot water swirl down a drain in the bathtub, feeling the cold chill in the air kiss your bare skin. I shudder at his absence.

*I'm doing this for us. I'll come back to you unharmed with what we need. I love you.*

My head still throbs and pulses from the concussion-induced migraine, but the void swims closer to my consciousness. The depth and shape of its existence helps me breathe normally again.

Down a vibrant corridor of black brick walls glimmering with wild flames, I follow a line of inmates, dragging their feet across the gravelly floor.

*Use every tool in your arsenal. You can do this.*

Cloudy rooms are scattered along the path, each one holding windows so that the soldiers may still enjoy watching Fun House Night. I watch with growing hesitation as men and women stray from the line, filing into the rooms of their choice.

Strange face after face. Scarred. Burned. Tattooed. I have to ensure the room I pick doesn't have Kaspias in it.

Poking my head in the fourth room I pass, a group of three soldiers chug from their bronze chalices as if competing in a race. Brown liquid drizzles down their chins, seeping into their beards. I study each of them as quickly as possible while they remain unaware of my presence.

The first soldier is shorter than me, not an inch of hair on his body, not even eyebrows. His matte black uniform is without any accessories.

The second soldier looks similar, but with a long brunette ponytail.

The third has black liner around his eyes, piercings that run in a long, neat line over his jaw bone, and silver bangles with jewels covering his black breast plates. He's bigger than the other two, both in width and length. Thighs that resemble Warrose's legs and a beefy chest that reminds me of Dessin.

He looks positively terrifying.

It stands to reason that he must hold important information.

They've finished their drinks and shift on their heels, rotating toward me. Three sets of eyes trace over my neck and chest like carnivores assessing their next meal. I stand up straight, confident, and deviously, unassumingly strategic.

The bald one says something in the foreign tongue I don't understand.

"I don't speak Old Alkadonian," I say calmly.

The two soldiers without jewels or silver bangles swing their focus to the tall, hefty male leaning against a blazing torch. The orange flame only illuminates half of his shiny face. Those black-rimmed eyes bore into me, trailing slowly up the length of my legs until he reaches my hip bones. The small optic movement feels like a league of cockroaches sneaking up the length of my ankles to my thighs.

Something about him strikes me as off. He uses the nail on his index finger to scratch the inside of his upper lip. He holds his hands outward, like he wants to say something, but doesn't know how to express himself. And his stare is directed at me, yet not focused on anything in particular. It's as if he's seeing right through me, visualizing a scene I'm in with a different conversation entirely. The sum of his body language makes my nerves recoil with caution.

"You're not supposed to be up here," the leading soldier says, accent compact and uneven. His tone reminds me of a child trapped in a grown man's body.

I lower my lids to give him a once-over. "Says who?"

"Commander Kaspias."

That fucking name curdles my blood.

With a single swipe of my tongue across my bottom lip, I tilt my head to the side, gazing up at the man in charge from under my lashes. My gaze shifts between his lips and his eyes. Over and over again. I force myself to imagine Dessin, picture his clenching hands, the width of his shoulders. It forces my pupils to dilate wide.

Each subtle shift in my form acts as a subconscious signal for him to find it all irresistible. *Ignore orders. Let me come in.*

"Do you want me to leave?" My words come out breathy, like the mere sight of him is making my heart race.

The other two watch him in suspense.

"No," he finally answers.

The corner of my lip tips up in a shy smile. I take one step forward.

"It can be our secret," I offer.

The soldier in charge lifts his chin, and those pupils flutter wider. He takes a seat on his large chair with armrests that look like angry gargoyles, facing the Fun House stadium. Flaming stars blast across the window. Sparks and the booming sounds of drums sound like the chaos of a natural disaster. I force my eyes away from the show. I can't let myself get distracted, worry about what they're going through. This is for all of us to get the hell out of here.

I take three more steps into the room, sweat drizzling down the stinging cuts on my back from the heat of the torches.

The other two men take a seat, impatient eyes bouncing between the show and my long legs. But the gruff, tall leader's gaze rests just above my shoulder. His hooded eyes twinkle as he plays with the piercings along his jawline.

"It helps that you've brought a friend."

I raise my eyebrows at him, blinking as confusion stops me in my tracks.

"I didn't—"

The movement of a shadow emerging at my feet has me spinning around, coming eye to eye with a freckled-cheeked, creamy-skinned redhead. Marilynn swallows as I gape at her with eyelids stretched past comfort.

"*No,*" I utter.

"Yes," she breathes out calmly. "You didn't lose everyone."

My breath gets caught in my throat.

"You didn't lose me," she adds, sadness lining her voice.

The muscles in my back tighten so hard they start to ache. I should make her leave. She of all people, can't be here in her condition.

But Marilynn shoves past me without waiting for any further confirmation, taking her seat on the bald soldier's lap. He slaps her thigh excitedly. With a flip of her hair, she flirts without words. Like she's the best damn actress in the whole world. Like she's genuinely enjoying this.

I unclench my fists, flick my gaze back to the leader, and grace him with a careless smile.

"Watch the show on my lap," he commands without an ounce of emotion.

With swaying hips and lowered lids, I make my way around Marilynn to sit myself on the lead soldier's leather pants. His muscular thighs cushion my bottom, but the rest of him is stiff and uncomfortable to lean against. The gems and silver bangles stab my throbbing back. He doesn't seem to give a shit as I wince.

His hands relax over the armrests at my sides. Cuticles picked, split, and bloody. Nails jagged and yellow. And if I'm not mistaken, each finger is crooked, leaving me with the impression that he's broken every bone in his hand.

Swallowing my discomfort, I stare blankly at the glass window, doing my best not to see the show beyond its smudged surface. I have one task. Only one. And the urge to succeed rips into my bones, pulsing like a live wire.

With a slow rolling of my hips, I try to detect his erection. My ass rubs against his pelvic bone, wiggling up his thigh. Nothing. No bulge. No indication that he's aroused.

The soldier seems hollow, like a vessel that lacks the basic male functions to be turned on. I try settling in, getting comfortable, allowing my limbs to loosen in his lap.

The lead soldier says something in Old Alkadonian to his comrades casually. From the corner of my eye, I see Marilynn running her hands over the bald man's forearms, caressing him.

I moan softly, then wait to feel him harden beneath me. One second. Ten seconds. I wait, and wait, and wait. Failure. *What the hell?*

The void flutters against my consciousness, grazing my thoughts with its flickering presence, like a gas lamp that's about to sputter out. My head still hurts, a dull ache that won't seem to go away. But maybe if I just dip my toes into the water, I can test out its potency.

I close my eyes, ignoring the fact that this man doesn't seem to have a weakness for me to prey on. If I'm going to extract information, I'll need something to exploit.

I strain against an invisible leash to merge with the void completely, skull thumping with a stabbing ache that only gets worse as I conjure what I need from his subconscious.

Most of what I find is useless, knives ripping through flesh, getting sized for armor, getting punished with a hammer to his fingers. I wince as I hear bones crunch. This man wasn't allowed to cry, if he broke, he'd feel the pain of another finger shattering. Which explains why his hands look wrong.

Nausea shreds through my stomach as I filter through his being quickly, quietly. Trying my best not to alert him with my impending absence.

His name is Roxal, Captain of the Vexamen Navy Guard. Eldest son of a peasant family in the southern village of Vexamen. *But what does he like? What's his sexual weakness?* I grow frustrated, begging for the right information to fall into my lap.

It practically hits me in the face as I stumble upon his time in the brothels created for the hardworking Vexamen Breed. Roxal visits the Bixez Tavern four times a week at sunset. He selects the same women each time. Oddly enough, they are the ones that don't judge him. Of all the scenarios I imagined, I'd never guess this powerful captain would be deeply embarrassed and ashamed of his preferences. But he is. I watch a memory of three women cackling at him before he bloodied their faces. His cheeks smudged with a shade of cherry.

Two specific, unique sexual preferences.

One: *Feet.*

He enjoys touching them, smelling them, fondling, kissing, and receiving sexual favors from them.

Two: *Being coddled by a mother (or someone who acts like a mother).*

I eject myself from his consciousness like a bat out of hell to keep from seeing why his second preference is so potent. I feel the deep ache behind that mask, like he's buried it deeper than a secret grave. Like no one can ever know he has a hint of hurt for the family he lost.

I can't feel sorry for this man.

Without wasting another moment, I run my toes up the side of his leg. His body tenses, gnarled hands clamp down on the armrests, and his chest puffs out at my back.

A sense of relief eases my muscles. Pausing for a moment, I spin to the side in his lap, tucking my knees to my chest so I can delicately rest my feet on his right thigh.

"I'm sorry," I say with a tired sigh. "My feet are so sore from walking around all day. Would you mind if I rub them?"

Captain Roxal looks genuinely, abruptly, joyfully *shocked*. Like this opportunity has never literally fallen into his lap before. He usually has to have the awkward conversation first, stammering over his words, dancing around the taboo topic, and waiting for their features to change.

He nods woodenly, his eyes burning a hole through my feet.

I hum my gratitude, reaching around my knees to my toes. Starting at the knuckles, I massage evenly, not exactly disappointed that this is a part of my ruse. My feet really are sore, scraped up, throbbing, and in desperate need of a massage.

Captain Roxal sighs jaggedly, hands trembling as he watches me instead of the show. Cheers entwined with guttural screams bang against the glass window, but he is completely oblivious to the outside world.

"I can—" the captain swallows —"do that for you…if you want."

I gush, thank him, place my hand over my heart in a fake swoon. And his chest deflates in blatant gratitude. Childlike wonder swims in his piercing eyes as he takes hold of my feet, rubbing my toes and heels with earnestness and precision. His breathing ramps up, and I feel his erection swell under me. It isn't easy to hide my disgust for this man. My body's instinct is to jump off his lap and run. I don't care about his preferences. Everyone is unique. It's the man that I have a problem with.

But this is what I must do.

I've lost my best friend.

All I have left is to get my family out.

And *this*, sitting in a murderer's lap, allowing him to caress my feet, is the cost of that.

"That feels so good," I purr, running my hand down his neck.

The captain nods with glazed, cloudy eyes.

And this is it. This is how I go in for the kill.

I place a kiss on his temple, inhaling the scent of copper and sweat. "You're being such a good boy."

His entire body shudders, gripping me tighter like a python attempting to suffocate its victim. And his shadowy eyes change, flickering to the innocence of a boy he's left behind. Sadness, pity, and repulsion twist through my center.

"Am I?" he rasps, continuing to bring my foot closer to his face.

"Oh, yes!" I say warmly, despite the cold, icky feeling in my gut. "You're behaving, and that makes me very happy."

The grown man moans in delight, rubbing his cheek against the top of my foot lovingly. I fight the impulse to snatch it away.

"I'm Mommy's good boy."

I scream...inside my head.

"Yep. You sure are."

Niles would have a plethora of terrible jokes and comments at this very moment. Thank goodness he isn't here.

"You know what would make me really happy?" I ask.

The captain gazes at me with an eagerness to please.

Okay, I have to do this part delicately. If I step out of line, he'll know. He'll figure it out.

"Tucking you into bed, kissing you good night, and reading you a bedtime story!"

To my horror, he starts grinding against me, nodding as he pants.

"Would you like me to talk you through it? So you can close your eyes, and we can pretend like it's really happening?" I add, watching his expression hesitantly.

Captain Roxal nearly gasps, like no one has ever presented this incredible idea to him before. "Yes."

"You're able to return home on leave from the prison, walking through the doors, you see..." I prompt him to fill in the blank.

"The caged tunnel that leads through the courtyard," he murmurs, nuzzling into my neck.

My skin crawls with invisible spiders in the space where his warmth mingles with my own. I need to pull this information without setting off any alarms, but at this point, I'm desperate to get the hell away from him.

"And as you walk through that tunnel, what do you see?"

The captain stiffens, and I immediately try to rectify my obvious prying. "Walk me through your day, sweet boy."

He settles back against me. "The swamp dawpers. They surround the cage perimeters until I leave, passing through the stone wall."

I don't bother asking the size of that stone wall. If it's surrounding the courtyard, it must be fairly large.

"Once I get home, will you put me to bed, Mommy?" Captain Roxal licks my neck, growing far more impatient.

"*Mommy?*" A thundering voice ricochets off the stone walls. "Have I died and gone to hell?"

I hop off the captain's lap, my alarmed gaze shooting to Dessin's broad, deadly frame blocking the doorway.

"Uh oh," I breathe, cringing at the scene I know is about to play out.

"Yeah. Uh oh," Dessin replies with iced-over indignation. His dark-mahogany irises shoot to the captain, then falling to the standing erection in his leather pants.

"*Out*, inmate! I'll have your fucking legs chopped off for walking in on this session!"

"Is that so?" Dessin unleashes a slow, cunning smile. "Then, before I'm maimed in front of an audience, tell me, did you have your hands on my girl?"

The captain smirks back. "And my dick pressed against her—"

I don't see Dessin lunge across the room, only the aftermath of his foot pressed against the captain's gulping throat. The sweaty, pierced man gapes up at Patient Thirteen from the floor.

"*Mine*. I. Don't. Share," he growls, a quick slaughter burning hot in his eyes. "I should cut your eyes out for even looking."

Chills pebble down the backs of my arms. To my right, Marilynn moves next to me, shifting away as the other two soldiers leave the room. Probably alerting the sentinels.

Dessin shifts his focus to me casually, like this is a normal routine in his day. And I know the captain won't fight back. Dessin has already paralyzed him.

"You trying to get my attention? Because you've got it." He continues to suffocate the man with his foot.

"I thought it might," I reply sweetly. But the footsteps down the hall rumble in our direction. I open my mouth and urge him to get out of here.

He lifts my chin, holding it in his fingers. "I should take you over my knee and watch you beg for it."

My nipples harden, poking through the thin material of my uniform.

"I got what we needed," I say breathlessly. "I have the details for outside of the prison."

Dessin's eyes widen, slightly surprised, slightly aroused. And the captain beneath his foot stops breathing.

"We have to go!" Marilynn shouts, signaling for us to follow her through the doorway.

Dessin jolts forward, his plush lips landing on mine with greedy pressure. I let out a small moan at his aggression, savoring his taste, his emotion pouring into me. And we take off after Marilynn, sprinting behind her down the long, torch-lit hallway.

Past the adrenaline, I have a single breath of a moment where I want to tell Ruth what I just had to do to get that information. I want to hear her laugh at me, teasing, and making light of something I'll eventually want to bury. The thought singes a hole in my heart cavity. Her absence is bruising, and I don't know how I'll ever live with this betrayal.

"And this is the nail on the coffin," Kaspias announces, standing in our way with a small unit at his back.

The three of us sway to a stop, unable to fight the effects of the magnet in our ears. I clutch the wall for support, feeling Dessin's hands gripping my waist. My stomach swirls, flips, and falls up my throat.

"We didn't do anything," I blurt out. But the writing is on the wall. It wasn't a sentinel killed this time. It was a fucking navy captain. One of the high ranking.

"Well?" Kaspias looks somewhere past us, raising his eyebrows.

"Captain Roxal is dead, sir," a young man announces behind us.

The hallway settles, falling eerily quiet. The sounds of fire eating through the air and the tips of the torches crackle around us.

Kaspias doesn't look angry. He doesn't appear upset. His sharp stare lands on Dessin, clear and elated. His mouth twitches before it shifts upward, rising into a lunatic grin. My back straightens at the sight of his disturbing happiness.

"My brother did it," Kaspias tells no one in particular. "I'm certain of it."

Dessin cracks his neck, shrugs. "And?"

More than one person flinches as Kaspias barks out a rough, cruel laugh. His large hands grab at air, like he wants to show us what he sees in his fucked-up head but can't because it isn't real.

"*And* I may not be able to kill you, but I can certainly torture the hell out of you for committing a federal crime!" His face lights up, biceps flexing, hands pulling at his hair in an attempt to have some sort of outlet for his childish excitement.

*No.*

I turn to Dessin, looking at him with the question in my eyes that matters. *Do we have enough information to make an escape now? Or would his plan rely on leaving in the dead of night?*

He shakes his head at me, and I might as well have just been kicked in the ribs. He can't expect me to watch him get tortured on stage. He doesn't really think I won't do everything in my power to stop it.

If he does, then this should really shock the hell out of him.

I kick my right leg back like a horse, sending the sentinel behind me flying backward with a breathy grunt. My body flings onto the soldier at my side, latching on to his back, and clawing my fingernails into his eyes until he screams like a small girl.

The object in my ear rings through my brain with a shockwave that throws my world into a tornado. But I throw all of my willpower into swinging my fists, biting flesh that gets too close to my face.

"I wouldn't do that, Skylenna," Kaspias exclaims past the violent outburst. I tumble to a stop, rotating through a shifting world.

As the dizziness clears, I see Dessin on the ground next to me. Blood on his knuckles and splattered across his face. He fought with me. But something doesn't sit right in my chest. An alarm goes off in my bloodstream. We look up at Kaspias at the same time, shuddering at who he has on their knees, arms pulled outward in chains.

Warrose tries to look at us through swollen lids and blood trickling down his forehead. Sweat glistens on his bronze skin, making his chest appear oily. A few soldiers hold his chains in four different directions like a leash for a rabid dog. I can imagine he wasn't easy for them to restrain.

"Warrose," Dessin grumbles.

"Hey, buddy," Warrose rasps, attempting to smile.

Someone quickly hands Kaspias a thick, rusty knife. His fingers curl around the cold metal, greeting it like an old friend.

"But you know what? Torturing you would only trigger an alter to come forward that could handle it. Right? If I'm not mistaken, you had to watch your mother die, didn't you?" His tone is vicious and taunting. The mention of Kane's mother gets a violent reaction out of Dessin. He jerks forward in the chains that have recently been attached to his iron collar.

"That's what I thought. The only way to really punish you would be to kill your oldest friend." Kaspias shrugs with a casual smile, pulling Warrose's hair back to expose his throat.

"No!" Dessin roars.

No words come from my lips. Only a garbled scream.

"Will the image of his blood streaming from his throat haunt you for life? Will the sound of his choking give you nightmares?" He's enjoying this. The grin, the twitchy fingers, the daring gleam in his eyes. It's as evil as they come.

Panic floods my mind as I try to reach for the void. But my brain is throbbing, searing with bursts of pain that seem impossible to overcome. The concussion and the distortive piece in my ear. It's blending together, dragging me further and further away from the void.

"Don't hurt him," Dessin grunts against the choking collar. "Please."

There is real fear warping his gaze. A look people don't often get to see.

"He just said *please*," Kaspias says to me with a small laugh, as if we'd both enjoy an inside joke.

"Kaspias." Dessin's eyes are wide and alert. "Don't do this to your brother."

Tears pool in my eyes. I study Kaspias's thoughtful expression, searching for any form of humanity left inside of him. *Please, Kaspias. Please, show me a heart.*

"I'll take Dessin's punishment." A soft voice travels to us from behind the unit of soldiers. The tone as delicate and smooth as a falling rose petal. They part evenly, allowing her to reveal herself.

I choke on a breath as Ruth steps into the light of the flaming torch.

## 35. "Where you go I will go, and where you lodge I will lodge; your people shall be my people, and your God my God."

## Skylenna

Kaspias chuckles. "That's adorable."

"No, really. I'll accept his punishment," Ruth says loud enough for everyone to hear.

Every emotion flashes behind my eyes. Shock, desperation, sadness, indignation, rage.

Kaspias's dark chocolate gaze flicks between Dessin and me. As if he's waiting for us to fight for her, beg her to stand down. Neither of us declines her offer. Neither of us has the words to interject at all. How are we supposed to feel about this? Does she think this sacrifice will make up for the betrayal? A part of me that still loves Ruth wants to scream at her to get out of here. That she doesn't know what she's offering.

The other part of me wants this bitch to burn.

Still, no words escape me.

All I can do is stare.

"You realize the punishment for a volunteer won't be death, but it might as well be, yes?" Kaspias asks, staring down at her skeptically.

Ruth sighs, keeping her eyes firmly locked with mine as she nods.

Kaspias watches her as he settles into his thoughts, working something out. An emotion flashes across his features, quick as a blink of an eye, and it's gone. He smirks, raising his eyebrows at me.

"No objections?"

I can feel Warrose's pleading stare clawing at my face to look back at him. My eyes fall to my knees, grating into the gravel. I try to keep my breath even despite the wild bull trapped in my chest. I can't decide between the vengeance boiling hot in my gut or the sweet, gentle Skylenna that first saved Ruth from Dessin's wrath on the conformists. She was so kind, so bright and accepting. I was excited to have a real friend.

But it wasn't real.

Without lifting my gaze, I shake my head.

A blizzard of feelings war against this decision, but I push it down in the depths of my soul, fighting the urge to cry at everything I feel.

"Very well," Kaspias purrs, signaling two sentinels. "Take her to the stage for the last performance of the night."

I raise my head reluctantly, catching Ruth's stoic gaze as she's being secured in chains. If I look past the betrayal, past the lies, all I can see is my best friend. My soul sister who would do anything for me.

And it's like she feels it. too, as tears rim her bloodshot eyes.

I take one last look at the tip of her upturned, pink nose, her perfect posture, and those curly lashes surrounding her soft brown eyes. A tear drizzles over her scattered freckles.

My heart cracks like a rock thrown into a glass window.

"Ruth," Warrose finally chokes out.

She makes a noise, a cross between a sob and a laugh. "I know you all hate me. I don't know how I could have done what I've done. But I do know that I love you all...my family. Maybe it isn't real for any of you because of my lies. But it was real for me."

And they tug her away, ushering her down the long hallway leading to the barbaric stadium. We're left sitting in shock, watching her thin figure slowly disappear into the darkness.

I inhale through my nose, sucking in the smoky aroma of the burning torches.

"We can't let this happen," Warrose grunts, voice cracking with a sob that is desperate to escape his iron hold on his sadness.

"She's made her choice."

Dessin and Warrose gawk at me as the soldiers force us to our feet. Did those words come out of my mouth? Yes, they did. It's impossible to sort through my murderous hatred of her lies. Those damning thoughts collide with the fond memories I have of her. The ones I've kept close when I need to feel the love of my family the most.

Before stepping into the blinding red and yellow lights, Kaspias turns to us with a half smirk. "Enjoy the show."

And we're left standing at the back of the stadium, waiting for the Ringmaster to calm the audience and announce the next round of entertainment. But my focus is nailed to the spot where Ruth stands on the side of the stage. She holds her head high, viewing that platform with determination. A pinched brow and a look that could slice through concrete.

I mentally grab myself by the shoulders, shaking until I rattle my teeth.

*What are you doing? It's Ruth! No matter the lies, those moments were real! She loves you!*

I squeeze my eyes shut, forcing myself to pick an emotion—*any* emotion—and fucking stick with it! Do I try to stop her from being humiliated and harmed on stage? Or do I pull my shoulders back and accept this form of revenge on the woman who gained my trust and stabbed me in the heart?

A sentinel jerks Ruth forward by her chain leash, causing her to stumble to her knees. She scrambles to the wooden table they lead her to. Its surface is slanted at a seventy-five degree angle. An incline that allows the crowd to see her strapped down, facing their boisterous activity. Her forehead, chest, forearms, wrists, shins, and ankles are locked down. Yet, she doesn't falter.

Ruth stares out at the audience in defiance. Unwilling to let them see an ounce of fear. Unwavering to remain strong in her solitude.

Just as I'm about to pick the emotion that is wrapped in the warmth and profound love of my best friend, I'm slapped with that one pungent visual of Ruth kissing Kaspias. The vicious fury that tore my skin from my bones. The way she clung to him, nibbled at his lip. The look on her face when she realized the jig was up. We finally discovered her face without the beautiful, loyal mask she once wore.

And I'm suddenly sure Kaspias won't let her get hurt.

It doesn't matter what emotion I choose.

They're lovers.

This is all a trick.

Dessin cocks his head in my direction, pinning me down with those close-set eyes turning a shade of bronze and gold in the streaming circus lights.

"Skylenna?" He lets a stream of alarm enter his voice.

"Kaspias won't let them hurt her," I say confidently.

I peer to my left, seeing Dessin's hand on Warrose's slumped shoulder. He's panting, trembling, flexing every muscle like he's going to rip the world to small shreds of paper.

"It's okay, Warrose. She may be a traitor, but I don't wish her to be tortured. She's Kaspias's lover. This is all to get a rise out of us."

Her stormy hazel eyes leak thin, hardly noticeable tears. "It's working."

"Ruth!" Niles's flustered voice stretches across the mass of the huddled inmates. He stands on a step leading to the stage, darting his focus from her to us and back to her again.

*Fuck. He doesn't know what's going on.*

"I don't think Kaspias will stop this," Marilynn says quietly behind me, like she knows something we don't. A warning.

I gulp, holding my breath in defiance. *She's wrong. She's wrong. She's wrong.*

"I think she's right, baby," Dessin says loudly enough to penetrate the thick plate of armor I've been molding around my breaking heart.

A soldier, the size of an ogre, tall with muscles as thick and broad as a horse, enters the stage holding an axe.

An *axe.*

Ruth's expression flinches, shuddering away from the image of strength and rebellion. Now appearing like a little girl in the middle of a battlefield. A place no child should ever go.

"*Dessin,*" I whine, snatching his wrist through the chains.

He stiffens, leaning forward to get a better look.

The blade of the axe is the size of a dictionary. Its handle is a thick pole of iron, matte black with dents and jagged markings, like it's seen the display of clashing swords in a war.

"*Dostërovex hiurëz dexezels!*" the Ringmaster bellows with a show of electricity that crackles across the ceiling and blue flames licking the edges of the stage.

"NO!" Dessin roars, veins bulging in his neck.

"What?" I yell. "What did he say?!"

Ruth's face breaks apart into a look of unadulterated terror. She cries out, shaking her head with burning red cheeks, fat tears rolling off her bottom lashes and puckered bottom lip.

"He said '*Remove her legs!*'" Dessin translates in a single, horrified breath.

I gasp, my mask of confidence shattering in the wind. I choke on a cry as Warrose roars at the top of his lungs, bucking like a bull against his restraints.

Within a small tunnel, in a single moment, Ruth looks directly in my eyes, straining to see me through a thick wall of tears. She mouths a single word. One that shoots through my chest like a spear.

"*Void.*"

The soldier walks to her, spinning the handle in his beefy hands.

"*Please, help me peek into the void! Only for a moment! Help me see what Ruth wants me to see!*" I silently beg that voice in my head that has guided me through the most dire of moments. "*Oh God, please help us!*"

A glimmering hand reaches out of the thin veil of air, hovering toward me.

"*Here, take my hand, Skylenna. Quickly!*"

Latching onto her wrist, I'm sucked into the darkness by an inhumane force. A loophole sneaking me past my splintering migraine, my brain sitting in a swollen shell of agony. I whirl past flickering moments in time, zooming through hours until we land on a setting in a hallway, the one that leads to the commissary. Kaspias is leaning against the wall, and Ruth asks him for food for me.

His only condition.

An injection he pushes under her arm. And as she asks him what it is, he smiles that wide, delirious grin. "Vexamen altered Mind Phantoms. You won't remember this. My brother won't even be able to catch the usual symptoms."

337

He gives it to her five more times after that.

We never noticed.

He chemically brainwashed her to believe she was a traitor.

The same way they altered my parents.

*"Go!"* The woman's voice detonates through the memory.

I fly through its smudged barriers, shooting past the void until I'm back in my own body, hunched and panting, twisting my head to gawk at Dessin in bleary-eyed astonishment.

"It was Mind Phantoms!" I scream at him. "She was never a traitor! That was Kaspias's trick!"

*Oh my god, what have I done?!*

I break into hysterics, screaming and crying, thrashing against my chains to break free. But as usual, Dessin is ten steps ahead of me. He's unlocked his chains, throwing them off his body. A dogpile of soldiers swarm him, launching against his bulldozing frame like a dozen wild animals.

"Go, Dessin! *Go!*" I wail, trying to break my own wrists so I can slip them through my shackles.

Hearing a violent cry from the audience, I look up to see Niles beaten and thrown off the stage. And that giant axe soars through the hot air, bashing into the bone under Ruth's knees.

The entire stadium goes silent.

Ruth doesn't even make a sound. She just looks at the blade splitting through her legs in quiet disbelief.

It's almost a clean break.

I vomit across the floor in front of me. Shaking. Gasping. Feeling the blood rush to my bulging eyes. *What have I done? What have I done?*

After the second swing, Ruth's legs fall off, hitting the stage with a wet, heavy thump.

Warrose cries out in agony.

*What. Have. I. Done.*

And there is so much blood. It sprays across the soldier's bare chest. It gushes from the uneven, gaping wounds beneath her knees. Dark, crimson rivers devour my sight.

And Ruth still does not make a sound.

# 36. Crushed In Spirit

## Warrose

My screams scour the earth.

"Dessin," I finally form words. "My—chains."

Dessin throws a sentinel off his back, eyes zoning in and out as he dissociates. His hands move swiftly, methodically as he frees me from my shackles and leash.

The crowd rumbles in victory. It surges like a ball of fire in my core, blazing through my lungs until I'm breathing puffs of smoke and steam. Nothing in my brain works right. It jumbles all thoughts together, fogging my sight, blurring all lines of sanity. The scene plays back over and over again until I'm dizzy with a cataclysmic rage. What the fuck have they done to her? It was all a trick. Kaspias truly made us believe she was a traitor. Ruth. *My* Ruth. My little rebel.

Skylenna's cries ring through my ears, but I don't stop running, don't stop shoving people to the ground. I'm a plague obliterating anything in my path. Elbows jab into ribs. Knuckles crack into the bridge of a nose, a cheekbone, a jaw.

I force myself to look up at her as I get closer to the stage.

She hangs from that wooden stand like a dismembered doll. Staring down at her legs on the floor, soaking in a lake of blood. Her face is ashen, draining of color.

Bile pressurizes in my throat.

Niles beats me to the stage. And what he does at first impulse makes me want to fall to my knees and cry like a little boy. It sends an arrow straight through my heart.

Nile—she scoops her legs off the ground. He tries to put them back on her body.

I race up the stairs to the stage, careful not to slip on the blood.

"Niles," I croak, holding back my tears. "I have to get her down."

He looks up at me in belligerent anguish, tears gushing down his cheeks to his neck. He looks as disheveled and incoherent as I feel. And the thing is, he still doesn't know she was never a traitor. He's letting himself come to her aid, no matter what.

"Bu—t" Niles hiccups on a sob"—her legs."

I don't listen to another word. All I can focus on now is saving Ruth. She doesn't even look up at me as I rip the straps off her paling body.

"I've got you, Ruth," I say in a shaky voice.

The only sign of life is a slow blink. A movement I'll accept as a glimmer of hope.

After tearing off the last strap, I hook my hands under Ruth's arms, half expecting her to grab onto my shoulders. She doesn't. She just…hangs in my grasp. The sight fills my eyes with tears.

"What do you need me to do?" Dessin is at my side, placing a hand on her back for support.

"Support her legs while I adjust her body so I can carry her in my arms," I say in a rush. "Gently. Please. Be gentle."

Dessin nods, wasting no time to angle his hands under her lower thighs, helping me lift her so I can cradle her to my chest, hugging her close. Her forehead grazes my neck, and it's cold. So fucking cold. Like melting ice against my skin.

"Move! All you fuckers either clear the path or die where you stand!"

I flinch at the sudden shouting voice. Helga Bee and Gerta herd people out of our way so we can leave easily.

"I'll find medicine," Marilynn announces in a panic. "What else should I find?"

"Clean cloths, hot water, a needle, and thread! I don't care what you have to do to find a needle, but I can't save her life without one," Dessin commands, sweat glistening across his forehead. "Also, a belt and alcohol!"

Rotating to face the opening path, I come face-to-face with Skylenna. Her usual glowing, golden face is now completely white. The whites of her eyes are as dark as blood, falling to where Ruth's legs once were.

"Do something to help or get the hell out of my way, Skylenna," I bark, red flares smudging the edges of my vision.

This briefly snaps her out of that lost trance. She stands up straighter, pulling back her shoulders. "I'll find blankets for her."

Niles leads the way back to our cages with Ruth's legs in his arms. Blood drenches his chest and pants, but he doesn't notice. He just keeps running. Just keeps yelling back at Ruth to hold on.

As we turn a corner, I look down at Ruth to check if she's still breathing. It's shallow. Labored. But she blinks away a single tear, and I have to battle the longing to cry with her. For her.

"I'm going to make you better, Ruth," I pant, kissing her once on the top of her head.

Dessin is careful to hold her legs up, adding pressure to her wounds to try and keep the blood loss at bay.

"Stop in the showers. We have to do this now. She's losing too much blood." He's right. My left side is soaked in vibrant color, painting my glistening skin in Ruth's gore.

Our actions blur together as we lower her to the shower floor. It's damp in certain areas and reeks of mildew and rusting metal, but it'll have to do for now.

"Where the hell is Marilynn?" Dessin raises his voice, signaling for me to sit next to him. "I want you to hold her right leg up and add pressure here—yes, that's right."

I hold her wound firmly, adding strength to a place that's pulsing riotously.

"Niles! I need you to hold her other leg."

Niles is standing two feet away from us, carrying Ruth's dismembered legs like he's clinging to the only hope we have.

"But..." he trails off, looking around for help. "What about her legs?"

He might as well take a gaff hook and rip my heart out with it.

"Set them down," Dessin orders.

Niles's face twists in despair as he gently lowers them to the ground. I have to turn away from the sight to keep from choking up.

"We're here!" Marilynn and Skylenna rush into the community shower. Their arms are full of white linens, glass bottles, and a toolbox. Skylenna is still shackled, trembling to hold the blankets up with her arms. "I pickpocketed the needle and small knives from a sentinel."

"Alcohol." Dessin holds out a bloody hand, accepting a clear glass bottle from Skylenna. He pulls out the cork and douses his hands in it. "Everyone, take turns disinfecting your hands and the area around us. We can't risk Ruth getting an infection."

I grab the bottle next while Dessin takes my place elevating Ruth's thigh. My hands shake as I dump a splash of alcohol over my skin. Blood smears and drips away. Ruth's blood. That axe. The desire to hurl snakes up my throat, pushing at the back of my mouth.

*How the fuck did we get here?*

"First we stop the blood, then I can surgically do my best to rectify the wounds," Dessin explains to us. His voice sounds so calm. How can he be so relaxed?

"How can you rectify this?!" Niles hisses.

Dessin ties something around Ruth's thighs, creating some kind of a tourniquet. I glance down at her face, watching the way she stares up at the ceiling, soft brown eyes drained of any emotion. Glassy and lifeless. Devastating to gaze at for too long.

"Support her head," I tell Skylenna.

"And cover her with a blanket," Dessin adds. "She's in shock. We have to keep her body temperature up."

Niles uses a knife to pick the locks binding Skylenna's body so she can move freely. And with that, she moves mechanically, cradling Ruth's head on her thighs, stroking her curly brunette hair as tears run down her cheeks.

"The bone is sharp and jagged on the right leg. I'll need to round and contour it down, otherwise her skin won't heal over it." Dessin pours a bucket of water over Ruth's wounds, giving me her leg back to hold so he can work. "Her nerves were severed. They need to be cauterized or buried in her bones."

"Just hurry," Niles pleads, looking down at Ruth's face with round, glossy eyes.

Dessin nods, cleaning her up as quickly as he can. Blood stops gushing down his arms as he tightens the tourniquet again.

"Get her to drink the honey of Sweet Nectar Valley," Dessin says.

Skylenna lifts Ruth's head slightly, giving Marilynn a chance to pour the milky substance past Ruth's lips.

"Drink it, Ruth," Marilynn whispers. "Please." And there's a shift in her features, something dead and drowning behind her grimace. Like she's reading a scene from a book that was already spoiled for her. Like she never anticipated how horrid it would make her feel, even though she already knows how it ends.

Some of the substance drizzles down Ruth's chin. But her throat bobs as she gulps it down.

After a few moments, Dessin makes a silent decision that the medicine has made its way into her system. He works as quickly and fluidly as I have ever seen anyone work under this amount of stress and pressure. He saws down her bones with a knife, taking away their sharp, piercing edges. His eyes are the color of wet bark, determined and impenetrable. Nothing could break his focus from the goal he's set for himself.

I'm grateful. So fucking grateful to have his genius on my side. To rely on his many gifts to save her. Yes, I've appreciated him in battle, in his many attempts to break us out of a bad situation. But this is different. This is Ruth.

We all turn our heads as he grates his knife against her bones, looking away but unable to close our ears to the sounds of scraping. It's like a fork clawing the smooth surface of a porcelain plate.

Dessin sets down his tools and works his fingers in her wounds, pushing and arranging.

"What's happening?" I ask, concerned with the pinching of his brow.

"I'm arranging her nerves. If I don't do this right, she'll be in a lot

343

of pain for a long time."

*Do it right. Please, Dess. Do it right.*

My hands and forearms grow numb as I continue to hold Ruth's thigh up, quivering with tension as I try even harder to hold myself steady.

"She's shaking," Niles comments, looking at Dessin with tracks of tears drying on his cheeks.

Dessin's focus slips to Ruth's face, flicking to Skylenna, then back to the nerves he's working on so diligently.

"She's in shock. Skylenna, get her pulse for me."

"Isn't shock a good thing?" I ask, gripping Ruth's thigh closer to my chest. "It's keeping her calm!"

"No." Dessin shakes his head without missing a beat. "Shock is the body's defensive response to a sudden drop in blood pressure. It constricts the blood vessels in the hands and feet, and then the adrenaline reverses, dropping blood pressure, which reduces oxygen and nutrients to vital organs. People die from shock."

A terrible ache wraps around my mind.

"*Fuck,*" I growl.

But his last words pop Skylenna out of the glazed fog she was settled into. Her emerald eyes snap up to Dessin, then fall back to Ruth's ashen face.

"Please, Scarlett. Save her." Skylenna closes her eyes, and prays out loud, whispering fiercely. "Protect my best friend. Don't let me lose anyone else. Please, Scarlett. *Please.*"

It takes me a second to remember the name. Skylenna had a twin who's no longer with us. She whispers frantically, kissing Ruth on top of her head, watching her tears drip into those dark, splayed curls.

Marilynn shouts the pulse back to Dessin.

"Talk to her," Dessin replies coolly. "Keep her awake."

"I'm sorry for believing the lie!" Skylenna sobs against her best friend's forehead. "I'm sorry for not being able to look into your eyes and know you'd never betray me. I'm a fool, Ruth. I should rot in hell for letting this happen to my best friend!"

Dessin wipes his temple with the back of his bloody hand. He walks us through every movement, every decision he's making. But nothing calms the web of nerves jolting around in my gut.

344

"*Vexëz! Vexëz!*"

I flinch around, seeing sentinels charge into the bathroom, pointing at us aggressively, as if ordering us to get back to our cages.

Dessin doesn't stop working, but he does glance up at me.

"I can't move her," he says calmly. "Do what you have to do. At all costs."

I turn back to four of the sentinels. My chin raises, my shoulders pull back. I wish I had my bladed whip with me, but I've never been one to back down to using my body as a weapon.

There are three sentinels that act swiftly, snatching Ruth's legs from the floor. They move like a night's breeze, in and out of the room. Niles bellows, tears splashing, veins bulging in his neck as he screams incoherent words at them.

"Let them go!" Dessin orders before Niles can take off running after them.

"But her legs…" Niles mutters wetly, blinking in devastation at Dessin's blood-splattered face. "They've taken Ruthie's legs."

"All that matters now is saving her life."

A couple more sentinels enter the room with the threat of harming us to return us to our cages. Whips, clubs, sticks flail around us.

Before I can stand, I ask Marilynn to hold Ruth's leg up for me. The floor tremors, the rhythmic sound of thumping feet cascades across the long hallway leading to this large shower. The doorway fills with the sight of prisoners bustling around us, pushing past the sentinels, and forming a circle around the small space where we're operating on Ruth.

"*Vexëz! Vexëz!*"

Dessin's tired, wide eyes flick up at the crowd around us, scanning their faces quickly before getting back to work.

"What're they doing?" I ask him.

"We're showing honor to our fallen warrior," Helga Bee says from behind me.

"They're giving me more time," Dessin responds.

The sounds of whips smacking against bare skin drop like a rock to the bottom of a lake in the bed of my soul. The inmates forming a protective circle around us grunt, but they don't part.

"I'm almost done," Dessin mutters, threading a needle and thread through her soft flesh.

I glance up at Niles. His face is wet, puffy, and he's staring at her wounds, yet completely zoned out. He doesn't even seem to notice the prisoners taking a beating for us.

I can't get the smell of blood, coppery and potent, out of my head. I see her hanging on that stage. See her legs hit the floor. I force my eyes shut against the disturbing memories. All that matters is that she lives through this. All that matters is that she survives.

Will she forgive us for believing Kaspias? We kissed the night before, and fuck, it was the best goddamned kiss of my life. I felt like a teenage boy being in the suffocating presence of my crush. Her sweet, floral taste. The way she softened in my hold on her, pulling that beautiful face closer to the bars.

I never expected my entire perception of her to be flipped around like this.

"You're not reattaching her legs," Niles gasps, staring down at her left leg sewn under the knee with his mouth hanging open. His eyes swim with new tears as they bounce from Ruth's slack jaw to the stumps remaining of her knees next to him.

Dessin finishes his last loop, tying off the last thread.

"I couldn't save her legs." He sounds genuinely furious at himself and his skills for that fact alone. "This was all to save her life."

I see the doubt written all over his face. He doesn't even know if he managed to do that.

"But...her legs," Niles mutters with a fist pressed over his mouth.

After a few moments, Dessin applies layers of cloth, bandages, wraps, anything to protect her sealed wounds. Then, we take turns cleaning our hands with alcohol.

"Let's get her back," Dessin instructs cautiously. "Support her head—yes, okay. On three."

We lift her as gently as possible. My chest splinters in agony as I realize how much lighter she is now. Niles lets out a choked sob.

A trail of prisoners follow us as we find Ruth's cage, dropping blankets to make her spot more comfortable. We squat slowly, terrified that any movement at all will make her scream out in pain. But she's still so quiet. So concrete in her shock.

It's immediately apparent that all six of us are staying in her cage tonight. Even though it's tight, cramped, and no one is getting a second of sleep, we settle in around her.

"We're not leaving you, my little rebel," I say in a hushed voice, holding her hand close to my lips, breathing hot air against her chilled, clammy skin.

Ruth's shallow breaths even out as she drifts to sleep. Dessin doesn't take his eyes off her, checking her pulse every few moments.

I zone out, fantasizing about meeting Ruth in another life, far away from here. A place where I didn't have to watch her suffer. A place she could be her sassy self in peace.

"Skylenna!" Dessin raises his voice in alarm.

I blink, surprised, at the blast of noise shaking me from my daydream.

Skylenna is halfway out of the cage, peering back at us with exhaustion and numbness clinging to her glistening eyes.

"I'll be right back."

# 37. The Bird's Nest

## Skylenna

I could have stopped it.

The brimstone walls blur past me, blending in with the flickering yellow and red bulbs. Voices, questions, screams, whispers, orders, sickles slicing through lungs, bodies swinging on nooses, conformists drowning patients, RottWeilens howling in the night, friends crying in pain, axes chopping through bone.

My veins leak a slow poison directly into my heart cavity.

It all comes crashing.

The stairwell takes me to the highest point in the prison.

And. It. All. Comes. Crashing.

Their looks of despair, of soul-shattering pain, of guilt as to why we didn't do anything to protect Ruth, of fear that we might lose her anyway.

They chopped off her legs.

I did nothing to stop it.

*Not a traitor. Not a traitor. Not a traitor. Not a traitor. Not a traitor. Not a traitor. Not a traitor. Not a traitor. Not a traitor. Not a traitor. Not a traitor. Not a traitor. Not a traitor. Not a traitor. Not a traitor. Not a traitor. Not a traitor. Not a traitor. Not a traitor. Not a traitor. Not a traitor. Not a traitor. Not a traitor. Not a traitor. Not a traitor. Not a traitor. Not a traitor. Not a traitor. Not a traitor. Not a traitor. Not a traitor. Not a traitor. Not a traitor. Not a traitor. Not a traitor. Not a traitor. Not a traitor. Not a traitor. Not a traitor.*

My heart stretches and tears like an old piece of cloth. I clutch my chest as I sprint those steps, not able to distinguish sweat from tears.

*What have I done?*

I get lucky as I reach the top level, the painted red door sitting in a daunting spotlight. The Bird's Nest. The looming rooftop. The tipping point for many prisoners in this prison. There is no sentinel guarding the area. Pushing the door open, I now realize why. It's too high in the clouds for anyone to successfully form an escape plan that involves scaling the walls or jumping.

*My fault.*

The air around me is thick and gray, obscuring any chance I have of seeing the edge of this towering perch. I crawl across the pebbled ground, being hit in every direction by fierce blasts of wind. Whooshing gusts toss my hair into golden whips around me. After a moment of moving blindly, my fingernails scrape against an edge, black bricks forming a waist-high wall.

*She didn't make a sound.*

I grip its chalky edge, holding on tight against the wailing breeze. I can feel the extent of the altitude without actually seeing the ground. It lights my nerves on fire, prickling my fingertips and toes.

*I did nothing.*

"I'm so sorry, Ruth," I cry out to the cloudy abyss, clawing my nails into the grainy surface until pain stings up my knuckles. "It's my fault!"

I could have pushed past the brain fog, forced my way into the void to see the lie Kaspias spun across our tight-knit family. I could have tried harder. And those horrible thoughts? I really had it in me to think such evil things about my best friend? I wanted to hurt her myself.

When she volunteered to take Dessin's punishment, I didn't have any objections. None.

I wanted Ruth to pay for the deep wound she carved in my chest.

But it was all a lie.

I scream to the wind.

How will we survive this?

How can my friends ever forgive me for letting this happen?

They're better off without me. Without having to hear my apologies. Without having to look at the guilt sliced into my face. Dessin will get them out of this. They'll be safe and happy.

And Ruth can live a happy life knowing that I got what I deserved.

*My fault.*

*She didn't make a sound.*

*They're better off without me.*

*My fault.*

I sob into my hands until my face grows hot and achy. I can't stop crying; it only manages to make the migraine throb harder.

"I love you, Dessin." I attempt to wipe my sore, gushing eyes. "I'm a coward. You—oh, god, you deserve so much better than me. I'll—watch over you for the rest of your life."

Climbing up on the ledge, adrenaline burns holes into every fiber of my being. My body sends off echoing alarms to back away from this drop, to go back inside.

"It looks like we'll have a similar ending, Scarlett. I hope you'll be on the other side waiting for me." I take a deep breath, close my eyes, and—

A hand seizes my wrist before I can shove myself off the edge.

It isn't thick and masculine. It's thin, frail, and feminine.

I tilt my head to the left and look into...my. Mouth. Drops. Open. I look into *my own* eyes. Emerald-green, long lashes, and straight honey-blond hair.

"It's just me and you now. I'm not going to leave you, Skylenna." Scarlett. My sweet, sad Scarlett. Her soft, full lips shift as she speaks. There's color in her cheeks, life in her thoughtful gaze. Her warm skin tingles into mine like it's made of electricity.

I can't move. My eyes don't blink. My heart stops.

"Is this...a memory?" I ask in a shaky breath.

"No." She smiles at me like she can really see me. Like she's really touching me. "This is real. I've been waiting so long for you to reach the part of your brain that can see me on the other side."

A powerful stream of wind roars around us as I stare at my twin sister.

"Wait, are you saying…"

"Yes, Skylenna." Scarlett delicately places a hand on my cheek. "I'm a spirit. You've finally accessed the part of your brain that can see all who have passed on."

# 38. Bonds Through Life And Death

## Skylenna

I slide off the edge and onto the roof's floor in a crying heap next to Scarlett.

"You're really here," I say through a gasp.

"I've always been here. I've heard every prayer. Every thought asking me to watch over you. I've never left your side," she says with that special smile she'd save for a rainy day.

And this most certainly is my day of storm.

I stare at her through the thick glaze of tears, memorizing the details of her face I took for granted. The way she blinks slowly, like she knows something I don't. The small ring of brown lining the outside of the circle of deep, forest green in her irises. She's always looked sick, though. The kind that makes your eyes puffy or your cheeks sunken in. With chapped lips, missing patches of hair, and the whites of her eyes always yellow or pink.

She doesn't look that way now.

She's healthy. Beaming with a soft white light. She's happy.

My Scarlett is happy.

"You're...okay?" She knows what I'm asking. At least, she should. It's been my greatest fear since she left me.

"I made it to heaven, Skylenna. And it's so beautiful here." She hugs her golden arms to her chest, looking up at the cloudy sky and seeing something I don't.

"But the Bible..."

"There are things in the Bible that were rewritten, misinterpreted, or taken too literally. Not to mention, it was written in a different world altogether. God knows my heart. He knew how much pain I suffered. He welcomed me home with open arms."

I cry into my hands, thanking God with more relief than I've ever felt. She wraps herself around me, breathing only love and light into my being as I shudder, and my sobs turn into bellowing wails. I tell her what I did to Ruth. I tell her about the day I watched Dessin die in my arms. About the asylum. About Absinthe and Albatross. And she holds me from behind, rocking me side to side as I get it all out.

"God gave you all of this to bear because you aren't any ordinary girl," she whispers against my tangled hair. "You are his warrior angel. You are cut from a cloth of the Almighty. You, sweet Skylenna, are the best there is."

Her words trigger a wave of reactionary goose bumps to rise over every inch of skin.

"You and Dessin were meant to change worlds. Can't you feel it?"

I can. Like an eternal flame that was lit in the base of my soul. The connection we've always had has felt stronger than just a childhood friendship. It has felt written in the stars. Biblically bound to our fates.

"And you want to know something else?" she asks, and it's so strange that it's my voice. A little rougher around the edges. A little different in tone. I haven't heard it in so long. Only in my memory.

"Yes."

"God gifted you with a family that would die for you. That would burn for you. That would hold your broken body in their arms all night to keep you alive. That would lose their legs for you. That would follow you into hell with no promise to ever make it out again. They have. They will keep fighting for you, just as you will change the world for them."

I have been so absorbed in my own faults; I haven't simply taken the time to appreciate my family for what they've done for me. Ruth deserves my love and presence while she recovers. She deserves me to help her get the hell out of here.

"Why am I suddenly able to see you?" I ask quietly.

"You've always been able to. We're told we can't at a young age, so our brains form that boundary. Experiencing something so horrific as what happened to Ruth broke that limit for you. The same way losing Dessin and Kane broke a limitation in your mind to access the void. Each trauma that leaves a scar on your soul allows you to surpass a new barrier. That's how you're able to perform these impossible wonders." She wipes my tears away with the back of her hand. "And now, after this terrible tragedy…you can see those who have died."

"Will I be able to see you again?"

"All you have to do is pray to me, and I'll come."

I smile against the violent gusts.

Scarlett turns me around to face her. "But Skylenna, you don't have much time left here. Use your gifts. Dig deeper. You and Dessin have the power of all the warrior angels that have come before you."

We embrace with a long sigh, holding each other close like I would in a dream. As if I'll never see her again. But at least now, I know I will. She's always with me. I'll find strength in that, even through the darkest of times to come.

As I walk to the big red door, I turn my head to see my Scarlett has dissolved into thin air. Gone with the clouds. Back where she belongs, at home, in heaven.

I reach my hand down to touch the iron doorknob, not even adding pressure, as the door snaps open, blasting wide so fast I have to jump back.

Dessin comes to a panting halt in front of me. Sweat-slicked chest, eyes alert and wild, with hands balling into fists.

"No…" he grunts, taking a cautious step toward me. "I didn't want to find you up here."

I stand my ground but am left speechless at his expression. His darkened gaze fills with tears as he takes me in. One fist rises to meet his mouth like he's doing everything he can to hold in a breakdown.

"Skylenna," he chokes out, struggling to catch his breath.

"I'm okay," I blurt out. "See?" I quickly pat my body to show that

I'm unharmed.

But it doesn't matter. I'm up here. I'm in the Bird's Nest.

"You *thought* about it. You were going to leave me, weren't you?"

I flinch at the first sign of real insecurity in his tone. Of real heartbreak.

I scramble to explain my lapse in sanity. "Seeing what happened to Ruth...I lost my mind, Dessin. I could have stopped it. I fucked up, and I thought everyone would be better off without me. It was a moment of true insanity."

He turns away from me, hiding his face, either in anger or because he doesn't want to show weakness. And it feels like someone has ripped out my soul and stomped on it.

"Dessin, I didn't do it." My bottom lip quivers, seeing him so torn up. "I love you, and I won't leave you. I won't ever leave you."

He spins back to look at me incredulously. "I don't think you understand. If I ever lost you, I wouldn't last the week. There are no alters my brain could split off to bear that kind of pain. There's nothing my mind could do to protect itself from that loss. I would simply stop breathing and find you again in the afterlife."

"Oh, Dessin..." My voice breaks, and I throw myself against him, roping my arms around his neck, feeling the way his warm frame tightens around me. He shudders as my breath grazes the space between his shoulder and neck. "I'm sorry. I love you. I love you so much."

"Don't scare me like that again, baby."

"I promise I won't."

He pushes me away only to crash his lips over mine, opening his mouth until I'm breathing his air, tasting his hot tongue gliding across my bottom lip. He breaks the connection, giving me fast, aggressive kisses on my lips, cheeks, forehead, jaw. I sigh against him, smiling through tears at the smoky sky.

"Scarlett made it to heaven," I say as he stops to look into my eyes.

"Come again?"

"When I was...on the edge of the roof. She came to me. Told me I can see those who have passed on now. I'm not sure how it works, but she told me she made it to heaven. She's so happy now." I'm panting, swallowing against a sandpaper throat.

He blinks, processing this news the way he always does.

"Do you believe me?" I ask.

He leans down to kiss me again. "Yes. I do."

I sigh, resting my forehead against his.

"Are you…are you able to…"

I know exactly what he wants to ask.

"I don't know how it works yet." I run my hands through his cowlicked, brown hair growing longer with our time here. "But the moment I do, I'll tell you."

He closes his eyes, listening to someone's thoughts running through his mind.

"Good."

"There's something else," I add.

"Tell me."

"Scarlett said our time here is almost up. To use my gifts. That we have the power of warrior angels and should dig deeper."

I can almost feel her skin still on mine. The sugary scent of blueberry pie.

Dessin mind races as he watches me. "I need you to promise me something."

I raise an eyebrow.

"If you have the window to escape without us, I need you to take it."

I don't even blink at his suggestion.

"No."

"Skylenna, listen to me." He grabs my shoulders firmly. "Ruth isn't in good shape. We're going to need help to escape with her. It just became so much more complicated than before this happened to her."

"But—"

"I won't leave without her," he says with a raised chin.

"We can get out together!" I argue.

"No, I don't think we can. The escape plan I have would kill Ruth. The sewage system is our best bet. That kind of bacteria and physical strain would cause her to get an infection or stop her heart. If we get you out, you can lead the armies here. Do you understand?"

I ache everywhere but nod sluggishly. Nothing about abandoning my family feels right. But if it's our best option to save Ruth and get everyone out alive, how can I refuse?

# 39.
# Somewhere
# Close To
# Heaven

### Ruth

My eyes peel open to see a yellow stream of chunky liquid. The lumps and fluid spew across the cold floor in front of me. There's a hand on the back of my head, tilting me to the side. Another hand stroking my arm. A voice murmuring in my ear.

I catch the putrid scent of sour bile and food coming back up.

The sound of vomit splashing across the stone floor.

I groan in the base of my throat as the last bit bubbles up my throat, burning across my tongue and down my chin. Someone wipes my neck and mouth with soft material.

Everything is a blurry, black pit with figures shifting around me. They're all so close yet so far away in the dizzy haze of my sight.

Signals of pain blast from my brain like a storm of radiation. I suck in a harsh breath, hissing through my teeth and throwing my head back in misery. A mix of fire and ice wrap around my legs, shooting acid up my hips and into my stomach. I must have the flu or strep throat. Maybe I was thrown off a cliff, breaking half the bones in my body.

I yelp before turning to vomit again. My hair is pulled from my face. A hand grips mine to keep me steady. To keep me grounded.

I'm shaking all over. Muscles vibrating like I'm sitting on an engine. Where does the pain begin and end? Why am I trapped in this dark hole of hellfire and pain?

*It hurts so bad. I can't take it! Someone, help me!*

I feel the echo of a cry leave my lips. A man's voice crackles against my cheek. A forehead is pressed to my temple.

*I'm dying. I need help!*

The pain becomes all-encompassing, roping around my shins and kneecaps like barbed wire soaked in kerosene.

"—*hurts!*" A word screeches out of my mouth with stinging anguish.

"Do we have anything stronger than that honey?!" a gravelly voice barks out.

"We need Dessin! Where did they go?"

A blubbering cry slips from my hold, slurring uncontrollably from my hammering chest. I cough gooey phlegm from my lungs, hacking until the muscles in my stomach cramp up, then cry harder.

I want to ask the figures around me why it hurts so bad. What's wrong with me? Who can stop this unimaginable anguish? I want to beg someone for help. Maybe even to kill me now. End this suffering.

But the only word I can say is "Why?"

"I'll get help, Ruthie!" *Niles.* I pick his voice out of the eternal stinging.

"I'm so sorry, little rebel. I'm going to find more medicine to make you feel better. We didn't expect the last dose to wear off this fast."

I blink through the glaze of tears pooling over my eyes.

"Warrose?" I hiccup.

I hear and feel him exhale against the side of my face. He's so close, his facial hair tickles my cheekbone. "Yes. I'm here."

"*Why…*" I mean to ask again, but the word is trapped in an air bubble sitting in my throat. I see the flash of a thick, sharp piece of metal. I see an audience jumping up and down, hollering, and beating their hands together.

Warrose stiffens without so much of a breath to leave his nostrils. Why isn't he saying anything? Why won't they tell me why I'm hurting?

360

But ignorance is only a temporary gift.

I see my legs detached from my body.

On the ground.

A pool of my own blood.

"My legs!" I gasp, eyes shooting wide open. "WHERE ARE MY LEGS?"

Out of the corner of my eyes, Niles covers his mouth and closes his eyes.

*Answer me.* Why isn't he reassuring me? Panic shreds my insides.

I try to wiggle my toes, roll my ankle, flex my calf. Nothing. I try harder. Clench my foot. Bend my knee. There's pain radiating up my shins. That means I was wrong, doesn't it? My legs are still here! How else would I feel pain down there?

I try to sit up anyway, try to see my bare feet. Straining my neck and using my arms to push myself an inch upward despite the sickening ache in my bones, I stare down at…

At *nothing.*

No toes.

No ankles.

No bottom halves of my legs.

"*No…*" I utter.

"Ruth…"

"Where are m-my l-l-legs?" I ask in a quiet, trembling voice. "Did they—"

I look into Warrose's swollen eyes. He's weeping. Sad, thin tears trickle over his long, black lashes. His lips part, but nothing comes out. No words at all.

"Did they take my legs?"

The question sits in the stale air alone, heavy and sucking all the life and hope from this cage. I silently beg for the answer that will relax the muscles in my back. But I keep seeing that axe. That man swinging his arms back. The blood streaming from the open wounds under my kneecaps.

"Yes," Warrose whispers with a grunt to clear his throat. "They've taken your legs."

I'm unable to blink as I stare at him through thickening tears. I wait for him to take it back, wait for him to give me a sliver of good news. But his expression is as bleak and hopeless as I feel.

I think back to why this all happened, remembering pushing past the soldiers to volunteer to accept Dessin's punishment. To save Warrose's life.

Of course.

I deserved this.

I betrayed my friends.

But my thoughts have been scattered. Warped. Clouded over with memories I can't attach to. All I feel is the love for my family and the confusion of why I betrayed them so heartlessly. I made one last silent request for Skylenna to sneak into the void and fact check my duplicity. Maybe it was baseless hope that I'm not the villain I believe myself to be. Maybe I was praying for a lifeline.

I just can't wrap my head around how I've been able to lie, cheat, manipulate the people I love most in this world. I'd never hurt DaiSzek. I'd never lie to Skylenna.

But it's true, isn't it?

"I deserve this," I whimper. The world grows cold and hateful. Black vines of bitter death snake around my vision. My pain levels skyrocket above anything manageable. This is what I deserve. "I betrayed my family! I deserve this!" I cry out with a burning throat.

"No," Warrose attempts to say, but my cries drown everything else out.

"They've taken my legs! I'll never run again!" I lie back down in a sobbing, hiccuping heap.

Niles and Warrose crowd me, holding my hands, trying to speak past my hysterics. But there's nothing they can say to bring me back now. I'm spiraling down, down, down. I'm sinking into the abyss of my agony and depression. I should be dead. I should be buried under this prison.

"I'll never—see the sun again!" I can't breathe. The cry has manifested into something crazed and delirious. "I'll never—*walk* again!"

*Can't breathe. Can't breathe.*

*I deserve this.*

362

*Betrayed them.*

*Can't breathe.*

Warrose and Niles's faces shift out of my sight, making way for a beautiful face surrounded by long honey-blonde hair. She looks down at me with wise, shining eyes. A gentle hand caresses my cheek, and she gazes into me as if she's unburying the secrets of my soul.

"Ruth." Skylenna's voice resonates through my entire being like a cosmic blast. Like the voice of God. She squeezes Dessin's hand as he looks down at me from behind her.

"I wasn't there for you when you needed me most," she says with both calm and serious lines hardening her expression. "Let me be here now. Let me bring you peace."

I swallow then blink. And the floor melts from under me. I slip backward, freefalling through the air, never looking away from Skylenna's soothing gaze. Her hair flies around her in wild, golden waves.

"Don't be afraid," she says with a voice that resembles all things holy and powerful. "You won't feel any pain where we're going."

I'm not afraid. The wind of the fall feels like dry water. Like tearing through layers of another world. It's guiding us to a place that robs me of all anguish. And all I can do is exhale.

Behind Skylenna's head, the darkness blots away. Pinholes of cerulean blue and fluffy clouds chase away the eternal black. And suddenly, my head is surrounded by tall blades of grass and the most incredible scent of lavender.

Skylenna brushes my hair away from my face. "Do you see that?"

I squint, my eyes involuntarily watering at the blasting rays of sunlight.

"You're seeing the sun again," she says with a smile.

I don't know how she's done it. But my entire spirit is levitating with the gentle allure of happiness. The kind that warms your cheeks and sends euphoric shivers down your spine. I take a deep breath, absorbing the floral aroma, the fresh air, the sunlight.

"Where are we?" I ask.

Her face lights up like a blooming wildflower. "The Ambrose Oasis."

She helps me sit up so I can take in the heavenly view. The purple wisteria dancing in the breeze. The vast meadow with oversized sunflowers, violet candytufts, and huge evergreen trees forming a protective perimeter around us. It's the meadow where we finally reunited with Dessin and Skylenna again. A little sanctuary for a small amount of time.

"It feels like heaven," I say quietly to myself. "Have I died?"

"No, you're alive. But I think God gave me a small piece of heaven, and this is it. To use for moments like this."

I look down to see my toes clenching around flower petals. My legs basking in the warm sun. With confusion wrinkling my brow, I slide my gaze to Skylenna.

"No matter what happens to us in life, I can always bring us here. Heaven is where you can see your loved ones again. And although Ambrose Oasis isn't quite that... at least you can run again, Ruth. Let me give you that much."

My hands press over my mouth to suppress a happy cry, although a moment flashes through me. The moment they found me kissing Kaspias. The moment I cut ties with my soul sister forever.

"I don't deserve this," I mutter from behind my fingers. "I broke our family."

"No, you didn't, Ruth." Skylenna pulls my hands away from my mouth so she can hold them. "You were manipulated with a stronger form of Mind Phantoms. The memories you have of betraying us aren't real. Kaspias deceived us all. But I should have known. I should have believed in your pure heart."

I study our entwined hands, trying to understand how this could have happened.

"I'm so sorry, Ruth. I let you down. It's my fault this happened to you."

"I didn't...betray you?" The memories feel real, yet I can't connect with them at all.

"Never," she replies sadly. "But deep down, you must have known something was off. You're the one that got me to look into the void for the truth."

I nod. "Everything aside from my love for my family felt detached. I remember being a spy or a traitor, but have no feelings connected to those images. Only to the ones of loving you all. I guess I was hoping you would discover I wasn't the villain."

"Not a villain." Skylenna's eyes fill with tears. "A hero. You're a fucking hero, Ruth."

"And…still your soul sister?" I ask.

She laughs wetly with tears forming rivers down her cheeks. "You'll always be my soul sister. And although I can't change what happened, I think I can help your mind suppress the false memories. May I?"

I invite Skylenna into my heart, my mind, my memories. It takes several moments of feeling her swim through each moment I've been given to feel ashamed over. The traitorous past of my fake relationship with Kaspias. The times I never actually shared any special information with him about my friends. It was all a lie. She detangles the thick web of fabricated moments, stores them somewhere deep in the back of my head. A place I won't find easily.

After it's all done, a great shadow shifts in front of us. DaiSzek steps around Skylenna to nuzzle his nose against my legs.

"Is he real?"

Skylenna grins. "I always thought he was a figment of my imagination. Now I know he's been real this entire time. A RottWeilen alpha shares an impenetrable bond with his pack. He's been saving me from trauma this entire time."

I rub my hands through his fur, feeling happier than I have in a long time.

"So, what do you say, Ruth? Want to run with us?"

I jump to my feet with a squeal, lurching forward and laughing as DaiSzek slows his pace to run with us through the tall grass.

I realize the depression, the pain, the hopelessness might swallow me whole when we return. But at least I have this.

To run one last time.

# 40. For Ruth

## Skylenna

"Where did you take her?" Warrose asks.

I let go of Ruth's face, sighing at how peacefully she sleeps in his arms. Her brunette curls are damp with sweat, her face is gray and depleted of color, and the rest of her body seems to shrivel in on itself. I force myself to look at Warrose.

"Ambrose Oasis," I reply with a long exhale. "She's running with DaiSzek there."

Dessin massages my shoulders, planting a slow kiss on the crook of my neck. There's still tension between us. In a way, I harmed his trust in me, in our communication by going up to the Bird's Nest. If the roles had been reversed, I would have a hard time forgiving him. But he's hurting, too, from Ruth's tragedy. I can see it in his cloudy eyes; he feels responsible for her. For all of us. There's guilt in his chest the same way it's sitting in mine. He understands my breakdown and why I felt like I had no way out.

"She's running?" Warrose eyes become circular and misty.

"Yes."

He slumps a little against the bars digging into his back.

"I can keep sending her there through the worst of the pain," I add sleepily, then turn to Dessin. "What's our main concern with her recovery right now?"

"Blood loss and infection."

Nervous energy clenches my muscles and curdles my stomach. I open my mouth to respond, but a hunched movement snags my gaze. Small sniffles and something dripping against a puddle on the floor.

Niles does his best to mop up Ruth's vomit with an old rag. But as he cleans, tears leak from his eyes straight to the floor without making contact with his cheeks.

"Niles." Marilynn touches the back of his arm.

He shrugs her off.

Sadness swells in my throat like a balloon about to pop. I swallow, commanding myself to be strong for him. "Talk to us, Niles."

He mumbles something, continuing to scrub.

"What's that now?" I ask.

"She won't make it through another Fun House Night!" he howls, his cries rushing through the halls of the prison. "Look at her!"

I look down at the bloody bandages and clothes wrapped around Ruth's legs. He's right. They make prisoners participate no matter what state of health they're in.

"I don't care what kind of plan you two have to come up with! Make *me* a fucking decoy to die here, I DON'T CARE! Just get Ruthie out! *Please!*"

My heart shreds into thin, lifeless strings as I look at Dessin. He's watching me with a hard, determined stare. Like he's waiting for me to come to the same conclusion he's already arrived at.

I have to get out first.

He was right.

If it's our best option, then nothing else matters.

I nod to him with my reluctant understanding. Letting the devastating reality of this new plan, new predicament, settle into my belly like rotting food. Leaving my family behind feels dirty and evil. I'd die for them. I'd gladly make myself the decoy to get them out. But looking down at Ruth's shivering, frail body…I know what must be done.

"We have a few days until the next Fun House Night. We'll have a plan," I say, looking into Niles's puffy eyes.

"Let's get some sleep. I'll take the first watch on Ruth." Dessin holds me in his strong arms as he arranges himself to have a clear view of Ruth, with enough room to check her vitals throughout the night.

"Wake me up when it's my turn," I whisper with my eyes closed.

"I will."

And I know that's a lie. With something this traumatic, his system won't be getting any sleep tonight.

# Dessin

I SPEND THE ENTIRE NIGHT working through different scenarios to get Skylenna out first.

But I only land on one that would be the most efficient. However, it depends on Skylenna. Her mind. The void. I still don't fully understand how it works, and I'm not sure she does either.

If she can force Kaspias into the prison void, maybe she can get him to sneak her out. He's a commander with high clearance. At this point, with all he's done, I don't give a shit if she fucks up his brain to get herself out.

*Neither do I*, Kane says near the front.

*About fucking time*, Kalidus adds.

I've been dissociating throughout the whole night. Performing surgery on Ruth that might very well have killed her was damaging to our system. The amount of blood, the complexity of rearranging her nerve endings, and keeping my hands from shaking was enough to send other alters racing to the front for different reasons.

And on top of everything, my heart nearly exploded in my chest as I realized where Skylenna ran off to. The Bird's Nest. I had my doubts, but seeing her face told me all I needed to know. She blamed herself for Scarlett's death. And this hit too close to home. It triggered an abrupt emotional response that she had the day she found Scarlett hanging in that closet. The day she tried to burn her house down with her inside it.

I should have figured it out sooner. But I was only focused on making sure Ruth survived the surgery.

A foul wrath races through my veins, pounding into my brain at the thought of losing Skylenna after everything we've been through. What the fuck would I have done? Would she really have jumped if Scarlett hadn't stopped her?

*She wouldn't have done it,* Kane says with unwavering confidence.

*How do you know?* I ask him.

*I know she probably thought she was going to. But we're soul mates. She wouldn't move on without us. I know her better than I know myself, Dess.*

I sigh, dropping my head to kiss Skylenna's hair, breathing her into my lungs, and closing my eyes as I fantasize taking her far away from here. Building a house in the Red Oaks and eventually giving her the castle she deserves.

Warrose's vibrant eyes shake me from the thoughts I've buried myself in. Ruth looks so small, withering away in his massive embrace. He circles her in his brawny arms, absently caressing her arm.

"How long have you been awake?" I ask in a low voice.

He shrugs one big shoulder. "Long enough to see you haven't slept."

I haven't slept much these days at all. How long will my body be able to keep up?

"How does her skin feel?" I lift my chin in Ruth's direction. "Hot? Cold? Is she running a fever?"

Warrose glances down, shifts his hand silently over her forehead, then to her cheek, and last her neck. "She's a little warm. But no fever."

I let out a breath of relief. "Good. And her pulse?"

He places two fingers on her throat, waiting silently in anticipation. "It's okay. A little weak."

"We need to get fluids in her system."

He agrees with a soft grunt.

I watch the way he moves her damp curls away from her face, how his brow wrinkles together as he gazes down at her. He blows out air with an exhale that tells me he keeps holding his breath.

"You really like her," I state.

Warrose doesn't look up at me. He merely bows his head once.

"Has anything else happened between you two?"

The conversation I'm starting feels a little out of our comfort zone. We don't talk about our attraction to women. Kane has discussed Skylenna, his one true love, with Warrose before when they were younger. They were far more open about their feelings than I have ever been comfortable with.

"We kissed the night before…"

My eyes fall closed. "Before Kaspias fucked us."

"Mm-hmm."

"And it meant something to both of you?" The question sounds moronic and obvious the moment it reaches our ears.

"Yes."

"And now?"

His eyes snap up to mine with mild aggression. "Now more than ever."

I'm happy to hear that. Even though I've been snippy and cold with Ruth, I…I *love* her, too. She feels like the sister I never had. And watching that axe crack into her legs was enough to split pieces of my soul off and throw them into a black pit of flames.

And worst of all, I wasn't there. I tried to break free too late. If only I figured out Kaspias's body language immediately. But he's the hardest person to read I have ever met, aside from Judas.

"We're going to get her out," I assure him evenly.

"How?"

"Skylenna needs to target Kaspias. Get inside his head. If she can get him to let his guard down, she can slip into the void. From there, if he can get us all out unnoticed, great. If not, he needs to get Skylenna out so she can bring the armies in that are probably waiting at the shoreline."

Warrose bites his lip in thought. "He won't be able to get us all out."

*I know.*

# 41. The Lineage

## Skylenna

"Skylenna, baby, wake up."

My eyes feel sticky and sore as I pry them open. Warrose and Niles are looking past me. I follow the direction of their eyes to the opened cage door, flinching at the unexpected figures standing there in silence.

"Help me with the trays," Dessin mutters in my ear.

The cooks from the kitchen hold out feeble trays with bowls and plates of food. A few more inmates behind them carry buckets of water and clean cloths.

After taking everything from their hands, they look to Ruth's sleeping body, bow their heads, and leave.

"That was kind of them," I say.

"It was," Dessin agrees.

Niles dips a white cloth in the bucket of water and begins dabbing Ruth's forehead with it. It breaks my heart the way he frowns at her appearance, blotting her cheeks with the utmost tenderness.

"We need to wake her so she can get some fluids in her system." Dessin pushes a tray near Warrose.

"Ruthie," Niles coos, kissing her knuckles. "Open your eyes. Just for a little while."

Warrose taps her shoulder softly, whispering something in her ear.

It takes her several minutes to stir, groan, whimper, then finally open her eyes. They're bloodshot, unfocused. She finally makes eye contact with each person surrounding her, wincing in pain, and finally gazing down at her bloody bandages.

"No," she whines.

"We just need you to eat something. Then you can go back to sleep," Marilynn says, and it's the first time I've noticed how hard she's trying to keep her facial expression slack and unmoving. A steel guard that she's taken time to build and strengthen.

Ruth sniffles, turning her head, closing her eyes, and letting tears drip down the side of her face. Her moans are threaded with both agony and devastation.

Warrose doesn't wait for her to come around. Instead, he lifts her head and signals to Marilynn to feed her. Spoonfuls of soup and a few sips of water later, they let Ruth settle back into Warrose's lap.

It's hard to watch.

Hard to listen to her groans.

Hard to stand by and do nothing.

"What good am I to you all now?" Ruth mutters against Warrose's thigh.

"What?" Dessin blurts out first.

"They've taken my legs," she whimpers. "I'm dead weight to you all."

I grasp at my chest to contain the pain. It radiates down my spine. How can she think that? How can I help her when she's feeling this hopeless?

Niles interjects, then Warrose, then Dessin. But a feeling hollow and gray fills my senses. That creeping suspicion that I'm being watched. An unsuspecting pair of eyes burning into me. I raise my sight to the corner of the cage behind Marilynn.

My posture stiffens. The hairs on my neck stand upright. And it's close to the same feeling I had with Scarlett.

He's here. But he's not.

An old man, appearing to be in his seventies with thin tuffs of white hair, olive skin, and wise, brown eyes watches me intently. He's dressed like a farmer, trousers rolled up mid-calf and a dirty cotton tunic with a drawstring around the neck.

I debate pretending he isn't here. But it's just as Scarlett said…I've reached a new level in my mind after Ruth's tragedy. I've broken a barrier that allows me to see this old man now. Someone who has passed on.

"She's very pretty," he comments thoughtfully.

I look away, hoping he won't realize I can see him. I'm not sure how this works. Do I have control over it? Is this invisible veil now lifted, and I can see them all the time? I wonder if I'll ever have these answers to my new abilities.

"I never got to meet her, you know. Died of a heart attack in my chair when she was a baby."

My breath hitches.

The old man laughs with a slow nod. His crow's feet pinching together like compressed clay. He has her smile. The one with the upturned, scrunching nose. I relax a little.

"That's my granddaughter. Can't you see the resemblance?"

My eyes dart between them, processing their similarities and their differences.

"I've been waiting a very long time to tell a family secret. I think now might be a better time than any." His voice is rusted over with old age and possibly smoking too many cigarettes.

"What is it?" Dessin's voice makes me twitch in his direction. Of course he's been watching me. He catches everything.

"I…" What am I supposed to say? Would she even believe me? Would she be willing to listen?

"What?" he asks again.

I'm torn whether to speak up or not. Dessin knows the truth, but Ruth is withdrawn so deeply into her own mind, she'll likely tune me out completely.

"Ask her if she still adds two raspberries to her tea," the old man requests.

I blink at him. Now everyone but Ruth is staring at me. I pull my lips behind my teeth, drumming my fingers against my thigh.

"Ruth? Do you still add two raspberries to your tea?" I ask.

To my surprise, her head shifts against Warrose's thigh, she blinks twice as tears soak the pant leg under her face. Everyone else seems to stiffen, too.

"Tell her Grandpa Monroe thought that was very sweet of her." He's watching Ruth now with a knowing smile. A warmth that can only be described as a grandparent's fondness for their grandchild.

I repeat his words carefully.

"Did you see that in the void?" Her voice is raw and beaten, yet she still doesn't make an effort to look at me.

"No," I reply quietly. A heavy pause impregnates my hesitation. "I've broken through the veil of the living and dead. He's been waiting a long time to tell you a family secret."

Warrose, Marilynn, and Niles shoot their startled eyes to Dessin for answers. But he only crosses his arms and smirks in response, pride rooted deep in his soul at the sight of me.

Ruth turns her head, moaning loudly at the sharp pains that small motion caused her. Those long lashes flutter before her swollen gaze meets mine.

*Please, please let this be good.* I can't bear to disappoint her.

"Oh, it is," Grandpa Monroe says. "Tell my granddaughter that there's a reason we've taught our lineage Old Alkadonian despite strict Demechnef laws."

"There's a reason your family taught their lineage Old Alkadonian despite strict Demechnef laws," I repeat slowly, watching the old man with my own questions hanging in the air.

Ruth's brow furrows. And even that causes her to wince.

I listen to his next words with anticipation gathering in my belly.

"His mother went through great lengths to keep your family small and unnoticeable. But even she knew that one day the significance of your real last name would defy the hierarchy," I announce, although my tone changes to question at the end. Where is he going with this?

Niles stirs in his seat, searching my eyes for answers the same way I search the old man's.

Grandpa Monroe clears his throat. "Tell my granddaughter she's made for greatness no matter her current situation. She will heal nations and change hearts."

I say his words, feeling itchy with a need to understand.

"Come on!" Niles exclaims impatiently.

"I am the bastard child of Malcolm Mazonist. My mother smuggled her pregnant belly away to the shrill society of Demechnef before anyone could notice. My granddaughter's true name is Ruth Mazonist, the heir to the Vexamen throne."

# 42. One Heart

## Skylenna

I crumple to my knees with a choked sob.

"What?!"

The group outburst rattles me. But Ruth stays perfectly still.

I crawl to her, holding her clammy hand in mine. "Your grandfather is the bastard child of Malcolm Mazonist. His mother escaped this country to hide her pregnancy in Demechnef. Your real name is Ruth Mazonist, the rightful heir to the Vexamen throne."

The group is deadly quiet at first. But Warrose whoops like a howling animal, running a hand through his hair.

Niles jumps to his feet with a gaping smile. "What?! WHAT?"

Dessin laughs in genuine shock.

Marilynn kisses Ruth on the head with tears gathering at the corners of her sapphire blue eyes. Although…she doesn't look surprised.

"Are you certain?" Ruth starts to cry, and I can't tell if it's out of happiness or pain or the unknown of her future.

"Yes!"

"Skylenna," Grandpa Monroe interrupts. "She'll struggle for a long time. It's true. But this bit of news will act as a beacon of light for her. A force of strength and motivation to survive her hardships. Never let her forget who she really is."

I bow my head. Unbelievably thankful that he picked his moment to share this with me.

Warrose wipes the tears and sweat from Ruth's face, looking both relieved and tortured as she shudders in his arms. Her cries stun us into silence.

"How am I supposed to be any good to anyone like this?" she finally verbalizes with a discouraging finality to her tone.

Warrose's jaw tics. "Your strength doesn't come from your legs, my little rebel. It comes from your heart. Your soul." He lifts her chin softly, forcing her to look at our family sitting around her. "This family is filled with misfits, broken bodies, and minds. But our hearts beat as one. We make up where the other lacks. Do you understand?"

I look around at all of us. Niles's burns. Warrose's scars that paint his body like tattoos. Marilynn's history with Vlademur Demechnef. Dessin's traumatic past in Demechnef. Kane's childhood. My childhood.

Ruth sniffs and squeezes her eyes shut so hard, tears run rampant. She nods twice.

"What do you need from us, Ruthie? Give us just one thing we can do to help you feel better." Niles leans forward, holding together his own suffering for his best friend.

Ruth doesn't hesitate. She closes her eyes, licks her dry lips, and exhales.

"I need a group hug. From my family."

I don't understand why this single request clogs my throat with the need to cry for the rest of my life. And it's not just me. Dessin's eyes fall to the floor, catching the light with a subtle shine. His Adam's apple shifts just as Niles has to look away, nodding like that request is the best one he's ever heard.

And in this moment, we look at each other simultaneously. It's in this stare between each family member, we understand the weight of this group hug. It was a source of humor when we first reunited. It was

380

something that brought smiles to our faces. It was a request that Dessin might have denied under any other circumstance.

But this is Ruth.

And as we gaze into each other's eyes, we know that this special momentthis hug, it's for all we've lost. It's for Ruth.

I hold my breath against the sob rising in my lungs as we scoot forward, encircling Ruth's body with our heat and love and sorrow. My right arm slides around Dessin's waist, and his left over my shoulder. My left hand finds the side of Niles's ribs, and he stretches his arm around Warrose, who is embracing Marilynn. And last, Marilynn slides her hand over mine against Dessin's back.

We huddle so closely together, foreheads almost touching, tears dripping around Ruth's sobbing figure, unable to keep her eyes open as we have this one moment.

There are no silly remarks from Niles.

No rude comments from Dessin.

Our hearts beat as one.

For Ruth.

# 43. Show Of Dolls

## Dessin

I'm going to kill Kane's brother.

If it weren't for the massive weight on my shoulders to stay out of trouble so I can keep everyone safe, I'd do that right now. I'd pull his skin off his bones and feed it to the Blood Mammoths. There are no words to describe the rage I'm keeping locked away, no adjectives to represent the fury that bubbles in my veins at the sight of Ruth so ill, so depressed, so weak.

If I didn't have to be strategic, I'd bring her the severed head of each soldier that cheered for her demise.

I want them all to burn for stringing her up like a doll and ripping limbs off like they were disposable.

The question has often risen from my contemplation in this specific type of captivity: is the asylum worse? Or better?

It isn't a question anymore.

"I can't fucking eat," Warrose grumbles as he pushes his plate away.

The girls asked us to go eat at the commissary so they could give Ruth a sponge bath. We needed to separate anyway. I've been getting stir crazy, pent up with so many raw, animalist urges to slaughter these fucked-up human beings. I can see the same crazed glint in Warrose's eyes as well.

"Neither can I," Niles agrees.

Although my stomach is in knots, constantly nauseated, I force myself to take a bite of the stale slice of bread on my tray.

"Eat. I know it's fucking terrible, but we'll need our strength," I say quietly.

They nod reluctantly, shoveling in food with a tight grimace. Watching their gloomy expressions, I do something that's more in Skylenna's wheelhouse.

"Ruth is royalty," I say.

I try to start a conversation. Raise morale or whatever.

Niles peers up at me from his slumped position over his food. Warrose keeps eating with an acknowledging grunt.

They don't respond. Now what?

"That's, um, crazy," I add.

Niles raises his head completely. Warrose stops eating.

"What are you doing?" Warrose asks.

"I think he's trying to chat," Niles muses slowly. "Or gossip. The intent is unclear."

"Why?" Warrose asks with an almost scared look on his face.

"Did Skylenna tell you to do it?" Niles's face isn't out from the dreary cloud it was under, but it's certainly taking on an entertained expression.

"No, she didn't tell me to do anything." I narrow my eyes with rising annoyance.

"She definitely did." Warrose pinches his mouth together like he's just diagnosed me with a terminal illness.

"I'm just talking." My forehead heats up. "What's wrong with starting a conversation?"

Niles and Warrose exchange a strange look. It pisses me off.

"Nothing…for most people," Warrose mutters.

"It's just weird when you do it." Niles smiles sympathetically.

They stare at me for several seconds before rumbling with unexpected laughter. I don't offer a smile in return. They fucked up.

"I'm never talking again."

They laugh harder.

Although they're annoying the hell out of me, I know Skylenna would be happy that I got them to laugh. I just won't tell her they were laughing *at* me.

"Hello, Beetle Brain," Helga Bee chirps, materializing out of thin air.

I flinch.

*I* actually flinch.

This does nothing to quell my *former* friends' amusement.

"What is it?" I grimace.

"New stock in the stadium. Honey of Nectar Valley. Go on and snag it before the other rodents get to it first."

The boys stop laughing and gawk up at her like she's a living, breathing angel. We ran out of it for Ruth, and she's been howling relentlessly in pain. We've tried everything.

I jump to my feet, grab Helga Bee's round, plump face, and plant a rough kiss against her forehead. She fusses and blushes, swatting me on the arm.

"Wait till we get a room, muscles!" She pats me on the back, ushering us out of the commissary.

"For the record," I holler over my shoulder. "I like that nickname better!"

"Too bad, Beetle Brain!"

I smirk as we race down the hall.

*I have a bad feeling.* Kane floods my consciousness with anxiety and apprehension.

*About what?*

We enter the musty stadium, smelling of blood and sweaty bodies. It's empty, and we're the first ones here. The iron trunk of supplies sits in the center of the stage. A glass jug that holds about a gallon of the Honey of Nectar Valley sits at the top.

"I hate to be that guy, but we're grabbing the whole thing," Niles suggests.

"Agreed." Stepping up on the stage, I feel the hairs on the back of my neck stand up. That alarm that I feel in the bed of my chest, traveling down to my gut, sounds off. Danger. A threat. Something to be cautious of.

*Grab it and go*, Kalidus orders.

I snatch the big glass bottle only for it to slip from my grasp, banging against the side of the iron chest.

Turning my hand over, I see the unmistakable shine of thick, greasy oil.

*Fuck!*

"Get out! Go back to the cage!" I command Warrose and Niles.

The veil of sleep falls over me like a ton of bricks. I feel the stage bang against my knees. Looking over my shoulder, past the spell of dizziness, I see Warrose and Niles on the floor with needles in their necks.

The grimy surface of the stage is the last image to fade.

# Dessin

"He'll wake up in a minute. Unless he's already awake. You never know with my brother."

My head is the weight of a building. Gravity lays against my lids like concrete, preventing them from lifting. Everything in my neuropathways moves like a slug. My muscles, heart rate, motor functions. What have they done to me?

I focus on the sounds around me. Footsteps. Heavy. A man, no, two of them. Metal grazing metal. Breathing soft and heavy, close to a snore. The sharp whistling of fierce winds hitting a window.

Allowing myself to relax, I tune into a special frequency, syncing with minute rhythms and sensations throughout my surroundings. There are five heartbeats in the room including my own. Two are fast as if they're in motion, and the rest are lethargic. The burning scents of propane, saline, hot coals, and other chemicals I don't recognize.

"Get them up. I don't have time to wait."

That voice.

*I know that voice.*

A surge of adrenaline dumps into my bloodstream. My jaw tics. The muscles around my eyes fight to wake up.

Why is it so hard to breathe? To shift my body? It's as if someone is standing on my chest, clamping my arms down at my sides. I press my back into something cold and hard. A wall. Granite.

"Good morning, brother," Kaspias says too close to my face.

There's a sizzle followed by a bright explosion of pain against my rib. I grunt through my teeth, not even able to jerk away from the burning of something hot against my flesh. Smoke fills my nostrils, and finally, my eyes pop open, flaring wide and alert as I take in the scenery.

Kaspias twirls a fire poker in his left hand, examining my drugged expression with malice and foreign intrigue. It's unsettling the way his eyes light up at my pain.

"Guess you all found out about my little white lie with Ruth."

A snarl rips from my throat as I try to jolt forward, roasting alive with the need to separate his jaw from his face. But my body is stapled to the granite wall. Literally. Metal molds around my waist, hips, legs, ankles, throat, forehead, and arms. I am bolted with no way of breaking free.

I suppose they've figured out I can't be trusted with the shackles.

"Dessin." Warrose's husky voice comes from my right side. I can't even turn my head to look.

"I hope you don't mind. I thought we'd have a *guy's day*. The females make us weak and tender. And by us, I mean you three," Kaspias taunts.

He brought Warrose and Niles here, too.

*Goddamn it.*

"What do you want?" I exhale to steady my rising anger.

"I hoped having your friends here might make you a little more compliant about accepting what I have planned for you."

"Stop toying with him, son. Let's get on with it."

My eyes shoot up to the corner of the room. That familiar voice steps out of the blanketing shadows, revealing the tall, spindly man. The one with raven hair and empty eyes. The man who walks with a cane.

The man who once grabbed Skylenna by the hair and told her how a woman should behave.

My nails nearly peel off as I grind them into the wall behind me.

"Masten," I say with a tone cold enough to chill the air. "The Demechnef Traitor."

# 44. The Demechnef Traitor

## Dessin

"I assume I'm speaking to Dessin." His distant eyes flick up to me with disinterest. "Your way of coming and going as a boy was always confusing to me."

I'll kill him. Not just for the way he once treated my girl. But Masten and I have a long-standing history. He knew me when I was a child. He helped train me into the sick son of a bitch I am today. He was the reason Kalidus split. With the constant bullying, name-calling, and belittlement that spewed from this man's mouth, we had no choice but to create an alter that could maintain confidence even through the constant ridicule and abuse.

At the sight of this demon, Kalidus presses dangerously close to the front, ready to take over at any sign of mistreatment.

"Not brave enough to face me without these restraints?" I ask in a low, deadly voice.

Masten scoffs softly. "Not ignorant enough is the better way to phrase that."

He is right. If freed from being bound to this wall, I'd act without a single thought. There would be no consideration for whether my attack would hurt the others. There is too much history here for rational thought.

"Then get on with it. Whatever you're going to do."

"My thoughts exactly. Your relationship with the female subject has posed quite an issue for us. We need the ultimate soldier who is loyal, dutiful, and complies without thought or complaint." He traces the wolf's head on the top of his cane. "But with you and that...*girl*, your only loyalty is to her. Your only care in the world is her."

*And his point is?* Kalidus says slowly, flooding my mind with a superior cockiness.

"I'd like to rearrange your priorities. It'll take some conditioning with the new Mind Phantom chemical we fashioned, but I'm certain that after this trial, we'll be able to...*fix* you."

My lungs tighten.

"And after that success, we'll be able to fix her."

A laugh booms across the room. Warrose's laugh. Dark and edgy like unfinished, onyx marble.

"You think that kind of love can be altered?" He chuckles again. "Then you're even dumber than you are ugly."

I smirk, though it doesn't touch the fire in my eyes.

Masten slides his glare to Warrose, revealing a subtle curling of his upper lip. My heart rate picks up at the simple movement. It was always a tell when we were younger that Warrose's smart mouth was about to earn him a beating.

"Any fantasy can be altered with the right motivation." Masten nods his head at Kaspias.

Kaspias takes one step forward, jabbing the bright orange end of a fire poker into Warrose's left side. He hits a sensitive part of Warrose's core, the space over his ribs, clustered with nerves that explode under the heat of the poker.

Warrose grunts, taking deep, angry breaths to absorb the pain. He channels it into silent rage. This isn't new to either of us. Those scars disguised as tattoos have taught him much about pain management.

Kaspias laughs irritably, glancing over his shoulder at Masten for further instruction. And I refuse to plead or beg for them to spare my friend. It's a silent understanding between the two of us. If they know our weakness, they can control us. We are easily able to withstand torture, so it won't be a problem to ice them out.

But something in Masten's glazed-over eyes makes me second guess myself. He is thinking of a way around our little arrangement. After all, he was part of the reason we grew so skilled with accepting torture.

"It looks like the other one is no stranger to fire, hmm?"

The other one.

I hear one word that comes out in a plea, the way a child who begged for a light to be turned on so they wouldn't have to sleep in the dark.

"No," Niles breathes.

"I bet he'd respond well to the poker, don't you think?" Masten directs to Kaspias.

"Please, God," Niles rasps, struggling against the impenetrable metal that bolts us to the wall.

My heart sinks into my stomach. Warrose and I could have easily made it through whatever they had to throw at us. But it's Niles. He isn't like us, but he is family.

The sizzle of hot metal burning into skin spears through the giant room like a stick of dynamite. Niles's screams follow, making me lose my breath.

"I'm here, alright? I can't go anywhere! There's no need to hurt him!" I order with a furiousness lining the edges of my words.

Kaspias pulls the fire poker away, grinning at the quick submission on my behalf.

"Just get the fuck on with whatever you're going to do," I add. I'm confident in my brain's ability to protect itself. We've been through so much already in our lifetimes.

"Good, I'm glad you see it that way," Masten replies as he prepares a glass syringe.

Niles moans in agony and what must be PTSD flashbacks. I'll do whatever they want just for them to stay the fuck away from my friend. I never expected that thought to cross my mind regarding Niles of all people. But here we stand.

"Hold still," Masten commands, sticking me in the neck with the syringe filled with yellow liquid.

"What is it?" I grimace.

"Let's call it a safety precaution. If you behave, I'll enlighten you later."

The chemical settles into my bloodstream, feeling cold and unnatural as it travels to my brain.

"This one, on the other hand, is the new Mind Phantom. I've added a twist to help your conditioning set in a little faster." He injects me again, this time, on the other side of my neck. I flinch at the way this one scalds like flesh-eating acid as it invades my body.

It happens fast. The quick ink that blots through my vision. The shouting of Warrose. The cruel, narrowing of Masten's eyes.

And I've been sucked into something I can't climb out of.

I'm back in Kane's childhood home, swinging the sickle into Sophia's chest.

# 45. The Call
# Of The Void

## Skylenna

"I want to die," Ruth mutters as she spits more bile from her mouth.

Marilynn ties Ruth's thick curls back into a braid so they don't get clumped with any vomit. Her pain level is so high that it's affecting her stomach. Nausea, diarrhea, migraines, body aches. We've all felt helpless while taking care of her. Watching her suffer is bearing witness to my heart being cut into tiny pieces, then set on fire.

After one final dry heave, Ruth slumps back down, letting us wash her half-naked body. She smells like captivity. Like dried blood, bile, sweat, and terminal illness. We thought that by cleaning her up, it might help her feel a little better.

But in fact, nothing can make her feel better.

She's depressed. Every time Ruth looks down, she sees the empty space where her legs once existed. And it only takes her a moment to process, but she ends up sobbing quietly into her hands for an hour.

"The boys should be coming back any moment," Marilynn says, trying to make her voice sound hopeful, even though the action is obviously foreign to her.

And that's the sad truth of this. Our hope has been waning significantly. Everything everywhere looks so grim. It's the feeling all living, breathing beings in captivity feel, isn't it? A complete loss of hope. Our world turns a shade of black, cold, and empty.

But no matter what, we do our best not to let Ruth see that.

"I want to die," Ruth repeats in a withdrawn voice. She has this dead look in her chestnut eyes, as if her soul is retreating far away, not bothering to give this body a second glance.

My hands tremble at the reminder of Scarlett. In a way, she looks like her at this moment. That same expression Scarlett wore when I left her to gather blueberries.

I won't bury another friend. I won't lose any more family. Stumbling toward her, I place my cold hands on her cheeks. They're hollow, ghostly without that radiant olive tone she usually wears so beautifully.

"Should I take you away for a while?" I ask.

"I guess." No emotion. No care for anything at all.

My bottom lip sticks out involuntarily, a natural impulse as tears gather in my eyes.

It only takes a few moments to lure her back to Ambrose Oasis. And only a few more to return to Marilynn, who watches me with exhaustion hanging over her soft features.

"We're in hell, aren't we?" I ask her.

She nods. "The ninth circle. Right in the thick of it."

As we watch Ruth breathing shallowly, I try to count back in my head. The minutes, maybe hours, of how long the boys have been gone.

"Shouldn't they be back by now?" I look at Marilynn with suspicion pinching my brows.

"Right? What else could they be doing?"

I turn my head down the hallway, waiting to see if I hear their voice or footsteps. They were only supposed to be gone for twenty, maybe thirty minutes or so. It feels like it's been a couple hours.

"Do you think I should go" A torrent of misery blasts through the void like a horn of war. Echoing through my bones like hellfire. I fall back against the bars of the cage, clutching my chest as a tidal wave of emotions suffocates the inside of the void.

"What's wrong?" Marilynn rushes to my side.

"Oh my god," I gasp, breathing through the fear, the hatred, the almighty downpour of guilt.

And I *feel* him.

It's tangible.

A rope connecting my life source to him.

I feel Dessin through the loud, violent energy sounding off in the void.

"Shit," I grunt, bearing down my teeth. "I think he's in trouble."

Marilynn doesn't waste a breath. She merely lifts her chin, straightens her shoulders, and nods toward the long, grim hallway.

"Go. I'll take care of Ruth."

My insides jolt with a sharp, electrical shock at the essence of Dessin's roars. I'd know it anywhere. It's the stinging reminder of his grunts radiating through the asylum as he was being tortured.

I'd argue with Marilynn about leaving the two of them alone, but the pull to find my soulmate is unbearable. It's an itch to escape my skin, travel the length of the void to find him. I nod to my friend, jump to my feet, and bolt through the hallway.

# Dessin

"ARE YOU GOING TO SWING it again or let her bleed out slowly?"

Skylenna stands next to Sophia's body, arms crossed, head tilted, and a wicked smirk I've never seen on her before.

Kane's mother bleeds out on the kitchen table. The sounds of her gurgling lungs fill the stale air, piercing my ears and leaving me with a haunting memory that won't ever fade.

I pull the blade of the sickle from her chest, painting my face with a look of indifference. Only...why is Skylenna here? Why is she smiling? Something isn't right. Uneasiness turns my stomach at the sight of her.

"Let's get the little brother in here!" She claps her hands.

What is wrong with her? Doesn't she see Kane's mother suffering?

"Skylenna…" I utter cautiously, as though I'm cornering an animal.

"Yes, there he is." She shifts behind Arthur standing next to her. "Are you able to kill him, or shall I?"

"Don't touch him!" I growl, anger flaring hot against my chest.

"He's too much of a burden. Wouldn't you want to get rid of him?" *What the fuck is she saying?* "NO. He's Kane's brother."

She laughs, then brings a knife to his throat.

"Do it!"

"Skylenna! Stop!" I take a step forward. "This isn't you."

An idea flashes behind her cold stare. She pushes Arthur away with a small shove and brings the blade to her own throat, pressing against her skin without a care in the world.

"Wait!" I shout. But she takes a step back, eyes desolate and buzzing with excitement.

"It's him or me," she says loudly.

My eyes leap from her to Arthur. He's scared, clutching his rabbit, pleading with tears streaming down his plump cheeks.

"Please," I beg, the word feeling foreign on my tongue. "Don't do this to me."

She grins, showing off her straight, white smile.

Everything in this room scorches my senses. The sight of red. It drips off the sides of the kitchen table. It puddles around the floor. It seeps from Sophia's lips. The smell of copper and death. The sounds of Kane's mother suffocating, convulsing, pleading for me to save Arthur.

"I'm not going to choose." I swallow, holding the sickle against my chest.

"No?" She presses the tip of the knife into her skin. Beads of blood gush around the blade, drizzling down her chest one drop at a time.

Conflicting emotions jet through me from Kane. He cries out for her, for his brother. I search her eyes for what I should do, questioning her actions, begging for mercy.

But the blood continues to stream.

"I know this isn't your heart," I say somberly. "I love you."

And Kane howls as Arthur hits the floor, never letting go of that rabbit.

# Skylenna

"WHERE IS HE?!" I PUSH my way through a crowd of inmates gathered at the entrance to the stadium doors.

Helga Bee pops up from her seated position on the stage.

"Where is Dessin?" I shout, eyes stinging with tears at the void blowing up in chaos.

She shrugs in confusion. "Thought they went back to you by now. I told them about the new stock of Honey in here. They ran off like they were gonna get it, but when I showed up, it was still here."

My hands clench into fists. A dead end. Where would they go? Did something happen?

Dessin's heartbeat hammers through the void. It's haunting, fast, and filled with morbid intentions.

"Fuck!" I screech, throwing my hands down to my sides. I spin in a circle, desperate to find any sign of him, catch a hint of a trail that will lead to my friends. "Dessin!"

Perplexed faces, sweaty bodies, and strobing lights make me dizzy as I jog aimlessly into the stands of organized seating. I feel it in my gut, in my bones that something is horribly wrong. After finding my memories again, learning of the deep, profound relationship we really have, it's been different between us. Like we were meant to breathe the same air, share the same thoughts, be fueled by the same power.

And something is disrupting that fuel.

It's like someone is sawing down the bridge that links me to him.

"Dessin!" I bellow with a red face and trembling hands. "DESSIN!"

A cold fingertip grazes my shoulder lightly, a touch that resembles the softness of a feather. I jerk around like a rabid animal foaming at the mouth, thrusting my hand forward to snatch the figure's wrist midair.

The girl yelps, fumbling back into the arms of a man appearing just as startled.

"Do you remember me?" The girl exhales shakily.

I blink through the warm wall of tears, focusing in on her bruised face. Familiar. Tan skin, copper hair, both matted and stringy, with a heartbreaking glint in her gaze. The kind that screams pity, and maybe compassion. The last time I saw them, they were dressed in white, surviving in a different setting of captivity.

"You're the two I broke out of the asylum," I say cautiously.

"Yes."

"What are you doing here?"

"Apparently the side effect of escaping the Chandelier City is to end up here," Niklaus answers behind the girl. His black hair is tied back in a bun, and somehow he looks stronger than before. Glowing ocean eyes like he's just seen war.

My swollen eyes shift between them. "I don't have time for polite conversation. I'm looking for someone."

I try to push past them, but the girl holds my wrist again.

"Drop it," I growl.

"I know you don't know me, but you've done so much for me the moment I needed you the most." Her voice is lined with yearning gratitude. "Let me do something for you now."

I watch as her brows knit together, and her bottom lip trembles.

"He's in the tower on the east wing. It's a dungeon they use to experiment on inmates."

Respite and terror wrestle in my core. Experiment? Haven't we had enough of that shit to last a lifetime? I pull away from her to go after him, but she tightens her grip.

"Don't hold back on them. It takes something extraordinary to unlock a mind like yours. *No one* will ever forget this day. Especially not me. Not ever." She stares into my eyes with a wealth of knowledge I've only seen in a few individuals in my lifetime. Dessin. Judas. Marilynn. Asena. The people of the ancient colonies…

And those eyes…there's something about the colors of her eyes.

"Who. Are. You?"

Her look of farewell is timeless, beautiful, and ethereal as she bows her head, taking Niklaus and disappearing into the shadows.

# Warrose

HE STARTED OFF MURMURING HER NAME.

"*Skylenna, Skylenna, Skylenna.*"

Now he says nothing at all. Every few minutes he makes agonized noises, the kind I used to hear from a dying animal in the forest. It's a guttural moan that is so unlike him, raking across my skin like a blanket of spiders. Sweat glistens his furrowed forehead. Every muscle is flexed and excruciatingly tight.

"Alright, that's enough! This has gone on long enough!" I fight against the bars holding me down, bruising myself until I'm a throbbing mess.

*What the fuck are they doing to him?*

"He won't make it out until his brain chemistry toward the girl changes," Masten says absentmindedly as he glances up at Dessin from an old book.

Niles pants next to me, still sickened and traumatized by the hot poker. I don't blame him; I'm shivering and wincing at the horrendous burns on my side. But all I care about right now is getting my friend out of his own personal hell.

"Dessin? It's me, buddy. Fight through this. You love Skylenna, and she loves you. Nothing in the world can corrupt that!" I shout with a sore throat.

But Dessin continues to make awful sounds in the base of his throat. And Kaspias fucking laughs. Before I can even open my mouth, Niles beats me to it.

"You think this is funny?" His snarl is shaped by torment and hatred. "That's your brother! You're hurting your brother!"

I watch as Kaspias glances between Niles and Dessin, and his expression goes taut, only for half a second, then morphs back into mockery.

"My family is here," Kaspias says proudly, hands on hips.

"No." The room swells with ice and wickedness. "Your family was Sophia and Arthur."

I jerk my head to look toward the doorway but can't move past my manacles. However, I don't need to see the woman standing there to know her intelligent, strong voice.

It's Skylenna.

She found us.

"Sophia's heart broke the day she thought you died in her arms after birth. She sobbed in her birthing bed, trying to breathe life into a child that was swapped with you. Begging God to give her baby back to her." Skylenna takes three steps forward, coming into my sight. "That was your mother, Kaspias. The same mother who used to tell bedtime stories to Kane and Arthur about the man you would have become. The same mother who cried at your grave every Sunday, leaving yellow tulips on your small grave in hopes it would brighten your day wherever you were in the afterlife."

Kaspias is on his feet now, gawking at her like someone has just dumped cold water over his head. "How the fuck did you find us?"

"Sophia and Arthur were murdered in the house you were supposed to grow up in."

Kaspias's veins bulge from his hands and forearms, though he doesn't move.

"Enough of this," Masten scoffs, rising to his feet with the support of his cane. "Maybe she won't be so mushy if she knew what you're doing to your *precious* brother."

Skylenna's head turns to Dessin, taking in the horrendous view of the way his body reacts to the gruesome images the Mind Phantoms have given him.

"Masten." She acknowledges the traitor with little surprise. "What have you done?" Her upper lip peels back.

"I'm fixing him," he declares proudly. "Now, he'll never look at you the same way again. He'll forever associate you with loss, pain, and hatred. Without the weakness of loving you, he'll be the perfect soldier. The world's greatest assassin. And you're next."

# 46. Into Dessin's Mind

## Skylenna

I stop hearing Masten's words, stop trying to make sense of his inhumane cruelty.

My eyes are fixated on Dessin. I watch his abdominal muscles coil tightly together, flexing and unflexing. He grinds his teeth with his eyes darting around under his closed lids.

*Whatever you're going through, you won't go through it alone, Dessin.*

My feet move to him like magnets, like a gravitational force pulling me in. Placing my hands over his clenched jaw, I allow the bizarre phenomenon happening in the void to swallow me like a collapsing ocean wave. And the fall is far more aggressive than I've experienced to date. It's a riptide, so strong, so forceful, I have to hold my breath.

Fog, chilled winds, and darkness storm past me, through me, around me as I finally part the seas of the void's strong borders. I stand upright in a room that strikes me with bad memory after bad memory.

Electroconvulsive therapy in the Emerald Lake Asylum.

My heart races in the doorway of the unventilated room, finding Dessin strapped down, practically levitating at the pulses of electricity zooming through his body. He's in his white patient's uniform, reminding me of our first meeting, the thirteenth room, my daily sessions with him that I so looked forward to.

As I take a step forward, I finally take note of who is operating the machine that's torturing him.

"No…" I breathe.

Long, honey-golden hair streams down her navy-blue conformist's dress. She fidgets with the remote excitedly, practically bouncing on her heels.

Three more steps, and I see her face.

Emerald eyes filled with poison and malice. Long, wispy eyelashes. High cheekbones.

*Me.*

I'm the one torturing him.

They're conditioning him to associate me with pain, with hatred. The way he saw Meridei or Suseas. Absinthe or Albatross.

My stomach shrivels, and I find that I don't want to fight the sudden (but welcome) downpour of rage feasting on my insides. Walking up to her, I snap her neck, quick with a loud crack, and the other Skylenna's body is dumped to the floor. I flip off the machine and unstrap Dessin.

"It's me, Dessin. The *real* me." Running my hands through his hair, I kiss his cheek. "I've come for you. The way you've always shown up for me. I love you. I love you so much."

His eyes slowly open and close, then open again. He focuses on my face, searching my eyes for answers. A look that says he recognizes me. An expression that softens my heart. His pupils turn the size of saucers at first, then shrink to tiny pinholes.

The thrust of his body into mine is so abruptly powerful, I can't even scream as we're thrown off the table, pelting through the air. My back slams into the tiled floor, knocking the wind from my lungs. I'm certain I've broken something after hearing a snap. But I can't breathe, can't scream, can't beg him to see me clearly.

His eyes flare and shudder with an overpowering *hatred* for me. Fire and brimstone merge with a carnal need to hurt me.

I blink up at him in shock.

His hands clamp around my throat, fingers curling all the way to the back of my neck. He squeezes with every ounce of strength he has. Blood rushes to my face, building in pressure.

"D-Des," I croak.

*Oh, God. What have they done to you?*

This is the void. I can change this. I can take us somewhere that will bring him good memories. With one hand, I reach up to his cheek, watching the moment his eyes shudder at my soft touch.

*I'll take you somewhere safe.*

I close my eyes, and we tumble through the void, piercing a veil of the sunny sky in Ambrose Oasis. It's a safe haven from everything he's recently seen. The sweet aroma of lavender and wisteria.

"What the hell is this?" he growls under his breath, looking around at a setting of perfection. Our place away from the evil we've seen. Our home when we don't have one.

"I've brought you to our special place. Do you remember it?" I ask, taking a step away from him in case he tries to choke me again.

Dessin remains perfectly still. "Yes."

I sigh in relief. "Good."

"But this is *my* place. Not yours. How did you learn of it?" His face is cold and unemotional. I have *never* seen him look at me like this.

I wrap my arms around my core to protect my heart from that horrible blow. But it does nothing to shield that sting his words have caused.

"Dessin, I think your memories of me have been altered." I gulp just looking at the revulsion hardening his features. "What do you feel when you look at me?"

"Disgust," he says evenly. There isn't a moment of hesitation behind the thought. The look chills my skin.

I blow out a steadying breath.

"Would it make a difference if I told you that I'm deeply in love with you?" My tone. It's pathetic. It's weak. It's heartbroken.

He nearly laughs. "I'd know you were lying. There isn't a fiber in your body that could ever love anything."

*What have they done to you?!*

"And what does Kane say about it?" I ask. *Please.* My Kane will see me through all of this, won't he? He's known me the longest. Loved me my whole life. He'll know this isn't real. *He'll remember me.*

He looks down in thought. "He agrees with me."

They've even gotten to his alters.

"It isn't a lie. I've loved Kane since I was a little girl. I fell in love with you in the asylum, even before I had my memories returned to me. You are my soul mate, Dessin." I wipe away a stray tear quickly, trying to keep myself together. But it's near impossible. I won't be able to survive it if he looks at me this way forever.

The air thickens with uncertainty, and there's a terrible stillness about him.

"Stop lying," he warns, taking a threatening step toward me.

A snarl rips through the space between us as DaiSzek takes a protective step in front of me. He lowers himself in a predatory stance, making it clear that he is willing to fight to stand up for me.

"What have you done to him?" Dessin asks in subtle horror.

"Nothing." My voice cracks. "He knows the truth. That we're family. He senses your desire to harm me again, and he's showing you that he won't let it happen."

Dessin shakes his head.

DaiSzek and I take a step forward. "Can I show you what's in my heart?"

"No."

Another step.

"I'm warning you," he grunts.

"I promise this is the only truth that exists." Before he can react, I place a hand over his temple, sending a memory spiraling into the depths of the void, linking through his thoughts.

The night in the thirteenth room when he had me in his bed, on my back, and my legs around his hips. He kissed me and said, "I've never wanted anything more."

Another memory scatters across his mind. When he burst through the door and found me in Albatross's cage. The next memory of me sitting on his lap by the lagoon, the night we shared our traumas for the first time.

Something on the outside of the void pulls us from those memories, sending a tremor through this slice of heaven.

Dessin takes a vigilant step away from me. Confusion, uncertainty, and frustration that begs for him to decipher which reality is the truth.

"We can't stay in here," I breathe. "We're in the Vexamen Prison. Our friends need our help."

Dessin exhales slowly, looking at me like both an infectious rash and a soothing touch. Like I might laugh in his face at any moment and return to the cruel individual he knows me to be. He nods once.

"When this is over, you'll know how much I love you. Because this time, it's my turn to help you remember *me*."

# 47. Heaven And Hell

## Skylenna

Returning to the room that has changed the trajectory of Dessin's heart, is like landing in a pit of molten lava and flames. I see nothing but red.

The color of blood as it gushes from a sliced artery. The stain on a carpet after someone has been stabbed repeatedly. The shade that dripped in a pool around Ruth's legs. The color on my hands as I held Dessin's body in that sand. The wet gleam of the sickle as it was pulled from his chest.

There's a serenity in understanding my new abilities better through this rage. It's biblical. It's being able to soar past physical barriers, to conquer the mind's limitations, and to manipulate anyone like a puppet. It's a gift from God to travel through a veil of life and death and act as a deliverer of evil souls. I understand it now as heat blinds me, thrumming through my veins with the thunder and lightning of the Almighty himself.

I turn to Masten slowly, taking my time to pin him down with my unblinking glare. Focusing in on him as he rises to his feet, gripping that wolf's head on top of his cane like he is considering using it to crack one of my kneecaps.

"You don't know, *do you?*" And I feel like a puppet as I direct my question to him. Like there is a devil and a god pulling my strings, working as one to funnel power through my lungs, into my bloodstream. A power no one has ever seen.

"Know what?" Masten asks with faked disinterest.

"That your fate for this will be much worse than death."

I stride toward him, closing the space of this dungeon with only one thought: to destroy. To obliterate all of his humanity in my wake. The void thrums through my fingers, vibrates my soul with a ticking detonator.

Masten forces out a laugh as I'm slowed down, feeling the weight of the magnet in my ear, blurring my vision, and obstructing my natural axis that aligns me upright on my feet. I sway for a moment, holding my hands out to break my fall.

But that gutting visual of Dessin being tortured by me rings loudly in my brain. It wakes me up. The ancient, dominant power of the void takes a hold of my equilibrium on its own, sending my entire body buzzing as I straighten myself and lift my chin.

I smile at him, as he has no control over me anymore. No one does.

"How?" Kaspias asks with uncharacteristic horror thickening his tone.

My strides close the distance, and just as my hands grip the sides of Masten's head, he falls to his knees with a thud in my presence. The connection is stronger than it's ever been. More potent. More alive with a black fire that can only be described as apocalyptic. End of times.

Like both a demon and an archangel, I drag Masten's consciousness into the prison void, although we don't stop there. We seem to glide right past it to a deeper location surrounded by screams, cries, moans, and an ache that resonates so deeply, I can only imagine that this is what hell would feel like.

And maybe it is.

Dropping him to his knees, I levitate above him, revealing every evil moment in his life in a show around us. Spinning images of the way he treated Dessin as a child, of the torture he cast on other children. It hits us like a meteor shower. All he can do is brace himself for the bone-shattering impact.

I am the judge, jury, and executioner of his actions.

One moment sticks out to me like a blinding spotlight in his memories. I see a massacre of dark fur surrounded by a symphony of swaying red trees. RottWeilens killed by chemical warfare in the Red Oaks. He even took the head of one and placed it over his fireplace.

It was…Masten.

The slaughter.

Soul survivor.

Masten is the spy that orchestrated the slaughter of the RottWeilen, leaving DaiSzek to be the last of his kind.

I look down at his cane, at the wolf head carved under his palm.

That shade of red blots out parts of my vision.

I point a single finger down at him, and it's as though my voice booms with a deep, divine echo. "You are condemned to this version of hell, Masten. You will feel the pain of every victim you've harmed. You will relive the suffering of the slaughter you caused in the Red Oaks. You will live here for all eternity and never escape these walls I have formed around you."

And his sentence has begun.

Masten curls in the fetal position, screaming in anguish, and retching until blood pours from his gaping mouth.

I let the void suck me out of that brand of hell, rushing back to the surface as though I'm underwater and have yet to take a breath of air.

Masten's comatose body falls to the ground in front of Kaspias, a prisoner of his own mind as he will never escape the oblivion I have sentenced him to.

"Masten?" Kaspias barks, kneeling in front of his shivering body.

"And what should I do with you?" I muse, already feeling the blanket of ice drape over me.

I'll undoubtedly reach hyperthermic levels at any moment. Therefore, I know I have to take advantage of Kaspias being in my direct line of sight while I still have a chance. My mind races with ways I'll wound him for hurting Ruth, for harming Dessin's mind in ways that may in fact be irreversible. I want to take him back to the day Sophia was killed, to the rabbit Arthur held onto as he took his last breath.

"Don't." A woman's soft, delicate voice reaches me as I stand over Masten's limp body. It isn't a voice I could soon forget, though I've only heard it in the void, through memories of Kane when he was only a child.

Sophia stands behind Kaspias with tears rimming her wispy bottom lashes. The glimmering light of the wild torches reflect off her round glasses. She wears a long, dusty rose dress with gossamer sleeves that end at the elbow and a flowy bottom that drags along the dirty floor. And I can see clearly the resemblance to Kane.

When I first met Dessin in the asylum, I remember thinking that he was the kind of handsome that was timeless, a striking look that doesn't belong anywhere.

That's Sophia. Small waist, bronze skin, and chocolate hair. A doll from a rare, refined collection. She looks into my eyes with nothing but respect and profound love.

Her glimmering ghost captivated my attention entirely.

"Thank you for loving my son and giving him a reason to keep living. To keep fighting," she says to me without looking away. "But now I must ask you for a favor that isn't quite fair, Skylenna. Though he doesn't deserve your mercy, Kaspias deserves one chance to see the path he could have had if fate were kinder to him as a child."

I swallow, unable to think of anything other than the fate Ruth has suffered at his hand. A fate he chose for her. She watched the crowd cheer for the axe to land under her kneecaps because of his demented trick.

"I have watched over both of my sons since I departed this world. I have seen the evil that tormented my boys. Kane was only a child, but so was Kaspias. The difference was, Kane had me and Arthur for six years of his life. To show him love and family. He had you to build a friendship with, then later to fall hopelessly in love." She takes a deep breath as the tears are let loose from her bottom lashes. "Kaspias has known cruelty since he was an infant. Every shred of kindness and the throbbing desire to have a mother and a family was beaten out of him. My boy never stood a chance."

Tears gather in my own eyes as time, for only a moment, stands still for Sophia. For the gentle mother who was taken too soon. I wish Kane could see her now.

"I can't just let him walk free," I whisper thickly.

"And you won't. You see, a warrior angel doesn't just have the ability to burn down the world. They may also deliver it from evil." She pauses, glancing at both of her sons. "Instead of dragging Kaspias to hell. You can also show him heaven."

# 48. "What lies in darkness."

## Kaspias

Skylenna's maniacal, stormy green eyes slide to a space over my shoulder for a couple seconds before she spears me with that cold stare.

The vicious, rabid energy in her expression has changed. No longer murderous, vengeful, and somewhat empty. She's pinning me with a glare that says she's never seen me before.

How is she still standing? Her balance should have her on her ass right now. I've never seen a prisoner fight this. I've never seen them stand so effortlessly for this long after it's taken effect.

"You want to fight?" I taunt with a challenging smirk. "Let's fight. I know you've been waiting to see if I can do it like my brother."

My jibe falls short, not even coming close to affecting her stoic face.

"For all you've done, I should make you suffer with Masten."

I can't help but glance down at my mentor passed out on the floor, trembling slightly with his eyes rolled back in his head. What did she do to him? If I had been raised and trained to know fear, I might back away from her.

But she's nothing.

My brother's weakness.

An uninspiring distraction.

"But Sophia wants something different for you, Kaspias. And after all your mother sacrificed, I owe her this much," she says with wet eyes and puffy cheeks.

The name Sophia used to get a rise out of me. It was used to trigger an emotional reaction, the need in a child to see their mother, to be loved by a parent. But every time I'd react, the beatings would get far more creative and eventually unbearable.

I had to stop thinking about her.

Had to stop imagining what she looked like. How she would take care of me. If the rumor of a mother's love was fact or fiction.

The concept of a mother eventually infuriated me. Made my lip curl and my stomach ache. I developed an irrational hatred of all mothers over time. I'd watch my fellow students walk their mothers on a leash to get some fresh air on nice days, and I couldn't stop the irrational fits of anger that I'd spiral into from seeing it.

I'm not stupid enough to not understand that it was a conditioned response. Of course, it is. But it doesn't matter because that is the price of winning wars. That's what Vexamen must do to stay on top. To dominate our enemies.

"Don't say her name again," I snarl.

I hate the sound of it. I hate the way it makes my heart stutter in my chest. The way I try to picture her face. It forms a ball of fire in my gut.

"For your sake, I hope this works."

I can't help but flinch and attempt to deflect as she slides a hand along the side of my face until she reaches my temple. Skylenna's pupils stretch wide, appearing demonic and comatose as the whites turn bloodshot, filling with scattered blood vessels and black clouds of smoke.

And it's like she's strapped a collar around my soul, dragging it away from my eyes as I sink, sink, sink into the darkness of my body. Sounds of wind, of water whooshing, of stars and planets shifting in the universe. It feels like being injected with the most powerful of drugs, ones that send you on your ass and detach you from your body.

I go limp as I flounder through the empty space, traveling at an otherworldly speed. I don't see her around me as we move, but I can feel her ethereal presence. Something about it makes me feel weak, like a little boy, like a prisoner unable to fight back.

I try to yell, to throw my arms around, to attack whatever force is controlling me like a doll soaring through this unearthly air. But I'm at her mercy, watching as pinholes of light break through the ongoing storm of endless night around us.

And suddenly I'm standing, shielding my eyes with my hand as a blinding stream of light burns my retinas, blanketing my whole body with warmth. I'm gasping for a single normal breath, fighting the light with watering eyes and quivering hands.

*Where the fuck am I?*

"Your brother showed me this place when I was a little girl. He taught me how to recreate it in my mind." Skylenna's voice travels to my ears from behind my shielding hand. "But I think it's more than that. I think your brother taught me to reach my hand to the skies and cut a slice from heaven, an oasis just grand enough to help me in this war."

I part two fingers to see her standing in the sunlight, surrounded by a meadow, tall grass, and swaying trees of purple flowers.

"I have no idea what you're talking about. What have you done to us?" I ask, finding my voice in a scratchy throat.

I was told her brain was different, just like my brother's. But hers was far more complicated to understand. Female subjects don't last long in this particular experiment that Crow Ivast created. The Mazonist Brothers were looking forward to studying her.

"Ambrose Oasis," she says quietly. "I think this has always been the place where I can do what's always needed to be done."

*She's fucking insane.*

"I know you didn't choose this life, Kaspias. And even though you should suffer for everything you've done to my family, I want to give you the memories you deserved as a little boy before this country corrupted your heart."

I glare at her in stupid confusion. Mouth open and eyebrows raised. Her nonsensical sentences are making me feel like I'm having a goddamned aneurysm.

Before I can insult her, a mirage of my childhood spins around us. The sight is gruesome, bloody, full of every lesson I was taught, even in infancy when the human brain isn't even formed yet. It's all here. The time I was forced to watch the meat carnivals that go on in the villages around our base. How I cried when my best friend, Creed, died of infection from getting a finger cut off with a rusted blade. The many sessions our instructors trained me to feel happiness at the sight of decapitation, at a person screaming in pain.

Skylenna watches it all in silent revulsion.

But I'm not fazed. Did she think I'd cry? Show even an ounce of emotion? This is nothing. It was necessary to build me into the unstoppable commander I am today. I see others go through these exact scenarios every single day.

However, Skylenna sees a memory of me crying for my mother in a dark cell at the age of four. I look away, avert my eyes to anything else. It's the only memory that makes me furious, hateful, resentful.

As she tightens her jaw, the images change drastically. She shows me a cottage in the woods. It isn't until I see my mother on a kitchen table that I realize what moment in time this is. I watch Sophia die, slowly, with small whimpers that escape her full lips. I watch as Arthur bleeds to death while he clutches his toy rabbit to his chest.

It's one thing to hear of these stories.

It's another to witness them play out before me.

And Skylenna closes her eyes, gripping my hands before I can yank them away. Without warning, every memory we just watched play out begins to drain from my mind, funneling down a black hole Skylenna created. And just as I panic from the loss of everything that's made me who I am, I'm blinking through new moments of my life.

Sophia holds me in her arms as a toddler, picking me up from my crib to kiss my wet cheeks and warm forehead.

Sophia scolds Kane for pushing me into a trench of mud before dinner.

Sophia hands baby Arthur to me to hold for the first time. Kane and I gaze down at him, making a pact to protect him no matter what.

Sophia cleans my scraped knee, dresses it with a bandage, and kisses it with a smile. Kane asks to go next, even though he wasn't the one to fall.

Sophia sends Kane and me to our room after we bring a goat into the house, and it shits all over her new carpet.

Sophia holds me.

Sophia sings to me.

Sophia loves me my whole life.

It all hits me like an earthquake happening inside my body, inside my aching soul, splitting everything I know apart. I watch my life play out with Kane—the times we'd play pranks on Arthur or the days we'd take him on adventures through the forest. I even meet Skylenna as a little girl. I watch them fall in love.

With an abrupt gasping sob, I fall to my knees in front of this strange, gallant, all-consuming phenomenon of a woman. How long have we been here? Decades? Centuries? Time has no beginning and no end. She's crying, too. Holding my face in her hands, seeing my life play out in front of her own eyes as well.

And I'm suddenly not the man I was before. I'm the man that Sophia raised, because everything else was drained from existence. Everything else was obliterated. And all that's left is the love I have for my two brothers and the mother who gave me everything.

# 49. All We Have Left

## Marilynn

"Niles," I gasp.

He's hanging from the wall with fresh burns on his sides, wincing as he tries to take deep breaths in and out. Warrose is next to him, staring straight ahead without blinking, as if he's in a trance.

I turn around, taking a step back as I watch Skylenna gripping the sides of Kaspias's face. He's on his knees in front of her, eyes rolling back in his head.

"Get us down, Mar," Niles pleads.

I nod with a racing heart, dashing to his side to unbolt the iron contraptions around different parts of his body. "What happened?" I ask him.

Niles grunts as I unlock one of his ankles. "They did something to Dessin. Something about making him see Skylenna differently. And then she fucked up Masten, not sure how. *Ow*, fuck, easy!"

Spinning around with a weight dropping into my belly, I see *him* on the floor. The man who harassed me, who tried to kill me, who made my life hell for so long. *Masten.*

"What did she do to him?" I ask.

Niles drops down after the last manacle is lifted. "Honestly, I don't know. He's been seizing like that since she touched him."

Every fiber in me is begging to ask her what happened. But I know that will have to wait until later on. Right now, we need to get out of here before anyone discovers what she's done.

Niles works on freeing Warrose while I unscrew all of Dessin's restraints. After unclamping his forearm, I glance up at his eyes that I didn't realize are wide open. I do a double take, scanning his flexed jaw, lowered lids, and bulging veins in his neck. It's as if he is choking on a fit of resentment, cold with brimming hostility.

*What happened?*

Working on his last bar, I shout over my shoulder, "Let's go, Skylenna!"

Not a sound escapes her. She just stands there, hovering over Kaspias.

"Leave her," Dessin orders, bitterness twisting through his words.

*What?* Tugging his last leg free, I glower up at his towering height. It takes me a solid moment to consider if this is actually Dessin. Why is there so much hate etched across his face?

"Dessin," I say carefully.

"I said, leave her. Let's go. *Now!*"

I flinch away from his thundering voice. What the hell is going on?

"It's okay. Go." Skylenna's voice is barely an octave above a whisper. A sound coming from far away, withdrawn and distracted.

"But…" Niles huffs, stepping toward her.

"Go," she repeats.

Warrose puts a hand on my back and taps Niles on the shoulder, guiding us toward the exit. I shuffle past Dessin, but before exiting, I glance back at Skylenna.

And time, though fickle and cruel, takes pity on them. For no more than a few seconds.

Skylenna looks back at Dessin, meeting his murky glare with a yearning that makes my own heart break. Her eyes are so red, they almost look like they're filled with blood surrounding her two emerald irises. Three tears slip down her gaunt cheeks, falling straight to the brimstone floor.

And Dessin is the one to finally turn away, jerking his head forward for me to follow him out.

# Dessin

THE IMAGE OF HER DEMONIC face won't leave me.

Not as I replace Ruth's bandages.

Not as I find medicine for her to take.

Not as Niles grills me with questions.

She's all I can think about in the worst way imaginable. Skylenna has been a demon sent straight from hell to ruin me and all I've lived for since I was a child. How could she stand there and pretend like she loved me? How could she act so innocent? So kind and gentle? I know her games and awful tricks. I've lived them for far too long. We all have. Every alter knows what she is capable of.

"I know it's hard for you, Dess. But you have to tell us what's going on in your head," Warrose says in a low but demanding tone.

Ruth tries to sit up to hear what I have to say.

"What's there to talk about? The demon is up to her old tricks again. That's the end of it."

Warrose raises his brows, meeting eyes with Ruth in confusion.

"What demon?" he asks.

I roll my eyes. "Don't make me say her fucking name."

He stares at me for a long moment, sorting something out in his head. He blows out a breath, running a large hand through his thick hair. "Oh Christ, man, tell me you're not talking about Skylenna."

Her name singes my skin like acid. I taste blood as rage runs red through my mind. I have multiple flashbacks of her evil antics that replay at the mention of her name. I've spent my life trying to avoid that trigger.

"Why?" Ruth asks weakly. "What did she do?"

I glower down at her incredulously. "What the fuck didn't she do?!"

Ruth recoils at my rising voice, and it makes me flush with shame. She's done nothing to deserve the side effects of my anger.

"She's made my life a fiery pit of hell," I respond reluctantly.

Warrose crosses his arms and sighs. "They've fucked up his memories of her. Created this emotional response."

"How do we fix it?" Niles's jaw drops.

"Ironically, I think Skylenna is the only one who can fix it now."

Red pours into my vision as I picture that demon's face again.

"Stop. Saying. Her. Name."

"You truly hate her?" Ruth inquires quietly.

*I'm practically drunk with hatred.* "With every fiber of my being."

How can they even ask these questions right now? They know what she's done to me. To all of us. She's the reason Kane lost his baby brother and mother. She's the demon that put us in the prison, that tortured me every single day in that asylum. She's the trigger for every alter split, every form of trauma that we have worked so hard to recover from. Why are they acting like the demon's spell worked on them? Did she convince them of her lies that she loves me?

"Do you all...*believe* her new story she's telling?" I ask slowly as if I'm speaking to unintelligent children that need hand-holding.

The group looks around at each other, hesitant to answer. As if they're afraid of making me angry.

"It isn't a story. It's your life," Marilynn finally says.

I scoff. "So, she has gotten to all of you. Was it Mind Phantoms?"

"It was. But not on us. The Mind Phantoms were given to you by Kaspias. Not her." Warrose watches me carefully with those piercing eyes that make me want to hit him. He's cautious of any movement I make. Like I'm some feral animal he's found scrounging for food in a ditch.

*If it were Mind Phantoms, we wouldn't all be affected by it,* Kalidus clarifies.

But Warrose is giving me that look he used to give us as a child. The one where he's waiting for me to solve a problem that he already knows the answer to. I rub my hands over my face, grinding my teeth against the confusion and frustration gnawing at my bones.

*Take a breath. You're okay, honey,* Kane's mother says, pushing to the front.

I'm not okay. Everything is pounding and rotting with an ache. My heart rate picks up as Warrose continues talking, something about Kane loving this girl his entire childhood. About protecting the demon. About meeting her in the asylum and falling in love. Disgust rolls through me like a rogue wave. My stomach heaves, and I wipe my hand over the sweat forming against my brow.

*Breathe with me Dessin,* Sophia murmurs, trying harder to reach me.

The dissociation affects my vision first. In and out of focus. I suddenly feel a disorienting amount of spaciness. Have I been sitting here staring at the floor for a few seconds or minutes? Hours? A few different alters crowd the front, flooding my thoughts and attention

# 50. Carousel

## Ballaviranoz
## The War Caster
## Non-human alter

A feral sound slashes through my throat at the humans who surround me with puzzled looks on their faces.

I'm in a dungeon. A fortress. Bars and charcoal ceilings. Flashing lights. Broken music. Sour stench of sewage, captivity, and dried blood. My narrowing eyes scan the cage swiftly, taking in every detail. Trapped. Bars. Cage.

The humans back away, shifting to the other end of these bars as I readjust my stance to crouch on all fours. My dragon form would terrify them. My reptilian eyes. My thick, black claws. But they know not that I have come to protect them. To guard them.

The male with bronze skin and eyes the color of gemstones calls me by my name. The name I have known for thousands of years. Ancient and heavy on any human tongue. I tilt my head in his direction, bowing my head slightly to reveal to this male human that I am no threat. He holds out one of his two hands, revealing to me the face of his palm. The delicate crease lines. The short nails that are not lethal the way my talons are. I sniff it, leaning forward to push my face against his fingers.

As I scan their faces once more, my sight clouds over, blurry and without detail.

# Ralek
# Emperor of Snakes
# Non-human alter

THIS PLACE...

The smearing black grittiness underfoot. The smoky atmosphere. The scent of burning souls.

This place reminds me of home.

But my dissociation is slow. I come in and out of consciousness. Blinking, swallowing, looking around with heavy lids.

As I come to, I grin at the alert faces before me.

"Hello, children," I purr with ophidian excitement. How long has it been since I've lurked around young mortals? My last memory of merging to the front was around Masten and Absinthe. My soul reason for splitting.

"I think they're rapid cycling," the one called Warrose says to the other confused faces. I've known this male since he was much smaller, much less carved like a stone statue. Does he remember me? How many human years have passed?

"Where am I now?" I ask, piercing him with my eyes that shine like two ruby stones smoldering from the heat of hellfire.

"Vexamen Prison. We've been captured," the brawny male responds.

"No Absinthe?" I inquire with a wicked tilt of my lips.

426

The large mortal studies me with narrowing eyes and a straightening back. His hazel gaze sweeps over my hands, the curling of my fingers, my relaxed stance.

"You're Ralek, aren't you?" He places a steady hand on the shoulder of the sickly female lying next to him. "The Emperor of Snakes."

"Uh, that doesn't sound good," the blond, pretty male mutters, rearing his head back.

"He's a demon alter. It's usually not all that pleasant," Warrose responds.

"I knew you'd recognize me, Warrose," I say in an eerie, demonic voice. "Have you seen your family since they abandoned you, child?"

His upper lip curls. It was always so easy to get under his skin. But I'll admit. He was never my concern or my usual target. Absinthe and Masten have always held the cake for my regular triggering.

"Why the need for a demon alter?" the sickly mortal girl asks. Her gaunt face is ashen and covered in an oily sheen of sweat.

"Absinthe was a cruel and religious tormentor to us as children," Warrose explains, like he has a bad taste in his mouth. "After she tried performing exorcisms of Kane, calling him evil or a demon, Ralek was split."

"I'd like to see her again." Pleasure swirls under my scaly skin at the thought of taunting her with my fiendish threats.

"I'm pretty sure Dessin maimed her during their last encounter."

My smile deepens. "Is that right?"

The muscular mortal's voice blurs together in a string of garbled syllables. My sight falters, and I suddenly am unable to follow the conversation. I'm a ship drifting away from the dock of this present moment.

# Absinthe
# Introject Persecutor

Dirty. Disgusting. Street rats.

"What happened to this one?" I point to the girl lying on the floor smelling like vomit and pathetic excuses.

The filthy young adults around me exchange looks as if I'm not asking them a question. As if I'm not looking them in the eye, gritting my teeth, and sneering at the dirt in their pores.

"We have to help them," a thick-boned, red-headed woman mutters, still not answering my question. Who let her walk around carrying this extra weight? Doesn't she realize Demechnef will have her thrown into the asylum for eating like a pig? Doesn't she care?

"How much do you weigh, girl?" I clip in her direction.

"Hey!" A young man with sunshine hair and doe eyes shifts in front of her. "That's enough."

"Absinthe." A husky, baritone voice snaps my attention away from the two disgraceful children sitting before me. "I think it's time you leave."

I ball my fist in front of him. "Talk to me again like that, boy, and I'll bloody that pretty nose of yours."

"What do we do to stop this?" the golden boy asks.

I scoff in his direction. How pitiful of him to ask. How sad and emasculating.

"Dessin told me once about a gatekeeper. It's an alter that controls when they switch."

I rev my hand back to hit the stupid boy, but a dominating presence collides with my position in the front. Overly confident. Strong minded. Ancient. My head throbs like a gushing wound at the chaos going on around the other alters. They need to stay still, leave this to me. I'm going to have to teach them a lesson when I return to the inner world.

*That's enough, old woman.* A mountainous voice takes over my thoughts.

Kalidus.

# Kalidus
# God of Storms
# Fictive Introject Alter

I'M ASSISTED WITH A MEMORY download from a memory holder.

I take note of who fronted before me. Absinthe. How she got out of the prison we locked her in, I'm not sure yet. But these small humans look at me in a slight panic. Perhaps more alters have switched? Perhaps we're having some sort of a meltdown?

"Be calm, humans. I will make certain Absinthe returns to her cell. My sincerest apologies."

This body is quivering, sweating, aching in several places. The migraine, the lack of sleep, it crunches down on our bones like a cancer.

"What has happened to this body to throw us into chaos?" I ask the mortal men and women around me.

I recognize Warrose as he runs a hand through his hair.

"You're rapid cycling. They did something to Dessin with Mind Phantoms. Made him believe Skylenna was the source of his pain and suffering."

"She *is* the source of it," I confirm. I've watched the way she's toyed with us over the years. She is the reason I split in the first place. A demon from hell like Ralek.

He sighs, nodding slowly. "Kalidus, right?"

"God of Storms," I add.

"I think I know of a way I can stop the cycling," he says cautiously.

I bow my head to give my approval.

"Cricket. I know you're the gatekeeper." Warrose leans closer. "We need your help to stop the carousel switching. Please come to the front."

# Warrose

MY CHEST ACHES FOR THEM as Kalidus dissociates. The trigger to call Cricket by name worked. He blinks slowly, as if he's about to fall asleep.

"Have you ever met Cricket?" Ruth asks.

I shake my head, but don't take my eyes off of the man dissociating in front of me.

"Never. But Dessin told me about an alter they called a gatekeeper once. This alter named Cricket controls switching, access to other inner worlds they might have for different subsystems, or even alters that contain certain traumatic memories."

I can't imagine what they're going through. In one fell swoop, Kaspias and Masten managed to erase everything good about Skylenna. They managed to corrupt the purest love any of us has ever seen.

They broke Skylenna and Dessin.

I clear my throat and make eye contact with Cricket. He's staring directly at me, unblinking, as still as a block of stone.

"Cricket?"

"My apologies. Our system has seen a high level of stress," they say flatly.

"How can we help?"

Cricket's emotionless eyes flick between the rest of us. This alter doesn't move like any alter I've been around; they're mechanical and measured. I've never actually met Cricket. From what I remember, the gatekeeper sees and experiences almost everything but rarely interacts with the outside world.

"I do not think you can help."

"Your system is under duress from the most recent experiment. Mind Phantoms. It was to make you all believe that Skylenna is your enemy. But in reality, she's the lover of Dessin and Kane." I steeple my fingers against my mouth, hoping that Cricket will be able to see past the false logic they've been given.

"I see."

"Do you think you can convince the other alters of this shift in their reality?"

They blink. It's a gesture of boredom, I think.

"That might be your reality, but it isn't ours. I hold many of the traumatic memories that are solely centered around Skylenna. As does Bloom, our memory holder. Since Skylenna is a prominent trigger, I am unable to process your request."

*Fuck.*

"What can you do to help the others then?" I demand, heat rising to my face as anger wells inside my chest.

"I can slow down the unwanted switching," they offer matter factly. "It would be best if exposure to this trigger was eliminated or kept to a minimum."

"Meaning what?" Niles says.

Cricket slides their focus to him. "Meaning stop saying her name. Stop bringing her up as a topic in conversation."

# 51. Darkest Of Heartbreaks

## Skylenna

Within a breath of a moment while my hands are pressed against his temples, years go by that play out the events of his entire life.

"She loved me," Kaspias mutters in the safety of Ambrose Oasis. "Sophia loved me."

The void flickers as my energy depletes. I don't know how much longer I can last here. My head swims with delirium and fuzziness. Everything starts to sway.

"Skylenna?" Kaspias rises to tower over me in the buttery sunlight.

I shake my head.

"What's happened?"

"We have to go back," I slur.

Kaspias nods, wiping fresh tears from his eyes. His hands find mine, and it's like being sucked into a funnel. A whirlpool. The void blasts us through its cold, windy airway, spitting us back out into the dungeon.

I'm a shivering puddle on the floor, hugging my knees to my chest, hissing out of my chattering teeth. This is going to kill me. I feel it. All heat is seeping out of my pores, leaving my body with every exhale. Even the beating of my heart drudges along, barely making an effort to pump anymore blood in my limbs.

"What can I do?" Kaspias kneels, tucking my hair behind my ears.

My vision clouds over. I can hardly keep my eyes open as ice hardens my spine, chilling my brain to its core.

"B-lankets."

He leaves the room, footsteps heavy and loud as they thump against the cracked stone floors. Unsure how much time passes, my eyes flutter open as he returns with dirty cotton blankets. He wraps them around my shoulders, tucking their edges under my chin.

"What else?" He keeps his swollen eyes level with mine, waiting patiently for my next request.

"I n-eed you to take m-me back to my friends," I say quietly. "And I'll n-need you to find a way to g-get us all out of here."

He shakes his head in disbelief. "Getting that many high-profile prisoners out is impossible."

My hazy eyes shoot up to meet his. "A-and you'll find a way. F-f-for your brother and everything you've just c-cost him. Now take me back to them. Please."

In his strong arms being carried through the long, grim halls of this prison, I feel safe. The same way I've felt every time Kane carried me long distances. I press my cold face against the armor on his chest, trembling belligerently as I try to block out the breeze brushing past my arms through the small holes of the cotton blankets.

"I'll do everything in my power to get you out of here," Kaspias whispers as we get closer to my cage.

"Okay."

"What the fuck have you done to her?!" Warrose's unmistakable baritone voice slams into my ears and startles my eyes to blink open.

Kaspias pauses. "It's what she's done to me."

I hear someone gasp. And my heart twists in my chest at the thought of Dessin looking at me right now. Tears bulge over my eyes as I realize that I can't help him right now. I can't make him remember me.

"Who should I leave her with?" Kaspias asks.

A violent sound of something slamming into metal rings through my ears, and I flinch in Kaspias's strong arms.

"Throw her off the fucking tower for all I care."

*Dessin.*

The fury behind his voice pierces my heart like a rusted dagger. A single puncture wound that leaves me infected and bleeding out.

"Dessin," Warrose scolds.

I hear Dessin panting with wild energy racing off his standing frame. And right now, nothing is more heartbreaking than the fact that all I want is for Kaspias to leave me in his cage. Leave me in his arms. I just want that hug only Dessin and Kane can give me.

"I'll take her," Warrose says softly.

There's clanking below me as Kaspias unlocks his cage, passing me gingerly to rest against Warrose's bare chest.

There's an awkward silence that stretches from Kaspias to the rest of us. All I can hear is the even breathing and heartbeat of Warrose's warm skin against my left ear.

I open my eyes again, finding Kaspias staring down at Ruth. A deep crease forming between his eyebrows. "I'll make this right."

As he walks away. Dessin growls, banging his fists against the metal bars.

"Knock it off!" Warrose snarls.

"Skylenna," Niles murmurs, kissing my forehead like he hasn't seen me in years. "What happened?"

I blink through the tears, through the pain of Dessin so close yet so far away. I exhale slowly, unraveling a shaky breath that sounds dangerously close to a sob.

"C-cold," I say.

"She must have done some damage in the void," Warrose explains. "Let's get her warmed up."

I let my eyes rest as Marilynn helps take off my uniform, pressing my damp skin to Warrose and Niles's chests. They wrap the blankets around us, creating a cocoon of body heat. Through the fading in and out of consciousness, Ruth holds my hand, Niles whispers sweet words, Warrose massages my cold feet.

"How can you all treat her like she's some sort of angel?" Dessin speaks, and it feels like a razor blade carving the skin and muscles off my bones.

"Because she *is* an angel," Marilynn answers. "You both are."

"Is this what you wanted?" Dessin's question is directed at me. I sense the weight of it, like a rock too heavy to skip across the water.

"What?" I mutter with a dry mouth.

"To isolate me from my friends. To leave me with nothing and no one."

With labored breaths, I force myself up, using my hand to push off Warrose's shoulder and Niles's thigh to grip the bars, facing Dessin in his cage. His blazing eyes shudder as they land on my naked body, my blue lips, my puffy, tear-streaked face.

Dessin looks away, taking long, staggered breaths.

"L-look at m-me," I command in a wobbly voice. He continues glaring at the floor. "LOOK AT ME!"

Dessin drags his glower from the floor to me reluctantly.

It brings me back to the Red Oaks. To the time he lit a fire on the shore of the lagoon. I took my wet dress off, and I dared him to look at my body.

"You. Are. Not. Alone." I wish I could still my body, stop it from shivering, stop the endless chill from freezing my veins.

He remains so still. Not even an ounce of compassion.

"If I w-wasn't sick right now, I'd go into the v-void, and I wouldn't come back until I found you. I would use my l-last breath to show you every memory I have of the two of us." I grip the bars, sensing my friends turning away to give me privacy as I bear my soul to him.

"I *have* every memory of us. Do you know how many alters have had to split off because of those memories?" He shows his teeth, grimacing at my naked body. Disgusted. Hysterical wrath unfurling in his bloodstream.

"I don't care about the fabricated memories that the Mind Phantoms gave you. I want you to s-see *ME*! I w-want you to remember when you watched Meridei whip me in the asylum. The rage you felt because all you wanted was to protect me. To—avenge *me*."

Tears flood over my bottom lashes, gushing down my red cheeks. I force the stammering away from my voice so I can get this out clearly.

"I want you to remember the moment you found me in Albatross's cage. How you maimed him for hurting me. For torturing me. I want you to remember the nights we slept under the stars, next to DaiSzek and a fire you built. The day you held back my hair as I vomited from the poison Meridei and Belinda gave me. Or the way you kiss me like you've been waiting your whole life just to touch me!"

I'm hiccuping now, choking on sobs as snot and tears coat my face.

"You *died* in my arms. My lap, my hands, my cheeks—I was covered in your blood! I told you I loved you for the first time on that beach. I burned down the asylum, exacted every threat you ever made to your tormentors, and lost my mind as I watched your body get lowered six feet under the ground." Pressing my throbbing face between the bars, I force him to see me. "All because I *love* you. I love every alter. I love every fragment of your soul. And through every obstacle, every tragedy, you've gone to hell and back just to be with me. Why? Because. You. Loved. Me. Too."

And for a small, minuscule fraction of a second, Dessin's eyes shutter, and he leans back. Away from me. Like he saw something in my eyes, he felt something. Touched a memory that has been preserved by the deepest layers of his mind.

I bawl so hard, Warrose has to wrap me in my blankets and hold me close until I pass out from exhaustion. From being so close to my soulmate, yet so far away. From the darkest of heartbreaks.

# Dessin

THE FOOD IN MY MOUTH has no taste. But I make an effort to look busy with each spoonful because I can feel their eyes on me. Warrose and Niles sit across from me, pushing their food around as they continuously look up to steal glances.

"Stop looking at me," I grumble.

"Do you want to talk about it?" Warrose asks.

"Not even a little bit."

I can't get her crying face out of my head. I've never seen her cry in all the years she's made us suffer. Never a single tear. Never a sign of remorse. She's only ever been capable of wicked amusement at my expense.

*Why put this act on anyway? What does she gain from it?*

"Did you feel anything after what she had to say to you?" Warrose probes, dropping his fork on the table.

I wish I could say no.

I felt...everything.

Every emotion known to man, and some unidentifiable ones. Saying I died in her arms? The devastation welling in her eyes? It made my chest grow tight. It sucked the air out of my lungs. What kind of manipulation tactic is that? And why did it cut my heart open?

"Anger," I respond.

"*Pfft.*" Niles rolls his eyes. "It was more than that. We all saw your face."

I keep my burning stare fixed on my food. Why do we have to talk about her at all? I should be focusing on our escape. But that demon's face captivates my thoughts like a plague cast down to punish me.

Warrose clears his throat, raising his brows at something over my shoulder. I turn around to look and immediately regret it. My heart races as I follow the tall blonde with dazzling green eyes walking into the commissary.

I blow out an annoyed breath.

"Relax," Warrose growls.

How can I? The bane of my fucking existence is locked away in close proximity to me. I can't escape her destructive presence. I can't get rid of this evil entity.

And to make matters worse, Kane's brother walks up behind her, placing a hand on her back as he whispers in her ear. The demon listens intently, nodding her head as he speaks.

I narrow my eyes as I catch the way his breath brushes over her golden hair. Why is he that close? Why does he have his hand on her lower back?

An emotion I've never felt around the demon surfaces, blasting through my senses like radiation poisoning. I ball my hands into tight fists until my fingers go numb. My stomach burns, flips, and ties into a knot. What the fuck is wrong with me?

*You're jealous,* Kane says in disbelief.

"No, I am not."

Did I say that out loud?

Kaspias pulls away from her, pausing to look into her eyes. Rage weasels its way back into my nervous system, prickling my skin and setting my teeth on edge. I jump to my feet, knocking my tray over in the process, sending it clattering to the floor along with the rest of my food. The bang is loud enough to draw the attention of a few nearby tables, along with *them*.

The demon and Kaspias.

They stop looking at each other to tilt their heads toward me.

I move without thinking, blazing my way through the scattered inmates blocking my path to Kane's brother. Bumping my shoulder past the last obstacle, I stand at eye level with Kaspias, glowering into his bark-colored eyes lined with black paint.

"Dessin," he breathes. And his brows twitch upward like he's surprised to see me. Or maybe it's deeper, more convoluted than that. He's…gazing at me like a puppy dog.

And the demon, well, she looks like she's two seconds away from losing it.

I part my lips to explain why I've approached them, but the moment I stare into those cold, green eyes, I'm the one that loses it.

My fist flies into Kaspias's cheekbone. A stabbing pain pings up my knuckles and into my wrist. Kaspias's face jolts off to the side at the sudden blow. The demon gasps but does nothing to comfort her new friend or to stop me.

My vision turns spotty at the act of defiance, and I start to stumble from the spinning room. The woman who ruined my life grips my elbow to help me stand upright; her touch sends fire racing over my skin. An electrical sensation buzzing across my nerves.

"Get your fucking hands off me," I growl, ripping my arm from her grasp.

The blonde demon holds her hand to her chest as if I sliced her with a blade. My laugh comes out harsh and cruel, the same way she laughed when Arthur died in front of me.

"What? Don't act like you suddenly have feelings that I've hurt."

The evil woman stares at me. A look that I can feel weighing down my shoulders, preventing me from taking even breaths.

"You could never hurt me, Dess. Because I know this isn't you."

"You're a fool if you think that to be true. I can, and I *will* hurt you."

The demon places her hands on the center of her chest. "You could cut my heart out, and I'd still love you."

I step away. My throat involuntarily bobs. Why can't she just stick with her wicked fiend routine? The soulless hellhound that giggled every time we would cry as children. The devil that made so many of us split.

"Stop," I grit out.

"I'd love you if you snapped my neck right here in front of everyone." She takes another step.

"I'll do it," I warn.

"I'd wait for you in heaven."

"*Stop.*"

Her steps close the distance until my panting breaths graze the top of her head. And as I let myself, only for a heartbeat, scan the details of her face, an intrusive thought bursts like an exploding star in my mind. A thought that makes me hate myself, utterly and eternally.

*She's beautiful.*

"You're my soulmate no matter what they do to us," she whispers.

My heart caves in on itself at that familiar word. *Soulmate.*

"STOP!" I roar in her face.

The entire commissary goes mute, stopping their conversations abruptly.

And for no reason at all, this has made my entire body shake with emotion. My muscles vibrate against my bones, my lungs pulse in and out as if the oxygen in the air refuses to go down my airways. I'm suffocating. My heart gallops and stumbles, churning and tearing. I lose my bearings as she holds her hands in the air, like she wants to touch me but is scared to anger me further.

The logic of it all sends a blast of more revulsion, more loathing down my spine.

She is a demon.

What trick is this?

Why do her words move my heart like a ship drifting without sails?

Sweat forms over my entire body, and everyone is watching me. Everyone is silent. I might start rapid cycling again if I don't get this under control.

*Get away from her,* Sophia warns.

*Do you want Kalidus to take over?* Cricket asks.

"No!" I snap.

I do as Sophia orders, storming out of the commissary. Faces rush past me as I search the prison halls for a private spot. Why don't I just kill the demon? I am an avenging alter. I should be able to do what I must to protect and avenge our system. What the fuck is stopping me?

Throwing myself into an empty cage, I scoot to a dark corner, putting my head between my knees and focusing on calming my breathing. But it isn't working. Nothing is working. I'm dying. I'm suffocating.

"Take my hands."

My head snaps up to see the demon's horribly beautiful face watching me with tears in her eyes. Why is *she* crying? How does she keep faking these emotions around me?

"Do it. Now."

I must have fully lost my mind. My hands reach for hers without a single thought of retaliation. Her hands are soft, small, swallowed up by my own.

"Squeeze until it goes away," she whispers, nostalgia swimming in her gaze.

I squeeze her hands hard enough to seriously injure. Enough to make her wince. Enough to make her gasp.

"Harder. I deserve it."

She does. She's ruined our lives.

"I should have found you sooner. I should have saved you," she sobs as I nearly break her bones, pinching her knuckles in my hands.

My jaw goes rigid. And as tears cloud over my eyes, my stomach sinks. *Don't show weakness in front of her!* But I can't stop them from distorting my vision. Something in me, deep and in the most foreign depths of my mind, recognizes the genuine emotions weakening her voice, breaking her heart.

*What is wrong with me?!*

"You are safe with me," she says wetly, sniffling through her sobs.

I shake my head, forcing my eyes to go dry.

"Say it. *Please.*"

*Don't fall for it,* Kalidus's voice is distant as he tries to knock some sense into me.

I swallow. "I'm...safe with you."

The words glow in my mind like shining beacons. They tug on a memory that feels invisible, thin, and delicate. A moment from another life entirely.

"Yes," she says softly, "you are safe with me."

My breathing evens out, slowing and regulating in rhythm. And with that, I pull my hands from her grasp, wiping my face as quickly as possible. Erasing the evidence of that breakdown.

I stand up, my shadow stretching over her crouched stance on the floor. Sad, pathetic, in a desperate puddle at my feet.

"Stay away from me."

Leaving her behind in that empty cage, I try to ignore the sounds of her muffled cries as they echo down the brimstone walls of the hallway.

# 52. Healing

## Ruth

"Mar, I can take over. Go get something to eat."

Warrose leans against the open cage door, arms crossed over his chest, nodding at Marilynn. She gives me a gentle pat on the shoulder, uncrossing her legs, and gives Warrose a smile as she leaves.

"You don't have to babysit me," I say with a dry throat.

"I'm only here because I like being around you."

"Oh."

Warrose smirks, lowering himself to sit on my right side. "I brought you soup."

My stomach gurgles at the smell of hot chicken broth. I nod, lifting my head to see the metal cup next to his thigh.

"Can I help you sit up?"

"Okay."

Pain floods down my legs as Warrose positions his hands on the back of my neck and the base of my spine. He angles me against the cold bars, using Skylenna's leftover blankets to cushion my back.

"We haven't had much time to talk lately," Warrose says.

"I don't want to talk about my legs," I respond bitterly, bringing the steaming soup to my lips to blow on.

Warrose looks down. "It killed me to see you kiss him."

*Oh.* Initially, I'm relieved to hear a change of topic. But the memory of my lips on Kaspias's mouth and the look on Warrose's face as he watched it all burn down in front of him—it stabs me in the gut.

"It killed me, too." Especially after our kiss. My god, that *kiss.* I close my eyes, remembering the way he clawed at the bars to get closer to my face.

"It made me think the night before was all a trick," he adds.

I swallow my first spoonful of soup. "I know."

"I'm sorry I believed the lie." Warrose glances down at the thick veins on the tops of his hands, trailing up his massive forearms. "I was blinded by jealousy."

My eyes raise to meet his over the steam.

"Do you hate me for it?" he asks.

"You were jealous?"

His bright hazel eyes shudder at the memory. "Insanely jealous."

For the first time in…I don't know how long, a smile creeps up my cheeks.

"What?" He narrows his gaze.

I shrug, my smile growing deeper.

"Does my jealous rage amuse you, Ruth?"

A blush blooms across my entire face, smearing down my neck. The thought of Warrose being jealous does warm my heart. Why? I really don't know. For a moment after the kiss, I did get insecure wondering if it meant as much to him as it did to me. Wondering if I'm even a good kisser. Did he think so? My thoughts completely spiraled out of control.

"Yes," I say.

Warrose smiles back, enthralled by the look on my face. However, he swiftly goes still, serious in expression. With one giant hand, he slides his fingers around my waist, stroking my uniform slowly.

"I never want to see your lips on another man again," he finally says.

My heated smile falls. I set the mug down. "No?"

"No."

His jaw tightens, and his hand stops moving on my side. It feels like he's holding his breath, waiting for me to reject him again. I hold his eye contact fiercely, because even if it's temporary, he probably doesn't realize how powerful, how womanly this conversation makes me feel. I don't have to obsess about how my body looks after the axe. I don't have to wonder if he finds me attractive anymore.

It's in that flaming stare that he undoubtedly does.

"Okay," I answer breathlessly. "Then you won't."

His Adam's apple bobs over the length of his throat. With a tight nod, Warrose leans over me, hovering like a tree blocking the sun. I meet his eyes, watching as he struggles to find the right words.

"I want to be the only man that you give your lips to."

I exhale and close my eyes, letting this single sentence slay the depression feasting on my soul, even if it's for this moment only. That sentence loops in my mind repeatedly.

And all I can do is nod to keep from crying.

I breathe in his scent that's buried under the aroma of this prison. His chest moves up and down erratically, and he's so close that I can see the light dusting of black hair on the center of his chest. Warrose dips his head, placing a light kiss on my forehead, then lowering his lips to graze mine until I feel his soft breath mingling with my own.

I hold my breath.

And he moves like he's lost his self-control. Two large and overpowering hands slide up the sides of my face as he brushes his lips to mine. The movement is hesitant and sweet, making butterflies run wild in my stomach. Tilting my chin up, I give him access to deepen the kiss, and so he does. It's just one kiss, but the base of his throat grumbles with a ravenous groan.

It's the desperation that reminds me why I can't move any further with him. The agony radiating down my thighs. The phantom pains in my ankles. The loss of all hope.

I break the kiss, touching his elbow so that he moves back to look into my eyes.

"Will you promise me something?" I ask.

Warrose nods.

"If you can't break me out of this prison…if it's too hard to escape with me…"

"No." He doesn't let me finish. His back straightens, and his angular chin lifts stubbornly.

"Make sure I'm dead before you find freedom again. Don't let me rot in this prison." My hands start to shake aggressively at the idea of being left behind.

"It isn't an option," he says low enough to sound like a growl.

"Warrose, please. I need to know you'll do what must be done!"

"How can you fucking ask me this?!"

Angry tears swell over my vision, and my face wrinkles with the cry that comes spilling out of my lungs.

Ever since this happened, I've had this constant nightmare of watching my friends run out of this prison without me. And no matter how hard I try, I can never crawl fast enough. I'm left behind, cold, and dying a slow death in this cage.

"I'd rather die than end up here all alone!"

His face contorts into a look of anguish as he gazes over the details of my face as I cry out, as I shake from debilitating fear. In a flash of movement, Warrose snatches my feeble hands, bringing them to his chest.

"Oh, baby girl. Don't you know? I'd never leave you. I'd cover your body with my own to protect you from a storm. I'd stay in hell for the rest of my life if it means I'd get more time to make you smile. Baby girl. Don't you get it? I'd die before I ever left you behind."

I gasp before letting my cry unleash from my chest.

And this beautiful man doesn't waste another moment. He curls his body around mine, careful not to hurt me. His giant hands cradle my head to his chest, spreading his body heat over me like a thick blanket.

"You won't leave me behind," I sob.

Warrose nuzzles his face in my curly hair, sighing softly against my scalp. "I'll never leave you behind."

# 53. What Comes Later

## Marilynn

Niles sits by himself in the stadium, hunched over his knees with his hands tightening in his hair.

I plant myself in the seat next to him in the first row that faces the stage. He leans back in his chair, noticing my presence with a quick glance.

"How're you holding up?" I ask.

Niles shrugs in defeat.

"You can talk about it," I say in a softer voice. "I know you're not one to bottle up what you're thinking."

"You want to know one of the first conversations I ever had with Skylenna in the asylum?" He stares off into the distance of the mocking red stage. Eyes unfocused and sad.

"Tell me."

"We talked about soulmates. And how once you find them, there is no life without them."

"Right."

"Well…I've now watched my sister grieve through the death of her soulmate, burying him, avenging him, loving him even when his heart no longer beat. And now? Now, I watch as she loves her soulmate who feels nothing but hatred for her." He balls his hands into fists. "And Dessin has done nothing but love her fiercely through her amnesia. Protected her friends. Kept us safe. How is any of this fair?"

"It's not."

"And what about Ruthie? I'm supposed to accept that my best friend will never walk again? Never be able to run in the early morning the way she did when we'd make camp in the forest? She doesn't deserve this fate!"

I turn my head to look at him as he crosses his arms, shaking his head while working out his grief. Exhaustion darkens the spaces under his eyes like smeared charcoal. His skin has lost its stunning golden glow.

We have to get out of here.

"You can't give birth in this prison, Marilynn."

I meet his hardened stare with the vertical wrinkle in between his brows. It's this no-bullshit look that seems to float deeper and deeper into my heart like a leaf drifting in the wind.

"We'll get out before then," I assure him.

At least, I think we will. There are a lot of details missing from the prophecy. I assume it's to make certain meaningful events happen at the right time.

"And once we're out?" he prompts.

"Once we're out, I'll raise him in Demechnef."

"It's a boy?"

Damn, I'm not sure if I should have kept that to myself.

"The prophecy says it will be a boy."

Niles doesn't move for several seconds. "I suppose Aurick will be happy he's having a son. An heir."

Before I open my mouth to respond, I observe the slight lowering of his gaze, the twinge of insecurity. "I'm not going back to Aurick."

"No?"

"No."

Niles rubs the back of his neck. "You'd go through your pregnancy alone?"

I smile. "I'm a strong woman, Niles. I've been alone for a very long time."

"And if I said I wanted to be there? To help?"

Every atom in my body jumps with nervous energy. It's like every bedtime story I've heard. Like déjà vu spinning around my head in a carousel.

"I'd say I wouldn't mind the company." Though I try to remain unfazed, my smile spreads. He matches my expression with a devastating grin. Stunning in every way.

"Good, because I am an excellent chef for pregnancy cravings."

My smile burns against my cheeks. "Are you really?"

"Absolutely. Midnight, freshly-baked cookies? Chocolate malts? Cheesy baked potato soup? We'll have a fully stocked kitchen on standby for you."

My stomach grumbles like a small animal.

We both laugh.

"You'd do all that for me?" *Have I ever smiled this much in my life?*

"No." Niles shakes his head, and his dimples appear in the shifting shadows. "I'd do all of that for you *and* your baby boy."

If only he could hear how my pulse races, how the blood rushes to my head at his sentiment. I bury my face in my hands and let out an excited giggle. I was supposed to keep my distance. I promised myself since I was a little girl. Why is this so hard?

"Well, that makes me really happy."

Just as I remove my hands from my face, Niles leans in and places a slow, lingering kiss on my cheek. His breath fuses with my skin, and the warmth of his lips burns into every membrane. It gives me delirious flashbacks to our kiss on that one Fun House Night.

"It makes me happy, too." Niles smiles against my cheek.

I pivot my head toward his face hovering so close to mine. Looking into his eyes, I see the anticipation dilating his pupils, lowering his lids. Tilting my chin toward his lips

"I'm calling an emergency family meeting."

We pull apart at the sound of Skylenna's voice. She's standing in front of us looking like a storm ran her over, disheveling her hair, whipping against her eyes and pink cheeks. It's evident that she's been crying for hours.

"Someone needs to find Dessin," she adds with a thick voice. "Then we can meet back at the cages."

# 54. A Single Moment

## Skylenna

"What's this about?" Warrose asks.

Niles and Marilynn sit down to the left of Ruth after finding Dessin and bringing him back to us. He's standing in the entryway of the cage, leaning on one shoulder, looking like a shadow of death, a grim reaper. His hands are trembling at the sight of me, though he won't raise his eyes to meet mine. In fact, he doesn't stare any higher than my legs.

"The Fun House is tonight," I announce. "Kaspias told me that the theme is called the Guzzle Ride."

"Shit," Warrose breathes, running his hands through his thick hair nervously.

"Well, that doesn't sound good," Niles says.

"They force the inmates to drink from an alcoholic hose. Then they must walk across a plank surrounded by a trench of fire. Many die from not being able to walk a straight line."

The moment my gaze falls on Ruth, I realize what I've said.

"I'm going to burn," she utters, her face turning a deadly shade of gray.

"No, you're not." Dessin takes a step into the cage. "And neither is Marilynn since she can't even drink alcohol with the baby."

My stomach drops. I didn't even consider that.

"Warrose, I recall you being able to drink any Demechnef captain under the table since the age of thirteen. You'll drink Ruth's share of the hose and carry her across the plank."

Warrose snorts. "I was already going to do that, but thanks for stealing my thunder."

"Niles and I will drink from Marilynn's share," Dessin finishes.

My spine aches, feeling feeble and unsteady at the sound of his beautiful baritone voice.

"It may not come to that." I find my voice buried under my splitting heart. "Kaspias told me he has a plan to make this right."

"And you believe him?" Ruth asks, somewhat hopeful in her drooping eyes.

"Yes. When I had him in that dungeon, I did something to him in the void. Something I've never done before."

"What was it?" Warrose asks.

"I took away the abuse and changed the trajectory his life would have taken if he had been raised by his mother. He's not the same man we knew. And right now, all he wants is to make this right. All he feels is remorse."

Five pairs of eyes blink at me. Their wheels turn as they process this information.

"You think he's going to help us," Niles muses skeptically.

"It's another one of her tricks."

Everyone turns to look at Dessin. And this time, he's glaring directly into my soul, searing his hatred through my bones like a branding iron.

Warrose cracks his knuckles in frustration. "Give it a fucking rest."

"It's not a trick," I mutter, losing my breath as I maintain eye contact with him.

"No? Only a demon should be able to rewire someone's brain."

"Or an angel." Ruth reaches out to grab Dessin's ankle. He looks down at her like he's trying to understand why someone is touching him. "Dessin? Can you come down here?"

He blinks, widening his stance defensively. But lying on the floor, her head on Warrose's lap, she looks so weak. Her hair has thinned, cheeks sunken in, and the beautiful brown eyes have lost their sparkle. Dessin sighs, bending a knee to be closer to her.

"Are you my friend?" she asks him.

"Yes."

"And haven't I already been through enough?"

Dessin nods solemnly.

"Then stop hurting me by speaking about my sister and the woman you love this way. I have been through enough. It breaks my heart to hear the poison of your words."

The muscles in my back solidify. I hold my breath involuntarily. It kills me that I'm not suffering alone on this. What they've done to Dessin, to the other alters, it's hurting all of us. His hatred, his distrust of me...

I understand how he felt when I was so angry at him about keeping Aurick's identity from me. I lashed out, refusing to speak to him. But in truth, this is much, much worse. Every beautiful memory we've ever shared has been violated in his mind.

His grim, dark-mahogany eyes flick up to me, then back down to her pale face.

"Okay, Ruth."

I let my eyes fall closed and sigh, feeling tender all over.

Ruth nods, squeezing his hand that rests on his thigh. "Thank you."

# Skylenna

THE LINE GOING INTO THE stadium is long, winding around the musty hallway.

"I feel sick," Ruth mumbles against Warrose's shoulder.

"Keep her legs elevated, and be extremely careful around her bandages," Dessin instructs, looking a little worried at Ruth's wincing face.

"You're not moving an inch the entire night, my little rebel." Warrose carries a lightness to his tone, like he's trying to keep her calm. "If I say anything inappropriate while I'm drunk, just ignore it and don't remind me about it tomorrow. Oh, and if you happen to observe Dessin during all of this, be sure to let me know if he's a sloppy drunk."

"I'm not," Dessin grunts.

I smirk before I'm brought back to reality, where my smile quickly fades.

"Not true. He thinks he's greater than thou because he considers the drink to be a poison that he would not choose to enter his precious body."

To our joy, Warrose's little confession has elicited a laugh out of Ruth. The sound is quick and small, but it's there like a pearl found in an oyster. Niles turns around to grin wide at Warrose.

"What's your point?" Dessin glares.

"You are a lightweight."

Niles snickers. "Let's get him a sippy cup!"

Dessin slides his intolerable glare to Niles, unflinching as he communicates his lack of humor and annoyance silently.

"Mm-hmm, yep, I'm just going to check on this line." Niles takes a step to the other side of Marilynn like a coward. She pats him on the back with a chuckle.

I focus on my breathing as I try tapping into the void. After what I did to Masten and Kaspias, it has felt distant, unreachable. I have to do everything in my power to reverse what they've done to Dessin.

Before he falls in step with the moving line, I hook my hand around his elbow, pulling him off to the side with a knot forming in my stomach.

"Get your goddamn hand off of me before I cut it off," he growls with clenched teeth.

*I know this isn't you, but that still hurts.*

Respecting his space, I remove my hand, placing it to my side. One breath in, one breath out. I count to four.

"I don't know what Kaspias has planned," I say under my breath.

Dessin stares down at me from his lofty height.

One breath in, one breath out.

"To the point," he grits out.

454

*I know this isn't you.*

"I mean, I—I don't know what's going to happen. And that scares me."

"Nothing scares you," he responds bitterly.

"There is something that terrifies me, actually." I look up at him. "Being separated from you knowing how you feel about me. How you're plagued with revulsion at the sight of me. That *scares* me."

"I don't believe you."

But again, something behind his eyes shifts, a glimmer of doubt.

"Soon, when I'm strong enough, I'll be able to give you every last moment they stole from your mind. But right now, all I can do is find something they might have missed. Something that will show you the truth of my words." Insecurely, I clasp my hands together and twist.

"I won't fall for your tricks." He blinks slowly, like this conversation has already lost his interest. A lie I can spot immediately.

I use all of my strength to call upon the void, but it answers with a long rope that ties me to Dessin. A bridge I need to cross in order to access its vast range of space.

And thinking back on the conversation I had with Dessin recently, I know exactly what I need to do.

Dessin's eyes widen in alarm as he sees me actively make the decision to do this, knowing it might end poorly for me. But it's the only option I have. The only way out.

Like I once did in that abandoned Demechnef building, I throw my arms around Dessin's neck, pulling my body flush to his in the fiercest hug I can muster. His large hands catch my waist up high, close to my ribcage, in an attempt to stop me or push me away. His form goes rigid, unyielding like a wooden board against my soft curves.

But I don't let go.

I hug him like it's the first time all over again.

And with the surge of emotions attached to the two of us, the void slams into me like a bolt of lightning, flooding my senses as I tumble into his subconscious. We float into a clear blue sky like a bird soaring over a magical village, the kind you would see in the pages of a mystical storybook.

The inner world.

But the void doesn't allow me to explore. It doesn't give me the chance to meet his alters, see their real faces. We travel over an ocean, through the clouds of a hurricane. It must be hundreds of miles as the rain drenches us in the sky. And this place isn't like our initial impression of the inner world. It's stormy and cold, waves crashing over each other in a gray ocean that moves violently like it's in the middle of war. And among the fog and sea mist, there's a tower.

It's a tall fortress made of granite, onyx, and ashlar, with the sides covered by thick layers of algae. It's a prison. I can feel the forbidden energy hanging in the air around it, shaming us for coming so close. But the void throws us at the foot of its entrance.

"I'm not supposed to be here," Dessin gasps, backing away from the sheltered doorway and into the pounding wall of rain and mist.

"What is this place?" I ask.

Dessin's eyes dart over the exterior of the tower. "This is where the *deeper alters* stay. I can't go near them. They're never supposed to have any contact with any other alters."

I remember the conversation he told me about them. It was one of our earlier nights in the prison, and he opened up about the inner world.

"The trauma they hold could bleed into other alters," I state in exasperation.

"Yeah."

I'd respect this boundary if the void wasn't drawing me into this prison like a fishing hook reeling me out of the water.

"Dessin, I think there is an alter in here that can help."

He shakes his head, sprinkling water across my face with the action.

"He doesn't have to come in."

Dessin and I turn our heads back to the entrance, refocusing our eyes on a woman I wouldn't have guessed resided in his hopeless place.

Sophia takes a step into the windy atmosphere.

Dessin stumbles back across the rocky terrain, mouth gaping open as he watches her.

Sophia's dress flaps in the hazy storm, rising and falling around her like a pink puff of smoke. She smiles at us sadly. "I had to keep something safe before they did their damage."

Chills blossom over my back.

"What did you keep safe?" I ask so quietly, it sounds like an expelled breath.

"Memories."

Dessin takes a step forward. "I can't be close to you and the trauma you hold."

"Trauma wasn't the reason I split," she murmurs. "I'm a memory holder. But my purpose is to protect the memories that have given us life. The small moments that have made the trauma worth the struggle."

Sophia moves toward him, and although Dessin fears this place, he doesn't shy away from her. Why? For the same reason I feel so nostalgic around her calming presence. For the same reason her energy reminds me of falling in love, picking flowers, or having a first kiss under a waterfall.

She reminds me of all the good things that have happened to us.

She reminds me of home.

"I think it's time I give a moment back to you," she adds, placing her left hand on his shoulder, and reaching her other hand out for me to take.

His breath hitches as my skin touches hers, shooting us both through the memory as if we're living it all over again.

# Dessin

"I WATCHED YOU DIE!" SKYLENNA screams in anger at first, but the meaning behind her words causes her bottom lip to tremble. And she breaks into tiny little pieces.

We're surrounded by dead Vexamen soldiers in the Hangman's Valley. DaiSzek and I followed the sixth sense that she was in danger. We knew exactly what to do.

And this is the first time she's seeing me since I died in her arms.

She coughs out a sob and tries to feebly pound her fists against my chest. I can't watch her fall apart any longer. I grab her hands before they meet my chest, drawing her against my body and walking us back until I'm pressing her against a tree.

My heart is a flurried storm of endless anguish. That storm doesn't calm until I rest my forehead to hers, silencing the noise of the forest, silencing the other alters in my mind.

Her golden face becomes blurry through the thin sheen of tears.

"I was so cold..." she whimpers, sending a thousand knives through my soul. "I wanted to die, too."

How could I ever make up for this pain I've caused her? How will I ever live up to deserving a heart as pure as hers?

"Forgive me," I grunt through the lump forming in my throat. "Forgive me. Because I'll never forgive myself. We never wanted you to hurt like this."

It was her plan when she was younger. Our Skylenna was actually willing to succumb herself to this custom form of hell just to be with us. Just to be able to protect us the way we've always protected her.

She cries harder than I've ever seen her cry, drooping in my arms as she bellows. I lock my hold around her, inhaling the sweet scent of her hair, feeling her heartbeat against my own.

*I love you, baby. I love you so much.*

"Please, don't leave me," she begs with a small voice, so desperate, so tortured, I nearly drop to my knees.

"I'm here. I'm here." Every muscle in my arms and back tightens, fiercely wrapping around her limp frame, determined to always hold her up at her weakest.

Skylenna howls against me, unraveling against my chest. "You were dead!"

"I was. And it killed me more watching you *watch* me die."

"I can't get the memory out of my head. I see your blood on my hands everywhere I go."

Fucking hell. Nothing in the world has ever cut me this deep.

"And I've become a monster. You—"

I dive my head forward, capturing her mouth with my own, cutting off her question with the uncontrollable need to taste her kiss again. And it isn't like any other time I've laid my lips on hers. It's tortured. It's traumatized. It's deeply, madly, ferociously in love with her. Through the tears dripping down her face, the blood and sweat splattered across our skin. Her arms wrap around my neck, and I tighten my hold on her waist.

"I fucking missed you, baby."

And I did. I missed the woman I love more than I missed having a beating heart. Because without her, I have no heart. Without her, I have no air in my lungs.

Skylenna Winter Ambrose is my whole world.

# Skylenna

I OPEN MY EYES AFTER SEEING into the special memory Sophia gave back.

She's gone. Like smoke spiraling into the air from a small fire. Disappearing into the ocean's breeze, back where she belongs to protect their system's precious memories.

And it's just us.

Dessin takes a step back with an open mouth and an agonized expression.

"That was…" he breathes.

"One of the best days of my life," I tell him weakly.

"I—" He shakes his head in muted shock. "That was real."

"Yes."

*Stop crying. Stop crying. Stop crying.*

"I…*felt* it. I remember." He looks me up and down as if seeing me through a new lens. His chocolate gaze rests over my lips, the curve of my neck, my hands, my long hair.

He remembers me.

Now I know why those words meant so much to them.

*I remember.*

"You were so emotional to see me," he says without the usual hard edge to his voice. He moves in my direction, using his left thumb to trace through the trail of my tears. "Is it because you love me?"

My eyes burn as I stare up at him through the spray of sea water and rain.

"Yes. Because you're my soulmate, and when I watched you die on that beach…there was no life without you. No sun. No warmth." I run my fingertips over the hairs on his forearm, savoring the fact that he doesn't pull away from my touch even though it's hard for him.

"This is…hard for me to accept," he grunts.

"Why?"

"I still remember how you tortured us our entire lives. I don't know how to move past it."

Dread turns my stomach sour. I wish I had the time and strength to help him right now. But this trip into the void has already cost me so much.

"We have to go back," I mutter.

Dessin looks into my eyes for a few more seconds, as if he might just find all of his answers there. He nods once, pursing his lips as he glances away.

Standing back in the hall of the prison after being sucked out of the void, the line nearly disappears into the stadium. I untie my arms from around Dessin's neck, lingering close to his face, sharing the same breath.

"We should get inside," he says, eyes fixed on my mouth.

"Okay."

But as he walks away, my heart crumbles. Everything from here feels uncertain. Life and death are a part of the same thread of fate.

"Dessin…"

He turns around, and for a moment, his gaze reminds me of the first time our eyes met in the asylum. The raw magnetism dragging us together.

"I won't give up until I return all you've lost. I'll love you until hell freezes over."

His lips part like some muscle memory wants him to finish that statement. Say the words we've always said. But he doesn't remember them.

I don't give him the chance to linger on it. My feet sprint to him, closing the distance as I throw my arms over his shoulder, jumping in for a kiss before it's too late. Dessin doesn't move as I press my mouth to his. Doesn't relax his stern muscles as I latch onto his shoulders, kneading my fingers into his back.

After the initial shock, he exhales into a brief pause, then grabs my face in his strong hands and deepens the kiss. It's both reluctant and fueled with exploding passion. His heart warring with his mind. I memorize his taste, his cedar scent, the softness of his full lips, and the calluses of his palms grating against my cheeks.

*And even then, Dessin.*

He breaks the kiss off abruptly, storming into the stadium without looking back.

I slump in the spot he left me in, arms shaking in the place he once stood. Depression forms a collar around my throat, squeezing until I'm panting in Dessin's absence.

"We don't have long. You're going to have to do everything I say and never deviate," Kaspias says, making me flinch back as he unlocks the collar around my neck.

"What?" I ask, rubbing my hands along the raw skin.

Kaspias smiles genuinely, rubbing his hands together. "There's an army at our border. And I'm here to execute your escape. You think you can lead them into battle to save your friends?"

# 55. Into Hell We Go

## Ruth

I tremble like a blade of grass in Warrose's arms.

"Are you shaking for me, my little rebel?"

I exhale. "Nope. I'm shaking at the thought of being dumped into a pit of lava."

"You think I'll get that drunk?"

"I do."

He snorts.

Across the stage are barrels connected to rubber hoses. Prisoners stand in several lines waiting to consume their share of the drink. The audience mingles among themselves as they wait for the plank walking to start. Soldiers wear hats that look like animal heads: pigs, goats, bucks, and something else...

I squint into the distance, going still.

"RottWeilen," I breathe.

Warrose looks at me quizzically, then darts his gaze to the audience and the many soldiers wearing hats that look like the heads of the

RottWeilen. That look just like DaiSzek.

"Why the fuck are they wearing those?" he growls.

Dessin steps forward with a scowl.

"They're celebrating the start of the meat carnival season," Helga Bee says, appearing to Dessin's right.

"And they're probably wearing those particular hats to taunt us," Dessin speculates.

Niles sighs. "Skylenna isn't going to like this."

I nod in agreement. This will definitely set her off. But as I turn to gauge her reaction in the line behind us, she's missing. I shift in Warrose's hold, trying to search the sea of inmates waiting for their turn in the lines. No waterfall of honey hair. No long legs. No Skylenna.

"Dessin?" I ask.

He raises his eyebrows in my direction.

"Did Skylenna not come in with you?"

Dessin's dark irises flick to the assembly lines, scanning the heads of hair, reaching all the way out to the entryway. His focus returns to me with a slight alarm wrinkling his brow.

"She was right behind me."

# Skylenna

"I'm not leaving without them."

Kaspias tugs me through a few hallways I've never seen before. His grip on my wrist is stronger than an iron shackle, and he doesn't loosen it even as I resist his pull.

"You're the only one not affected by the devious little piece inside your ear anymore. Remember when you fought the dizziness in the dungeon? That shocked even Masten. Your friends don't have that luxury," he explains.

"So?!" I grind my teeth against the frustration growing hot in my chest. "I don't care. We can still get them out!"

Kaspias shoots me a look with those black-rimmed eyes. "If I try to get them out with it still inside their ears, the walls encasing this prison will cause it to shoot through their brains like an arrow. Is that what you want?"

No. What? Of course, not…but…

The hallway shrinks around me, echoing the drumming of my racing heart. I'm out of breath, eyes pleading at the open space as we sprint. There has to be a way to free us together. Isn't there?

"Kaspias…"

*I can't leave them. I can't leave them. I can't leave them.*

"My brother would want me to get you out," he hollers back.

Fuck. I know he would! I made a promise to him. But you know what? No. NO! I hiss, throwing my weight into my back leg and freeing my arm from Kaspias's pull.

"I won't leave my family behind," I pant.

Kaspias stumbles away a few steps, straightening his posture and looking so much like the man I love, yet nothing like him at all.

"There's word of a RottWeilen pacing the perimeter of Vexamen's shores." His words sink like an anchor. "They say it's bigger than any RottWeilen in recorded history. Our archers have been given orders to shoot him down with Sapphrine Oil from afar."

I shake my head, the word "no" shaping my lips.

"He's yours, isn't he?" he asks, lowering his chin.

I swallow, nodding.

"If leading in the cavalry is your best chance to free your family, wouldn't you take it?"

Exhaling feels dangerously close to releasing venom from my body. My shoulders sag forward, and even my face melts into submission.

"Are you sure you can get me out?"

"I'm sure. There's really only one area I can see being a problem. But…" Kaspias stares deeply into my eyes with determination. "I won't let you down, Skylenna. I'll give everything to get you out."

# Ruth

"WHAT SHOULD WE DO?" WARROSE asks Dessin, trying not to sound alarmed. "We're up next."

Dessin zones out in the grand theater seating the Vexamen soldiers. And I can't help but wonder if even a small part of him still loves her. If there's even a fragment of that affection left in his mind that can verify all we've said.

"The de" Dessin cuts himself off. "Skylenna can handle herself."

I blink in surprise at his use of her name. The act of saying it causes tendons in his neck to strain, but he still said it. Warrose glances at me with parted lips.

"We're next," Niles announces nervously.

I inhale deeply, trying my best to slow my pounding heartbeat, but the thick aroma of candy apples, popcorn, and sweat makes me cringe. Bursts of fire explode from torches surrounding the stage for dramatic effect, sending heat waves tumbling around us.

"You're going to stay calm for me, okay?" Warrose tilts his face toward me, nearly grazing his nose against mine.

"Okay."

"And if you get scared, I want you to close your eyes."

"Aren't *you* scared?"

At this point, my limbs are pulsating with anxious energy. The lower half of my body aches and throbs, and I'm faint with unrelenting nausea.

He stares into my eyes like he's waiting to see if I can figure that out for myself. His expression is nothing short of calm and confident.

"No."

We step up to the barrel and hose. My skin bubbles and prickles at the sight of Dessin and Niles kneeling to receive their serving, then to take Marilynn's hose, too. I'm lowered a few inches as Warrose goes down to a knee, nodding at the sentinel holding two hoses.

I massage Warrose's left shoulder anxiously. "What should I do to help?"

"*Mmm,*" he hums in the back of his throat. "That. I'd like you to keep doing that."

I relax a little knowing that I'm able to do something helpful. My hands knead against his skin with purpose, trying to ease his tight muscles.

I watch with building tension as he accepts the first hose, taking long gulps and not even flinching as the potent liquid drains down his throat. The scent of the alcohol burns the edges of my nostrils, even though I'm not the one drinking it. A drop drizzles down his chin as he nods at the sentinel, giving the first hose back to receive the next serving.

"Oh, God," I breathe in sharply. "Are you sure you can handle the next one?"

Warrose rolls his eyes with a cocky smirk but doesn't respond as he continues to take efficiently large gulps. I stop massaging his shoulder and start caressing the curve of his neck. Slow, intimate strokes. I run my fingers upward, skimming under his hair to his scalp. That soft, dark head of hair is like silk; I become mesmerized by fondling those thick strands. He's rough around every edge, from his calloused hands to his bristly facial hair, bulging muscles, thighs that might be made of tree trunks—all except for his hair and his eyes. These two features are made of satin and midnight dreams.

"That's going to get me hard." Warrose drops the second hose from his mouth, taking deep inhales to catch his breath.

"From touching your hair?" My lips twitch into a half smile.

"Yeah."

I ignore the mental image of a tent forming in his pants. "I think your hair might be softer than mine."

"Did you just give me a compliment?"

"Don't get used to it."

Warrose chuckles, low and gruff. As he turns his face closer to me, I instinctively use my thumb to wipe away the trail of alcohol that ran down his chin and neck. His eyes lower as he follows my every movement.

That smoldering look sends a rush of wet heat between my legs, and my gaze shudders over his full lips. The desire to taste that alcohol on him is making my mind swim with delirium. His face is so close, and that mouth would feel so good against mine.

"You good, War?" Niles nudges us from behind. "They're having us wait on the edge of the stage until the drink kicks in. Then I think we're walking the plank."

"Did he just give me a nickname?" Warrose raises an eyebrow at me.

I snicker. "I like chicken coward better."

"Me, too."

It's another beat of a moment that his weighty gaze burns deep into my soul, a look that I've never seen in a man's eyes before. And I can't help but stare right back.

"Are you ignoring me because I'm drunk?" Niles pops his head around to our left.

Warrose's eye roll is slow and exaggerated.

"Are you already drunk?" I ask with a laugh.

"Perhaps." He boops my nose. "Perhaps not!"

Dessin shows up to my right, nodding his head in the direction of the inmates gathering to wait for the Ringmaster to announce that it's time for the plank.

"What about you, Dess? You drunk yet?" Niles bumps Dessin with his shoulder.

"He's really sticking with these nicknames," Warrose mutters close to my ear.

"No," Dessin mutters, irritation pinching his brow.

"How do you know if he's drunk?" I ask.

Warrose shrugs. "Hard to tell. He would just get all broody and talk about Skylenna."

I can tell Dessin hears Warrose's comment by the way the tendons in his jaw tic. But he doesn't retort. I'm sure he's experiencing conflicting feelings with hearing her name.

We stand in a circle on the stage, being bumped and crowded by the mass of warm inmate bodies cluttering in the same area. I grip Warrose's back with as much energy as I'm able to exert without passing out. Everything hurts, but at least the adrenaline is making me numb.

As time passes, Warrose's eyelids droop as performers throw sticks of fire around the stage, entertaining the crowd until we're ready to walk.

"Warrose?" My voice pulls him from the deep thought he was

working through. He slides his slightly glazed over eyes to me.

"Hmm?"

"Are you sure you can do this?"

He flashes me a devastatingly handsome smile. "Yes, I'm sure."

"How drunk are you on a scale from one to ten?"

"A seven."

"I'm a fourteen!" Niles laughs, doing a little fist pump.

"That's not something to be proud of, Niles," Dessin scolds, and even his words are a little slurred.

"You always smell so pretty." I turn my head back to Warrose, just now noticing his nose nuzzled into my hair, breathing in with his eyes closed.

"What do I smell like?" I smirk.

"Roses and money," he says huskily. "Like a queen."

I laugh. "Well, that's not so bad."

"What do I smell like?" Warrose opens his eyes, pulling away from my hair to give me a look that makes my thighs tremble.

I pause to think.

"A cow's ass! *Ha-ha!*" Niles throws his head back and busts out laughing, eavesdropping *again*.

Warrose clenches his jaw, but Dessin steps up first.

"You are two seconds from being thrown off the stage," Dessin hisses.

"By whom?!" Niles's eyes go round.

"Me."

"Shutting up, sir."

The stage trembles as it opens rectangular gaps in the floor with thin metal planks stretched across their centers. We stare as the audience of soldiers rumble their feet in anticipation. The percussion fills my ears, making it hard for Warrose to focus on one thing.

The Ringmaster begins to yell in excitement.

"*Feizëx! Feizëx! Feizëx! Feizëx!*"

"What're they saying?" Marilynn asks.

"Fire," Dessin and I say at the same time.

And this time, Niles really does shut up. His face goes a sick shade of green.

"We'll go first," Warrose announces to the group, becoming more alert as we watch the pits fill up with molten lava, bright yellows and oranges swirling under the planks.

I jerk in his arms as tufts of gas and flames explode from the lava. Sentinels pour liquid into each rectangular pit, encouraging a blazing wall of fire that climbs to great heights, licking the sides of the planks.

"Oh, Warrose." I hug him tighter, pressing my face against his warm chest.

"I want you to close your eyes until it's over, okay?" He places a quick kiss on my forehead. "Keep your face against my chest."

I nod and try to steady my quivering limbs. If anyone can do this, it's Warrose. He's a tank of a man who can obviously handle his liquor. And besides, it doesn't look like they gave these inmates that much to drink. Our group seems fine.

Putting my thoughts to shame, the first prisoner steps up to the plank, slips, and immediately falls to his death. His limp body plunks into the lava and flames like a boulder being tossed in a lake.

"Shit," I breathe, tucking my face against his chest once more.

Helga Bee and Gerta shuffle through the crowd, waving us down.

"Hey! Come on, you two need to get to the front!" Helga Bee bustles through the lines of inmates, throwing elbows to reach us.

"Why?" Warrose asks but doesn't object as they place their hands on his back, pushing him forward.

"The longer you wait, the hotter the planks will get! Your feet will burn!"

*Wait.* The planks are metal. A conductor of heat. *Oh, no.* What about Niles? This is going to be hard enough for him as it is! I whip my head to search for Niles through the crowd.

"Niles!" I screech, raising my chin above Warrose's bulky shoulder. "Niles! You have to get to the front of the line! *Niles!*"

"What's wrong?" Helga Bee asks, pushing inmates aside to get us a spot in the front.

"You have to get our friends up here, too! Niles is a burn victim! *Please!!*"

Gerta nods with fierce determination, and they leave to go find him.

The line moves faster than I'm prepared for. The inmates don't walk the plank one at a time, they follow each other across like a line of ants. Warrose's feet move forward steadily, if I didn't see him drink from those hoses, I might not be able to tell he's drunk.

"Close your eyes, baby girl," Warrose breathes against my cheek.

I squeeze my eyes shut, feeling my stomach dip as I can tell we've now stepped onto the plank.

"It'll be over soon," he says gruffly.

"Is it hot?" I ask.

"The metal is warming up. But it's not burning my feet."

*Thank God.*

From what I can tell, Warrose walks in a straight line. Steady. Composed. With the graceful agility of a cat. My muscles loosen their grip, and I soften my hold around his neck. Maybe this isn't as bad as I thought it would be. Maybe

We stumble forward, and Warrose curses, hugging me to his chest to keep balance.

"Hey!" he grunts.

The plank shakes underneath us. The prisoners bump into each other as they grow frantic and drunk. A panic breaks out among those that are crossing this well of fire. Shoving. Screaming. The melting sounds of bodies flopping into the vat of lava. We're suddenly jerked back and forth, wobbling side to side as Warrose fights to keep us upright.

"Don't you dare open those eyes," he growls in my ear.

"I won't!"

But it's too tempting. I have to know what's going on. Not just to satisfy my creeping curiosity, but to quell the motion sickness swirling in my gut. If I have to start heaving, that will definitely wreck his focus, throwing us off balance.

I peek out of one eye, watching what takes place over his shoulder.

Inmates are being poked and stabbed with sticks from surrounding sentinels and soldiers climbing on the stage to be a part of this bizarre and demented circus.

An animalistic noise rumbles from Warrose's throat as he's stabbed in the side with a dull spear. I gasp as a small trickle of blood slides down his hip.

"Warrose!"

"I'm okay."

Something hooks and latches onto my hair, dragging us down to the right. I yelp at the sting that rakes across my scalp. A female inmate with crows feet surrounding her frightened, beady eyes uses my head to keep herself upright.

"Let go!" I scream.

Warrose headbutts the woman, a crack through the air between us, and she tumbles off the metal strip. I groan against his shoulder.

I hear Dessin shout something from the end of the plank behind us. Warrose nods, taking a deep breath.

"It's going to feel crazy for a minute, but I promise I won't drop us. But Dessin's right, I need to clear the path." He sounds confident and ultimately fearless in what he's about to do. I have no room to question it. His calmness is like a steel shelter in a storm. Unbreachable.

"Okay."

With one arm, Warrose yanks a spear from a sentinel, tugging so hard the glorified guard is thrown into the flames with a high-pitched shriek. He uses the spear to spin around in a circle, batting inmates away from us and not stopping even though some fall to their deaths. He's doing what he must to get me out of this. To protect us both.

Warrose moves like a tiger, bulky in size, but attacks with the flow of a snake. His thick legs kick outward to defend us from the mob of fumbling bodies. And once he gives himself enough room, he throws the spear back to Dessin, hissing as a few wild flames stroke his ankles. A few strides across the remaining distance, and we're on the other side of the stage. Panting. Grumbling curse words.

"You're hurt," I whine.

*I'm sorry I couldn't walk this plank by myself. I'm sorry you're hurt because of me. I'm sorry I've been so useless to everyone this entire time. Why did this have to happen to me? Why, Warrose?*

"It's a scratch," he brushes me off but then catches the way I'm looking at him. The way I'm beating myself up internally over this. "Ruth?"

"I hate myself," I mutter while shaking my head.

*Don't you dare cry again. Don't!*

"Talk to me," he rasps, still a little out of breath.

"You shouldn't have had to carry me." My chest roasts with self-loathing. How am I supposed to live my life needing this much help? All I've ever wanted was to be of use to our family. To be able to fight. To run faster than the others. To do something. ANYTHING!

Warrose surprises me by smiling wide.

"What?" I try not to take offense to his satisfaction.

"Baby girl, I would have carried you in perfect health."

My eyes turn round and glossy. *No more crying. I am not weak. From now on, I'm going to put on a strong face. It's the least I can do.*

"You mean it?"

He nods with that same smile that makes my skin tingle. I bite down to keep the tears from rushing to my eyes.

"Why are you making that face?"

"I'm trying not to cry." My voice comes out in a squeak.

He laughs, rough and beautiful. "It's okay to cry, Ruth."

"Not anymore," I explain. "Not for me. I can't let myself fall apart again."

He lifts his chin, looks off to the prisoners scurrying across the heating metal.

"Then when this is all over, I'll take you somewhere safe. Somewhere you can finally let yourself fall to pieces, okay?"

I blow out a strained breath. "You won't want me in pieces, I can promise you that."

"Oh, yes I will." He touches the tip of his nose to mine. "I'll just have to mix my pieces with yours. We'll make a beautiful puzzle."

# 56. Pyrophobia

## Marilynn

"It's a real bad sign if the stadium is spinning, isn't it?"

"Shit," Dessin says through an exhale. "It isn't good, Niles."

I have no doubt Dessin will get across that plank unscathed. Warrose just put on a show for everyone with how quickly he was able to maneuver every obstacle that was meant to throw him into the pit of heat. And we all know Dessin is better.

"Why do you say my name like it's a dirty word?" Niles pokes Dessin in the side.

I try to hide my smile from both of them. It isn't the time for Niles's poorly-timed humor to surface, but it's too funny not to enjoy.

"Because the name gives me a spike in cortisol levels. And it sours my stomach," Dessin replies, preoccupied with watching the line disappear across the stage.

"But why?"

"Niles, stop." I laugh into my hand.

"No." He looks down at me with betrayal creasing his brow.

"You're pretty."

I laugh again.

Dessin turns to face me. "We'll need to be on either side of him. He's shitfaced."

"A Niles sandwich? Hot."

Dessin looks at me, ignoring our shitfaced friend. He inspects the spear Warrose threw to him with hazy eyes that are working overtime to see clearly. It reaches the height of his chest, made of black crystal.

"We're up, let's go," Dessin orders, waving Niles and me to walk in front of him. "I'll keep the line from overrunning us. You just focus on getting him across safely."

Stepping up to the edge of the plank, the heatwaves alone nearly singe the hair off my arms. Chemical bursts of lava bubble and pop from the pit. And my god, that fire roars to life, as if it senses Niles's presence.

"No," Niles utters, sounding completely sober.

"Niles, I'm right here. I promise we'll be quick."

Involuntary tears drizzle over his cheekbones as he stares at the flames in debilitating shock. He doesn't move a centimeter.

"I can't move," he whispers.

My stomach twists in knots at the sight of him. The careless, drunk humor vanishing from his eyes like a dying candle.

Sentinels throw their whips out toward us for holding up the line, and we all hiss as the lashings bite into our warm flesh.

"Go, Niles!" Dessin barks.

"I can't."

Bits of rocks are thrown by the enraged audience, cheering and booing as we cause a traffic jam. The arena is a carnivorous zoo of sweat, unrelenting heat waves, and thick puffs of smoke that burn our lungs. It's overwhelming to all five senses, beating down on Niles like a torrent of rain from a monsoon.

"I can't," Niles says again, shaking from head to toe with a wet face from both tears and beads of perspiration.

I try to tug at his wrists, but he flails away from me, grunting like a child having a fit. His face pinches together, creating new lines on his forehead. He doesn't even seem to notice the way the whips slash into his flesh, or the small rocks grazing his scalp, smashing into his shoulders.

"Please, Niles!" I yell over the terrifying symphony of people screaming as they melt in the pits. "We just have to get across, and it will be over!"

"*I can't. I can't. I can't. I can't. I can't. I can't.*"

My panicked voice doesn't reach him. My sweet, golden boy is trapped in a nightmare brought on by the heat flaring across his skin. I look up at Dessin with bulging eyes, pleading for him to have one of his ideas.

Dessin's stoic gaze finds mine, staring into my soul as a decision unravels throughout his thoughts. He moves to Niles's side with a calm grace that appears like he's unhurried, unafraid, tranquil in every sense of the word.

"You're thinking about that day on the beach," Dessin says to Niles in a low voice. Meanwhile, he catches the end of each whip in his muscular hands, yanking them toward the pit and sending sentinels screaming to their deaths.

Niles doesn't say a word. He pants shallowly and silently sobs.

"I get those flashbacks, too." Dessin wraps a hand around Niles's neck, urging him to look up. "But you became a warrior that day, buddy. And I need that warrior fighting by my side today. Do you understand?"

Niles blinks away the hot tears that drench his face.

"You're my comrade. My friend. My brother. I need you to show up for me." Chills race down my arms, pulsing through my fingertips as Dessin stares intently into Niles's beautiful eyes.

"I am?"

I do my best to shield flying rocks, letting them tear the skin on my arms as Dessin smirks, giving Niles's neck another squeeze.

"You are. Will you be the warrior I need by my side today, Niles?"

The gray, feverish storm clears over Niles's face, replaced by a look as fierce and protective as a lion guarding his pride. He rises to his feet, reaching out his hand for me to take. Relief soothes the nerves in my chest, setting my shoulders straight.

"We have to run," I yell at them so they can hear me over the ruckus. "The plank is really hot now!"

The boys nod as we sprint, my hand clenching around Niles's knuckles to make sure he doesn't fall. The metal sears into the sensitive underside of my feet, but we move quickly, never leaving our skin against the panel too long.

I hear Niles yelp as the fluid limbs of the fire reach too close to his legs. I tug him along faster, keeping my eyes nailed to my feet as they move in a straight line. *Almost there. Almost there.*

A firm hand snatches my wrist, pulling me to the end of the line. I lift my eyes off the ground, seeing Warrose and Ruth looking down at me in relief.

"We made it!" I screech, jumping up and down!

Niles matches my smile.

"Wait…" Warrose shouts, looking over my shoulder to the pit.

Niles and I turn on our heels, searching for Dessin, who was supposed to be right behind us. And he's there, still on the plank, burning his hands and knees as he tries to free himself from something jagged and black tying his leg to the metal plank.

"Dessin!" Niles bellows, taking off in the direction of the fire.

I freeze at first, not believing what I'm seeing. Niles. Niles, who's mortified by the flames, runs back to them to save his friend.

I throw myself forward, following Niles back to the plank.

"Keep the other prisoners from pushing us off! I'll free him!" Niles demands.

I push ahead, stepping over Dessin's crouched body, snagging the spear so I can fight off the mass of shoving bodies trying to get past Dessin.

I can hardly feel the burning of my feet as adrenaline strengthens my body, fuels my arteries with power. I throw my weight into each defensive movement. Looking over my shoulder, I notice the detail of barbed wire fashioned into a whip, which was used to hook around Dessin's leg, nailing it to the path. His legs turn bright red as the heat no doubt injures and melts his skin.

"It's nailed into the metal!" Niles grunts, trying to find a way to unwind the barbed wire.

"Just get out of here!" Dessin retorts, sweat making his face shiny.

But Niles doesn't listen. Doesn't respond. Instead, his expression changes into something calm and determined. With his bare hands, he uses all of his strength to pull the contraption free from the hot metal. That soft flesh rips from the tiny spikes, fresh blood spurting out around

Dessin's leg, dripping into the flames with a sizzle.

Niles grinds his teeth, grunting against the fiery pain burning his knees, tearing new wounds into his palms and fingers as he finally breaks the hold of the whip, untwisting it from around Dessin's calf.

"Go!" I shout, pushing away more inmates that try to rush us.

Dessin helps Niles to his feet, guiding him to the exit as I follow behind.

Once we're to safety, we stand in a circle, a bubble of silence that separates us from the chaos of this Fun House Night. Dessin looks down at Niles's blistered, shredded palms still gushing with bright puddles of crimson. His forearms are covered in thick webs of blood that drip down to the tips of his elbows.

And Dessin stares at it all with parted lips. Niles shifts on his feet like he's embarrassed or uncomfortable being under the spotlight of Dessin's focus for this long. As I look back, I see Dessin blinking, exhaling slowly, then doing the most unexpected thing I could have imagined.

Dessin takes a step forward and hugs Niles, causing our golden boy to release a heavy sob.

"Thank you, my friend," Dessin whispers.

# 57. Swamp Dawpers

## Skylenna

Kaspias faces the rusted metal door as I change into the new leather bodysuit, the color of roasted red peppers or oxblood wine. It's covered in brass buckles, straps, and black armor plates cover my breasts, shoulders, and ribs.

"Are you listening? You need to follow these directions exactly, Skylenna. The Vexamen villages are not ones you want to get lost in."

I secure the next three buckles across my waist, tightening the leather until it's snug yet still breathable. The body suit belongs to Persecuting Caretakers, trained guards that taunt inmates sentenced to the prison basement until they starve or contract a deadly disease from the rabid rodents. Kaspias brought us to an empty room so I can change and not be recognized when I leave.

"I'm hearing every word," I answer.

Once I'm through the gates, I should veer right through the Foul Falcon Forest, stay there until sundown, then pass through the village town square of Madmaz, staying away from street torches that attract the spine-toothed eagles.

"They'll send out units to find you, probably accompanied by hordes of Blood Mammoths sent to catch your scent of blood if you get injured," he goes on, pulling something long and dark out of a chest attached to the wall behind him. "Keep yourself from being wounded, and head north out of the village, toward the north side of the East Vexello Mountains. You'll find the shore that your reinforcements are gathering near."

I take a breath. *I can do this. It must be in the prophecy that I've already done this.*

"Put this cloak on to cover your hair. And I suspect you've been missing these." After pulling a dark silk cloak over my shoulders, he hands me a pair of leather gloves with spikes running along the knuckles.

"Demon's Teeth." I smile, remembering the day Garanthian gave them to me to hold for the day I'd learn how to fight. And now I can. Now I can lead the fight to my friends.

"Lead your army through the East Vexello Mountains; you'll find rebellions already formed there that may want to fight with you. If you go straight through the villages, it'll be a trap, and everyone on your side will die."

"Got it."

"You ready?"

I pull the satiny hood over my head, tucking the strands of blonde hair away from my forehead, and nod quickly. Kaspias hands me two daggers and assures me that he left Dessin's weapon's belt hidden in his cage until they get to escape.

The stale air chills my damp skin as we keep fast strides through the empty hallways of the prison. He gruffly nods to a few sentinels on guard at different posts; they salute to him sternly, bowing their heads as the commander and his Persecuting Caretaker walk with purpose.

I lower my head, letting the soft hood hang over my eyes so that I am not recognized. My pulse contracts wildly under my skin, hammering into my throat, making a noisy racket in my ears.

Moving down the long and twisty stairwell, I tune out the screams pinging around from wall to wall. The void pushes memories against my mental barriers, tempting me to watch all of the evil that has happened here. But I pull back my shoulders and focus on my breathing rhythm. *In and out. In and out. Slower. Relax. Focus.*

"There are three towers that are connected around a square courtyard. That's what makes up the prison. The towers are built on small brimstone mountains. The only way down is to scale the length of the side after we sneak out of a side door. I know it's unconventional, but if we take the soldiers route of the designated pulley system, there will be too much traffic, and you might be caught."

I jog to keep up with him as we must have already gone down a dozen flights.

"Is scaling the side of the small mountain what you were worried about?" I ask.

It doesn't sound ideal considering how weak this captivity has made me. The lack of sunlight, inconsistent nutritious meals, and physical activity. Not to mention the constant state of abuse. But I'm willing to jump off the side of a cliff to save the ones I love. I can do this. I will do this.

"No, actually." Kaspias sounds hesitant, like he's unsure if bringing it up is even worth the headache. "I'm concerned about the swamp dawpers."

The name sours my stomach. "Cousins of night dawpers," I say, recalling Helga Bee giving us this information, though she was unsure if they were merely rumors.

"Yes. They only attack if they catch the scent of a prisoner. Soldiers can come and go without setting off that barbaric alarm system, but your scent will set them off."

We round another flight of stairs, breathing heavily from the lack of breaks.

"How am I supposed to get past them?"

He shoots me a look over his broad shoulder. "I've given them a feast at the other end of the courtyard, by the tower furthest from us. They should be distracted long enough for us to get past them."

"Good." I pause with a thought creeping in. "What if that doesn't work?"

"It will be difficult to get away from them," he admits, scratching his beard. "They are trained to leave the prison gates and hunt down the stray at all costs."

*Great.*

Kaspias motions for a wide, rusted door with slight exhaustion drooping his shoulders.

"This is the side door." He latches something heavy on to the toe of my boots, then black straps on to my elbows and hands. "Hooks to scale down."

I look down at the heavy metal formed into sharp, curved nails sticking out of my shoes. *Is this all we get to keep us from falling to our deaths?*

"It won't take as long as you might think," he justifies.

But that doesn't ease the burning knots forming in my stomach. I'd say I'm a good climber, based on the many times Kane and I used to find tall trees to scale when we were children.

Kaspias swings the rusted door open, and the wind is so fierce, it sends the bulky piece of metal flying wide with a bang against the brimstone.

I shield my eyes against the sweltering sun. It's a bright, cloudless day with a ferocious breeze that is begging to send me falling and breaking my neck. I peer down at the courtyard between the three monstrous towers. It isn't that far of a climb, but my stomach still dips and gallops around in a panic.

"I'll go first. Follow my lead," Kaspias commands.

At first, the climb down is agonizing as we fight against the treacherous winds. My hold on the hooks that dig into the unmoving brimstone mountain is shaky and unstable. But after several minutes of matching Kaspias's steps exactly, I create a sound rhythm of movements.

As we lower closer to the black gravel ground of the courtyard, I see the mob in the distance. They have the same shape as a night dawper. Tall, spindly, and grim, like elongated corpses. Yet their skin isn't gray, it's the color of a newborn baby before it's been cleaned. A shade of pink, like a new scar or fresh burns from a fire. There's a white, gooey film that layers the top of that rosy skin. It's as if their pores are oozing pus-like excretions. And their mouths are much wider, too, a wicked clown's smile with long yellow tusks, the kind a walrus has. Even with these differences, their beady eyes remain the same.

Helga Bee told us briefly about the terrors of these demented creatures. Their saliva is acidic and meant to soften and eat through flesh so that they may eat their prey down to the bone. They can sniff hot organs from a mile away.

Fortunately, at this moment, they seem very distracted. There must be a hundred of them fighting viciously over a pile of bodies. *Human* bodies.

Kaspias grips my waist, helping lower me to the ground.

I jerk my head in the direction of the feasting swamp dawpers.

"They were already dead," he explains coldly.

I huff, clenching my jaw. "They were prisoners, weren't they?"

He doesn't answer, swiftly removing the hooks from my boots.

"And you didn't think they deserved a burial?"

His black eyes snap up to meet mine. "My only concern right now is getting my brother and those he loves out of this hell. Is that okay with you?"

I stare down at him, seeing the raw nerve of fear and uncertainty and guilt in the abyss of those eclipsed eyes. I don't push him any further. I'll just be happy if this all works out the way we want it to.

"Be very quiet. We must be ghosts as we pass them." Kaspias stands, turning to the forking silver shimmering paths of concrete that connect to each of the three towers. I crane my neck to see their peaks, but they get lost in the blue sky, swallowed in the atmosphere.

*I'll come back for you, Dessin. I swear to God, I'll come back to save you all.*

"Now!" Kaspias whisper-yells, tugging me along to jog quickly but soundlessly along the path.

The courtyard is square and surrounded by giant walls that reach the height of the abandoned Demechnef building I once roamed, and the shade of black licorice with a subtle shine in the buttery sunlight. Ahead of the three towers connected by the pathways is a steel prison gate that looks like our cages. Bars crisscross to make up a wide door that can rise or fall upon entry.

We use the tips of our toes to move without noise. And it's working! *It's fucking working!* The mob of swamp dawpers is feasting in a heap of growls and snarls, attacking each other as they eat mindlessly. I crack a smile to Kaspias, and to my surprise, he smiles back. The first real expression of happiness I've seen from him. And oh, he looks so much like Kane with his cheeks stretched and those eyes gone round.

The skin on my bicep rips apart, screeching in pain as something scalds through my leather. A whipping sound whistles through the air. Kaspias flinches, clutching my arms against a stream of blood. His expression morphs from concern to shock to a surge of overwhelming dread. He looks up at the bird's nest near the prison gate, and there it is. An archer pointing their crossbow in my direction.

"They were supposed to be switching shifts!" He squeezes my arm in a rage. "No one was supposed to be up there!"

The sound of bones crunching and blood slurping goes eerily quiet.

No more chomping of tusks through dead flesh.

No more snarls.

No more territorial growls.

The attention of every swamp dawper turns to us slowly, nostrils flaring wide as they take in the potent scent of my blood smearing across Kaspias's palm.

"Run!" he cries, nearly pulling my arm clean out of its socket.

We race in the direction of the gate, panting, sweating, muscles contracting in our thighs as we aim for that gate, those bars that are…opening.

"Why are they opening the gate?!" I shout, dodging the arrows that whiz past our heads.

Kaspias watches that large steel gate rise. "They know you won't get far, and they like to give the swamp dawpers a challenge."

*Fuck!*

It hastily dawns on me that Kaspias is now deemed a traitor. He'll be tortured or killed for helping me make an attempted escape, won't he? He'll have to run with me. Find the army with me. And something about the notion gives me small comfort. At least I won't be alone. At least I'll have him to help me navigate the dangers of this strange country.

Kaspias grunts loudly as an arrow lodges into his hip. I hiss at the way he keeps sprinting, determined not to let it slow him down.

"Almost there!" I shout over the warring wind, the dreadful sound of swamp dawpers running with thudding feet behind us. Gaining as their speed exceeds our own. I can't give up! I have to do this to get my family out of here! God, I wish DaiSzek was here more than anything.

Kaspias yelps, causing my entire body to pulse with even more adrenaline. A swamp dawper closes the distance on him, nipping at his ankle.

"No!" I scream.

One drop of their saliva will eat through his tender skin and muscles and tendons! What are we going to do? How will we get out of this one? There must be a way to heal him once we've escaped.

But something in Kaspias's black-rimmed eyes flickers, shifts, alters the trajectory of his thoughts. He looks blankly at that gate now hanging wide open, then back at me.

"Kaspias…"

We make it to the exit with three more giant strides, and instead of crossing that glorious threshold with me, Kaspias shoves me from behind, sending my body hurtling, airborne and whirling, past the steel gate.

Spinning around on the gravel to look back at him with a gaping mouth and tears stinging my eyes, I am a cold, numb statue as he forms a wall in that gateway. Arms clasping the top of the gate overhead, legs spread wide, and he cries out like a small child. A little boy who never had his mother to comfort him in the dead of night.

"Kaspias, no! Come with me!"

Although the denial churns my insides with determination, the fate of all rests over that potent gaze flooding with tears. The swamp dawpers fight to feast on him, no longer caring about me on the other side of this wall. Their giant tusks puncture irreparable damage to his organs, shredding his tan skin right off his flexed muscles.

And I watch Kaspias Valdawell get eaten alive.

Saving my life.

"Tell my brother I love him!" he wails as he holds that stance strong and true. "Tell him I'm sorry, Skylenna!! Tell my brother I'm sorry!"

I break into a devastated cry, holding my hands over my mouth as the gore and horror fill my sight. As I witness Kane's brother bear it all.

And that's when I see it. When I see them…

"They're with you now, Kaspias," I choke out. "Sophia and Arthur have come to take you home!"

Right there, on his left and right sides, Arthur clings to Kaspias's pant leg, and Sophia caresses her son's cheek. She looks at me with sorrowful eyes, mouthing the words *thank you.*

And though it scorches my soul to run away from him now, I still hear his screams follow me into the depths of the Foul Falcon Forest.

*"Tell my brother I love him! Tell my brother I'm sorry!"*

# 58. Alone

## Skylenna

The Foul Falcon Forest is grander in size than I anticipated.

As the silvery moonlight creates pinholes of stars and rays of glimmering light through the leaves overhead, a cold, humid wind sweeps through the uninviting forest. I've spent twenty minutes running through the muddy ground, sticky and littered with soggy plants, which tells me I've already made it a little over two miles with still more land to cover.

*Tell my brother I love him! Tell my brother I'm sorry!*

I rub my raw eyes and then cover my ears against the repeated echoes of Kaspias's screams. The void lashes against my being as if in punishment. I changed a man's mind with a flick of my wrist. I played God. And even after everything he's done, that pit in my stomach only grows as I replay the way he died. The way Arthur clung to his pants. The way Sophia held him until he passed.

*Thank you, Kaspias.*

The humid air is filled with the scent of earthy moss, fresh rain, and potent whiffs of rot. Whether it's dead animals or plants, it's strong and hard to ignore. Each tree is uniquely different, thick and curly, like giant roots forming their own trees, twisting around each other like contorted acrobats in a circus. Their leaves are the color of dull charcoal, big and wavy, about the size of my face. And the only noises aside from my heavy breathing are the creaking of old wood, similar to footsteps in a condemned house, cats hissing, falcons quietly squawking, and the occasional moan (though I can't tell if it's from a human or animal).

Since it's already night, I decide to make it through the next village as quickly as possible. DaiSzek has brought an army, and I need more than anything just to see him again. To know that we will go to battle together to get our friends out.

Reaching an opening, I find the orange glow of torches in the distance. And the village is not at all what I pictured in my head.

There are wide sandstone streets lined with black marble trim and matching pillars holding enormous flaming torches. A piazza with grand, black pearl steps, statues of naked men and women made of red aventurine, and trickling fountains that look aged and cracked around the edges. I jog soundlessly toward the village, keeping an eye on each torch I pass through the piazza surrounded by altars, stages, perhaps a small library, and a bell tower.

The town is as quiet as death rotting in a coffin.

No whispers.

No footsteps.

Not even a heartbeat.

Perhaps there is a curfew. Maybe a cultural choice to stay indoors when the sun goes down. Or what if it's the spine-toothed eagles? Do they hunt at night? As if to answer my puzzled thoughts, a whoosh of wind and feathered wings slap against the night air above me. It's fast, a quick dip of an eerily large bird taking flight.

Kaspias told me to stay away from the torches. They attract the birds.

Carefully, I slip into the shadows, tiptoeing my way toward the East Vexello Mountains that stand proud on the midnight horizon. Being out in the open is a wounding shock to my nervous system when I've grown so accustomed to the perimeter of my cage, the stench of body odor and urine, and the brutality of violence in the prison. But I'm almost to real freedom. I can practically taste it on my tongue. And although it's sweet and satisfying, the sword of guilt still stabs at my chest continuously, not allowing me to feel even a moment of true relief.

My friends are still in that fucked-up prison.

I sprint a little faster, ducking and weaving through the darkness to make it out of Madmaz without being seen.

A whistle rings high and in perfect pitch from across the piazza.

I slam my back against a black marble pillar to stay out of sight, waiting with a thumping heart to see if I'm not alone. Was it a bird? A human? I don't know which would be worse. I—

The pillar supporting my back vibrates, shaking my bones and rattling my teeth. I spin around and watch the top roar to life with red flames, swallowing the oxygen in a blue gust. And the aftereffects of being caught under a pillar of fire are not delayed or slow in action.

I am swarmed with screeching eagles that are the size of a large dog. Wings stretch wide, an umbrella blocking the light of the moon. Red beaks and white heads. And there are several dipping down to find me, filling the skies with their bizarre squawking and powerful wing flapping.

I fight the scream that wants to tear out of me as I sprint away. I hear voices, doors opening, and maybe an alarm going off in the distance. Sweat forms rivers down my skin as I race away from the village, taking a flock of outrageously big birds in my wake.

*Where do I go? I can't outrun them for long!*

"*The drains!*" the woman in my head shouts.

I veer to the left, seeing a black hole on the edge of the sandstone street that must lead to a drain system underground. I thank the woman silently, then take a nosedive through the opening without another thought.

And for three days I sit alone in the dark, murky water, waiting for my opportunity to escape once again.

# 59. Traitor

## Dessin

**W**e stare in silence at the skeleton on display in the center of the stage. The bones aren't white because they're still covered in blood, tendons, shreds of muscle, and bits of skin. And in a medal plaque at its gnarled feet reads:

*Here lies what is left of Commander Kaspias Valdawell*
*Traitor to all of Vexamen*

"Traitor?" Niles asks.

Warrose places a hand on my shoulder. I shrug it off.

"Does that mean he managed to get Skylenna out?" Ruth asks weakly.

I take in a breath. "I guess so."

Kane is no longer anywhere close to the front. Cricket, our gatekeeper, ensures he stays deep inside the inner world for this. Though I've switched alters many times to cope with the stress of our new reality. Kaspias hurt our family, caused irreparable damage, scars that may never be healed, and cost me the woman I loved. Yet, he was still Kane's twin brother.

And that means something to all of us.

My mind spins with questions. Why would he help us? Why save Skylenna? The part of my mind that has been soiled by the Mind Phantoms believes it's because she was the traitor all along. He helped her because she was just as evil as he was.

But I shake my head against the dark thought.

The memory that Sophia saved where the *deeper alters* lie gave me much clarity, much to think about regarding Skylenna. So many traumatic memories we all hold are tied to her, and she never seemed to age in any of them. Once I was given a sliver of the truth from someone in our system, it was much easier to believe. Easier to accept.

The way she cried for me after seeing me again. Her emerald eyes were bright red and gushed an endless supply of tears. She could hardly talk. The supreme, unyielding sadness made her entire body shake. God, I could feel the pain and heartbreak from miles away, couldn't I?

Nothing killed me more.

And that kiss.

Fuck, that kiss was world-ending. Her body leaned against mine like she'd done it a thousand times before. Her lips had mine memorized, and she understood me in ways that could only be described through her passionate touches.

Skylenna is wholeheartedly in love with me.

I have to do everything I can to recover my memories. To find her and learn all I've lost. What must it be like for her to look into the eyes of someone she would die for only to have them stare coldly back at her? To hate her with every fiber?

It's been a few days since we now know she escaped. A few days for me to wonder how I would feel if something terrible happened to her. A few days to watch Ruth and Niles wither away at their imaginations running wild with possibilities of her demise.

"Dessin?" Niles inches toward me cautiously, looking at the skeleton that was once Kane's brother, then back to me.

"I'm getting us out. *Tonight*," I say, taking one last look at the strings of meat hanging off his bones. I don't know what happened to him. But at the very least, some day, I can tell Kane that his brother died a hero.

# 60. Long Live The King

## Skylenna

As the sun rises, A burst of burnt amber and apple cider light filters through the hole of the underground drain pipes that reek of a molding mummy, a basement of mildew, and the sodden aroma of my growing dread.

I haven't been able to leave this narrow, gray passage due to a storm of soldiers, Blood Mammoths, and beasts of all sizes searching for me. They've shouted in foreign words, only exposing one I actually understand: *Skylenna*.

Chunky sewage and dirty water collect around my thighs and hips, and occasionally that horrid creek brings dead animals, like mice or kittens floating like rubber duckies in a child's bathtub. Mushy and decaying.

And I'm sitting in my own piss and shit.

My stomach is empty, grumbling, chewing on itself as I starve and grow dehydrated to the point of dropping dead. My skin is pale and pruned. My mind is swirling with doubt, and the fear of failure won't seem to leave me be! The nightmares grow more powerful each time I close my eyes. Ruth dying. Niles dying. Never seeing Dessin again. Being killed before I can reach the army. It's all there.

But as I stretch up to my tiptoes to look out the hole blazing with the morning sunrise, the village is finally quiet. No more stomping hooves or shouting soldiers. It's quiet and...hopefully, safe to flee. As if I even have a choice anymore. Another few hours in this hole, and I'm dead.

I lift my arms to grip the edges of that drain hole, but my God, I'm so terribly heavy with the disgusting water soaking through my leather. My boots feel like they weigh fifty pounds a piece.

"*Arrrrgh!*" My arms tremble as I pull myself up another few inches. It's agony. I'm weak and hungry and exhausted. My boots splash back into the gray water as I let go, huffing and grunting from the energy I wasted.

"*Fuck!*" I hiss, my bottom lip jutting out in frustration. "I can do this. I have to do this!"

Jumping again, I use the muscles in my thighs to give me some added height in hopes I won't have to use as much strength to pull myself up. But gravity hits me like an avalanche.

Again, jump, pull, shake, slip.

Again.

Again.

Again.

Each attempt is more pathetic.

Again.

Again.

Again!

I fall backward, hitting my head, and chunky water spatters into my gasping mouth.

"*Oh, god! Oh, god!* I'm going to die down here! Oh, god. Please, no. Protect my friends. Protect Dessin. Please, I don't care what happens to me. I could die in this hole knowing my family would find freedom."

"Protect them yourself."

A voice that still haunts my dreams, still sends distress escalating into my core, echoes along the stone walls of the drain tunnels.

My eyes search the darkness now filling with the early sun, landing on a man who used to seem so tall, so frightening to me.

His five o'clock shadow, dark shiny hair, and sea-green eyes. His leather jacket and dimpled chin.

Jack Ambrose stands above me, holding out his hand.

"No…" I mutter with a dry mouth and burning eyes. This tunnel of rainwater, debris, and rusty air shrinks around me.

In an instant, it all happens so fast. The memories of what he did to me. And then the truth that the void showed me. He loved Scarlett and me. Our mother loved us, too. He was a victim of these experiments, and he even ended his life to make sure they couldn't use him as a pawn to hurt his little girl anymore.

"You deserved a good daddy, Skylenna." His deep voice breaks along with his face, pinching together in a frown. "I'm so sorry they took that away from us. I love you. I've loved you your whole life!"

The sound of my father crying turns my body to mush. I cry with him, watching the big man drop to his knees, sloshing the nasty water around us. And I throw my arms around his neck, remembering the sweet moments we had before I turned six. The days under the Red Oaks. The scripture he'd read me on Sunday while I ate vanilla ice cream. He was once a good father.

"I love you, too!"

My father holds me close while he breaks apart softly, stroking my matted hair down my back, giving my cheeks soft kisses. We deserved to always have this relationship. We were robbed of it.

"You don't have much time, my sweet daughter." He separates our embrace to hold my face in his warm, calloused hands. "You need to get to DaiSzek. There's a bond between you two that goes beyond logic. It's in your blood, linking your souls, and giving you a language no one else other than Dessin can understand. Once you find him, the enemy is doomed to fail."

Goose bumps prickle up the backs of my arms. The sound and shape of his name quickens my breath and ignites my soul. The urge to find him, to hold my big, furry boy is overpowering. It laces my blood with something stronger and more ferocious than adrenaline.

"You are a warrior archangel sent from God himself to strike down the evil in this world. Be that angel now. No mortal body can contain what lies under your flesh and in your soul."

My pulse skitters in my throat like a jack rabbit's heartbeat. I give my father one last look, one last hug. "I'll always love you."

"Always," he replies with fresh tears swimming in his eyes.

My muscles buzz with new energy as I look to the hole streaming with daylight. This time, as I jump, I throw my arms back, swinging them upward, and use my feet to claw against the slimy wall. I kick so hard that I'm able to hoist myself onto my elbows, eyes watering as the light blinds me. Panting, I wiggle out, thrusting myself forward until my boots are free of that dingy hole.

And as I stand, rubbing my eyes against their natural adjustment, I see that my father is no longer here. He did what he needed to do.

As the adrenaline subsides, I feel the sting in my left bicep. The slash of torn skin where the arrow hit me has been opened back up from my many attempts to free myself from the drain.

And blood is dripping down the tips of my fingers.

It's mixed with the sewage water, splattering on the sandstone street. Like a knee to the gut, I recall the other monsters that are looking for me.

Blood Mammoths.

Those awful products of generational incest, big like ogres, long hair, and no ears. They're inhumanly strong, impossible to escape if they catch the scent of blood...

I bolt toward the end of Madmaz village, focusing on the East Vexello Mountains. The army that lies just beyond their glorious peaks. I've been through too much to be captured now.

Sprinting past an execution stage with a guillotine and rope for hangings, the void adds pressure to the back of my mind, begging me to stop, to see, to witness all that has happened here. Something horrible. Something that will likely kill me, too.

But I let DaiSzek's face fill my mind with sloppy kisses and belly scratches. This is my one step, my one goal to achieve, and *the enemy is doomed to fail.*

Leaving the borders of this village, alarms sound off behind me. Loud bells clanking together. And the ground rumbles with stomping feet. It isn't just the sound of soldiers running about. It's the heavy, ogre footsteps that shake the earth. The clumsy, erratic race of Blood

Mammoths. Blood thirsty. Crazed.

And I am their target.

Sweat drizzles down my temples. Fire weakens my legs with each stride. I'm probably not even running as fast as I think I am. My stomach has been empty for days, and I'm running on nothing but determination.

I make the mistake of twisting my neck to see a cluster of ugly, barbaric Blood Mammoths galloping wildly through the confines of the village, gaining on me with ease. Their raven hair flies around their face cages like stringy flags, and their bodies are even more terrifying in the daylight. The waxy chests are covered in boils, blisters, and sores. And their faces…crooked. Distorted. Slobber and drool spills down their chins.

*Fuck.*

I wish Dessin was by my side. He would know what to do.

The East Vexello Mountains grow in size as I race closer to them, hiking up sandy hills, tripping into dunes and ditches. Tears swell over my eyes as I realize my body is unable to keep going. Unable to take any more exertion. I taste coppery blood coming from bursting vessels in my lungs. I feel like a bag of bones, a chunk of meat ready to collapse, to drop dead. When the Blood Mammoths catch me, and they will, I won't be able to fight back. I'm not even certain I'll be able to access the void to hurt them the way I did last time I was chased.

*There's a bond between you two that goes beyond logic. It's in your blood, linking your souls, and giving you a language no one else other than Dessin can understand.*

A divot of sand and rock catches my boot mid stride, and I go flying, slamming to the ground on my hands and knees. I cough and hack, accidentally inhaling the sand.

*There's a bond between you two that goes beyond logic.*

Every time I've ever screamed in terror, DaiSzek has been there to defend me. But I have no energy to scream. I have no air left in my lungs to give.

*…giving you a language no one else other than Dessin can understand.*

Soaked from head to toe in sweat and blood and drain water, I close my eyes in that dune of sand. I ignore the stampede of Blood

Mammoths growing so close I can practically smell their oily skin and meaty breath. I give myself over to the angelic nature that my father spoke of. To the divine magic that clearly links me to my supreme protector.

I open my arms to the sky.

I feel the tingling sensation of my love for my guardian, stronger than a mountain, faster than a storm, and filled to the brim with the fire of a dragon. Fear slips from my grasp as the breeze picks up, blasting against my sodden skin. It's telepathic as it soars through the void, through a bond that can't be explained with words.

And with a single pulse of my mind, I need no words, no thoughts, not a single scream.

Because I can feel him racing through heaven and hell.

I can sense the wave of terror he brings, the will of the Almighty God himself.

And as I open my eyes to the daylight and backdrop of the obsidian mountains, all I see is the venomous glow of crimson eyes and midnight fur hurtling toward me like a lion on the hunt. DaiSzek leaps over as the Blood Mammoths dive into the dune of sand, following the scent of my blood, only to be led into the jaws of the greatest beast there ever was and ever will be.

DaiSzek devours them in a savage wrath of fangs and claws and puddles of blood.

The sand is soaked in red, littered with heads and fingers and arms, all separated from their bodies. My boy stands there above the carnage, looking back at me with those cinnamon eyes, and I can't help but choke on a sob of relief. Because I know he feels it, too. Being apart from him for this long was like missing an arm or leg. Missing my heart from my chest cavity.

And as I bawl in a fit of gratitude and love for my boy, he jumps over the massacre, leaping into my arms like a puppy that's come home to his mama.

# 61. Through The Valley

## Skylenna

"Oh, my baby boy! Oh, I love you, DaiSzek!" I cry into his thick coat of fur. "I missed you so much! I'm so sorry we left you behind."

Adding to the painful throb in my heart, DaiSzek whimpers against my chest, pushing his head so hard against my sternum, I collapse on my butt.

"I know, buddy," I whimper with him. "I know."

He feels so good against my tender, pruned flesh. Warm and soft, throwing his full weight into my lap. I laugh with tears dripping down onto his head, scratching his belly, and leaving a thousand kisses across his snout.

"We're going to get Dessin back, I promise you. He'll be so happy to see you again. He needs you to save the day for him, too."

I wish to God I could take him back to the prison now and storm it together. I wish I didn't need an army. I wish I wasn't so damn dehydrated and weak.

With the edge of my cloak, I clean his mouth of the clotting blood and ropes of skin hanging from his chin. He looks up at me attentively, lovingly, full of adoration and a tenderness most humans may never see in an animal of this great destruction.

"How I've missed those big, cinnamon eyes," I coo.

An object thumps in the sand next to us, sounding off with snarls and growls. An animal. It attacks the dead bodies around us. I turn my head with DaiSzek, blinking rapidly to make out what has invaded our special moment.

A smaller dog-wolf with copper fur and pointy ears like a little gremlin.

Knightingale shakes half of a dead Blood Mammoth the same way she'd play with a chew toy. Her whole muscular body whips back and forth to shake that corpse in a fit of anger.

"Knightingale, stop! They're already dead!"

DaiSzek barks at her like he's translating for me.

The stocky Ginger Wrathbull turns to us with perked ears, then drops the body with a thud. After a moment of staring at us, she wiggles her butt and tail frantically, and with that, she skips over to us in joy.

"Hi, little girl," I laugh, petting the top of her heavy head. Her fur is short and sleek, unlike DaiSzek's. She's smaller, feistier, and apparently out of breath.

I laugh again. "Did he leave you behind? Is that why you're tired?"

She curls her upper lip and snarls at DaiSzek in response. My sore frame relaxes being around these two cuddly creatures. A rush of dopamine floods my senses as I sag against them, feeling a heaviness tug at my eyelids.

"Dessin should be here," I tell them sleepily. And before I can adjust to what's going on, Knightingale is nudging her wet nose against my shoulder, pushing me onto DaiSzek's back. I drape over his broad shoulders and elongated spine like a limp weighted blanket.

We're walking now, with Knightingale occasionally poking her snout against my fingers to make sure I'm okay, into the valley of the East Vexello Mountains.

And with these two by my side, I haven't felt this safe, this protected, in a very long time.

THE VIBRATIONS WAKE ME UP.

The deep grumblings against my chest and cheek startle me actually. The feeling is all too familiar. An animal growling at a nearby threat. I've felt and heard it come from my boy all of the many times Kane and I would play alone in the forest. Even as a pup, DaiSzek was always looking out for us.

My eyes are sticky and sore as I bat my lashes, forcing my lids to peel back. And immediately, I can see we're surrounded. They aren't close enough for Knightingale's frantic snapping and showboating to seriously harm them, but they're there.

Men and women dressed in multicolored layers of wool and fur, with massive axes strapped to their backs. And these people are huge. Tall, even the women over six feet, and the men reminding me of bears.

I sit up from on top of DaiSzek's back, straightening hesitantly.

*"Deveëxeq nioëx beaxious be ne qeúsez!"* a man with long braids and dark skin shouts to me with a hard scowl and proud stance on a hill to my left. We're in the center of the valley between the two mountains now.

A woman that looks like his daughter jabs her axe in Knightingale's direction, trying to tame or frighten my Ginger Wrathbull. Only she doesn't know that Knightingale has a bad temper, an eagerness to prove herself, though she is smaller in size.

"I wouldn't piss them off if I were you," I say with a raw throat. "You may manage to kill us with your numbers, but provoking them will only ensure that they will take down at least half of your people first."

"You are from Demechnef," the leader says.

I sigh in relief. "Yes."

"Why are you wearing the clothing of a Persecuting Caretaker?"

I look down at my uncomfortable red leather bodysuit.

"I…" Should I tell them the truth? "I escaped."

The leader lifts his chin, looking to his daughter to silently communicate something.

The young woman with matching braids steps forward and says, "Do you know Helga Bee and Gerta?"

My eyes shift between the many faces staggered through the valley, still holding their weapons, crossbows, torches, and some even camouflaged in the greenery.

I nod once.

"Prove it."

I look away, thinking about my time spent with them.

"She told me about Bunny Moon Tag," I say. I hear Ruth's laughter and Niles's snide humor as we'd catch each other on that stage.

Collectively, the people of the rebellion start to smile, laugh, slap each other on their backs. I take it that our prison friends mean a great deal to this large family.

"Are they alive?" she asks now, losing one side of her smile.

"Yes."

Her strong shoulders relax. "And you are their friend?"

"I am. They've helped me more than I will ever be able to repay."

"Then you are a friend of ours!"

The people around me throw their axes up, whooping their celebration, and I slump a little against DaiSzek's back.

"I need your help." My cracked, raspy voice hardly makes a dent in their outburst of conversation. However, the leader holds his hand up for those around to be silenced.

"I'm on my way to any army on the shore, maybe you've seen them already. My friends are in the Vexamen Prison. They're important to ending this war, this reign of terror from the Mazonist Brothers." At this point, I may faint if I don't get something in my stomach, but that isn't important right now.

"You are brave enough to start a battle with the Vexamen Breed?" he asks with narrowing eyes.

"And I am strong enough to win. God is on my side. I have the last living RottWeilen fighting with me and the armies of the seven ancient colonies that come from the other side of the Midnight Sea." I lick my chapped lips, beginning to shiver in the crisp breeze of the lowering sun. "Helga Bee told me of your rebellion. And if you're anything like her and Gerta, you aren't afraid of raising your swords. You aren't afraid of looking the devil in the face and fighting alongside your brothers."

The leader hops down from the jagged hill he was perched on, walking to get closer to me. I hold my hand up to Knightingale, prompting her to stand down. Though she releases small, annoyed growls anyway.

"If we strike at the Breed, we will effectively be breaking our treaty. Our homes will be invaded. Our people thrown in prison. Our lives become theirs." The leader is only an inch taller than me, but he's solidly built with a square jaw and prominent brow that makes him look mean and angry.

I pause. "Only if we lose."

He cracks a smile, nodding like that answer was what he hoped to hear.

"When do we ride?"

# 62. Strength In Numbers

## Skylenna

The sun burns red on the ocean horizon. A hot piece of coal hovering over the crashing waves.

I'm not sure what keeps me awake and alert. Maybe the nerves of seeing hope in the form of soldiers scattered along that shoreline. The fantasy of running into Chekiss's arms. The perfect picture of success that I've made it this far, I've honored my friends by not dying along the way.

"Are we almost there?" I ask my furry travel companions.

DaiSzek chuffs, trotting around a crusty crack in the sandy earth. He picks up his pace with excitement, racing forward. I feel the spray of ocean mist, a sensation that might have me sick and breaking down if I wasn't so sick and tired already.

But Knightingale hops next to me with the giddiness of a puppy, so I lift my head from DaiSzek's thick neck and look to the dark wall forming a heady perimeter across that sandy shore.

Only…it's not a wall.

It's populations of soldiers in clusters talking, sitting, eating, setting up tents, sharpening weapons, docking boats, and training with swords. And they're all so different. The Demechnef soldiers stick out like sore thumbs to the far right of the shore with their gold tassels and maroon uniforms. But the rest are rugged and ancient and beautiful to look at.

The Stormsages are sporting their northern attire, yet peeling off their heavy coats and furs.

The Nightamous Horde appear like sultry death in their black straps of leather and revealing transparent clothing. Though this time, they wear charcoal breastplates and helmets.

Then there are the Druidalas Kin with their heavy robes and long wooden staffs.

The Naiadales with their clothing made of shrubs and vines.

The Faecrest colony in shiny bangles and beige clothing, holding golden spears.

And off in a small section surrounding a fire is Judas with his people of Crimson Cres. They wear silver armor, old and antique, like stoic white knights. And I suppose they're all spies of the city, now gathered for their greater purpose.

"You really did it," I whisper to DaiSzek.

He gathered the colonies. He brought our armies.

"Child?"

I shift my focus across the masses of people along the border, landing on a man rising from the log he was seated on. Chekiss steps toward me, boots sinking in the sand, arms rising from his sides in complete astonishment.

"Chekiss!" I choke out, sliding off of DaiSzek's back.

He races toward me, but the second my feet land, my knees quake under my weight. The world tilts and rotates unnaturally. I'm feeble and hungry and disjointed in my ability to stand upright. I tumble to my knees, feeling Chekiss's warm, fatherly arms wrapping around me.

"Are you hurt?" he asks huskily.

"No." I blink slowly. "Yes. I haven't eaten or had anything to drink. My arm was hit by an arrow."

"What does she need?" Runa stands behind him, blocking the tangerine rays of the sunset.

"Runa," I murmur with a smile.

"She must be delirious if she's happy to see me," Runa comments with a glib smirk.

"Soup! Bring hot broth and bread!" Chekiss sits me down gently, brushing my hair away from my face. "Rest your eyes, child."

"I can't," I say helplessly.

"You're safe now."

"No. We have to get them out."

But my vision is shaded and blurry. My face goes numb. My lashes crisscross over my vision. And the last thing I feel is DaiSzek lying down beside me.

I WAKE UP TO THE stars twinkling over my head and a mug of steam hovering under my nose.

"Drink. It's soup," Chekiss says.

I sit up against DaiSzek's sleeping body. I remind myself of a street child the way I guzzle the warm soup. Chicken and other vegetables. Hot broth. Salty and delicious running down my throat.

"*Mmm!*" I sway back and forth, feeling delighted as I slurp from the mug messily.

"Tell me he's alive, Skylenna." I lower my mug to see Chekiss's weathered face in the light of a fire to my left. He looks older somehow. Tired and ill with worry.

"Who?"

"Niles. Tell me my son is okay." His rusted voice trembles with his chin and bottom lip.

"Yes," I breathe. "For now."

Chekiss deflates a little, rubbing his dry hands over his face. He really does appear sick, from his worry lines to the weight he's lost. His dark skin has lost some pigmentation, eyes are sunken in, and as I reach over his frail hands, they shake.

"I've been taking care of the kids while you were away," he says softly, then smiles to himself. "Or I suppose they've been taking care of me."

I follow his sight to Knightingale and DaiSzek sleeping with twitching paws as they dream about running and fighting.

509

"Thank you," I say after another sip of soup.

"You're alive."

I look over Chekiss's shoulder at the leader of Demechnef in his general's uniform and slicked back hair. Those arctic blue eyes shudder as he stares at me.

"I am."

As other soldiers gather around to see me again, Aurick simply stares at me with an unreadable expression. Though it's full of strong emotions, I can't figure out why he's looking at me like this.

In three long strides, he dumps himself at my feet, throwing his arms around my shoulders. I pass my mug to Chekiss before he can knock it over.

It's a tempting notion to shove this man off of me. But before I do, he shudders against me. Not crying, not laughing. He just shudders.

"You're hugging me," I comment, sounding like Niles.

"I'm fucking glad to see you."

*Why?* I narrow my eyes at Chekiss over his shoulder. He shrugs at me with one lifted eyebrow, bringing my mug to his mouth to sip in silent judgment.

"You're the one that sent us out there to be captured," I remind Aurick.

"I know!" He shudders again. "That's all I've been able to think about since you six didn't come back. In one fell swoop, I lost everyone who means a damn to me."

*Please.* He's talking about Marilynn. I'm not stupid.

"I really never thought they'd outsmart you, too. Honestly, it never occurred to me that you would be captured."

I roll my eyes. "Don't let Dessin hear you say that."

Aurick holds me tighter, and for a small moment, I almost feel like he does care about me. Not just as an experiment, but as the friend who gave me a home when I was left out in the cold. He buries his face against my shoulder, running his hands up and down my back.

*Yeah, Dessin would really hate what's going on here.*

"Is he okay?" Aurick grumbles against my shoulder. "Are *they* all okay?"

I wonder why he doesn't want to ask about Marilynn directly.

"They're alive. But Ruth is in bad condition."

Chekiss sits up straighter at this.

I give Aurick's shoulder a gentle *pat pat*, offering him the hint that this hug has lasted way too long, and now it's getting uncomfortable. But he doesn't budge, only latches on a little tighter.

DaiSzek snarls next to me, his lips curling over his razor-sharp teeth with one eye open, glued to the man hugging me past his welcome.

Aurick releases me quickly, shifting backward with his hands up to show DaiSzek that he isn't a threat.

I smile, patting my furry buddy on the head. "Good boy."

"I'll let you get your rest." He stands to walk away, but I dig my nails into his ankle urgently.

"I'm not resting anymore. We must get them out of the prison. *Now!*"

The guilt of being the only one to escape is poison to my heart. I should have stayed behind. Dessin should be the one here, leading the masses to our rescue. He would know how to command these men and women. He wouldn't rest until he broke us out of confinement.

"It'll all be fine. We're working on it," Aurick says with a dismissive wave of his hand.

"*Working on it?*" Steam pulses from my ears. "I just watched my best friend's legs get chopped off by a rusted axe! Were you *working on it* then? Or how about when the love of my life was brainwashed into believing I'm a demon from hell sent to torture him? Where were you and this army when they were starving us for weeks? How long will you be working on it before they die horrible deaths in that hellhole?!"

I've gathered an audience of different members from the ancient colonies. They surround us one by one, listening intently as I raise my voice in a fit of anger.

Aurick's glacier eyes move through the audience insecurely before answering.

"After we mapped the layout of the prison, we sent a small but formidable unit to rescue your friends. They're on their way there now," Aurick answers in a stern tone that tells me to stop questioning his authority.

I narrow my eyes into small slits. "A small unit?"

He nods twice.

"They'll never make it out," I exhale in defeat. "A *small* unit?"

"My husband will get them out." A few members of the Stormsages open their bodies to allow Asena to step forward. She looks like a white wolf queen in her armor made of white scales and gray pelts, with a heavy cloak made of animal skins and furs.

"Asena," I utter.

"Garanthian and my son took our strongest, stealthiest warriors to break your friends out." She gazes into my spirit with those wise, almond eyes. "They will not fail."

I know she might believe that. But she hasn't seen what I've seen in that insidious place. Doubt and more guilt fill my lungs as I hold her gaze with uncertainty.

"There are swamp dawpers, and the place is crawling with sentinels and basically the entire force of the Vexamen Breed." I shake my head and rub the space between my brows. "Even if they manage to get them out, they won't make it back to our camp. We have to bring our army and be there waiting to defend them."

"No." Aurick stands tall, like the egotistical leader he is. "Their numbers far exceed our own, even with the added forces of the ancient colonies. We're safer if we wait this out and come up with a better plan of attack."

"With all due respect, Mr. Demechnef…" Runa appears behind me, looking to her left at Rydran, from the Naiadales.

"We follow the Fallen Saint into battle. Not you," Rydran says, with a few of his own men forming a crowd behind him.

Aurick looks genuinely confused. "But I'm the one who brought you all here. I'm the one who has gathered your people, even you said it yourself! They haven't gathered in hundreds of years!"

"No," Asena says sternly. "*He* has gathered us. As predicted by our sacred prophecy. The last of the mighty RottWeilen, the alpha of all alphas. He was always meant to unite us for a greater calling."

Everyone looks at DaiSzek, who now sits up, watching us with attentive eyes.

"Well…still…" Aurick still looks like he doesn't quite understand. "You need my army, too. And Demechnef will not fight without proper planning. We refuse to walk into a slaughter."

My face boils with heat and hatred for this man. After everything we've been through…how can he still be this asshole? How can he wait any longer to rescue my people? What could I possibly say to change his mind?

An intrusive thought enters my mind like an unwanted house guest. "Shouldn't you do it for Marilynn?" I probe.

He shifts on his feet unnerved. "She would want me to be smart about this. And she can take care of herself."

"Can she?" I stand up, and so do DaiSzek and Knightingale. "Did you know they ripped all of her fingernails out?"

Aurick winces, staring at the ground in an attempt to school his expression into submission.

"Did you know they starved her, even though she's…" I trail off, realizing it isn't my place to tell him this.

"Even though she's what?"

Not even the waves of the ocean make a sound as we stare each other down.

Is this a secret I should keep until Marilynn's ready? Can I get him to send his soldiers to rescue my friends without spilling this last detail? As I watch his skeptical face and think of all the ways my friends are hurting right now, I decide this is a matter of life and death. For all of them.

"Even though she's pregnant with your baby, Aurick."

Gasps, throat clearing, and feet shuffling echo around us. But Aurick doesn't move, doesn't blink, doesn't even breathe. He stares at me as if he's been frozen in time, unable to catch up to the present.

"What?" he chokes out.

"She's pregnant," I say through my teeth. "So, if you won't ride with us to save my family, at least do it for the heir of your precious dynasty. Do it to get your baby out of that prison, Aurick."

I don't think I have ever seen this man so disheveled, so uncomposed. He's unable to close his mouth or blink. All color drains from his face, leaving his skin a clammy shade of green.

"Red's pregnant?" he finally asks.

I nod with a lump forming in my throat.

Aurick stumbles backward, being steadied by a few of his soldiers holding him upright. With only a few words, I've managed to turn his world upside down.

"I'm going to be a father," he mutters to himself in a strained, absent voice.

"No, you're not," I reply darkly. "If we don't come for them…they may not make it out alive."

His furrowed brow smooths out as determination takes hold of him. Those piercing eyes slide to me without blinking.

"We'll prepare the carriages tonight and leave at first light tomorrow."

My shoulders, arms, and neck sag in bone-chilling relief. *Thank God!*

Runa throws her white hair off to one shoulder, slapping me on the back. "Darling, Skylenna. I have seen you transform through every season, haven't I?"

"I guess so." I shake her hand, nodding to Asena and Rydran as they go off to prepare.

"Let's get some baths and then off to sleep, child," Chekiss says quietly. "I'm going to see my son tomorrow."

ASENA AND RUNA DRESS ME AT FIRST LIGHT.

They include different warrior offerings from each colony. A linen tunic, metal corselet, scale armor of dull iron plates, leather bindings to hold it all together, brass-colored pants, and leather thigh-high boots. It's heavy and clanky, but I've never felt more terrifying.

"Thank you," I say as Runa paints black markings over my eyes, brow, and cheekbones. Staring into a small mirror, I look like both a demon and an angel, foreign and ancient. My hair is pulled back halfway with small braids that are clamped together with white silver clasps, intricately designed.

"Oh, we're not done yet!" Runa grins, nodding to Asena standing behind me in the small tent.

"We have some gifts," Asena adds.

"What else?" I ask.

Asena holds out a war helmet, designed with flying dragons in blood red and gold. Then a headpiece of black diamonds shaped into claws or icicles that run down my forehead.

"These come from another world, gifted to us. From special heroes who gave everything to save their people. That's Vindawolf's headpiece that she wore into battle," Asena explains, pointing to the dark tiara now on my head. "And that's Dragas's helmet. You can give it to Dessin when you see him."

I look to her curiously.

"Dragas is a warghost, the most lethal warrior who has ever fought on any battlefield. Vindawolf is a great master of beasts. It's said she is the only being alive that can command any creature. Even ones that are alphas like your—"

"RottWeilen," I breathe.

Asena kneels before me. "DaiSzek is a descendant of the last living dragon that fought alongside our Fae king and Elven queen."

"DaiSzek and Knightingale," I say absently.

"Yes." She nods, touching my hand to get my attention. "It's said that the last living RottWeilen can breathe fire like his ancestor. But only if he has a strong enough bond with his pack. The fae king, DaiSzek, used to merely close his eyes and imagine his enemies burning for his dragon to know when to strike. Do you think you have a bond like that?"

My jaw drops open. I feel rude for laughing, but I do. It comes out like a cough.

"DaiSzek can't breathe fire," I snort. "We'd know it by now."

"Have you ever asked him to?" Runa lowers herself to eye level with me.

"Well, no…"

"If he is the true alpha of his species, the last of his kind, then it should run hot in his blood—dormant until his pack rides into battle, believing he can torch a path through the blood and clashing swords." Asena grabs my hands. "When you get out there, *dashna*, you'll know when it's time."

I can tell how passionate she is about this, so I don't argue it any further.

"These were DaiSzek and Knightingale's swords, saved for the next warrior angels who took their places." Runa pulls two gleaming swords out of a silk sleeve. Their handles are wrapped in shimmering leather and onyx stones. Matching. Huge. Sharper than DaiSzek's teeth.

"How am I supposed to fight with this? Don't get me wrong, it's beautiful. But it's heavy, and I don't know if I'm that…"

"You won't be holding it alone," Asena says with that motherly tone. "Knightingale will fight with you. She'll appear when you need her most."

Goose bumps rise across my whole body, prickling my skin like tiny needles.

"Okay," I say quietly.

After sheathing both swords in my belt, we exit the tent into the early morning sunrise. I blink in surprise at the forces dressed in full body armor, some shiny and new, others in vintage, as if they've traveled from the past to be here. They stand with their hands on their weapons, watching me quietly as they wait. Aurick steps forward to speak, only to appear confused and agitated as he comes to understand that they aren't looking to him.

They're looking to me.

I let my alert eyes wander over the warriors of different races and magical heritages, forming a stadium around me as they wait for my parting words.

A storm of adrenaline and tingles race through my body. My mind blossoms with emotion, sentiments I need to announce while I have their attention. It's now or never.

"I know this war is what your prophecy has always predicted. But this is more than just words on a piece of paper to me. This is my family trapped behind those bars, taking lashings, being drugged, and abused." I walk the perimeter of the circle they've fashioned, only DaiSzek and Knightingale pacing at my sides. "When you fight with me on this day…don't do it for the faceless, nameless ancestors that wrote those words and predicted our actions. Do it for Niles, who has walked through fire to save his people. Do it for Ruth, who lost her legs because her loyalty is unwavering to those she loves. Do it for Dessin, who has lost the only good memories he has ever known in a fucking experiment!"

My heart hammers in my throat as I stare into the many eyes that follow me.

"And do it for me. Because my rage, my heartbreak knows no bounds. I may not know how deep my power runs, but I can promise you this. Those who stand in my way will see my true face. Judge, jury, and executioner. Those who raise their swords against us, will watch as I bring heaven and hell with me!"

The crowd of ancient colonials roars, throwing their fists and weapons in the air.

"And who will be my sword?" I scream over the sounds of crashing waves and stomping hooves. "Who will run with the will of God and free our brothers and sisters?!"

The army erupts into a whirlwind of emotions, screaming and grunting and bellowing to the sky in the greatest war cry I may ever hear in my existence.

And we're ready.

Because off in the distance, we see something that Runa can identify before anyone else. It takes me a moment to remember what that darkness in the skies means.

We waste no time. I climb onto DaiSzek's back and lead our army.

# 63. Midnight Rescue

## Dessin

I'll admit, it's taken me too much time to figure this out.

The object they use to throw off a prisoner's equilibrium is *not* a magnet. Every day in the showers, I tilt my head to let in water. Once I'm out, I let the water drain, and it carries away the residue of a white solidified chemical. The same look as taking a pill and watching it dissolve in water.

This entire time, they've put a slow-releasing capsule in our inner ears, working with the natural chemistry of our body to release on moments of defiance to authority. This must have taken their savants years to test out and learn the correct way it would filter into the bloodstream. Once the frontal lobe of the brain displays an impulsive action to misbehave toward authority, the capsule is triggered by the change in brain chemistry. It releases into the bloodstream, affecting the cerebellum, which is what gives us balance and coordination.

Before our cages close, I create a funnel with items I found in the stadium and commissary and a bubbling solvent that I first test out on myself. Only a few drops, and it sizzles the inside of my ears like crinkling paper. It burns, is uncomfortable, and I'm having trouble hearing now. But the dissolving white substance comes pouring out of the side of my head.

One by one, I extract it from Marilynn, Warrose, Niles, and Ruth. The only one to give me a hard time is, of course, you guessed it Niles. Warrose and I are the only two who complain of hearing loss, but it's fucking worth it. We're no longer tied down by a choking collar and leash.

I give Marilynn and Niles a list of supplies we'll need for the journey. Protective wrapping for Ruth's legs, water, food, and a few other items. And as I secure a bag in my cage, a strip of black leather and shiny metal catches the light of the red and yellow bulbs in the far corner. Hidden in the shadows is my weapons belt.

"Shit," I exhale slowly.

"What's wrong?" Warrose leans against the entryway of my cage.

I turn on my heels and dangle the belt in front of him. Those hazel eyes sparkle with childlike giddiness as he realizes what it is.

"How the hell did you get that back?"

I examine the sharp tools and weapons with pride and have visions of myself using them to break us out of here. They're flipping images in my mind, slashing through sentinels, sending throwing knives through the air to take them out one by one. I haven't felt like myself in a long time. I'm a wild animal that is not used to being caged without a way to freedom.

*How did it get into our cage?* Kane asks.

But he's quickly swept away from the front as I recall Kaspias's body, or what was left of it, being gawked at and defamed on the main stage.

It was him, wasn't it? Kaspias really was trying to help us.

I secure the belt around my hips, standing eye to eye with Warrose.

"Looks like Kane's brother did one last good deed before getting Skylenna out." I wish those droplets of emotion didn't enter my voice without invitation. But my tone is edgy and weighted like I need to clear my throat. Warrose lifts his chin in understanding as he hears it, too.

Before he can say something to try and get me to open up about the whole ordeal, I hold up my hand to stop him. "I'll be ready to talk about it when we get the fuck out of here."

The calm smile that used to comfort me after a beating when we were children spreads across his cheeks. He rubs his hands together, making a dry, sandy sound. "When do we leave?"

Niles and Marilynn return to their cages, hiding the supplies they've gathered.

"Midnight."

IN THE EXACT MOMENT OUR ward's night sentinels switch shifts, Niles picks each lock in impressive silence.

Sneaking into Ruth's cage, we all agree it's best if he carries her for this. The rest of us will need to fight if it comes to that. Without exchanging any words, Niles gently circles his arms under the backs of her thighs and around her ribs, lifting until they're out first. The rest of us—form ranks around them. Warrose is in the back to defend if anyone sneaks up on us, and Marilynn and I lead the way.

In the community shower, there's a laundry chute. A tunnel that drops down to a washroom. In the washroom is a plumbing drain that filters out on the ground behind the east tower. From there, we'll run through the courtyard, and I'll rig the pulley of the iron gate to lift. I believe there are dangerous creatures guarding the courtyard, but those can be dealt with by using a sentinel as bait.

It's all laid out. There, of course, is room for error, but we're running out of time. Ruth won't survive another Fun House Night.

Shuffling quietly through the prison halls, we pause mid-step as a Blood Mammoth crosses over to the next hallway. The giant being drags his feet lazily across the serrated floor. Chains clink together. And his oily hair sweeps behind his footsteps.

We hold our breath, then continue on, dashing on our toes to make it to the community shower. Each moan, grumble, or snore from the sleeping inmates that we pass makes us flinch with heightened senses. The crackling music, flickering lights, I dig my nails into my palms, scraping my teeth against each other.

*You're going to get them out, Dessin. No one is as masterful at escapement as you,* Kalidus says coolly.

I glance behind me at the obvious stress and fearful expressions plaguing our group. What would Skylenna say to them now to give everyone some reassurance? I hate how I don't know the real her like I should. I hate that I can't sort out my own feelings about her. At least I can go back to that kiss before the Fun House Night. At least I have one memory to hold onto in moments of doubt.

"*Dessin*," Warrose whispers in an alert voice from behind us.

He points over his shoulder to a Blood Mammoth trailing behind us, slowly, aimlessly, as if he doesn't even see us in his line of sight. I motion the group along to move faster; we need to put as much distance between us and that thing as possible.

We don't have much farther until we get to the showers. And I'd prefer not to get into a bloody fight before then because it would draw way too much attention.

"I'll go down the chute first to make sure it has a safe landing before we have Niles and Ruth make that trip," I whisper-yell to Marilynn. She nods, understanding that when I'm gone, it'll be up to her and Warrose to be on guard in case they run into any other Blood Mammoths.

My strides are cut short when I notice a group of three sweaty, bulbous bodies blocking the entrance of the showers. Seven feet tall. Cages that sit on their heads like masks. Sores that ooze creamy fluids. The Blood Mammoths have us surrounded, sniffing the air like dogs, distracted, and clueless that we're only a few feet in front of them.

I dig my heels in, holding my arm out to stop the others. It takes three seconds for gasps to break out between Niles and Ruth.

"God fucking damn it," Warrose growls under his breath.

I consider hiding us in the vacant cages around us, but what would be the point? We'd be stuck there. Escape failed. And I do not fail. Pulling my shoulders back, I look down at Marilynn. "You take one. I'll take the other two." I crane my neck to make eye contact with Warrose. "You take the one behind us, and make sure they don't get near Niles and Ruth."

For a split second, Warrose gazes through the flickering lights at Ruth's pale, frightened face. Tendons in his jaw pulse, and he flashes that indomitable gaze back to me with a sharp nod.

Ragged, animalistic panting comes from a few paces ahead of me.

They've finally noticed us waiting here like sitting ducks. Their chains rattle back and forth as they shove each other to get to us first. Heavy, thumping feet shake the ground with the same vibrations as a stampede of elephants. I hand two katanas to Marilynn, lightweight and easily wielded, toss a spiked mace to Warrose, and for myself, a ring sword.

Niles hugs Ruth close to his chest as they prepare for impact.

And with their last three giant steps, the Blood Mammoths jump to throw their full weight into us as a way to use brute force to their advantage. But before I can even flick my wrist to use the ring sword as a small tool to slice into their main arteries, a snowstorm of white blasts from behind them.

Terrifying white, furry heads with unhinged jaws soar through the air over the Blood Mammoths' heads, clamping down on their shoulders and throats in an explosion of snarls and fangs and fireworks of clotted blood. Six bodies of White Wolves' attack without mercy, ripping into muscles and meat, overpowering the Blood Mammoths from the element of surprise and their savagery of strategic attack.

A smaller wolf goes for the Achilles' heel, wiping them out by the legs. The others spread out with planned precision as if they're operating from a telepathic system of aiming for the weakest points to strike.

And it's over before it's even begun.

Blood Mammoths scatter the floor in heaps of spurting arteries, splayed, exposed nerve endings, and glistening strips of flesh detached from the bodies.

Our group stands in mute shock as they finish their work, ensuring the enemies are dead.

*What the fuck is going on?*

"Should have known ya wouldn't have waited for a rescue!" A gruff, northern accent plunges from the darkness, walking up behind the white wolves.

*Of course.*

Garanthian grins, hands on hips, with a few men and women dressed in Stormsage-themed warrior attire. His carrot-red beard is longer than last time, twisted into messy braids and metal fixtures.

I smirk back.

"I'm not the type to wait like a damsel," I say, letting him hug me with a manly slap on the back.

"Who is this?" Niles asks in a quivering voice.

"The Stormsages, from the ancient colony in the North Sapphrine Forest," I reply.

"And how the hell did you manage to get this pack of white wolves in here?!" Warrose kneels down to scratch the head of what looks like the alpha. He's beaming at the large creature, letting his tan fingers disappear in the fluffy white fur.

Garanthian is about to answer before I stop him. "Do you have a better way out of here than the sewage pipes?"

"There's a hidden fire escape in the commissary. Let's go!" His son waves us forward.

I nod to the others, feeling a desire to thank God for this divine intervention. A better alternative to making us all trudge through the sewer in hopes we can manage to escape without waking the prison.

"There's a pulley system we can leverage that'll drop us in the courtyard," Garanthian explains as we run. I notice a few dead sentinels they clearly had to kill on the way. They must have been as silent as a night's breeze because we never heard any sign of violence or struggle.

"And what about the security measures in the courtyard? I heard there are foul beasts down there. I was going to throw one of the sentinels down to distract them," I say through a few deep breaths.

"Swamp dawpers." Garanthian nods his head, then smiles down at his trotting wolves. "My pack took them out. But there may be more coming. We'll have to be swift."

As we turn a corner, one of the smaller wolves rubs against me. I grit my teeth, missing DaiSzek terribly. I'm always confident in my ability to dominate in a fight, but with him…we become the epitome of violence and terror.

I hope Skylenna has found him.

"Niles." Warrose dips his head in Ruth's direction. "I'll take her for now."

Niles's upper body is shaking a little, and his forehead is shiny with perspiration. He smiles at Warrose and places Ruth in his arms gently. "Just for a little while."

We open the door to a tar-black sky with a blurring wall of rain. The clouds are the boisterous size of krakens and slopping wet sea monsters, carrying a cataclysmic amount of rain. The kind of rain in biblical tragedies with flooding rivers, uprooted trees, and fat drops of water that hold the weight of falling rocks. Yellow lightning forks across the sky, crackling and popping, booming into the earth with its shrieking thunder.

It takes several minutes to be lowered on a wooden pulley in the blustering winds carrying the scent of dirty rain and landfills full of manure and rotting fruit. We're drenched as we hold on for dear life, braving the mighty storm like a small boat in a hurricane. The platform we stand on quakes and rumbles, making Ruth bury her face in Warrose's shoulder. We're so high up, but the view doesn't frighten me. What's bothering me is the thought of failing. Especially since the Stormsages have come all this way with their pack of wolves to help us escape.

*Do you think when all of this is over, Skylenna will help us recover those memories? And maybe we won't have such conflicting feelings about her anymore?* Kane paces near the front, filling me with anxiety and a feeling of loss.

I shake my head. *I can't think about that right now.*

But I do anyway. I remember the taste of her lips, the smell of her hair, even the musical notes of her laugh. Though…I don't know how I can remember something I've never heard.

I want to know her.

I want to stop obsessing over the thought of being with her.

"My men have already taken out the archers, but once we hit ground, we need to stay low and exit quickly. I have two men holding the gate, but we attracted the sights of a few spine-toothed eagles on the way in." Garanthian watches the bizarre skies carefully. "I suspect they've gone back to their nests by now to take shelter from this apocalyptic weather."

"Okay."

The wooden platform thuds against the rocky terrain, slanting at an angle to which we hop off, scrambling toward a slippery stone path that leads toward the iron gate. I squint my eyes through the soft fog filling the night air, focusing on the two young men squatting and gritting their teeth as they keep the gate from coming down.

"Holy shit. We're really getting out," Warrose whispers.

My heart radiates with longing and joy and throbbing anticipation. I get to see my boy again. I get to ask Skylenna all of the questions I've had since we kissed. But I steady my breathing as we crouch low, jogging lightly toward that rusting exit. The wolves are even more quiet next to me. They're in a predatory stance, surrounding us in a circle they've formed to protect the humans.

"When we drop the gate, it'll likely be loud enough to wake up the ranks on standby. We'll have to run like hell through Foul Falcon Forest!" Garanthian hisses loudly to the rest of us.

"Come on, ya cock hairs! This thing is bloody heavy, and we're practically drownin'!" the young man holding the right side of the gate whisper-shouts.

We're cautious enough not to slip as we thump through puddles that go ankle-deep. And if it was not for the whooshing sounds overhead that aren't quite the same as the murderous, incessant winds, I might not have noticed the giant flapping wings swooping down above us.

"CAAAH!" An eagle the size of a small lion whirrs past us, snapping its sharp beak at Ruth's hair. She slams her hands over her mouth to muffle her yelp just as Warrose ducks out of its line of sight.

"The hell?!" Warrose grumbles to the sky.

And that's when we all see them. So many of these large birds circling us, they could be mistaken for a trembling roof over the courtyard.

"That's them!" Garanthian doesn't bother whispering anymore. He pushes me in the back, shoving the rest of us along to forget about the notion of being quiet. We run like hell.

The squawking acts as an organic alarm system, sending reverberating echoes against the brimstone walls, and it happens too fast. There isn't enough time to process how they managed to react with the right weapons or fill the courtyard with both Blood Mammoths and new swamp dawpers.

They appear in the yellow flashes of the splintering lightning. Archers taking their positions along the tops of the walls that surround the courtyard. The crazed, rabid beasts come from all angles, and we're now left with a choice. It's fight here or die running.

Warrose passes Ruth off to Niles, and we form a protective wall around them. The fight breaks out like a collision of two apex predators sprinting in the same direction. The wolves attack the beasts without an ounce of fear, soaked from the rain, and smeared in blood from their earlier wins. They are the first line of defense.

And as I fight four sentinels at once, my stomach is punctured with a blast of fury and heartbreak as one of the wolves gets shot down with three flaming arrows, whining at high frequency.

"NO!" Garanthian roars through the thudding rain.

The wolf tries to rise back up and keep fighting, but the swamp dawpers attack ruthlessly, ganging up on its weak points, drawing a heavy cry from Ruth as she watches helplessly.

*Fuck. We're outnumbered!*

"Form lines!" Garanthian's son commands the pack of wolves, pointing for them to help usher us toward the gate. And they do, well trained and fierce as they fight the enemy while backing us toward the two men still holding strong.

"Make a run for it!" Garanthian shouts to us with the dominating tone of a true leader.

I jerk my head to Niles first. And he obeys without question, sprinting through the trembling gate as the men struggle to keep it up. I nod to Marilynn next, then to Warrose as they keep the wall strong, fending off arrows with Garanthian's men swiping at them midair before they can hit a target.

"Go, son!" Garanthian hollers over his shoulder to me.

I back away with a few more steps, slipping under the gate.

They've formed a strong enough wall that they are good to follow me now. I form my hands around my mouth to increase the volume of my voice.

"We're good, let's go!"

Just as Garanthian looks back at me to exit, seven flaming arrows land on their newest targets. The two men holding the gate. It comes crashing down on their bodies, crushing their bones and impaling their backs.

"FUCK!" Warrose screams in agony.

"Get them out!" Ruth begs in a hysterical cry.

My jaw locks as I try to lift the gate. "Help me!" I beg the Stormsages, signaling for them to lift. But they don't move. Even one of the wolves looks back at me with a look of honor that could almost pass as a human expression.

Garanthian bows his head to me.

"I can get you out!" I bellow through the storm. As Warrose comes to help me attempt to lift the impenetrable iron, Garanthian holds up his stiff hand.

"Garanthian!" I grunt, using every ounce of strength to lift this fucking gate.

"Dessin." Marilynn places a hand on my shoulder.

"NO!" Are tears seeping from the corners of my eyes? My heart is collapsing on itself as blood rushes to my face and muscles.

"Go, son," Garanthian says calmly, bowing his head once more.

And searing into my brain for the rest of my days, the alpha of the pack bows his head to me, too. In a chaotic outrage of soaring arrows, chomping teeth, and disembowelment—they join the rest of their pack to keep fighting a battle they will never win.

"Garanthian!" I scream through the bars, pressing my face against them with a helplessness I'm not used to feeling.

Warrose and Marilynn have to pry me off the gate as I struggle to hang on.

"We have to run!" Warrose tries to bark some sense into me.

And he's right. I know he's right. I have to think about keeping them safe, no matter the costs to those who came to save us. Those who have only ever shown me kindness.

We charge through the mud and the splashing puddles, hearing the fighting of wolves and beasts and clashing swords lower in volume, until it finally goes silent.

# 64. With The Strength Of A Thousand

## Dessin

"We shouldn't have left them behind." My hands are shaking with guilt and shame. Their faces were so serene, at peace with the decision they've made.

"Dessin, we have to keep running. They're following us!" Warrose slaps my back in encouragement, pleading with his glistening, sorrowful eyes to get me moving again.

I straighten my back and wipe my face of the splattered blood smearing from the drops of rain. I nod reluctantly, leading the sprint through the dark, muddy forest. Warrose runs with Ruth in his arms now, Marilynn keeps a good pace next to Niles in the back.

*Clear your mind of these fucking memories.*

*Go, son.*

The look that alpha gave me sits in my stomach, churning and twisting into nausea.

*Forget it!*

My eyes water at the mental images of those boys being crushed by the weight of those iron bars. *I could have freed them!*

Bloom comes close to the front, drawn in by the fact that I now have a memory that's disturbing my performance.

*I'm fine!*

We run through this rotting, mucky forest aimlessly, taking turns I'm unsure if we're supposed to take. I've never been in Vexamen before. My understanding of its geography isn't like how I know my way around the many forests that surround the Chandelier City.

That wolf got hit by those flaming arrows. He tried to get back up to keep fighting. Why can't I stop thinking about this? Why is this ripping my stomach to pieces?

Warrose matches my strides on my left side, holding Ruth who is silently whimpering into her hands.

"Reset your mind on getting us to Skylenna and DaiSzek. Think only of them," Warrose instructs.

His sentiment jolts my heart back to life. A brief, fleeting memory of Skylenna holding DaiSzek as a puppy skips over my mind, and it comes from Kane.

*Did you see that?* Kane shifts closer.

Fondness, longing, and deeply rooted love penetrates my heart cavity. Through all of the demented memories I have of her, that moment pierces my veil of hatred. And nothing sounds more motivating than running to her right now.

*I'm coming, baby.*

"Gahhh!" Niles wails, his body flopping into a puddle a few strides behind us.

His leg is entrapped in something that blends into the earth. Dark green with slimy skin. Huge jaws.

"Forest gator," Warrose says. "Here, take her." He passes Ruth off to me. She reaches her arms out, wrapping them around my neck, trembling like a dry leaf in the autumn wind. I hug her close to my chest, needing this comfort more than she probably realizes. It grounds me to swallow the dishonor down my throat and concentrate on saving our family.

Warrose rushes to Niles's side, bashing the reptilian creature over the head with his mace. It takes three swings before those wide jaws unlatch their grip on Niles's calf. He moans, rolling away from the hideous beast as it retreats back to the swampy area it crawled out of.

"You alright Niles?" I call out.

He's panting as Warrose inspects his leg, dumping a canteen over the bite marks. Niles inhales through his nose as he gets back to his feet, testing to see if he's able to hold his own weight.

"It wasn't too deep, just broke the skin," Warrose assures him.

"I'm okay," Niles says, cracking his neck. "Let's keep going."

Warrose comes back to my side to hold Ruth again, but I shake my head, tightening my grip around her. "I'll hold her for a while longer. You keep watch for more animals until we find our way out."

Warrose locks eyes with Ruth for half a second, then turns away to take the lead.

The harder I run, the tighter Ruth's body coils around my neck and shoulders. She shields her eyes in the crook of my neck as Warrose slays more stray beasts that block our path or try to sneak up on us. And although sprinting with someone in my arms isn't ideal…it sparks a feeling in Kane.

*It feels like we've been here before*, Kane says with a feeling like nostalgia stirring inside both of us.

It's the act of carrying someone while we run. That's the trigger. The feeling of being responsible for a trembling woman in our arms.

*I think I've carried Skylenna before. I don't know. It feels like I have.* Kane grows impatient and agitated by this thought.

"We're going to make it out of here, Ruth," I promise her through controlled panting.

She leans the side of her head against my shoulder, looking so sick, so weak. "I believe you."

The eerie forest opens up to us, and we pivot through the fog until we see a rocky terrain of small, scattered mountains that look more the size of sharp hills. As I peer farther to the left, I see an area I wish I could have avoided looking at. A setup of red-striped tents, stages, firepits, and cages.

The Meat Carnival.

I shudder, but as I look closer, I notice that every cage is empty…

"I hear them coming!" Marilynn shouts from the back.

I look to Warrose as we both listen, finding the distant sound of a stampede, both human and animal. The trajectory of that noise tells me they've cut around Foul Falcon Forest. They're going to catch up to us.

"We need to get on the other side of these rocky hills. The shore is where our army is at. If we can at least get close, they may hear us in distress!"

Our group is dripping in sweat, taking erratic breaths, and looking so goddamn tired.

But we can't stop to rest. Not even for a moment.

Weaving through the flat valleys between the short, rocky mountains, our strides become shorter and slower. The uphill effort is leaving everyone waning, in need of water, and sleep. I instruct everyone to be careful where they step, watching the shiny shale rock as it's slippery while the rain hammers down against it.

The sun comes close to the horizon, just barely peeking out its orange glow. And I can somewhat see its distant reflection over the glassy surface of the ocean.

"We're getting closer!" I yell back to them.

Marilynn and Niles look like they're close to passing out or vomiting. Pale faces with sunken eyes and gaping mouths, but God love them because they keep going. I've never been more proud.

Warrose scans the smoky skies with pinched brows.

"What is it?"

"*Duck!*" he shouts.

Following the sheer squawk, we bend downward just as a spine-toothed eagle swoops through our group, attempting to grab someone with its yellow claws.

And everything, through our exhaustion and constant running, seems to explode into violent chaos. Flaming arrows soar through the rain, piercing the atmosphere, then dropping down toward us.

"Seek cover!" I yell. We all dart away from the line of fire, stumbling and falling. I stay on my feet, being as careful with Ruth as I can manage. She screams against my shoulder, and I pat her on the head to let her know we're okay.

I look to our group, fiercely inspecting everyone for injuries. Niles covers Marilynn's body with his own, Warrose bats at the birds with his mace, managing to injure three of them.

"We need to get to higher ground!" I point with my chin to the hill that's covered in nooks, caves, and covered passages.

Everyone scrambles to their feet, huffing and puffing to climb to the wet bedrock. I grimace as I pass Ruth off to Warrose, seeing silent tears blend with the rain down her cheeks. She feels like a burden. Helpless and powerless.

As we hike upward, I glance at our bloody feet. We're all barefoot, running through the forest, and now digging our toes into razor-sharp shale, butchering that tough skin. But no one complains, begs to stop, or makes a fuss. We're all running on no sleep, adrenaline, and the overpowering desire to make it to that army. To never have to return to the Vexamen Prison again.

The higher we get, the better view I have of the landscape around us. My stomach tightens at *the entire fucking army of Vexamen* barreling toward this desert land of gravelly hills, pits, and narrow valleys. They're storming every inch of the area with wild animals on leashes, cannons, carriages, and Blood Mammoths. And off into the foggy distance, my blood runs cold at the daunting, large cage being hauled. I can't see what's inside it. But it's clear that whatever it is, it is grander in size than DaiSzek.

I turn, scoping the wet granite, divots, and an opening that forms into a tunnel. It's the perfect shelter to cut across. I point, gesturing to the others. "Through there!"

Wiping the rain from my eyes, I wait until everyone is safely inside the lengthened cave, ducking my head to follow behind them.

"How're we going to get out of this one, Dess?" Niles asks from the middle of the line.

My throat shifts as I gulp. My bones ache with the same question. But as the person leading this escape, I can't show weakness. Can't show doubt.

I confidently say, "We're almost there."

A sudden heat wave funnels through the entrance behind us. It's our only warning before the walls collapse, and an explosion skyrockets us out of the small shelter we obtained. Our bodies, brushed with fire and debris, are forcefully ejected, tumbling down the hill in a torrent of screams, rocks scraping through skin, bones banging against hard edges, and my vision swirling with colors and the flipping bodies of my friends.

As the movement comes to a screeching halt, I blink furiously against my blurring sight. A hot gush of red pours into the corner of my left eye, and the only sound I hear is a constant ringing.

"*Call-out-t to m-me!*" I yell with an involuntary slur. Blood hangs in a string of drool from the corner of my mouth, dipping into the mud under my jaw as I cough.

My ribs implode with each jolting contraction. Sharp daggers pierce my brain. And for a single heartbeat, I wonder where I am. *Is anything broken?* My mind goes into survival mode, forgetting about our current situation to determine if I'm dying. I roll my ankles, bend my knees, shift my hips. Nothing broken, I don't think. But my entire body will swell and bruise tomorrow, if I live that long.

*You will*, Kalidus commands.

Dust and smoke construct a new atmosphere between all of us. I can't see past its towering barrier, can't breathe in its toxic particles.

"I feel—like I just gave birth—to my *brain.*" The voice isn't recognizable through the ringing in my ears, yet I know it's Niles. Because *of course* it's Niles. And through the pain of my pulsing jawbone, I smile.

An object cracks into my cheekbone so hard, my head whips to the side from the brutal lashing. More blood and saliva spray from my mouth. As my head turns back to the source of the attack to see what hit me, I only have a second for my distorted vision to process the soldier on his knees, swinging his sickle back to aim it for my chest.

A freckled hand loops around his neck, swiping a wide blade through his major arteries. A shower of crimson liquid drenches my left arm and collarbone.

"I heard you already died that way once," Marilynn says as the body plops on the ground next to me.

I take her hand as she helps me to my feet. "I did. A second time would have lacked creativity."

"My thoughts, too." I smile with a wince, wiping the blood from her forehead.

Niles walks up behind her, massaging his shoulder. He looks pretty beat up, but he's standing, breathing, awake, and walking. That's a win.

"Where's Warrose and Ruth?" I ask them with a spike of panic.

"*Here!*" Ruth calls in desperation. "Help him!"

Despite the gashes in my feet, I run across the wreckage that is similar to shards of glass, following Ruth's voice through the fog and smoke.

"There!" Niles shouts, pointing to a figure lying still on a slanted rock. Warrose is unconscious on his naked back, still holding Ruth to his chest.

"He slid to the side so he wouldn't roll on top of me!" Ruth sobs, trying to reach around and point to his back. "I think his back is injured."

I gulp as I lift his limp shoulder, and sure enough, the skin has been ripped off in slivers from the fall. Blood coats my fingers while I gently lift him to see if anything else is seriously harmed.

"Marilynn, get some water," I say in a low voice.

She hands me a canteen, and I use it to splash cold water in his face. Warrose gasps, flinches, then opens his eyes to glare at me angrily.

"It's going to hurt like hell, buddy. But I need to know you can keep moving."

My friend groans, guttural, coming from the depths of his core as he sits up. The stomping of feet, wild hissing, and snarling comes closer. Warrose nods, hardening his face in an attempt to show no weakness.

I take Ruth from his arms once more, jogging over the boulders and carnage stretched across our path. I peek at Ruth's bandages, now sopping with fresh blood. Her shoulder is dislocated, and she has pieces of gravel lodged in a few of her open wounds.

"I'm good," she murmurs in a slight haze. Probably coming in and out of shock.

"I know you are."

*Please, God. Help us find a way out of here. I can't let them die. They're my responsibility. My family.*

As we run and jump over pits and volcanic holes, bits of the army finally catch up to us. Warrose slays a few swamp dawpers that jump out from our left sides. Marilynn takes on two soldiers with double-edged swords, and she wields her small weapons with more speed than I've seen from a warrior in battle.

But it's not enough.

A flaming arrow spears through Niles's arm. He howls in sudden shock and pain, staring at me with eyes that ask *what should I do?*

Watching his scarred arm dripping blood takes my soul into a death grip. I open my mouth to encourage him, to assure him, but I'm out of options, and we all know it.

"Retreat to that trench!" I shout, pointing to a narrow valley that's evenly cloaked by surrounding hills.

And as Warrose looks at me with raised eyebrows, I silently communicate to him that we have no other plays here. We have to stay and fight. We can't keep running.

His Adam's apple stretches over the length of his throat as he bows his head to me. Understanding that…this is it. This is where we die. Together.

My only regret is that I don't get to know Skylenna the way I am supposed to. I don't get to hear her laugh the way I can almost hear an echo of it in my memory. I don't get to hold her one last time. I don't get to *remember* what it was like to love her.

Diving into the muddy, slimy trench, Marilynn breaks off the arrow logged in Niles's shoulder. He holds his brave face intact, fighting the urge to wince and cry out.

We fight them trickling in one by one. A Blood Mammoth rakes its unnaturally long, yellowed nails across my chest before I open its chest. Warrose bashes in the skulls of two more soldiers, Marilynn takes a knife to the cheek, withstanding fresh blood seeping down the side of her face before breaking the man's neck.

And Niles shields Ruth's body with his own, shivering against the trickling rain and flood of entrails being dumped around us with each kill.

I lose my ring sword after throwing it across the trench to behead a

Blood Mammoth that makes a beeline for Niles. He nods his thanks, and I reach into my belt for another weapon. My fingers brush something jagged, like a dusty rock.

My stomach does a flip as I speculate if it's what I think it is…

I pull it out of the pocket it rests in, examining the ash-colored stone in my palm.

*Shades were once fae or elves. They turned into dark, vengeful spirits that haunt these lands.*

My conversation with Qilan, one of the elders from the Nightamous Horde.

That *is a shade stone. The only object that can call to them. So, if you should ever find yourself in dire need of help, rub the stone until flecks of ash and dust float into the wind.*

He gave this stone to Skylenna and me.

*And help will come.*

Whether I believe in that mythology or not, I witness my family being cornered by an entire army. Warrose is soaking with sweat, rain, and gashes pouring out blood. Marilynn fights more soldiers than she can handle.

*Skylenna, if you can hear me…I need help. I need* you.

And I rub the stone.

# 65. The Shade Storm

## Warrose

"What are you doing?" I yell to Dessin after stabbing a soldier in the eye.

He's just *standing* there. Marilynn and I are holding up the line alone. And Dessin is standing among the bodies holding something small in his hands. He rubs his fingers over it.

"Help us!" I shout again.

Dessin finally looks up at me with a cloud of black dust traveling in a vortex around him.

"I am," he says.

That ominous cloud travels high, cutting through the hail and rain, polluting the atmosphere overhead. There are whispering words of vengeance that spiral through the entity, carrying a weight of hatred and venom.

The fighting slows down as the soldiers look up to the sky, afraid to breathe in the thick substance flying through the air. And the attack isn't normal, it isn't human. It's supernatural as shadowy figures shoot out from the funnel of smoke, scampering toward our enemies in a feral attack. They slice through soldiers and swamp dawpers alike, moving the fight away from us as we scramble to understand what the fuck Dessin has done.

"I called for help," Dessin explains, which doesn't actually explain anything at all.

I hook my weapon on my belt as I lift Ruth from Niles's arms to further retreat back. She quivers against my slippery skin, gripping the back of my neck as she kisses my cheek.

"Thank God you're okay," she gasps.

"I'm not going anywhere, baby girl."

"Fall back!" Dessin guides us away from the heavy smoke.

"How much time will this buy us?" I ask as we run into the open desert.

"I'm not sure."

The rain morphs into thin waves of mist against the sun rising behind the East Vexello Mountains. We're almost there. It's so close, and hopefully the army will see our signals like a smudge of charcoal in the sky.

It isn't long before the army strongarms the wall of shadows, forcing their way through in numbers far greater than anything I could have ever imagined.

"If we don't make it through this..." Ruth speaks close to my ear as I run with her.

"Don't."

"Warrose, I need you to know—"

"Ruth!" I bark, losing my temper. "I told you that once we're away from all of this, we can go to pieces together. You're going to tell me whatever you feel when you're ready, when we're free."

She nods with a sniffle, wiping her eyes.

Although there's that doubtful part of me that fears the worst. I may die today without ever hearing what she wants to tell me.

# 66. At The Darkest Hour

## Dessin

Amushroom cloud of fire bulldozes into us from behind, cracking the earth with its grumbling impact and sending us flying. The explosion is bigger than the last, closer perhaps. Except this time, we don't roll down the side of a dangerous hill. We land in front of a gooey swamp and a bald cypress tree. The woody projections of the roots bulge from the black waters, giving us something to hold on to as we try to lift ourselves from the earthy rubble.

Using my elbows to hold myself up in the swampy gunk, I twist my body toward the haze of everyone dressed in matte black armor, bearing their swords in our direction as their mouths gape open in a battle cry.

Through my aching ribs, brittle spine, and brain throbbing in a nest of burning embers and shards of glass, I wobble to my feet. It isn't a choice whether or not I should let the stampede of these vast numbers run over my family in a brutal killing. I will stand against thousands of men without giving it a thought.

To my right, Warrose rises with me, having already handed Ruth off to Niles. Marilynn steps up to my left. She doesn't look afraid staring into the sea of murderers. The harrowing image of the angel of death sweeping the land to find us waiting. She watches patiently, taking a deep breath and nudging my hand with hers.

"I've waited my whole life to see this," she whispers.

Is this how her prophecy predicted our deaths? How could she possibly look so calm about this? Where is the fear that should wrinkle her forehead?

"How do you like these odds, Dess?" Warrose asks with a paling face.

I smirk with unease knotting my stomach. "It's not fair to them."

"Let's not make it easy on them."

I nod, appreciating my oldest friend standing by my side in the face of imminent death, never failing to rise against greater numbers with me.

The earth quakes around us as the army speeds up, flooding the open lands with stomping hooves and beasts sprinting ahead as they plan to end our lives first. And though I can feel time pushing against us with an iron fist, it also slows. A moment spread wide, bearing itself to face me as I realize…the earth quaking under my feet isn't coming from their angry mob of an army.

The faces of the many soldiers closing in on us stare over my shoulder, losing the fierce look on their faces. And as we follow their frightened gazes, I finally see what's shaking the core of the very ground we stand on.

Appearing like a god of death and hell in the distance, DaiSzek sprints with the force and speed of a world-ending meteor.

And Skylenna stands on his back, riding him as she bears her sword.

# Skylenna

THAT APOCALYPTIC PUFF OF black smoke over the desert lands of Vexamen only meant one thing.

It wasn't something the Nightamous Horde had to tell me.

It was something DaiSzek and I felt in our very core.

It was a call for help.

And as we raced into the face of an army larger than our own, DaiSzek and I showed no fear. No hesitation.

Our army follows behind us. Knightingale sprints as fast as she can yet is nowhere close to the otherworldly speed DaiSzek takes on. Wind beats against the front of my body, sending my hair and braids shooting away from my face like a long, golden flag. I grip DaiSzek's long coat of fur, praying we aren't too late, buzzing with anticipation of saving Dessin's life.

The atmosphere of rain slaps against my cheeks, bringing the scent of deep water and blood spiraling up my nose. And something between DaiSzek and I changes as we see the horizon of an army aiming their sights on a small swamp in the distance. I feel an undeniable pull to them, like fishhooks cutting through my navel, dragging me to my soulmate. A bond that shoots fire down my spine as I ride DaiSzek into a war that will make history. That will fulfull a prophecy. It's electricity transferring from his back into my hands, charging me with combustions of power. It ripples through the air around us.

"We need something stronger than just our fight, Dai," I tell him as we eat away at the distance between us and the bald cypress tree.

*DaiSzek is a descendant of the last living dragon that fought alongside our Fae king and Elven queen.*

I gaze down at him. Those cinnamon eyes turning a bright shade of crimson.

*It's said that the last living RottWeilen can breathe fire like his ancestor. But only if he has a strong enough bond with his pack. The fae king, DaiSzek, used to merely close his eyes and imagine his enemies burning for his dragon to know when to strike. Do you think you have a bond like that?*

His heavy paws beat into the earth like a drum of gods. The world rattles and shivers in fear at the great RottWeilen unleashing his fury, unraveling a power no one has seen in a thousand years. And it all clicks together as I hold onto his mane. Watching with gritting teeth and burning eyes as the army comes into focus, growing so near we can taste their adrenaline running thick in their pores.

*DaiSzek can't breathe fire.*

*Have you ever asked him to?*

*Well, no…*

His strides quicken, practically levitating off the ground.

*If he is the true alpha of his species, the last of his kind, then it should run hot in his blood—dormant until his pack rides into battle, believing he can torch a path through the blood and clashing swords.*

"Am I your pack?" I ask him with drops of rain splashing in my eyes.

My boy growls, revving up to sing his song of demise.

*DaiSzek, used to merely close his eyes and imagine his enemies burning for his dragon to know when to strike.*

"I've felt the connection to you since the day I found you as a child. You've always been mine. And I've always been yours." My eyes water as the feeling bursts like lightning through my soul.

*Do you think you have a bond like that?*

"I love you, DaiSzek. I think we've always known this would be our moment. This is what we were meant to be." And it simply feels like the right move to jump onto my feet, standing along the bulky length of his spine as I unsheathe our swords.

Twenty paces away from the small swamp, my family looks back at me, breaking my heart as I see their faces warped with the notion of one foot in their graves. Ready to die with honor. But there's a glimmer of pride beaming from Dessin's dark-mahogany eyes as he gazes upon my warrior stance, riding the back of the last living RottWeilen. In a single moment, he takes in my face painted like the reaper of Vexamen souls. The chains and armor and giant swords being raised by my fists.

And as if in slow motion, I toss him the sword of the fae king. And just as I do, their spirits reveal themselves to me. The warrior angels that came before us ride into battle at our backs, bowing their heads to me. It's only now I realize the voice in my head guiding me through the prison has always been the soul of the elven queen, Knightingale. And even now as I wield her sword and ride the greatest monster alive, she's with me. Dessin catches the bulky sword, filling him with a divine power that can only be gifted by God himself.

*When you get out there,* dashna, *you'll know when it's time.*

I do now. The front lines of the Vexamen Breed bolt toward us. DaiSzek doesn't seem bothered because it's time. And we both know it. My entire frame is lit with a force stronger than the gravity that moves the universe. Trembling, sweating, and levitating from the tips of my toes off DaiSzek's back. I lean my head back with a smile contorting my face, and I close my eyes slowly, letting them roll back in my head as I believe in what the alpha of all RottWeilens is capable of.

I imagine my enemies burning to the ground.

DaiSzek takes a deep breath in, and I feel the exhale before I see it. He roars like both a king of lions and a massacring dragon. The legend hunches his shoulders to his ears with a force of air that blasts from his jaws detonating blue flashing sparks, and within a blink of an eye, dark red flames ignite, the color of his glowing eyes.

The fire is massive in size, dwarfing the army, and emanating a callous fury as it engulfs charred pathways through several lines of defense. DaiSzek's body goes taut and hard to the touch with the scorching wrath of a dragon, the dominating energy radiating off of us in a musical dance of annihilation.

The faces of those who barely survive the blast are more shocked than if they saw the devil himself rising from the dirt to take them to hell.

Catching up behind us, Knightingale and a storm of white wolves make a head-on collision with Vexamen beasts like swamp dawpers and grinalie bears, wasting no time in their slaughter. The army of Demechnef rides in the wake of the smoke and flames being extinguished by the mob of dying soldiers, putting out the flames with their bodies. And even though we didn't take out the entire army, we sure as hell made a dent in their forces.

Stormsages fall in line first, then the Nightamous Horde. And as they create an impenetrable wall on the left and right sides of DaiSzek and me, we slice through the limbs of these soldiers like slabs of butter. In the thick of the fighting, I jump off of DaiSzek's back, beheading anyone that charges me. My nerves come alive, remembering every moment I trained with Kane as a child. Feeling the grief and depression from when I lost Dessin. The guilt from Ruth's moment with the axe. The pain of watching Niles throw himself into the flames.

I'm a lethal assassin in the calm of night, slithering through the falling bodies and sharp weapons. Blood splashes across my face as I take down a man three times my size, feeling the presence of another towering figure coming right up behind me. His shadow blankets the sunrays that glimmer off my ancient sword. I swing the blade like a whip lashing through the wind, throwing my weight into the attack. But as I see the brown eyes looking down at me, my arm halts to a stop, pausing just before it touches the skin on his tan neck.

"*Dessin,*" I exhale in a rush. Every bit of passion under my skin is rushing to the surface.

He slips his sword into his belt, and hesitantly slides those giant hands around the sides of my face. I melt despite the pumps of adrenaline coursing through my veins. His touch softens the universe into submission.

"You came back," he says, furrowing his brow.

I nod with watering eyes. "And I brought heaven and hell with me."

Dessin blinks as he glares down at me with confusion and intense emotions flashing across his vision. "You *love* me."

"Always."

A soldier comes up behind me, but not before Dessin uses the tip of my sword to impale him. We break away from each other, staying close as we fight back-to-back. An unstoppable force that conquers the weapons that rise against us.

With Dessin by my side, I can do all things.

Bear all things.

Endure all things.

# Niles

"DaiSzek just breathed fucking *FIRE!*" I scream in Ruth's ear, hugging her chilled body to my chest within the curly roots of the swamp tree.

"Good, you saw it, too," she says in a shiver. "I thought I was hallucinating."

I bury my nose against her wet hair. We've both lost some blood, probably have concussions, and I can't imagine how great her pain is right now. However, the cavalry has come! Soldiers in orderly lineups march on as Skylenna makes a blazing trail through a sea of fried corpses. It's astounding and surreal to see before my very eyes!

"Help has come, Ruthie."

"Thank God. I wasn't sure how much longer I'd last."

I dab at the tears dripping down her cheeks, kiss her temple, and hug on her some more. We're going to get through this. We have been through too much for that to be our tragic ending.

"We deserve a happy ending," I tell her.

"I don't think that's in the cards for me," she chokes out.

"Oh, Ruthie!" I pull her ice-cold hand to my lips, breathing hot air against her fingers. "Don't you see him? You think I haven't noticed the vibrant light that shines between you and Warrose? Sure, he's rough around the edges and eats like a brain-dead barbarian, but you've found your soulmate. And he's currently slaying any living being that tries to harm us."

She watches Asena toss him a razor-bladed whip and sees how he comes to life as he manipulates his favorite tool of destruction. The bronze muscles across his back flex and contract, hurling his body into a lashing that removes three heads at once. And those movements are positively bestial, a predator much faster than his prey. He's a leaf in the wind as he rotates his movements around each attack, avoiding even the slightest cut or jab.

Marilynn isn't far ahead of him. She stands out with her cherry-red hair and lips like a drop of blood on a piece of parchment. Her deadly presence twists around like a viper with her small hand blades. She's fluid and packs *a fucking punch*. I wish I could be the man to help her, fight with her, but if I'm being true to myself…sitting here with Ruth, holding her, protecting her, is where I want to be.

Off into the distance, another army of mountain men and women with heavy axes and hulking bodies swarm around us. They remind me of Helga Bee and Gerta, helping us from all angles, supporting each colony for our seven forests. And to my surprise, Hangman's Valley has its own colony. One that lacks a human population. Beasts of all sizes and colors enter the fight, gravitating toward Warrose to be commanded into the combat.

The clashing of swords and screaming men get a little too close to Ruth and me after a few minutes. It sends the hairs on my neck standing straight up. I scoot backward, closer to the bald cypress tree, hiding us away until the war is won, and this nightmare has ended.

Warrose and Marilynn are overrun, fighting too many at once, and that makes the snowy eyes of a nearby Vexamen Breed General that much more terrifying.

"Ruth," I say in a warning tone.

The general slips past the defenses around us, charging toward us with his face covered in white scars and bruising blemishes. He's wider than a Red Oak tree trunk, bald, with a mouth that is pinched and shaped like an asshole.

"Oh God," Ruth gasps, seeing the man target us, too. "Warrose!" she screams, though it's drowned out by the hectic noises of war around us. "*Warrose!*"

I attempt to continue scooting back, but it's a failing effort as the goliath general trudges through the swamp water toward us. Reaching around his back, he plucks out two war hammers with flat heads the size of my face. His eyes the color of an ice storm bounce between Ruth and I, twirling those hammers between his fingers as if they weigh a pound a piece.

I act quickly. Or, at least, I set Ruth down and unsheathe the dagger Dessin gave me somewhat in a hurry. I focus on my lessons with Dessin and Warrose, how to defend myself against an attack. I must make them proud, and even though my shoulder is pierced with that stick of wood from the arrow I was hit with, my body becomes a numb, trembling vessel.

"I won't let him hurt you, Ruthie!"

*It's all about confidence*, Dessin once told me.

I do a little twirl of my dagger, flipping in my hand, then pointing it at the general with a calm and collected smile. I am a master of this dagger. No one is faster than my hand with this sharp blade of swift death.

*Think to yourself, I am Niles Offborth, and I am not afraid.*

It's true. I'm not frightened of this big, stupid bald man. I am Niles Offborth, and I have been trained by the greatest warriors the world has ever seen. With a plunge forward, I jab at the general, forcing him to take a single step back. Pride swells in my chest at the small win. I jab once more, causing him to pivot to the left, avoiding my attack.

*I can do this.*

*I am not afraid.*

Blood pumps like a wild fireman's hose in my arteries, causing my internal organs to vibrate through my core.

"Niles?!" Marilynn screams from several paces away from us. And I make the terrible mistake of glancing at her, trying to fight her way through the crowd of bloody, burned bodies.

The general attacks without hesitation, slamming the head of his war hammer against my shoulder, pinpointing the wound of the arrow stem. I grunt and fall to my knees, pulling the throaty sound from the pit of my stomach. My arm zings down to my fingertips with an injection of torment.

Before he can swing on me again, I use my position in the slimy swamp water to slice across his ankles, then as he doubles forward, I stab at a major artery above his hip. The general pierces my ears with his snarl that sounds more enraged than hurt.

The war hammer in his left hand blasts into my dagger, knocking it out of my hand and into the murky water and mud. *Fuck. Shit. No.*

"Run, Niles!" Ruth cries.

*Run? I'd never leave her.*

The general swings his heavy weight into my shoulder again. This time, it's so hard and direct, the stem of the arrow comes jutting halfway out of my shoulder blade. Blood spills down my chest as I cry out. *Broken.* Something is broken or shattered or hanging on by a string.

Through the fat tears welling over my shuddering eyes, that fucking hammer rears back again, whooshing through the humid air in a straight line to my face. And I know, by the power behind that handle, by the muscles in this barbarian's arm...this swing will crush my face. This swing will kill me.

I pray I'll see my father again. I pray that my friends won't mourn me. I pray—

The tip of a long, golden sword clanks against the hammer's blow, halting a single centimeter away from my face. Sparks beam from the collision, and I cock my head back to look up through the sheer mist of rain at the lean, inky-haired leader of Demechnef stretched in front of my beaten body to block the killing blow.

"Ah, shit," I hiss in sudden gratitude. "Fuck me!"

"I'm a little busy saving your ass," Aurick Demechnef answers with a strained smirk. He kicks his boot into the general's chest. His sword moves so quickly it makes sounds similar to a wind chime or a flute as it slices into a wrist, across the belly, above the knee. He's a master swordsman, defending my helpless ass like it's a child's game.

After skewering the general through the right side of his chest, Aurick turns to me, slicking a hand through his professional, midnight hair. His smile hardly touches his icy blue eyes as he raises his perfect eyebrows, offering me a hand.

"Your first war, huh?" he mocks.

I grab his hand unenthusiastically. "Oh, fuck you. It's your first, too."

His chuckle is cut off, stopped too early with a loud popping sound. An egg cracks against concrete. The dark river of blood that spills from his scalp down the side of his face leaves us both momentarily immobile.

*What?*

Aurick's radiant aqua eyes seem to short-circuit, losing focus, then return back to me with nothing but foggy confusion.

"Was I hit?" he asks absently.

"I-Aurick...I..." Shooting my startled glare over his shoulder, the general drops back to the ground with his war hammer coated in a few strands of black hair and blood. He got one last hit. *Aurick*...he shouldn't have turned his back on him.

From here, there is only one sound that punctures the symphony of howling, feral animals, and the gory sloshing of war at its peak.

Marilynn screams, and it's a hacksaw to my chest. That singular cry stretches like hot lava through my trembling frame, blackening my insides. It wakes me up from a brief paralyzing shock, and I reach for Aurick's shoulders as I stand before him.

"W-was I *hit*?" he asks again. And the confusion in his rapid blinking gaze twists my face at the start of an ugly cry.

I nod slowly. "Yeah, man."

"Charles didn't deserve it." Aurick trains his eyes on me with a moment of lucidity. "I'm sorry, Niles."

A lump forms in my throat as Marilynn sprints with high knees through the gooey swamp, grabbing Aurick's midsection as he slowly loses his ability to stand. I help take on his weight, never breaking eye contact as the shock tightens its claws around his mind.

"I-I can't feel anything," he stammers.

That blood just keeps gushing, forking paths into his left eye, along the bridge of his nose, drizzling into his parted mouth. And I don't know why, but I try to wipe it away for him. I try to clear his vision and make him clean again.

Marilynn presses her fist to her mouth to stifle her sobs.

"Don't be sad." His eyelids drift down, then snap back open. "I'm sorry."

The red-headed beauty doesn't ask what he's sorry for. It seems she already knows.

Aurick is quiet for a long moment, shivering in the chunky water coming to my thighs as we sit among the ash that floats down like tears, and the screaming of dying souls that spreads through the barren land.

His clammy, pallid hand reaches for mine in a rushed movement. And his lips tremble as he pins me with a stare that captures every ounce of my attention.

*"Take care of them."*

Those wintery eyes, bloodshot and glossy, go lax in their sockets. They don't blink as they stare into the rain. Because there is no longer a spirit behind them.

Aurick Demechnef is gone.

# 67. That Old Serpent Called The Devil

## Skylenna

The Stormsages make up for the fact that Dessin and I have stopped fighting.

Marilynn's cries break our concentration and send us pivoting in her direction. She's kneeling in front of Niles, hunched over and trembling. *Why would she be crying? Did someone...*

"Dessin," I blurt out in terror, praying we haven't just lost one of our own. "Niles! Is it Niles?"

Dessin is tall enough to stare into the distance over the war and fire and pools of blood around us. His war-stricken eyes quickly flick back to me, and he shakes his head. Although his reaction isn't severe enough for it to be someone in our family, it still holds a certain crushing weight. I push through the massive cluster of men and women, bumping into thrusting elbows, dropping bodies, and moving carriages. Finally standing in a clearing close to the bald cypress tree, it's clear who Marilynn is hunched over. I lose my breath at the sight of him.

Aurick Demechnef lies against her lap, not moving, not breathing, not blinking. His silky ebony hair is sopping wet with blood, and Niles is reaching over his limp frame to close Aurick's eyes. I feel hollow and in disbelief at the thought of his chest no longer moving.

Though there are many disastrous memories of this man, he was still my friend in that blizzard. He brought me closer to the love of my life by getting me a job at Emerald Lake Asylum. He was there when I had no one else, regardless of his ulterior motives.

I feel my lungs sag into my chest as I look through the fog at the leader of Demechnef, now fallen. Dessin appears at my side, silent and staring, too, like he also needed that moment to process the gravity of who we have lost.

"Dessin!" Warrose runs to us, using his bladed whip to cut through the crowd ambushing him. He's pointing to a location off in the distance. "Dessin, *look!*"

We rotate at the same time, searching the sea of madness, though it's hard to miss. There's a bronze cage behind the many lines of Vexamen Breed soldiers. It's the size of a small building with bright amber eyes glowing from between its bars. And it's opening, unlatching locks from the bottom.

"It's a Dralutheran! Get DaiSzek out of here!" Warrose's thunderous voice sends a shockwave down my spine as my eyes widen toward Dessin.

*What does that mean?*

To my dismay, Dessin's face loses color, and he's suddenly searching the battlefield for DaiSzek, shouting his name. Tendons and veins bulge along his neck. His head twists and turns as he tries to locate our boy.

"What's a Dralutheran?!" I ask in a shriek.

We've never worried about DaiSzek with another creature before. I've seen him dominate the most fearsome of creatures. Even when he was a pup, he defeated a night dawper that stalked me near the Red Oaks! *And he was a freaking pup!*

"Dralutherans are just as rare as a RottWeilen nowadays!" Warrose finally reaches me with a bloodstained hand on my shoulder. "They're reptilian leviathans that only hunt apex predators! Nearly indestructible skin, and extremely intelligent."

And in this instant, a creature steps out of the colossal cage opening. It's a petrifying blend of a basilisk and a wingless dragon with seaweed green scales that glimmer to a shade of amethyst against the light of fire. Its short but powerful legs move with the speediness of a spider, reminding me of the claws and stance a crocodile has. And it sniffs the air through the slits of its stubby snout, flexing its purple tongue over those spiked teeth as it catches the whiff it's looking for.

The only other apex predator in this land.

DaiSzek.

The gigantic creature sets its amber eyes on a target and doesn't hesitate to blast through the lines of soldiers to get to it. The earth rumbles under my feet, vibrations quaking my innards and thrumming hard against my beating heart.

I finally spot Dessin sprinting through walls of opponents, cutting them down as he screams, "DaiSzek, *NO!!!!*"

Our boy is a mere fifty feet away, tearing apart a loaded cannon as he comes to a screeching stop, locking his sight on the Dralutheran. Those RottWeilen eyes flash to a blazing ruby red. Upper lip curling back to reveal his mountainous teeth. And he crouches low before bolting in that direction.

Dessin roars over the noise, begging DaiSzek to stop, to come back, to retreat.

But DaiSzek flies like a stallion, frothing at the mouth to protect us all from this new antagonist. Nothing on earth could stop him from meeting this challenge.

*"It is what killed the last dragon,"* the spirit of the elven queen, Knightingale, whispers to me.

My stomach convulses with doom. DaiSzek leaps and soars over the cinders and rubble, conquering his obstacles with ease. *What can I do? How can I stop this?*

I swivel to Warrose, gyrating his whip around us. "Cover me while I do this."

"Do what?" he asks without missing a beat.

I tilt my face to the sky, conjuring that feeling that consumed me as I rode DaiSzek's back into battle. I connect with it the way I would reach out and hold Dessin's hand, using the void as a crutch to stabilize myself. It's a tangible entity, warm and thrumming in my lungs and soul. Its lava spurting through my bloodstream, filling my brain with an electrical charge.

And I breathe life into the image I create in my mind.

My enemies burning.

The Dralutheran engulfed in flames.

A mere second away from a collision, DaiSzek unhinges his jaw to roar; an ear-splitting sound devastates the battlefield as a pummel of fire eats up the air surrounding the Dralutheran, taking out units of the Breed along the way. Those seaweed-colored scales heat up like glowing coals, turning red before brightening to coral with flecks of embers popping from its tough skin.

Endorphins fill me up from impact. Power. Elation. Seamless destruction.

But as I observe the great flames, my stomach takes a dip. The Dralutheran is only momentarily occupied by the bright lights and scorching heat around its body. It swats at the infernos like that combustion is an unwanted pest. And after the initial beat of surprise, the beast huffs, lunging forward to clip DaiSzek in the side with a scaley claw.

I cry out while DaiSzek flips to the side, looking so small compared to the gargantuan beast. But he doesn't stay down for long. He attacks without hesitation, using his teeth to snap at the ankles, the places near the gut where vital organs subside.

DaiSzek tries everything to no avail.

"I can't watch this," Dessin grunts, rushing to my side.

I shake my head back and forth, as if the motion will make this all go away. I was accepting of this way before I knew DaiSzek had a true competitor. Where did they find this thing? What are its weaknesses?

"Warrose!" Dessin barks over my head. "What can we do?!"

In two side steps, Warrose is by our side, looking uncharacteristically dumbfounded.

"Dralutherans are fucking rare. They haven't been spotted in over a century. I don't even know where Vexamen could have found one, much less capture it!"

This can't be happening. *No.* There is always a way. Dessin can always find a way.

"Weaknesses?" I choke out, watching the horror show while wincing, yet unable to turn away and spare myself the violent images.

"Not any that have been recorded. They usually are isolated and never enter combat. So no one has ever really gotten the chance to study them." Warrose pauses, giving his whipping arm a break as a flood of the Nightamous Horde swarms the area around us.

"But it's the Dralutheran that killed the last dragon." I turned to Dessin with balled fists and crazy eyes. "It defeated a dragon!"

"How do you know this?"

"The elven queen told me."

"She did?" He looks both fascinated and skeptical. "Isn't she…"

"Dead. Yes. But they've both been here fighting with us. The two warrior angels that came before."

"Ask her Skylenna!" He shakes my shoulders after DaiSzek crashes into a bed of explosives.

"DaiSzek, get out of there!" I scream.

I'm not sure if he hears me or he realizes what he's fallen into, but the brave RottWeilen leaps away from the stacks of ticking time bombs, barely missing the destruction as it booms toward the sky.

As he shakes himself off, releasing a cloud of ash from his fur, a unit of heavily armed soldiers surround him in a circle. Dessin and I both stiffen in shock at their brazenness of getting so close to him. Two long spears are thrown strategically from two separate angles, sticking into his back with the precision of an arrow. I jolt beside Dessin as DaiSzek howls to the misting sky.

"Hey!" I scream, gripping Dessin's arm with my nails.

"Marilynn! Warrose!" Dessin orders them over without any context, yet we all *know*. Because the moment Marilynn stands to Dessin's right side and Warrose to my left, we take off in a race of vengeance. Several members of the colony fall in line with us, but Dessin, being an avenging alter, doesn't slow his pace. This is what he was made for. This is what he lives for.

With a final leap toward a soldier with his back to us, Dessin throws him backward, directly into my arms. And I act on the fumes of my temper, snapping his neck swiftly. We fight together as if it's all choreographed. Selected moves and countermoves, lethal hits, and ways we maneuver our bodies to kill at an inhumanly fast rate. Bodies drop around us. All of this without the use of our swords. We decimate every soldier attacking DaiSzek with nothing but our bare hands.

After the path is cleared, I fumble over the bodies to DaiSzek, who is fighting to stand up with the spears poking out of his back and sides.

"I've got you, buddy!" I pant, throwing my arms toward him.

His cinnamon eyes flare wide at something above me, pupils dilating, his irises growing a fiery crimson once more. A shadow slithers over me, daunting and cold. But before I can rotate to fight the beast I know is creeping up behind me, DaiSzek hurtles himself over my head with every ounce of energy he can muster and lands on the arm of the Dralutheran! His growls and snarls are warped and messy, muffled by his efforts to rip into the creature's indestructible skin.

I scream something incoherent as the scaly creature rakes his claws into the side of DaiSzek's tummy, spraying his hot blood above us like a sputtering shower.

"Let him go!" I cry, observing our archers and best swordsmen attempting to take the monster down. But DaiSzek is thrown as if he weighs nothing more than a sack of flour. Air puffs from his lungs as he lands on the hard ground with a thud.

Dessin jumps in front of DaiSzek, covering his core by making his body a human shield. The monster screeches at the back of Dessin's neck, warning him that it will kill anyone to get to DaiSzek. It lifts his crocodile foot, hovering it over Dessin in an attempt to squash him.

And I'm running in a frenzy toward them.

*I'm going to lose them both! I'm going to lose them both!*

With a violent jerking of DaiSzek's leg, he kicks Dessin in the stomach like a horse, launching him away from the Dralutheran's foot. The sound that follows is deafening. A stomping of that scaly foot over DaiSzek's leg. Quick. Sharp. A wet *crack!* And my mountainous boy lies there, yelping like a puppy in agony as his leg is broken.

Dessin howls against the symphony of war around us. Because the pain of this beautiful boy detonates through our souls, feasting on our organs, blistering our hearts. And I can't breathe. Can't move. Can't do anything other than grasp at my chest to keep my heart from tumbling to the ground in pieces.

*Knightingale, help him! Oh god! Please help him!*

"I can't lose my boy!" I'm bawling as I scream into the void, both real and in my mind.

The beast is working toward a deadly blow, twisting the energy of this battle into heartbreaking loss and sickening anticipation for what comes next. Because our men do everything. They try everything. This thing is unkillable. A cockroach that lives through a nuclear explosion.

*Knightingale! PLEASE!*

She appears in front of me with the grace of a shadow, at a height of five feet and eleven inches. Radiant bronze skin, long coffee-colored hair, and white paint drawn in intricate streaks across her face. Her red leather corset is decorated with gold buckles and belted straps from her neck to her ankles. And those pointed ears that are clearly not human.

"*I am not the right Knightingale that can help him,*" the elven queen says with a voice of gilded iron and expensive silk. Her wise eyes bore into me, waiting for me to understand her meaning.

"What?"

But there's a figure off in the distance, staring, like a lighthouse calling a ship home. There's a sensation creeping over my body as I let that magnetic energy pull my gaze away from the elven queen through the sea of the dead and the living, the bloody swords, and the dismembered limbs.

My eyes land on Knightingale, the Ginger Wrathbull, standing a few hundred paces away from this massacring carnage. She stares at DaiSzek with those doe black eyes; the fur spiking in a strip down her back as she witnesses the leader of her pack being beaten down and annihilated before her very eyes.

And though she's an animal, I can see a potent idea rising to the front of her mind. A decision. She swipes her focus to the pile of explosives that are being used in the cannons. A hollow pit forms in my gut just as my mouth falls open.

"Knightingale!" I shout in terror.

Those dilated eyes switch over to me, then to DaiSzek in his slow death, then back to me.

I shake my head.

But it's the way she's looking at me, like she wants me to understand. She will bear no other options. The pain of watching her alpha, her only friend, be pummeled in a slaughter, is something she cannot stomach.

"Wait!" I scream to her. "Just wait!"

Dessin scrambles to his feet to set his sights on who I'm yelling at.

557

Knightingale lifts her snout proudly in a quick posture of honor. And her decision is made; her legs shoot into action, and she's sprinting like an award-winning racehorse toward the pile of bombs. Without missing a beat, she picks one up with her mouth, the size and weight of a brick, and swipes it through a sweltering torch. She huffs and snorts in pain as the fire ignites the outer shell, licking at her snout and tongue.

But my brave, misunderstood Ginger Wrathbull doesn't let that stop her. She barrels toward the Dralutheran, picking up speed with her pointy ears pressed back and the fire eating away at the sides of her lips and fur.

I screech and cry like a dying banshee, but Dessin holds me back. Arms wrapped around my waist, I can feel him shudder against me as I thrash and fight to stop her.

"Wait!" I scream through rivers of tears pouring down my cheeks.

DaiSzek looks up at the commotion through slackened eyes and the ache of his broken limbs. She chuffs and barks as he spots her zooming through the crowd, taking damn near flying strides like a cheetah before she reaches the grand beast.

And it…it happens too fast.

The Dralutheran lowers its head to the ground to greet her, opening its jaws wide and welcoming to enjoy a quick meal of this small, yet heroic animal. There's a gap of a few seconds as she takes a hurried dive into its mouth. Those jaws close around her. Her copper-furred figure disappears into that darkness.

Dessin and I freeze with gaping mouths.

The Dralutheran has but a moment to blink its reptilian eyes. It implodes from the inside out, spraying everyone in a fine, pink mist. The skies weep with its disintegrated fragments, skin, innards, and, of course, DaiSzek's friend, Knightingale.

# 68. Scorned

## Skylenna

The aftermath leaves me in the form of a block of stone. Frozen. Muted. A human vessel of nothingness. Dessin's arms go slack around my waist with my sharp nails still biting into his forearm.

We blink through the cloud of pink smog and floating ash. My ears ring, tuning out the war. My chest shrivels in on itself, warping my spine, beating against my soul with bony fists. The shock that takes over is a cage that wants to lock me down and protect my mind from irreversible trauma.

But I still see her running like an angel, flying on the wind with purpose. I can feel the swell of determination she emanated wanting to save her best friend. I smell the outcome of her demise.

"Skylenna?" Warrose's face fills my vision.

There are so many sounds. The cries of death are like an untuned violin. Wind and rain. Metal puncturing meat. Teeth snapping at limbs.

"DaiSzek can't defend himself!" Warrose tries to reach me again. Dessin's arms unwind around me as this seems to break through the impenetrable glass of our shock.

A swarm of soldiers hold tall shields as they close in on the wounded RottWeilen. Slow marches to ensure he doesn't attack from being cornered.

A searing filter of red fills my vision. My nostrils flare as I turn my head to the right, slowly, like a possessed doll coming to life. In the distance, closer than before, the Mazonist Brothers riding like kings in a merlot-rusted chariot. Their old, weathered faces smile down at me. They watch DaiSzek fall from glory like a theater performance.

And they're resting in the safety behind their army.

"Protect our boy," I grit in rageful daze to Dessin.

"Skylenna..."

"I'm coming with you." Marilynn touches my elbow, still covered in Aurick's blood.

"As are we, *dashna*," Asena says with the conviction of the white wolf queen she truly is. And along come the remaining members of her pack, stained in red and black against their fluffy coats of snowy fur.

Dessin blinks at her, parting his mouth to tell her something that weighs heavy in his heart. But it's as if Asena already knows what he's going to say. She bows her head as if she already knows whatever it is he wants to share.

"Did they fight well?" she asks.

"The best I've ever seen," Dessin says.

Runa shows up with a wide grin of defiance, followed by Bellanne from Faecrest colony.

I turn back to Dessin, trembling with an energy that conquers all and quiets my mind.

"Protect. Our. Boy."

I wait for no one as I make my descent on the twins that have enforced evil and unforgivable cruelty on their nation. The leaders who are to blame for the death of Knightingale. The rulers who kept us locked in prison.

The dead brothers who will carry the brunt of my retribution.

Because a scorned angel is far more frightening than the devil himself.

Jumping over piles of bodies, severed limbs, and burned carnage, I feel the other women tread behind me. They clear a path as my arms twitch and shiver with pent-up hostility. The thought of Knightingale springing into the darkness as it closed around her, running with a flaming explosive, singeing the inside of her mouth...I can't unsee it. She was so brave. So small compared to DaiSzek, yet fierce with her conviction.

We've lost Aurick.

We've lost Kaspias.

And although they were not always friends, they lost their lives for *us*.

My brain splinters and curls at the corners, reaching for the void, channeling every tear I am going to spill from this day forward as I endure flashbacks of this day.

Malcolm and Maxwell are dressed in their most royal attire, with jewels and robes and smug smiles that begin to fade as the women around me slay their best defenses to get me closer. Their white brows rise cautiously, darting their eyes back and forth. Swamp dawpers are sent in to attack from every angle, but between my ancient sword removing their heads and Asena siccing her white wolves on them...all that's left is their supreme guard.

The most powerful of Vexamen Breed commanders just like Kaspias.

My mind flashes through the void like a whip, and I snatch the guards before Runa and Marilynn can touch them. My unit halts behind me as the commanders go stiff, eyes rolling in the backs of their heads. I dominate their souls like a bad omen, filling their bloodstreams with my authority as I sink my claws into the essence of their brains.

*"You are mine now,"* I command in a voice that echoes with darkness and a lack of humanity.

The supreme guard drops to their knees.

*"Eat your masters."* I grin with bloodshot eyes. *"Slowly."*

Those around us watch the show of cannibalism in horror. The Mazonist Brothers are too old, too weak, too fucking spineless to defend themselves against the now bloodthirsty guard. It was too easy to summon this violence, to get what I wanted from the void.

And even though my body quakes and pulses with hypothermia clutching at my nervous system, I watch the demise of the men who have ruined so many lives. I relish in their screams, the choking sounds that gurgle in their throats as teeth rip at their necks.

"You're a fucking terror, Skylenna," Runa utters next to me.

I glance at her, though my vision goes fuzzy around the edges, and I lose my breath.

"She really is." Dessin stands to my left with crossed arms and a look of astonishment as he pairs me to the scene of flesh-eating guards ripping Malcolm and Maxwell to shreds.

"Dessin," I croak thickly. My body fills with ice as I gaze up at him and lose stability in my legs. With bloodstained arms, he folds around me, scooping me against his bare chest.

"What's happening?" he asks.

"She gets hypothermia when she controls someone from the void," Marilynn answers.

Dessin uses a hand to lift my chin. Dark-mahogany eyes dart back and forth between my two eyes as he searches for a solution.

"Why haven't they stopped?" I whisper hoarsely.

"Who?"

"The war. I've destroyed their leaders. Why hasn't the war ended?"

He looks around, clutching me closer as he realizes the violence is its own entity. There is no stopping it or slowing it down.

"They've been brainwashed since they were young, Skylenna. I don't think they'd stop until their hearts no longer beat."

*But I've killed their leaders…*

I stare off into the distance at our armies defending DaiSzek lying on the ground, breathing shallowly with spears sticking out of his back like a porcupine. Niles and Ruth snuggle against him in tears as the war goes on.

"It was supposed to end…" I mutter against Dessin's hot chest.

"I know."

"I'm *so* cold."

"I know that, too, Skylittle."

My glistening gaze shoots up to those chocolate eyes softening around the edges. Kane looks down at me with both anxiety and confusion twisting his features.

"Why how are you here?!"

His Adam's apple stretches the length of his throat. He shakes his head, looks around, and holds me tighter to his chest as if he's trying to summon the answer to that question as well.

"You needed me."

I nod with my vision blurring from the river of tears. "Yes."

I blink in surprise as Kaspias appears in front of me. He's surrounded by a soft, glowing light. One of warmth and eternal love that can only be described as something holy. And holding his hand is my Scarlett.

"He's right, Skylenna. You need him." Kaspias steps closer, though no one sees him. "It's always been there; don't you see it? You've both been preparing for this day since you were children."

*What are you talking about?*

"God gave you two a place that you'd need one day. One that you two grew to know as home," Scarlett says.

I close my eyes, needing no time to search for the answer they've given me.

Ambrose Oasis blossoms in my vision with a light so luminous, it should blind me. The swaying purple wisteria. The meadow of long, luscious grass and calming lavender dancing in the wind.

"They were all children once, just like me." Kaspias reaches for my hand. It's no longer covered in scars and burn marks. "You are warrior angels sent by God himself with the power to reverse the trauma and evil done to them."

Fear skitters up my neck as I look into Kane's eyes. This will take more power than I've ever exerted. It will likely kill me. But maybe, with Kane and Ambrose Oasis, we can do this.

"Kane?"

His breath is shallow as he glances down at me.

"Will you go somewhere with me? You were right, I do need you. And I know you won't remember all of the moments we've spent here, and one day I'll work endlessly to give those moments back…but right now, I need you to do this with me."

His full lips part as he tries to decipher my choice of words. "Okay."

My aching, frozen body sinks deeper into hypothermia as I drop us into the void, funneling down, down, down until we arrive in Ambrose Oasis.

I never realized the connections stemming through this location before. It has a million strings, wires, flailing vines linking to the many minds around us. I reach my hand out to slide it into Kane's. His warm fingers curl around my hand, squeezing gently.

"I think I've always needed your strength to do what comes next." Feeling the void thrumming through me, I bind with the links, grasping at the minds of every Vexamen soldier on the battlefield. Kane goes rigid next to me, sharing in this experience.

And I do what was done to Kaspias.

I change their childhood, one memory at a time. Twisting their fate with the palm of my hand. Giving them mothers, brothers, sisters, pets. School. Playtime. Best friends. Toys. Desserts. Happiness. Lovers. Heartbreaks.

I kill the violence that was inflicted on them.

I stone their trauma into submission.

And Kane fights their demons with me. We erase the abuse, the beatings, the days of starvation that helped mold who they are.

And with life drumming like a heartbeat into Ambrose Oasis, I feel the war go quiet on the outside. It simmers from boiling to flat, motionless water.

The sons and daughters of Vexamen are altered, draining their horrible memories into the void, being vanquished in Ambrose Oasis.

As we wipe their slates clean, I droop into Kane's arms. The purple wisteria fades. The smell of lavender and honeysuckle vanishes. Kane holds me in the smoke and rain of the quieting war. Swords stop clashing. The screams have softened to quiet moans.

"Kane?" I choke.

"It's Dessin."

I peel my eyes open to look at him through my swollen lids. We're sitting in the mud, hearing the thudding of dropping weapons. Vexamen Breed holding up their hands in surrender.

"Dessin."

"Yes, Skylenna."

"Take me to DaiSzek."

The ground falls away from supporting my backside as Dessin lifts me. My eyes are closed, but I can sense the crowd parting for us. Kind words. Victorious cheers. It's all a fever dream in the fogginess of my mind.

"I think he moved—where is he?" Dessin asks someone.

"Over there," Warrose responds close to my head, his voice sounding drained and loaded with a cry he's suppressing.

As Dessin moves in the direction of wherever DaiSzek was moved to in his wounded state, my eyes pop open at the sound of our boy whimpering in agony.

"What's wrong?" I jolt upright against Dessin's chest.

Gazing down at DaiSzek, wounded and weakened, I see Niles and Ruth sitting close to him. And many warriors from the other colonies are down on one knee. Even the white wolves bow close to them.

"What is it?" I ask again.

"He's…" Dessin's voice catches. "He's found Knightingale's ashes."

"*Oh.*" I press my hand over my mouth, but my face tightens together as I let out a cry. "Oh, my boy."

Gently, Dessin lowers me to the ground near DaiSzek's head, sitting among the piles of gray soot and ash. His snout is covered in open gashes, blood, and debris. The spears are still lodged in his back.

"He wouldn't let us remove them," Ruth says wetly, sniffling into the back of her hand.

Dessin assures her we'll take him somewhere we can stop the bleeding and bandage him with clean cloth and water.

I lean down to DaiSzek's face, brushing my hand over his head softly. His whines vibrate under his fur, humming through my fingertips. And I break apart with him, tears bursting free as we cry together for our fallen friend. For the small Ginger Wrathbull who fought so bravely. For his friend that followed him everywhere.

And the world feels it, too. The sky sheds flecks of snow and ash though it is not winter. A white blur descends around us as the war has finally come to rest.

"I loved her, too," I tell him through a sob.

"As did I." Dessin places a hand on DaiSzek's paw, using his other to rub circles over my back.

The audience remains silent as we sit in Knightingale's ashes, heavy with exhaustion. The weight of all we've given up, all we've endured crumbles around us like a gentle apocalypse.

"Dessin?" I look up to him through my gushing wall of tears.

"Yes?"

And I bow my eyes in sadness, speaking words that ultimately hold a different meaning. Words that I will never forget.

"Hell has finally frozen over."

His brows knit together as his own gaze glitters with tears. He swallows, then nods his head. "Hell has finally frozen over."

# 69. Rebuilding The Broken

## Four Months Later
## Skylenna

Once we returned to the Red Oaks, we slept for three days. Medical professionals checked on us frequently, patching up DaiSzek, and ensuring we were hydrated and fed. Ruth spent time in the infirmary, undergoing reconstructive surgery and getting the medication she needed. Warrose didn't leave that hospital room.

Marilynn and Niles moved into Aurick's estate. She said that's what he would have wanted for his son. We didn't question her on how she knew the gender so early.

Once we were recovered from the war, physically anyway, we began building a house that surrounded the giant Red Oak tree closest to the lagoon. The same one Kane and I would climb as children. The one that Kane made the beacons from. Even though he still couldn't remember our special life together, he agreed to start building anyway. Chekiss helped after I insisted he live with us.

I was too weak and detached from the void to return it all in one fell swoop. My nerves were shot. My emotions numb and broken. But Dessin and Kane were patient and understanding. Although we never touched. Never kissed. When we fell asleep at night under the stars, he would turn away from me. I thought I escaped hell when I left the prison.

I was wrong.

Sleeping so close to my soulmate, yet feeling so cold and unwanted had left a gaping hole in my heart. I tried every night to climb into the void, take him to Ambrose Oasis, and show him everything I cherished so deeply.

I fucking tried.

Most nights I'd wake sobbing hysterically. And Kane would come to the front, claiming he hated seeing me cry. The feeling confused him, although I know the truth. It's the same words Kane has used since we were children. He always said his heart would wilt with my tears. It was the one thing he hated most in the world.

There were times when we'd eat around a fire in silence, and Kane would look up at me, and for a minuscule moment, he'd recognize me. There was a flash, a glimmer, where he would part his lips and straighten his back and say, "I thought I remembered something."

But it would fade like the ocean pulling its water away from the shore.

And some mornings, Dessin would ask me to share a memory. I'd tell him about the time I first hugged him in the abandoned Demechnef building, or the time he pulled me out of the Isolation Tank. He was always so quiet after I finished. He'd stare blankly into the sunrise, unresponsive and deep within the walls of his own thoughts, then he'd go about building our home without another word about it.

That always broke my heart.

The dismissiveness of my most treasured recollections.

I'd walk out to the lagoon and cry into my hands. Sometimes, DaiSzek would join me, leaning against me so I could muffle my cries into his fur.

Every other day, I'd visit Ruth in the infirmary. I'd bring her wine and treats, and we'd kick Warrose out to hang out while we gossiped. We'd cry about traumatic memories from the prison, about the aftermath of our realities. I'd do my best to pull her out of her depression even though I was wrestling deeply with my own. Most of the time Marilynn would join us, and Niles would go have a guy's day, because, in his words, he was *one of the boys now!*

And now, after four months, with the help of many colony members, over many long days of cutting wood and building a layout based on an old blueprint my dad made long ago we have a house!

It's a massive cottage with a thatch roof, tall oak pillars, a stone base, and a front porch that stretches over the cliff. The perfect spot to drink our morning coffee and watch the sunrise over the lagoon. It's heaven, and my dad knew it.

"Skylenna."

My mind wakes gradually, but my eyes remain closed. I shift under the covers, rolling away from the noise.

"Someone is at the door."

I feel Dessin climb out of his side of the king-size feather bed. The front door creaks open, and muffled voices swim back to my ears along with the midnight breeze. At the distinction of a woman's voice, I sit up in bed, wiping my face and blinking away the blurry sheen of sleep.

*What time is it?*

Something white nudges the bedroom door open, trotting inside, then leaping to jump on my bed to greet me.

I snicker. "Were you sent in to wake me, Kira?!"

The white wolf queen steps into the doorway, illuminated by the glowing moonlight shining through the window. "I'm sorry to disturb ya slumber, *dashna*."

"Is everything okay?" I make a feeble attempt at combing through the ruffled waves of my bed hair.

Asena sighs, glancing at the wolf snuggled between my legs.

"I have someone who wants to see ya, dashna. Someone who has been under my care for many years now."

My sleepy gaze slides through the moonlit doorway to Dessin, shirtless, arms crossed, and looking just as curious as I feel.

"Who?"

She sits on the corner of my bed and reaches for my hand. "Do ya trust me?"

I nod.

"Then I think ya should see for ya-self."

It's three in the morning as we follow Asena through the Stormsage Keep.

The hallways are flooded with warmth from the torches and fireplaces. The air smells like roasting chestnuts and hot apple cider. It reminds me of the night we spent here. That dinner, I learned the city had a stronger hold on my eating habits than I realized. Kane was gentle, kind, and patient as I worked through it. He held me close as we fell asleep.

This all makes me tilt my head in his direction, walking slightly ahead of me with the glow of the aged sconces shimmering across the side of his face. His eyes are zoned out, mouth parted, body going through the motions of following Asena through the keep.

"Kane?" I ask.

It takes him a little longer to respond. He reacquaints himself with this location, then peers down at me.

"Hmm?"

I wonder if he switched because this place is a trigger for him.

"Hi," I say, then lean closer to him. "We're in the Stormsage Keep. Asena is bringing us to meet someone who has been asking for me."

Kane lifts his chocolate-brown eyes to Asena's back, covered in furs and cloaks. He gives me a thankful smile but doesn't say anything. His strides even out. He faces forward to continue walking in silence.

My stomach turns into a bitter puddle of acid.

*I miss talking to you.*

*I miss the way you'd reach for my hand.*

*I miss you so much, Kane.*

"We stayed here once after running away together," I blurt out in a low whisper.

There isn't a hitch in his pace as he cocks his head in my direction, glancing at me with a crease in his brow.

"I had a breakdown in the dining hall because I was trying to ration what I was allowed to eat. My mind was still stuck in the ways of the lady-doll regimen. You were the one that helped me realize what a problem it had become when you encouraged me to eat until I was full."

I twist my hands together, wringing them out like a wet towel. Does he care? Could he possibly remember flashes of this? Does he feel what I'm feeling when I repeat the memory?

Kane's expression is usually so readable. So easy to dissect the emotions morphing his features. But right now...he's a stranger to me.

"And now? Is eating still a problem?" he asks, but it sounds like he's trying to make conversation to be polite.

I bow my eyes and frown.

"No. Not anymore."

"I'm glad."

*Me, too. But that wasn't the point. I wanted you to feel something. Look at me the way you used to!*

Asena stops in front of the door at the far north end of the keep. She lifts her chin to me with a defiant look of strength. "Do not be mad at me, dashna. I was not sure if ya would come. But I have come to know her after much time and do not think ya will have another chance."

My blood runs cold. "What did you do?"

Who is *her?*

Kane stiffens at my side, taking a protective stance toward me.

Asena pushes down on the dulled silver handle, using her shoulder to shove the door open. It scrapes against the floor as she opens it wide to reveal a bedroom. I find myself retreating inward as I glance around hesitantly. There's a large cherry oak bed with ten-foot posts and a sheer canopy. It's covered in white furs and wooden accents. Dim with the light of two fireplaces going.

It doesn't exactly smell great in here...

Like a neglected infirmary. Saline and bodily fluids. Ash. Dust. Something similar to the way our cage smelled after Ruth underwent surgery. Death warmed up.

Asena observes me with cautious eyes. Waiting. Bracing for impact. My eyes then go in a frantic search of the giant bed, skimming over the ruffled sheets, the hand hanging off the side, the wolf resting its head on a lump in the center. I take a guarded step forward, tilting in to

571

get a better look.

"Do ya know why I've called ya *dashna?*" Asena's low voice greases the air. "It means *daughter*."

There's only one image in that bed that makes me back away.

I don't need to even see the face that's turned to the side in silent slumber. All it takes is the mess of golden waves that look like the hair of a mermaid. They're splayed out across the white pillow, a pool of honey around her head.

It snaps my neck upright. My breath hitches in my throat. Goose bumps pebble over my arms and legs. The air drops twenty degrees, yet my forehead and palms go damp with perspiration. I'm burning up, shivering, swallowing down a heavy lump in my throat.

"Asena…"

"She wanted to see you before…"

My feet blunder back again, making my movements jerky and unpredictable.

*"I remember you. You're the little monster I made a few shiny coins off of."*

That moment in the cemetery comes screaming back to me with pitchforks and rebellions gathering in my head. Her eyes were spiteful and without any love for her children. And for the first time, the void purrs in anger.

"What is she doing here?" I ask through my clenched teeth.

I know everything I learned from my trips into the past should make me less inclined to kill this woman. I know. She suffered from the Mind Phantoms the same as my father, the same as Charles Offborth. I remember it well.

But the last time I really saw her in person was the day she looked at Scarlett like a poisoned insect.

"She's sick, *dashna*."

I see the memory curdle in front of me, showing me the ugliness of its insides.

*"Scarlett deserved everything that happened to her. She's nothing to me. No daughter of mine."*

Sick? I dart my eyes back into that large, comfy bed. And this time, I focus a little harder on her face. It's oily, pale, and bony. Her breaths are fast and shallow, like tiny, useless pants.

"What's wrong with her?"

Kane moves to place a hand on my back in a small show of support.

"That chemical ya government injects to control ya people. It's like a slow-releasing poison if abused for too long." Asena looks back at the sickly woman huffing and puffing in her sleep. "I'm so sorry I lied to ya, *dashna*. But her story should be heard by ya before she passes on. *Please*."

Passes on? She's dying?

I don't know what to think. How to feel about seeing her again. It's a firestorm of thoughts and memories warring against my barriers. The void flickers on like a lightbulb I thought had burned out.

I see the conversation my parents had after we were born. I see how our mother's face was beet red, gushing tears, and the desperation on her face to keep us.

*"I can protect my babies. I will protect Skylenna and Scarlett."*

She fought so hard to ignore the prophecy Judas gave them. To defy the plan Sophia was making. All because she wanted to raise us right. She wanted to give us the home and parents we deserved.

*"I can't leave her!"* she wails into the void. *"I can't separate my babies!"*

"We can go if you want," Kane says in my ear.

I give him a side-long glance. He looks concerned and a little unsure about this situation. But not in the way he would if he remembered all that has happened to me as a child. To Scarlett. That might be what hurts more than this impossible decision I'm facing.

The fact that Kane can't understand how devastating this is for me.

"I'll see her," I finally announce.

Asena's body sags in relief.

"Would you like me to wait outside?" Kane asks.

Even though he doesn't know why this is one of the heaviest moments of my life…I *need* him right now. God, I need him more than anyone alive. If he had all of his memories, he would have never even thought to ask that question. I shake my head, and he follows me in.

It takes me several seconds to sit down on the soft fur chair next to her bed. But I can't help but stare down at her, studying how much she looks like me. Older. Sadder. A few scars on her clammy face.

I take a shaky breath in while I sit down.

The creak of my chair has her cat-shaped eyes opening slowly, like she's trying so very hard to pull herself out of a drug haze, a feverish coma. The whites of her eyes are a dark shade of yellow, covered in so many burst blood vessels.

Those wrinkled eyelids stretch back in drowsy surprise at the sight of my face. Her gasp rattles in her chest from phlegm and unwanted fluids gurgling in her lungs. I hold my wince as her breaths turn to small wheezes.

"Scarlett," she croaks with a dry mouth.

It's like someone slams their fist straight through my chest. I shake my head slowly.

Her face pinches together in shame as she looks me over with more lucidity parting the clouds of confusion in her eyes.

"Baby Skylenna," she rasps.

"Hello, Violet."

My mother's eyes pinch close, squeezing tears out of the corners. She blows out a stuttering breath and nods, like even though she knew this day would come, nothing could have prepared her for the way her heart would react.

"Do you remember the last time I saw you?" I ask her with a pang of pettiness and the urge to rub salt in the wound.

"Yes," she whispers.

"And do you know what happened when we walked back home?"

Violet looks like she might die right here, right now, simply from a broken heart.

"I know how it ended." She bites down on her chapped lips.

"Do you, though?" My best efforts fail to calm the simmering hate in my stomach. "How about the times before the end? When she'd bang her head against the drywall in that closet in your old room? Or when she'd spend hours in the bathtub scrubbing her skin raw *'to get them off of her?'*"

Tears are running down both of our faces now. But mine are brewed in animosity, and hers are infused with guilt. However, witnessing her cry sends a nostalgic shiver racing through my nervous system. She cries the same way as Scarlett. The same scrunched nose. That soft frown that looks more like a pouting child. The splotchy, rosy pink that spreads from the tip of her nose down to her neck.

It brings me back, softens my heart, pacifies the boil in my gut.

"I t-tried to put her pieces back together," I choke out, holding the leash of my sobs tightly. "I wanted to be enough for her. I-I wanted to be enough for her to live!"

"That is not on you, my sweet girl. Her fate is a tragedy *I* must live with. I should have fought Vlademur harder. I should have taken my own life rather than be a pawn on his board." She reaches her frail hands out to me, clenching my fingers so hard, her knuckles turn white. "You both deserved a stronger mother. I am *so* sorry, Skylenna."

I would be lying if I said there isn't a small part of me that wished she was as strong as Niles's father. But the outcome would have been the same, wouldn't it? Niles was still traumatized by Demechnef, whether Charles participated or not. It would have happened regardless.

"If you've been sick from the Mind Phantoms, why have you waited so long to reach me?" I ask, using the sleeve on my arm to wipe my nose.

"I didn't want to distract you when the prophecy said there was a war coming. One that you'd win. And…I didn't have the words. What could I possibly say? There are no apologies in the world that could redeem me for what I did to my child. Drugs or no drugs. I was her mama. I was her *mama*!"

Violet breaks out into a coughing fit, wet and filled with mucus. Kane puts his hand on her back, helping her sit up to get it out of her lungs. Though the fluids seem endless, eventually she lies back down from exhaustion.

"There was one thing I did want to tell you, though. One thing I can die in peace knowing that I did for my family and…Kane's family, a great justice."

At this, Kane and I lean in.

"In my days of being conditioned and injected by Demechnef, Vlademur took a liking to me. He kept me as a companion. Had me around for years." Her emerald eyes glaze over as she dives into these memories. "I gained his trust so I could do what needed to be done."

"What did you do?" Kane can't help but ask.

"He was quite meticulous about things. He read the same Bible. Slept on the same pillow. Clutched the same string of rosary." Her eyes dart back and forth between the two of us. "So, I laced them all with a low dose of poison. Aurick's father did not die a slow and agonizing death from natural causes. He suffered slowly, by my hand, so I could have a front row seat to watch."

I let go of her hand to press it over my mouth. Something like pride and gratitude enter my soul, like seeing an old friend again when they come home from war. Relief. Satisfaction.

Vlademur wasn't terminally ill because that's what fate had in store for him.

My mother, Violet, tortured him. She gave us the justice we all deserved from being under his thumb, a victim of his malicious ideas and experiments.

Violet Ambrose dominated the original puppeteer.

Violet Ambrose was the real master of the game.

Kane gulps loudly, replacing the place where my hand once was with his own, gently gripping her knuckles. "Thank you. Not just from me, but from my family. Thank you, Mrs. Ambrose."

"No, Kane," she coughs, slipping her other hand over his. "Thank *you*. You protected my girls your whole life. You loved them. You cared for them. You gave my little Skylenna the childhood she deserved. Your mama would be so proud of the man you have become."

Tears drip from Kane's bottom lashes directly onto Violet's fur blankets. He doesn't try to hide the effect her words have on him. No, because that's not Kane. Kane is gentle, warm, and compassionate beyond comparison.

"I-I don't remember doing any of the things you speak of," he stammers, then moves his eyes across the room to me. "But I'd like to. More than anything. I want to remember so badly."

He may never understand how much hope he's just given me. I want to reach into my chest, rip out my own heart, and pass it over to him. *Here. Take it. I'll give you whatever you want for the rest of our lives. I'll dive into the void, and I won't come back until I have your memories.*

"Take good care of each other," my mother says, scratchy and breathless. "There are so many couples in the world that will never have what you two share. They'll never get to grow old together."

Kane looks down in thought.

I wish he could remember how much he has already taken care of me. It's my turn to look after him. To cherish. To provide. To protect.

"I don't want to put any pressure on you two, but I had Asena fetch this from Jack's house." Violet reaches into her nightstand, plucking something from the top drawer. "Jack wrote letters to me on the rare occasion. He said that Kane asked for his blessing and permission to marry Skylenna…at the age of seven."

Kane and I both release a surprised chuckle.

"And then again when Kane was nine. And again, at eleven. And then when he was nineteen."

My quiet laughter is replaced with more tears.

Violet smiles to herself. "Jack's words in his last letter were *'I didn't tell him… but he had my blessing that first moment he asked for her hand when he was seven. He wore his nicest clothes, slicked back his hair, and brought me a bouquet of wildflowers he picked in my backyard.'*" She laughs, shaking her head. "These are our wedding rings. And per Sophia's request, I had her diamond added."

Violet holds a necklace with her thumb and index finger. It holds a husband's gold wedding band and a wife's wedding ring with a pear-cut diamond.

I silently melt in my seat.

It's perfect.

It's two symbols that hold so much history.

So much meaning.

Kane lets her lower the chain and rings in the palm of his big hand. He does his best not to react to this beautiful gift. I'm not sure he even knows how to respond.

I, on the other hand, focus on the ill woman in bed staring at us weakly, yet with so much love in her eyes. I unleash a strangled sob, throwing my arms and half my body over her.

"Thank you, Mom."

Violet gasps before she weeps with me, arms trembling as she circles them around me, softly patting the back of my head.

"I love you, Skylenna," she cries.

"I love you too, Mama!"

After several minutes of crying, of apologies, of sweet words, we leave her room to let her rest. We walk back to our house in silence, basking in the sunrise that edges through the leaves. Kane holds on to

577

those rings in the palm of his hand like his life depends on it.

And as I come to the front door of our house, I pause before entering. The trails of my tears are dry on my cheeks, but I can feel a new supply preparing to burst free.

"Skylenna?" Kane raises an eyebrow from inside the house.

It's the chill of déjà vu again. That tug of nostalgia as I strip my clothes off in front of him, tossing them onto the wooden panels of the front porch.

"How good of a swimmer are you?" I ask, reliving that night Dessin jumped in the water, making me think he broke his neck and drowned.

Before Kane can answer, I spin on my heels, taking five long strides until I'm springing into the air, plummeting to the flat, shiny surface of the lagoon.

I wait underwater with my eyes open, beaming with excitement as he breaks through the surface hands first in a graceful swan dive. And I don't give him any time to look around for me. I snag his hand and pull him in the direction of the waterfall.

*This is where it should happen. This is how he would want it to happen.*

Kane doesn't fight the pull of my hand against his, drawing him under the beating downpour, into that sacred nook of ours where the world stops and time bends to us.

We bob to gasp for air against the light mist spraying us and the shiny limestone wall covered in moss.

"What the hell?" he gasps, wiping the water from his eyes.

The urge to cry puts me in a headlock, clawing at my insides. I swallow that lump, though I can't control the watering of my eyes.

"Kane, I'm sorry for the way I'm about to do this." Tears, tears, tears. "I wish I had the patience to give each moment back gradually. But…"

"What?" He swims closer.

"But I really *need* you right now." My voice cracks, and I shudder past it. "I'm so alone, and I need you. You're my best friend. My soul mate. And I can't live another day in a world where you don't call me honey or Skylittle. Where you don't hold me at night, remind me of funny childhood memories or my embarrassing moments. Where the man who's supposed to know me better than anyone…doesn't know me at all."

Kane's chocolate-brown eyes line with tears. He nods, swimming so close to me that only a small trickle of water can pass between our stomachs.

"Can I kiss you?" I ask so pathetically, it pains my own ears.

"Of course you can," he breathes.

I use my hands to slide around his wet neck, pulling myself up closer to his towering height. And it's as though his lips act on muscle memory. Because they move the way they did when he was in love with me. I open my mouth to him, whimpering as he slides his tongue past my lips, tasting me gradually.

"I love you, Kane Valdawell." I kiss him over and over. "I'll say yes to you giving me that wedding ring when you remember again."

And with that, I use the void and Ambrose Oasis as a shelter for him to experience each memory like it's the first time. One by one, I let him swim among every conversation we had as children, every fight, every scraped knee, every time he pulled me from that basement.

Through each precious memory he collects, I kiss him deeper, feeling his hands explore my body with far more interest and excitement than before.

Dessin switches to the front so that he can experience the asylum again. Only the times he shared with me. For me. About me. I flood his consciousness with my love, with every feeling I had about him when we first met. He goes back to the time he held my hair back after Meridei and Belinda poisoned me. He sees how I threw my body over his while they tortured him. He remembers threatening Meridei as I was whipped. He relives the night he made love to me in his bed.

I drain myself giving everything to him.

And as he lifts my nightgown in the water, I don't object but beg and plead against his lips to take me the way he used to. Kane lowers his breeches, nudging the head of his cock at my entrance. And it's beautiful, so fucking beautiful because we're both crying tears of relief. With each second he spends in the void, in Ambrose Oasis, he kisses me deeper.

"Skylittle," he cries against my lips. "I love you, honey."

With a jolting thrust of his hips, he pushes his full length inside of me, pumping the very breath from my lungs with the sudden impact.

"I'm so sorry I left you all alone," he pants against my lips, wet with tears and the taste of his mouth. "I'm here now, honey. I've got you."

"Tell me you remember me, Kane!"

He thrusts harder, forcing waves to crash over my shoulders, piercing me with his love and his kisses that make me go limp and boneless in his arms.

"I remember you." He slams to the hilt. "I remember you sitting in my lap in that treehouse, running your hands through my hair. I remember our first kiss under this waterfall."

I moan as ecstasy permanently buries itself in the contours of my soul. *He remembers me. He remembers it all.*

"I asked your father for permission to marry you every chance I got. I want you to take my name. My hand. I want you to have my babies."

"Yes," I groan, rolling my head back. "Do you want to get me pregnant, Kane?"

He looks up at me through heavy lids and glazed eyes. "Yes. God, yes. Let me fill you with my cum."

I ride against him, feeling the coil wind up tight inside me, ready to snap like a rubber band. He fucks me faster, pounding me into the limestone wall vigorously, like he's making up for lost time. And I can feel his cock twitch, pulse, and swell inside of me as he gets ready to release. With a muffled growl, he bites down on my shoulder, marking me, and the sharp sting sends me spiraling with tiny explosions in my lower belly. I come with him, losing my breath as I feel him gush into me.

And once we're done, Kane carries me back up to the house, to which Chekiss excuses himself to visit Niles, catching the hint. Kane dries me off, lays me in bed, and buries himself inside me again. This goes on for hours. He makes me laugh as he explains that he's trying to be thorough, coming in me as many times as it takes to put a baby there. After a while, and after he makes me breakfast, we fall back asleep in each other's arms. I dream of Ambrose Oasis, of the treehouse, of running through the forest with Dessin.

The sunset blasts amber light through the window, gleaming through the Red Oak leaves outside. I stir awake with a nudging of the void grating against my mind, my happy thoughts.

Ignoring it, I curl against Kane's chest, cherishing the rhythm of his heavy breath. Feeling eternal love and the yearning to see his eyes open. I kiss up the center of his sternum, his throat, his hard jawline.

"We slept all day," I purr against his lips. "Let's make dinner, then go back to sleep."

He smells so good. The spicy cedar and forest. I nuzzle my nose against the prickly facial hair below his cheekbones. I missed touching him. Missed getting to express how much I love him. How long has it been since they fucked up his head? I exhale, kissing his plush lips again.

Though, he doesn't react. Doesn't show any sign of rousing awake.

"Kane?" I bite at his neck playfully, then tickle his ribs because I know how that always gets him to snicker.

Not even a smile.

I press harder.

Nothing.

"Kane?!"

"I'll never forgive myself for this part."

The void projects a tall, familiar figure in the doorway. I jump to sit up straight, protecting Kane's sleeping body with my arms over him.

"Who's there?"

Kaspias Valdawell moves toward me, wearing an expression that makes my stomach shrivel up in fear.

"They told me to do it, Skylenna," he says like it's an apology.

"Do what?!"

My heartbeat rattles in my throat. It swells against my lungs, causing me to huff hysterically.

"Kane…my brother…he isn't going to wake up."

I stop breathing.

"I gave him an injection before we started that altered round of Mind Phantoms."

"SPEAK. *FASTER*."

"This injection was a Mazonist fail-safe. An untested experiment to ensure that you two would never be together again… It"— he exhales, shaking his head—"it sends him into a coma the day you two become intimate again."

My blood turns to acid as every atom in my body grows ice cold. I glare at him, then look down to Kane's sleeping body. No. *NO!*

"How do I fix it?!"

"I'm so sorry, Skylenna." He looks down at his brother in anguish. Regret. Remorse.

"TELL ME HOW TO FIX IT!"

"I wish I knew."

I'm standing on the bed with a burning face and clenching fists.

"I can't go through this again, Kaspias. I WON'T GO THROUGH IT AGAIN!"

But the doorway is empty. Darkness drowns out the bedroom as the sun goes down, stealing all warmth, all comfort, all sight in its wake.

"This was supposed to be our happy ending! No! We deserved these years together! After everything we've given up!" I'm screaming at God now, looking up to the ceiling. "How could you do this to us? Haven't we done enough?! This was supposed to be our happy ending!!"

And again, like before, when Dessin and Kane thought I was the demon that ruined their lives, I'm left alone in the dark. But this time, Kane isn't here to pull me out of the basement.

He's motionless in our bed.

Eyes closed.

Heart still beating.

Kane Valdawell is lost in a coma.

And I have no way of getting him out.

*To be continued in…*
*Wait, is there an epilogue?!*

# Epilogue

## Twenty-One-Years Later

I stand in front of our house, watching them through the window. This is a part of my daily routine when I come home from the city, and I don't have the slightest idea as to why I do it. Glaring through that wide window always rustles a feeling in my gut. Is it anger? Jealousy? Pure bitterness? I never take the time to analyze it. Why would I? I've felt it like a fire threatening to smother me since I was old enough to understand the dynamics of our household.

In truth, I don't know who I am without this cynicism. It's shaped my personality, my brain development. The resentment molding into my spine like a parasite has made me an impenetrable wall to the kids at school that like to pick on me during history lessons.

Why wouldn't they tease, poke, and gawk at me and my brother?

The chapters that cover our parents are never ending and so fucking dramatic, to say the least. Krimson believes the stories, though. His heterochromatic eyes, brown and green, always gleam with admiration at the tale of how our father faked his death. The first time we heard it, he went home and sobbed for hours, hugging our mother's waist and soaking her dress in tears.

But I stopped crying from hearing the bullshit in the first grade. Why?

Niklaus Demechnef.

That's why.

He drew a picture of my dad in an asylum uniform being manipulated like a puppet on strings. He did all of this to make the class laugh as I sobbed in my hands while our teacher was trying to comfort me.

I stabbed him with a pencil.

And even though Aunt Marilynn and Uncle Niles were called in, they didn't blame me for my outburst and made him apologize for taunting me. The harassment from their son was only the beginning.

I unclench my hands before walking into the house. Staring at her hovering over that bed for too long isn't good for me. It sparks a hatred for my mother that I know is toxic and unwarranted. She's good to me, kind, and does her very best to give me and my twin brother, Krimson, the best life she can, even though she raises us all alone.

"Stop staring at them like a stalker," Krimson hisses, bumping into my shoulder on the way to the front porch.

Stalker. Peeping Tom. Creep.

If the shoe fits, I guess.

"I'll go in when she stops talking to his limp body."

Krimson twists his head sharply to scowl. "Shut your goddamn mouth, Sapph. Have some fucking respect!"

I bow my head in shame. I hate when he gets mad at me. Krimson is the sweet boy that my mother says reminds her of a specific alter. The one she's known since she was a child.

A shadow passes through the kitchen as Krimson steps through the front door, setting his bag down with a clunking sound.

"Your kid was gawking through your window again," he announces.

My mom chuckles, turning the corner to greet me at the door.

"Are you gawking again, Sapphire?"

I sigh. I'm surprised she didn't say my full name. She loves to, even though I go by Sapph.

No one ever understands why I cut my name short, why I don't shake hands and announce my full name, why I don't claim it with pride and acceptance. Do I want to be stared and whispered about? Do I want to endure rumors on the state of my mental health?

*"Maybe she's like her father, maybe there are other alters living in that head of hers."*

*"Look at those different colored eyes. That must mean something, right?"*

Hello, my name is Sapphire S. Valdawell.

The daughter of Skylenna Ambrose and Dessin and Kane Valdawell.

Buy tickets to the freakshow.

Everyone's waiting to see if the spawns are freaks too.

*To be continued in…*
*The Novella between books 4 & 5:*
*The Fortress and The Figurine*
*A story of Warrose, Ruth, Niles, and Marilynn*

*Then…*
*The fifth and final book of the series:*
*The Clock and The Carnival*

# Acknowledgments

I'm so sorry you had to wait this long for The Doll and The Domination. Originally, I wanted to release a book every three months. But guys, no one fucking warned me. Dark romance authors get it BAD. It's just expected of us to lie down, be still, not fight back while we're being kicked.

My first thank you is to the readers that never judged me. That only sent the sweetest messages. I know it seems small, sending an Instagram message or leaving a comment. But do you have any idea how much light you brought to my aching heart? Just as my words have the power to bring you a friend like Niles, or a soulmate like Dessin or Kane? Your words had the power to keep me from drowning. To keep me writing.

I love you so fucking much.

Hi Momma. Once again, thank you for supporting me against all odds. For sitting in my office, drenched in tears while you let me read the darkest scenes without context. I hope my love for you lives on through these books forever.

To my Ruth, Anna, for always bragging about me being an author, even though my name is considered a dirty word in this industry. Watching your face as you read the scenes we've talked about as kids is the greatest reward in life.

To my littlest bubsy, Lou. When you came back into my life, it taught me to be a better human being. To talk less and listen more. To show patience and kindness above all else. Your year was clouded in a shroud of darkness that brought me to my knees and kept me praying every night. But hear me now, this too shall pass. This is that plot twist, that momentary pitfall an author writes before that main character sees greatness. If you're going through hell, keep going. I'll carry you the rest of the way.

Thank you to my older sister, Lacey, who read my book despite your aversion to all things dark and filled with horror. When I first read your poem about 9/11 as a kid, I knew I wanted to be a writer just like you. Thank you for planting that seed.

Thank you to my cover designer, Stefanie Saw. To my format designer, Amy Kessler. And to my editors, Ellie, Debbie, and Christine. I'm beyond grateful for your talent and hard work!

To my incredible beta readers: Danielle Caballero, Kayla Watson, Stevi Bakos, Laura Pena, and my superb sensitivity readers Neo Heuperman, and Mia Brandshaug (who has been my #1 cheerleader since day one)! Don't forget to check out the Instagram page she runs @thepawnandthepuppet! For my cousin, Nate. In this book, Ruth's journey was not without inspiration from the day I found out about your accident. That pain was real. In my eyes, you're a king for surviving stronger than ever, and continuing to face adversity with a smile.

And a special thank you to Emily Harnish, my sweet system with DID that sensitivity read to ensure I represented Patient Thirteen to do him justice as well as all systems.

# About the Author

Brandi Elise Szeker has had a million stories in her head since she was a little girl convincing her baby sister there were killer clowns in the trees that came out after dark. She has four rescue dogs, Louis, Cali, Stella, and Nova. You can find them sprinkled throughout the series so that her love for them will live on forever. And some days, she lies awake at night wondering if she writes the most beautiful love stories, maybe one will find her too. Texas is where she currently resides, but one day, she'll be deep in the mountains, under the stars, writing a thousand more books that will both break your heart and give you life.

**To learn more about Brandi, visit her at:**
**Author website & newsletter:**
www.brandibookthought.com
Tiktok & Instagram:
@brandibookthought
Author Facebook Page:
https://www.facebook.com/brandieliseszeker/
Spoilers Facebook Group for TP&TP:
www.facebook.com/groups/thepawnandthepuppetspoilers/

Also, do me a favor? Please. FOR THE LOVE OF NILES, leave me a review? Reviews are what fuel this writing machine! You want the fifth book, don't you? Beat it, kid! Run, don't walk! Five stars or it didn't happen!

JK, really just leave a review even if it was poo poo.

Made in United States
Troutdale, OR
12/23/2024

27230162R00357